TAYLOR CALLAHAN, CIRCUIT RIDER

TAYLOR CALLAHAN, CIRCUIT RIDER

WILLIAM W. JOHNSTONE

AND J.A. JOHNSTONE

PINNACLE BOOKS
Kensington Publishing Corp.
www.kensingtonbooks.com

PINNACLE BOOKS are published by

Kensington Publishing Corp.
119 West 40th Street
New York, NY 10018

PUBLISHER'S NOTE
Following the death of William W. Johnstone, the Johnstone family is working with a carefully selected writer to organize and complete Mr. Johnstone's outlines and many unfinished manuscripts to create additional novels in all of his series like The Last Gunfighter, Mountain Man, and Eagles, among others. This novel was inspired by Mr. Johnstone's superb storytelling.

All Kensington titles, imprints, and distributed lines are available at special quantity discounts for bulk purchases for sales promotion, premiums, fund-raising, educational, or institutional use.

Special book excerpts or customized printings can also be created to fit specific needs. For details, write or phone the office of the Kensington Sales Manager: Attn.: Sales Department. Kensington Publishing Corp., 119 West 40th Street, New York, NY 10018. Phone: 1-800-221-2647.

PINNACLE BOOKS, the Pinnacle logo, and the WWJ steer head logo are Reg. U.S. Pat. & TM Off.

First Printing: June 2022
ISBN-13: 978-0-7860-4908-0
ISBN-13: 978-0-7860-4909-7 (eBook)

10 9 8 7 6 5 4 3 2 1

Printed in the United States of America

Chapter 1

Texas 1875

There wasn't much to the town of Nathan, if anyone ever called it a town. No post office, no bank, not even a church. The lack of the latter never stopped a man like the Reverend Taylor Callahan. Why, the last town the lean, broad-shouldered, dark-headed man on the white horse had preached in, a little burg in the Creek Nation, his so-called church had been inside a livery stable, and the only reason there was a roof over the heads of Callahan and twelve women, six kids, and three full-blood Creek men plus one quarter-breed was because of the thunder-head that whipped up all of a sudden.

Nathan, Texas, didn't even have a livery stable. But there wasn't a cloud in the sky on that hot summer day.

By Callahan's quick count, the little burg on the banks of the Red River had four saloons, six cribs, and something that billed itself as Honest Crockett's Gambling Emporium. There was, allegedly, a ferry, but no one seemed to be working it on this day, so Callahan eventually stopped ringing the bell on the Indian Nations side of the river and swam his white horse across. Sometimes, that river could resemble the Red Sea, but the rains must have held off, and Callahan and his gelding made it across with hardly a struggle.

There was also a dead man on Nathan's one street. As Callahan rode toward the corpse, he thought how this might explain why there was no ferry operator, that he had up and got himself killed. The body lay face-up, spread-eagled, with a bloody hole in the center of his chest, eyes open, left hand clutching what appeared to be a writ, and a badge pinned to his vest that read Sheriff's Deputy.

So much for the dead ferryman theory.

The gelding snorted and fought the bit, which was understandable—Callahan didn't particularly care to gawk at corpses himself, but long ago he had developed a curious nature.

A long-barreled Colt, probably a .45 caliber, remained holstered on the dead deputy's right hip. His right hand, now being sniffed at by a mangy dog, looked like he had been pointing, perhaps at the man who had put the bullet in his chest.

"Scat," Callahan told the dog.

The cur looked up.

"Scat," Callahan barked, with more force, and his eyes turned cold and mean. The dog quickly turned away and trotted toward the alley between two of the cribs.

Callahan studied the town, which didn't take long. People were inside the saloons and gambling hall—it might have been too early for business in the cribs—and muffled voices traveled through the open windows and doorways, but no one came outside to greet the stranger in town. He looked at the edge of town, where the street dead-ended at a cemetery. No one was digging a grave, either. Callahan meant to just glance at the cemetery, but he couldn't help but notice what had to be four recent crosses. He could tell because they weren't dry-rotted or wind-blown or knocked down by coyotes digging up some supper to be found in the shallow graves.

A door finally opened, banging shut, and Callahan turned his attention to the closest crib on the other side of the street.

A woman with patches of clothes covering most of her wares leaned against a hitching rail in front of her picket hut, smoking a cigarette, red hair disheveled, her face almost matching the dead deputy's in terms of paleness.

"Man needs burying," Callahan said.

The prostitute took a final drag on her smoke before flicking it into the dust. "Reckon so," she said, and let out a ragged cough.

"Might there be an undertaker in this metropolis?" Callahan said.

"Nope." She pulled out the makings and started working on another cigarette.

"Too bad." Callahan tilted his head toward the cemetery. "From the looks of things, an undertaker could make a killing in this little burg." He smiled at his joke. Undertaker. Killing. He started thinking of how he might use this in a sermon down the road.

The woman didn't seem amused.

"I could give him a funeral." Callahan jutted out his jaw toward what was labeled "Boot Hill," but wasn't high enough to keep the Red, when it felt like flooding, from washing away the dead. His plan was to tell her how much he typically charged for preaching funerals, not that a soiled dove had a say in these matters, but it was also highly unlikely that Nathan, Texas, had a mayor or town council, either. He could bury the poor soul and maybe get a meal. Someone was frying up salt pork in one of the saloons, and he bet some place served coffee as well as forty-rod whiskey. Maybe get a little grain for the gelding, possibly pocket a dollar or two for his troubles, and be on his way to . . . well . . . wherever he wound up.

The woman coughed out something, but Callahan couldn't catch what she said. He turned back to watch her strike a match against her thumbnail and take a few long drags on her new smoke, exhaling through the nose.

"Ma'am?" Callahan said.

The woman flicked ash and spit. "Said, 'Your funeral.'"

"I just preach them," Callahan said.

The woman coughed out her guts again, pulled hard on the cigarette, exhaled, spit, and said, "No. I meant . . ." She had to cough more before she finished. ". . . meant it'll be your funeral. If you move that law dog."

Callahan let those words sink in. *The roads people take,* he thought. He could've stuck to the Texas Road or crossed the Red at Doan's, farther west. He could've turned east in the Indian Nations and explored Arkansas, or west into Comanche and Kiowa territory and likely got his scalp lifted. Instead, he found himself here on a hot afternoon with a corpse a few feet away, and his horse not enjoying the scent of a lawman cut down in his prime.

"Easy, boy," Callahan said, tightening his grip on the reins, then backing the horse a few feet from the dead man. He looked back at the woman, and let her finish her smoke. When she flipped that butt away, he waited for her to cough up what was left of her rotting lungs, but she just wiped her mouth with the back of her hand and yawned.

"You just plan on letting him feed the buzzards and ravens?" Callahan said. "It might curb your business."

She shrugged. "I could use a leave of absence."

If it weren't for the fact that a lawman was lying dead in the street, Callahan might have laughed at that comeback. It came out much better than his undertaker-killing quip.

The batwing doors of the saloon across the street squeaked open, then started the rat-a-tat banging on the hinges. Spurs jingled.

"There's the man you gotta talk to," the haggard, hoarse woman said, and she gave Callahan a quick nod before pushing through her door. He heard the bolt shoved into place after the door closed, though neither door nor lock would keep anyone, or any cockroach, out.

"This is my lucky day," a voice drawled on the warped planks underneath the awning of the saloon. "We gets to kill two lawmen in one day."

Callahan thought: *Speaking of cockroaches . . .*

Twisting in the saddle, Callahan eyed a man in striped britches with two ivory-handled Remingtons on his hips, ribbon tie, red shirt, gray hat, pale eyes, and a blond mustache waxed and twisted. He couldn't have been much older than twenty. The man's hands rested on the butts of his revolvers, and a toothpick bounced up and down between his thin, pale lips.

Moving the reins into his right hand, Callahan slowly brought his left hand to his unbuttoned Prince Albert, then slowly pulled away the coat to reveal two important features, or lack thereof, about his wardrobe.

No badge.

No guns.

He smiled. "Hate to disappoint you, son," Callahan told the punk, "but the only law I know is the Word. The Truth."

The toothpick catapulted about a foot and fell onto the dirt.

"Preacher man, huh?" the punk said.

"That's about the size of it." Callahan's head tilted toward the corpse. "And I'd like to see that this man gets a proper funeral." As proper as could be had in a Sodom like Nathan, Texas. "A prayer and a song. I'd dig the grave myself."

"Well . . ." The gunman stepped off the planks and into the dust. "The problem, Preacher Man, is that me and the boys got us a bet." He turned slightly toward the batwing doors. "Ain't that right, boys?"

A veritable Goliath pushed through the doors. He wore buckskins and a slouch hat, and carried a sawed-off shotgun in his massive hands. The wood strained against his two hundred and fifty stinking pounds as he moved to the right of the punk. A smaller man, in a black hat and red and white polka dot bandanna, came out next and moved to the leader's left. This one had a revolver on his right hip, and he was smoking a cigar.

"What's the bet?" Callahan asked.

"See how long it takes before there ain't nothin' left of Deputy Giddings but his bones."

Callahan raised his head, as though thinking, which he was. He wet his lips, then laughed, and slipped out of the saddle. Still holding the reins, now in his left hand, he knelt by the corpse, and pried the writ from the left hand. He didn't read the paper, but looked at the fist.

"He hasn't come out of rigor mortis," Callahan said. "It's a hot day, fairly humid this close to the river, and this is a land of insects. That'll make him rot faster." He glanced at the writ, and then pressed the paper against the dead man's cheeks. "He's been dead, what, six hours?"

The cigar smoker pulled a pocket watch from a vest pocket, glanced at it, shrugged, and answered, "More like eight."

Nodding, Callahan rose, and kicked the dead man's closest boot. "That sounds right," Callahan said. "His feet ain't stiff yet."

Smiling, he asked, "Might I inquire as to what each of you bet?"

"Two days," said Goliath.

"One," said the punk.

"Two-forty-seven Wednesday," said the cigar smoker with pride. "I'm all for being specific."

Callahan nodded. He didn't even know what day it was.

"Well," he said, and read the writ, nodded, and dropped it between the dead man's legs. "Which one of you is Johnnie Harris?"

"That'd be me," said the punk.

"This warrant says bank robbery and murder, and with the Indian Territory just a ferry ride away, if you can find the ferryman, I don't think you'll want to wait around to see how long it takes this poor gent to be nothing but bones. You see, he ain't even bloating." Callahan pressed his right boot on the man's stomach and laughed. "Boys, you should have seen some of the bodies back during the late war up in Missouri. I've seen a midget swell up till he's about the size of . . ." He stopped, stopped and picked up the writ, read some, and looked at Goliath. "I take it you're Big Jim?"

"No," said the cigar smoker. "That's Wolf. Those fool

lawmen can't get nothing right. The name here is Bigham. Not Big Jim."

"That's good to know," Callahan said, and he went on, pointing at the dead deputy's face. "Nothing leaking from his mouth or nose." His head tilted slightly. "Or ears." Shaking his head, Callahan removed the boot and pointed at the face. "You gotta wait till he turns green. Then, and I'm guessing in a week or so, when he starts becoming red—that'll be on account that his blood's rotting, like all the rest of him inside. The way that Major General in the Heavens made man is remarkable. He swells up to double, quadruple his living size, then shrivels up to practically nothing."

The three killers looked dumbstruck, which was Callahan's intention.

"You ain't no preacher," Johnnie Harris said.

"Oh, I beg to differ but I most certainly am. Ordained even. Not grounded to any one church, I'm a circuit rider. The Reverend Callahan. Taylor Callahan. Taylor was my daddy's ma's maiden name, you see."

He wet his lips, studied the deputy's body again, and said, "But you do have to take into account the carrion. They might accelerate the proceedings. But this close to an establishment that'll be attracting all sorts of gamblers and wayfarers—I bet the lights are blazing till sunrise—that might scare off the buzzards, even some of the bugs." He turned and pointed at the crib. "And I bet that lady makes a lot of racket in her business. She sounded like a locomotive with her huffing and coughing. That'll scare off a lot of those that eat the dead, so, that could add to your time here."

"You talk too much, Preacher," the punk said.

Wolf wasn't looking so tough or big now. He coughed, spit, and wiped the dribble off his chin with the hand that didn't hold the shotgun.

"All I'm saying, boys," Callahan said in an even tone, "is that I'd like to bury this man, say a few words over him, and be on my way."

"We're gonna bury you, Preacher, after we see how long it takes your corpse to . . . to . . . to . . ."

Callahan finished for him. ". . . skeletonize."

The punk spit, and drew the Remington on his right hip, but, for the time being, he kept the barrel pointed at the dirt.

"I am not here to harm you lads," Callahan said. "But I can declare the winner of your bet, so you needn't wait and risk capture and a triple hanging, or lynching if this dead man has many friends. The winner is either Wolf or Mr. Bigham. I've been on the road so long, I'm not sure as what day it is. So you boys can light out, and figure out who won the bet . . ."

"It's me!" cried out Bigham.

Callahan smiled politely. "I'll see to our late deputy, give him a few kind words, and six feet of sod to cover him till we all go home."

"You're going home now," the punk said.

"Johnnie," Bigham said, "he ain't got a gun. And he's a preacher."

"He talks too much."

"Most preachers do," Callahan said with a laugh.

"You've talked your last." Johnnie Harris let the punkiest smile cross his face. "But I tell you what. I'll give you more of a chance than we give that law dog. Grab his hog leg. Let's see if you can shoot as straight as you talk."

"Johnnie . . ." Wolf pleaded.

Callahan looked at the holstered revolver on the dead man's hip. Shaking his head, the preacher glanced at each man. "Boys, you don't want me to take a gun in my hand. I haven't touched a Colt in, gosh, ten years?"

"You better touch this one," Johnnie Harris said, "because after I fill your belly with lead, I'm a-gonna kill that horse of yourn, too."

Callahan dropped the reins. The horse, as though understanding what was about to happen, trotted over to the nearest water trough and began slaking its thirst. Callahan stepped toward the dead man and looked at the holstered revolver. His eyes raised toward the punk.

"You don't really want me to do this, do you?"

"I'm gonna count to five," the punk said. "At five, I'm cocking my piece and killing you and the horse. I promise you I won't draw till I say five. One."

Callahan waited.

"Two."

He reached for the revolver, waiting to hear the next number, but the punk was cocky, or wanted to drag out this dime-museum play as long as he could.

An eternity later, he said, "Three."

Callahan pulled out the Colt. Yes, a .45. Heavy. But the balance felt good.

"Four."

His finger slipped into the trigger guard, and his thumb rested on the hammer.

"Five!"

The first bullet shattered Johnnie Harris's right wrist, causing him to drop the .44 Remington into the street. The second splintered the stock of the shotgun Wolf wielded, and the giant touched off both barrels, which splintered the far column and sent that side of the awning crashing down, showering the behemoth with the thatch, straw and sod that served as the awning's roof. The recoil of the shotgun must have pulled the big man's shoulder out of the socket, and Wolf screamed like a horse-kicked coyote.

The third bullet struck the holstered revolver on Bigham's hip, ricocheted into the boardwalk, and left the cigar smoker on his knees, clutching his stinging right hand and yelling out all sorts of blasphemies. By then, the punk was trying to find the other revolver, but he must not have been ambidextrous because he grabbed for the gun with his ruined right hand and cried out in pain when he couldn't pull it even half an inch from the holster.

Then he saw the cavernous barrel of a .45-caliber Colt staring at his forehead, and he fell to his knees and cried out for mercy.

And it came to pass, Taylor Callahan would say a few nights later at a revival in Denison, that the honest citizens of Nathan, Texas, emerged from their places of business, even the ramshackle saloon whose patrons the three bank-robbing scoundrels had been tormenting. As honest, Callahan decided, as could be found in a town like this.

"Mister," a man in an Abe Lincoln hat cried out, "you can have all the whiskey you want . . . on the house."

"Mister," said a small man in a sack suit, "you won't even have to pay for any of my gals. You've saved the day, our lives, and our reputation as the most honest town in Texas."

"Whatever you want is fine with me, sugar," called out

a woman—but not the prostitute with that awful cough—from one of the cribs.

"What I want," Taylor Callahan said, "is to preach a funeral over this servant of the good folks of this county or some county in this state."

"That's what we want, too," said a drummer.

"Let's all gather at Boot Hill," someone said.

"No."

Callahan pointed the Colt between two saloons. "Up there. Far enough and high enough from the Red River so this man won't be disturbed."

"But . . ." The tinhorn looked at Boot Hill. "Like as not, his family'll dig him up in a week or so and bury him where he'll get flowers and attention. Maybe even a real stone with fancy words."

"Today, he's getting flowers and attention at a new cemetery."

"But the ground's harder up on that mess of chalk," cried out Abe Lincoln.

Callahan smiled. "And so is a .45-caliber bullet." He cocked the piece. "Ask Johnnie and Wolf and Bigham about that."

The town of Nathan, Texas, fell quiet.

"Who wants to make the coffin?" Callahan asked.

When no one volunteered, he started to raise the Colt.

It turned out to be a really nice funeral. Bigham had a real good voice, and so did one of the prostitutes. Two of the tinhorns agreed to escort the prisoners over to Bonham, and the town took up a collection and gave a rawhide poke to Callahan, but the circuit rider took out only two dollars, and told the tinhorns to make sure they gave it to the sheriff in Bonham with instructions to see that it went to the dead deputy's kin or charity of the sheriff's choice.

"Well, you deserve more than two dollars," said one of the prostitutes.

Callahan had stuck the .45 in his waistband. Now he drew it, examined it, and said, "Well, I'll tell you what, folks. I'll take this hogleg, keep it out of the hands of some miscreants like Wolf and Johnnie or Bigham. And if someone has a box of .45 shells, I'll take that, too. Put one in the left saddlebag, and one in the right." He grinned. "For balance. We need balance in our lives and in our travels."

Actually, what he thought was he could sell the Colt in Dallas or Fort Worth and have enough money to pay for a hotel bed or a supper of steak instead of bacon.

"You might need that Colt and ca'tridges more'n just for balance," the coughing soiled dove said. "Johnnie Harris . . . he got three brothers . . . and they's meaner and crazier than their kid is by a long shot. The boy didn't shoot down the lawman. It was the big cuss that done that. And from what I heard from Bigham, the boy didn't even shoot down nobody when they was robbin' that bank."

"That ain't true!" the wounded Harris snapped, but Callahan could tell a lie when he heard one.

"But 'em other Harrises, they won't give even a preacher no chance."

A townsman agreed. "You might be safe," he suggested, "in . . . South America?"

Chapter 2

Weeks later, upon reaching the fork in the road, Taylor Callahan reined in the white gelding, pushed up the brim of his black Boss of the Plains, kicked free of the stirrups, and swung his left leg up, hooking it over the horn. After a yawn, he stretched out his arms while the horse did its business.

He had kept meandering south, watching the country dry up, and feeling the days turn hotter. *Well,* he thought, *that's what happens when you ride south. Although, if I took the advice of that guy in Nathan, and kept riding to South America, I hear that the seasons flipflop down that away, so it'd be cooler. 'Course, by the time I got to South America, especially on this tub of glue bait, it'd be summer down there, and I'd just be sweating again.*

This day had been particularly oppressive, he had been riding far, but he could still push on another few miles. Even the lackadaisical white gelding he rode wouldn't mind that. On the other hand, there was a bit of shade in the patch of grass and rocks, but not many thorns, betwixt the two caliche pikes, one turning straight south, the other veering left where Callahan had a mind to go. All the way down to the ocean. Well, when he had mentioned *ocean* all those long miles behind him, up in San Antonio, the saloon owner, who had paid him seven bits to swamp the place and give him a personal preaching, then let him sleep in the storeroom for the night, that scalawag had corrected Callahan.

"'T'aint no *ocean,* Parson," the Texian had drawled. "No *sea.* It's a *gulf.* Gulf of Mexico, to be precise."

"He might not see nothin' more than the Corpus Christi Bay, exactly," commented the bartender.

"With that nag he's ridin'," said the chippy, "it'll be a miracle if he reaches the Nueces."

"I wouldn't give it no further than the Salado," said the cowhand, and everybody laughed, even Callahan, since the Río Salado stretched just a few rods down the pike.

But, Callahan and Job, which is what he had come to call the white gelding, had made it this far. That'd be Job of the Land of Uz, Job of the Old Testament, Job of the patience . . . because that horse had no hurry in him.

Which Taylor Callahan didn't mind one bit. And the Cherokee in Tahlequah had told him that the gelding wasn't going to win any match races when he and Callahan had made the deal.

But Callahan no longer thought about San Antonio, or the ocean, gulf, sea, lake, mud puddle, whatever it turned out to be, because he had reached a fork. Which always had him recalling what his favorite pappy always said, no matter if he were stone cold sober or drunk and on his way to getting drunker.

"When you come to a fork in the road, boy, you study

'em trails real hard, and you make sure you go down the right trail, because the wrong turn can get you lost forever."

He wondered whatever happened to that particular pappy. Obviously, he had taken a wrong fork. After all, one fine morn during hog-killin' season, his favorite pappy left the farm on a mule, bound for Centerville, and never came back. Which wasn't the first pappy to do that. 'Course, Pappy Number Three had good reason to ske-daddle. Why the very morn after he lighted a shuck for parts unknown, the Clay County sheriff and a dozen or so of Centerville's best riders and two of the finest shots in all of Western Missouri come looking for that particular pappy. But all they found was Callahan's ma-maw, her sighting down a squirrel rifle, and letting them know that lessen they had rid all this far to help with the butcherin', they'd be smart to ride back to the main road and not come a-botherin' the Callahans no more.

Callahan was the name of Callahan's birthin' pappy, one of the two daddies he never met. The first pappy, the one who had nothing to do with the begetting that brought Taylor Callahan into this world, had catched the rheuma-tisms or load of buckshot—depending on who was doing the storytelling that particular night—and died shortly after marrying Callahan's ma-maw, back when she had lived in Kentucky. The second pappy, being the one who mar-ried the recently widowed daughter of Fergus and Fiona Fleming—sounded like that medicine-wagon team Calla-han had watched up Little Rock way—was responsible for Taylor Callahan's being here, and had named the baby after his mama's maiden name, his mama hailing from one of the Carolinas, North or South, nobody knew for sure, just that the family had farmed in the western part of the state, around what once was Cherokee country.

Then came the other pappies. Course, Callahan's ma-maw being a respectable woman, the other pappies came after Callahan's birthing pappy got struck by lightning, not knowing no better than to come out of the woods during a thunderstorm carrying an ax on his shoulder. Some of his pappies had been good, but most of them were meaner than the Widow Morley—till, as must happen to all men and women, the end come for Ma-Maw Callahan, which is what folks called her, even though she had wedded Youngers and Washburns and Palmers and even a no-account Lingham, plus maybe some others that Calla-han had forgotten after all those years.

Callahan had suggested that they carve into her stone. She Outlasted Eight Husbands, but the stonemason just carved her name and R.I.D., which he offered to correct, but Callahan laughed and said his ma, and all his pappies, and most of Clay County's finest would find *RID* appro-priate.

Back in those days, those same fine, outstanding citi-zens were happy to be rid of Taylor Callahan, too. Couldn't blame them for that, neither.

He wondered what Clay County's finest would do if they saw him now.

They'd laugh. That answer came quick enough.

Sometimes, the way fate had played its hand in Taylor Callahan's life made him laugh, too. Most folks would have made it even money that Taylor Callahan would have been hanged, by legal or by lynching, long before now, shot dead or gutted in some barroom brawl or battlefield during the recent unpleasantness, which, a decade after the hostilities ceased, wasn't all that recent.

Yet here he was, an ordained preacher, spreading the Word.

That shade sure looked inviting, so Callahan dropped from the saddle and led Job toward it. He tied the horse up to a tree branch, removed the saddle, setting it down in the sun, blanket on top. Wouldn't take long to dry out, not in this heat, not without a cloud to cool things off. Rolled out his bedroll, took saddlebags and canteen, and sat down on the blankets, blessed the water, drank it, opened the saddlebags, and pulled out the Good Book from one and Milton from the other—good balance, that way—for his afternoon reading.

Supper was stale crackers, beef jerky, and coffee, which was packed in the bag that carried Milton. The horse got corn, which was packed in the bag that carried the Good Book. Again, all for balance, like the .45-caliber Colt on one side and the box of cartridges on the other. Taylor Callahan was a man who appreciated balance . . . balance in the world, balance in the saddle, or saddle bags. Why, back during the unpleasantness, in those dark days and nights during which Callahan had again lost his way, he had balance on his hips, two Navy Colts, and underneath his shoulders, a pair of .31-caliber pocket Manhattans.

But now he had balance in his life. No place to go to, and no one to run from. Just drift, like a circuit rider, which is what he had come to call himself. He was taking a circle, a long circle, seeing the elephant, as the saying went, with no ties binding him to one congregation or any particular town.

It was a good life.

Which would have been better had he ever learned how to make decent coffee.

When darkness came, he stamped out the fire he had used to make his coffee. It wasn't like he needed any heat, the one thing Texas had a monopoly on. Most places where Callahan had ridden, the air cooled off when the sun sank, but not in Texas. It would stay hot till a norther blew in sometime around November, if he got lucky.

He rolled out a lariat around his bedroll—a cowboy had taught him that on the trail to Abilene back in '69, saying it would keep the night crawlers and night slitherers away. He rubbed down the horse and gave it the last of a carrot a farm woman had given him three days earlier.

After muttering a prayer and a big thanks to the Major General in the Heavens for getting him through another day, Taylor Callahan closed his eyes and drifted quickly into a dreamless sleep, Milton on his left, the Bible on his right. For balance. And, in case he rolled over during the night, the books would stop him from rolling off the bedroll and onto caliche.

The rattling woke him up.

Not the most pleasant way to greet the dawn, not like hearing coffee boiling. Or a songbird chirping. Rain pattering on a tin roof. Or that gal up in Sedalia who could recite most everything Juliet ever told Romeo. What was her name?

The whirring of the rattles intensified.

Every muscle in Callahan's body tightened, but he managed to slowly turn his head and open his eyes.

A man, he decided, never stops learning, and here's

something that cowpoke on the trail to Abilene had not told Taylor Callahan. Sure, that lariat had done its job. The coiled rattlesnake had crawled neither over nor under the piece of hemp, but, from now on, if he didn't die soon, Callahan would remember to throw a wider loop, as the cowboys liked to say, far enough to keep a snake out of lethal striking distance. This particular rattlesnake was no less than six feet away, and from the looks of him, or her, and the number of his, or her, rattles, it had to be about four feet long.

Those eyes were hypnotic.

Job, the plug gelding, wasn't helping things at all. The snorting, screaming horse kept stamping its hooves, pounding the caliche and scraping the bark on the tree. Had Callahan left the reins on, that horse would be swimming across the bay, gulf, ocean, all the way to South America by now, but Callahan had put a halter and rope around it before turning in, and Job hadn't managed to pull down the scrub of a tree yet, but he sure kept trying.

If Job always had that much enthusiasm, Callahan would have seen the ocean, or gulf, or bay, by now, and likely have been halfway to California, or Florida, depending on which way Callahan had decided to travel. The problem right now was that the rattler seemed to think it was Taylor Callahan who kept causing such a commotion, the tree and the horse being off to Callahan's left, and the rattler on Callahan's right, and Callahan lying there in the path of those fangs.

In the olden days, the hell-roaring years, Callahan could have drawn his revolver and blown a hole right through the viper's flicking tongue and knocked off the head, but gunplay was a thing of the past. Why, he hadn't pulled a trigger since Nathan, Texas, weeks ago.

So Callahan eased his right hand from beneath the covers, and crept ever so gently until it touched the book.

The rattling seemed to intensify, and so did Job's irritation.

Callahan checked to make sure his fingers and thumb still worked. He clamped down on the Bible. Or was it Milton? Bible on the right or Milton? He mixed things up, for balance, naturally, and waking to a coiled rattlesnake ready to sink fangs and venom into your nose wasn't good for remembering picayune things.

The horse squealed louder, and Callahan wasn't sure how much longer that rope would last, or if that horse would trip, fall, and break a leg, leaving Callahan afoot in an empty, hot, dry land, which would be a pity, unless the snake, of course, killed him quickly.

He could pray, not for deliverance, for that struck him as cowardly. The Major General in the Heavens likely had millions of miracles being requested right this moment by women giving birth, mares birthing feisty colts, old-timers suffering from the grippe, and drunks waking with the most awfullest hangovers, and Callahan did not wish to add to the General's lists of things needing attention.

He moved, pretty fast for someone out of the fast-moving trades of rogues.

The snake, not exactly slow of mind or action, struck like lightning.

Chapter 3

Human beings, if Taylor Callahan still could be considered of that pedigree, never got too old to learn something new. On this morning, as the sun broke through so that Callahan saw the light, he learned that a fat Texas rattlesnake packed quite the punch.

As a lifelong Westerner, he had seen rattlesnakes, but usually they got out of his way or he got out of theirs before any harm was done. Or they were already dead. He remembered the rattlesnake-skin tie Captain Carbine Logan wore when he led his Confederate Irregulars up in Missouri and Kansas during the late unpleasantness, as the ladies like to call those four years of butchery. But Texas rattlesnakes had an ornery streak, and Callahan knew that the moment it stopped rattling. And the circuit rider had always been able to predict a demon's next move.

Just before the rattling ceased and the serpent struck, Callahan tilted his Good Book up.

The sound of the rattler's head hitting the leatherbound Bible reminded Callahan of the impact of an Enfield rifle's bullet into a log wall. Later, he wondered what he would have done had the rattler's fangs become stuck in the cover, but during the brief bit of dawn excitement, Callahan was too preoccupied to do any speculating. He sprang to his knees, as the Bible rocked backward. Spotting the stunned rattler, he grabbed it by the tail while at the same time springing to his feet and he whipped the snake like he was winding up to pitch a horseshoe for a ringer ten miles away. He let go, holding his breath while muttering a prayer, and watched.

The Major General in the Heavens let the sky lighten just enough for Callahan to see the rattlesnake spinning, descending and hitting the fork in the trail. It skidded or rolled a few feet, and quickly recoiled and let the rattles sing again—barely audible because Job was still having a conniption.

Callahan caught his breath, amazed that the reptile recovered so quickly. A snake like that would live a long time, he figured. And it had some brains, too, even after smacking a thick, hard, well-read Bible with its pointed head. Uncoiling, it began slithering at amazing speed, and reached that proverbial fork in the road.

Unlike Callahan the previous day, this critter did not stop to contemplate, cogitate, consort, constrict, or console itself. It kept right on commuting . . . down the left fork, toward the bay, gulf, ocean, cistern, whatever. A few moments later, it had disappeared.

Callahan sighed heavily, told Job to shut up, then walked over to the white gelding, and began humming to the animal, then singing, next rubbing its neck. Horses, even a worthless nag like Job, knew when danger had passed, and the gelding calmed down, despite Callahan's out-of-key hymn, and Callahan decided that this was a fine time of morning to hit the trail.

Before the heat started sucking the life out of everyone and everything in this wasteland.

After saddling the white horse, he let Job eat, and looked at his Bible before sticking it in the saddlebags. The Major General in the Heavens had a way of letting you know that your commander was on top of things, all the time. The Bible was heavier, wider and thicker than Milton. Had he put that collection on that side of his bedroll, there was a fair to middling chance that Taylor Callahan would be snakebit and not long for this world, and the way few folks traveled through this part of the country, he might be bleached bones before anyone took notice of him.

He chewed on a bit of jerky for his breakfast, washed it down with water, tugged on his Boss of the Plains, and swung into the saddle.

"Which way do we go?" he asked Job and did not wait for an answer. The rattlesnake had made that decision mighty plain.

"Pappy Number Four wasn't much of a father, but I recollect something he said that struck with me for all these years," Callahan said, trying out his preaching voice though it was a bit early to be testing those voice muscles, especially without any coffee for his breakfast. "'Taylor,' he says, 'only a fool follers a rattlesnake down a hole.'" That was after a hound had taken to digging after a snake disappeared near a stump in the field. Pappy Number Four then kicked the dog and sent it howling toward the barn. Which was another reason that Callahan never cared much for that particular pappy. "Boy," his father said, turning to look at the gangling teenager in the eye, "if you ever see a snake go one way, and you got a choice, you go tuther.

Serpents lured Adam, or was it Eve? Musta been both of 'em. That's what they do, whether they can kill you or just catch mice. They's lurers. Don't ever let 'em lure you."

So Callahan reined Job down the pike that didn't head straight to the Gulf of Mexico. The rattlesnake, well, he could see that ocean. Maybe, he thought with spite, one of them birds—pelicans, or something like that which he had seen drawed up real fine in one of those illustrated newspapers—would eat that rattler for dinner.

Besides, from what all Callahan read and heard, the Pacific was a whole lot bigger and a whole lot prettier, majestic even, than that little patch of blue off the Texas coast. He might get that way in due time. He would keep south on this road, then turn west at some point. Why, he could travel through the territories of New Mexico and Arizona, places he had never seen, land that had to look— if those pictures in those illustrated magazines were anywhere near the truth—a whole lot better than this big patch of nothing.

San Antonio, even that lawless dot on the banks of the Red River called Nathan, offered a whole lot prettier things to see than this country. But maybe things would change.

They didn't. The country just stretched on. The only change was the heat. It kept getting hotter.

Around noon, he thought he was seeing things, and he might have been, with all the sweat that had streamed into his eyes. An elephant was walking north on the southbound trail, but Job did not care a whit about the big beast.

Callahan closed the lids over his eyeballs tightly, shook his head, and let the apparition come into better focus.

Well, it wasn't an elephant after all, but it was moving, raising a bit of dust, and it was coming toward him.

Whatever it was, Job didn't seem to mind. It certainly wasn't a rattlesnake.

He tried to guess at how far away the stranger was, but he had yet to figure out how to guess distances in this flat land. He kept riding, and it kept raising dust.

Ten minutes later, Callahan shook his head and laughed at his stupidity. An elephant? Hardly. It was a cart, pulled by a donkey, with a thin man in pale duds and a straw hat walking alongside the ass.

"Hola," the man called out when some hundred yards, or perhaps fifty, separated them.

"Hola," Callahan said warmly, depleting thirty-three and one-third of the Spanish lingo in his vocabulary.

He reined in Job, took off his hat, and waved.

The man waved his hat and prodded the donkey with a stick. The cart was empty. That could mean, Callahan figured, that the man was coming from a town after having sold his wares. On the other hand, it could mean that the old gent—his hair was white, as was his mustache and goatee—could have been going to a town to fill his cart with supplies to bring back home.

What was the last town Callahan had seen?

The heat had wiped out most of his memory.

The man and the ass and the cart stopped, and they stared.

"Hola," Callahan said again.

"Hola," the old man said.

Those fools at Babel sure had made getting directions or a bead on where a wayfarer was a whole lot harder.

"Do you speak English?" Callahan said, and wondered if he really had tried to sound like a Mexican when he had asked the question.

Whatever the man said probably meant that he understood not a word in English.

"Gracias," Callahan said, and he had just one more Spanish word left.

That word brought light into the man's eyes, and he spoke rapidly all sorts of words, some sounding like music, others like a rattlesnake's warning, and he gestured with his stick and his hand, pointing south, and then at his leg, and then at Callahan's horse, and then at his leg, or it might have been the toes of his sandals, and kept talking and talking, and Callahan looked at the old man's sandals and wondered how a man could walk so far with shoes like that.

When the man stopped speaking, he pointed again down the pike, and looked up at Callahan and spoke again, this time in a more hopeful tone. Well, it sounded that way. How it would have played in Babel, Callahan didn't know.

"Gracias," Callahan said and smiled.

The man made the sign of the cross and spoke reverently at Callahan, pointed the stick south again, and let out a heavy sigh, as if relieved.

"Adios," the man said, and he tapped the donkey with the stick, and the old-timer, the old ass, and the cart squeaked past them and moved north.

"Adios," Callahan said, nodding and grinning at the

fellow wayfarers, and using up the last of Spanish that he knew.

"Vaya con Dios," the old man called out.

Callahan turned around, smiling, and said, *"Vaya con Dios."*

He told himself he'd have to learn the meaning of that phrase. He said it again, three more times, just so he would be unlikely to forget it. Providing the sun didn't suck out all of his memories before nightfall came.

Vaya . . . con . . . Dios. Three more words. Add to that and Callahan would double his Spanish vocabulary.

He watched the old man and the donkey and the cart, decided to take another swig of water from his canteen, then looked at the long, pale road.

"That row ain't gonna hoe itself."

He heard his ma's words, and figured that the road wouldn't be traveled any unless Job got back to walking, so he gave the gelding a kick, and heard the hooves on caliche and kept riding south.

An hour or so later, he saw something else, not an elephant, and not an old Mexican man with an old ass and an empty cart. He knew what the man had been saying, though he had forgotten all of the white-haired man's words except *Hola, Adios, Gracias* and *Vaya con Dios.* It didn't take as long to recognize what he saw, and he kicked Job into a gallop. The horse had to be surprised. He hadn't been put into a lope in quite some time.

Once he reached the figure, Callahan reined hard, and the gelding slid to a stop, kicking up bits of caliche and a cloud of dust. He swung out of the saddle, letting go of the reins, trusting the horse not to wander off. Quickly, he removed the canteen, then let his boots carry him to the man on the side of the road.

Man? Callahan wondered. *Or corpse?*

Kneeling, he slowly rolled the man over, and the man let out a gut-piercing scream.

Not a corpse.

Callahan turned to make sure the shriek hadn't frightened Job, but the horse didn't even glance at the side of the road, just snorted and began dropping a load of manure into the dirt.

"Go ahead, you low-down bushwhacker," the voice on the ground said, and that took Callahan back a number of years. "Kill me. I'm done for anyhow."

Chapter 4

He ought to be dead. In fact, Tommy Browne wished he were dead. Especially after some imbecilic stranger turned him over and sent fifteen million longhorns stamping on his left ankle. He cursed and screamed in agony, and when he could see straight, realized he still had a chance.

"Go ahead, you low-down bushwhacker," he told the dark-haired stranger through gritted teeth. "Kill me. I'm done for, anyhow."

Maybe the man had mercy in his heart. There certainly was something different about his eyes. Clear, like he knew everything anybody needed to know. Or maybe Tommy Browne's head was just fogged over after baking in this furnace for what seemed to be eternity.

Perhaps he was already in Hell.

He tried another tack, asking for mercy, not being belligerent. Which anyone in the county and most of this part of Texas would say took a whole lot of doing. The Brownes were said to be belligerent. Mainly because they were.

"How 'bout a drink of water?" the stranger said.

Tommy wanted to cry. Probably would have, but if

his pa found out he had wept, especially shed tears in front of some stranger, and a man instead of a woman, Ol' Vernon Browne might have granted Tommy's request and killed him right then and there. But Tommy's pa had to be back on the ranch. Of course, Vernon Browne might drag Tommy to death anyway once he learned that his no-account son had let his favorite new colt run away. After it had tossed Tommy onto the hard ground, rolled over him and crushed his ankle and maybe the rest of his leg something good. The last Tommy had seen of the colt—and that was through eyes blinded by tears caused by the most hurt Tommy had ever felt—it was loping off, that fine saddle leaning on the colt's left side, the horse heading north, away from the Browne's ranch.

Vernon Browne admired that saddle something fierce, too, but the way it had looked, it likely would fall off in two or four miles.

Either way, Tommy was as good as dead.

"I said kill me."

He reached for his revolver, only to remember it had flown out of the holster when the colt started bucking. Tommy would have crawled for it and maybe ended his misery, but just trying to turn his leg left him screaming. Besides, he had no idea where the Colt had fallen. He couldn't see it on the ground anywhere, and crawling through rocks and prickly pear didn't appeal to him. Like he could move anyway with his leg busted up so fine and good.

He closed his eyes, sighed, and decided he couldn't blame God for torturing him so. He deserved it. All Brownes deserved it.

The sun baked his eyelids and he wet his cracked lips.

He heard boots on the pale rocks, the horse's hooves moving, more steps, and then a shade covered him. A hand, then an arm, moved under his head, and he felt his upper body lifting, ever so gently, and when Tommy dared open his eyes, he saw the stranger. And his heart exploded when the stranger's right hand brought up an uncorked canteen.

Tommy practically smelled the water.

The canteen came to his cracked, bleeding, dirt-caked lips, and Tommy felt precious water pouring into his mouth. Not enough, though. The canteen came away, and Tommy coughed, then reached, cursing as his hands grasped for the canteen, but caught nothing but air. His leg protested against the quick movement.

The stranger's voice, still calm, said, "Not too much." No more words came till Tommy's eyes opened. "Not too fast."

"Just . . ." Tommy swallowed. "Just a little more?"

The man's empathetic eyes brightened, but the canteen did not move for another undeterminable amount of agony. Finally, it came back, and Tommy tasted the glorious joy of warm water.

Again, the water stopped flowing too soon, and this time the man corked it and set it near the road.

He pushed back his flat-brimmed, open-crowned Stetson, wet his lips with his tongue, and said easily, "Name's Callahan. Taylor Callahan. I'm a circuit rider."

"A judge?" Tommy asked sharply. A lot of those crazy sodbusters in False Hope kept threatening to bring the law down on the Browne ranch.

It had been a long time since Tommy Browne had heard

such a robust laugh. The stranger's eyes even teared over, though Tommy didn't think anything he had said was that funny. When the man could breathe again, he shook his head, that smile never dimming, and said, "Not hardly." He then said: "Preacher."

He didn't look like a preacher, nothing at all like the priest in False Hope. Tommy began to suspicion that this Taylor was a lawman, maybe a Texas Ranger working secretly, in disguise as a preacher—though the man's collar wasn't white, not like the padre's back home.

"Well, we got a preacher already," Tommy said, challenging the man called Taylor. "At least, the Meskins do."

"I see. Where's that?"

"Huh?"

The man smiled again. "Your home?"

"Oh." Tommy hoped the man might give him some more water. When he didn't, Tommy asked, "I could use some more water—something stronger if you got it." He flinched, feeling a sharp pain in his ankle.

"Where's home?" the circuit rider asked again, but explained. "I have one canteen, and it's about empty. So I need to know how far I have to take you."

"You ain't gonna kill me?"

"That ain't my line of work."

The man's face changed then, a haunting covering those clear eyes, and Tommy almost swore he heard the man thinking, but not saying, *anymore*.

Tommy pointed.

"False Hope's about seven miles south."

"False Hope?" the circuit rider asked.

"Well, it's real name is Falstaff. But that don't fit. We call it False Hope."

"That's where you live?"

"Nah. That's the town, which it ain't much of one. Our ranch headquarters be four miles south of it, but that's the closest saloon and general store that we got."

The man studied the land. "This road leads straight to False Hope?"

"Yeah."

"Seven miles?"

"I think." He swallowed, making it loud and dry, and closing his eyes as though in more pain that he was, hoping the stranger would take the hint.

"Is there a doctor in town?"

"Ain't big enough for no pill roller," Tommy said. "Folks gets hurt, they doctors themselves."

The preacher sighed. "Seven miles."

"I think," Tommy said. "Ain't exactly sure. I was riding Pa's new colt. Ain't ten miles, I know that. Might be six, even five, but seven feels right."

The man nodded and let Tommy have a short swallow of water. He could have kissed the preacher's forehead right then, but that would likely torment his ankle.

"So," the stranger said, and this time he took a swallow of water himself. "What happened to you and your pa's colt?"

Tommy told him.

"When did it happen?"

Sighing, Tommy asked, "What day is it, Preacher Man?"

The man's smile was genuine. "Honestly, I don't know."

"Well," Tommy said, "honestly, I ain't right sure. Yesterday. Maybe the day before. My mind's kinda foggy, and my leg hurts like a son of a—" He sighed, swallowed, and whispered, "Sorry, *padre*."

The man's face had turned serious. Even the eyes no longer seemed to be inviting. "You've been baking here, night and day, for a day or two?"

"I reckon."

"And nobody has passed by?"

Tommy turned his head, tried to focus on the spines of the closest cactus, and mumbled, "Well, some Meskin come by . . . I dunno . . . must've been this mornin' . . . yeah, had to be."

"And he just left you here?" The preacher seemed incredulous.

"No, suh. I just wasn't gonna let no bean-eater carry me back to False Hope or all the way to San Pablo. By Jacks, that scoundrel would likely toss me in the back of his cart, haul me into the desert, and feed me to his donkey, let the coyotes eat my bones."

"I see," the preacher said.

"No, suh, I don't think you do see. Where you hail from? You don't talk like no Texan."

"Missouri," he said, pronouncing the last syllable as *uh* instead of *ee*. Which, from what Terry Page, foreman at the Browne ranch, who could tell the difference between a Missouri Reb and a Missouri Yankee, said, put the circuit rider on the right side, as far as the Brownes were concerned, but the traveler needed a bit of a history lesson.

"Ain't you ever heard of the Alamo?"

The eyes beamed again. "I recollect a tale or two. Crockett, right?"

"Yeah, and Bowie and Travis and a bunch of other patriots who got butchered by Meskins. And that bean-eater with the cart and the donkey, for all I know, he shot poor Colonel Davy hisself."

The man nodded. "Could be. Could be he fought alongside Sam Houston at San Jacinto, too. Lots of *Tejanos* did."

"Huh?"

But the stranger was standing now, looking off on the other side of the road, then up the lane toward San Pablo, which had to be a two days' ride from here, and back toward False Hope.

"Which way did your horse take off?" the circuit rider asked and turned his head to see Tommy point.

"Away from home, eh?"

"Yeah. Chuckleheaded son of a—" Again, he cut off the curse.

"That says something about that colt," the stranger said, removed his black hat, and wiped the sweat off his forehead with the sleeve of his shirt. He moved to his horse, a white gelding, that Tommy's pa would have shot to make glue—about all it looked good for—and Tommy watched as the man untied a black coat from behind the cantle. The coat was thrown over the man's left shoulder, and next he reached into one of his saddlebags, and pulled out a knife. A moment later, the circuit rider squatted beside Tommy, rolling up his coat, and sticking it under his head. That's when he must have noticed Tommy's empty holster.

"Where's your iron?" the man asked.

"It fell out while I was trying to keep from eating gravel."

The man smiled, reached his left hand—the one not holding the big Arkansas toothpick—and rubbed the inside lining of the tooled holster. He brought his fingers a few inches below his nose.

"Hog grease?" the stranger asked.

"Makes my draw faster."

"And makes your six-shooter easier to lose." He grinned. "You want your holster to be snug, keep it secure while you're at a gallop or on a rank colt."

"What would you know about that?"

"Not a thing," the man said, and then untied the thong Tommy had to secure his holster on his thigh. Before Tommy realized what the tall man was doing, he had cut off the rawhide with his big knife.

"Hey—what the—"

But this gent Taylor was standing and tossing the string on Tommy's chest. "Don't lose that. I'll need it." The man stepped over Tommy with ease and began walking around the flat, miserable ground. Tommy turned quickly and reached for the canteen, but the clear-eyed man had eyes in the back of his head.

"It's out of reach, Tommy," he said.

Stifling a curse, Tommy turned back to watch the parson as he peered around some catclaw, then used his boot to kick around a clump of grass. The man studied the ground, walked a bit south, then west, then made a beeline twenty or thirty feet away, knelt, and let his left hand disappear behind some prickly pear. It came back into view holding the nickel-plated .45. The man walked back, stood over Tommy, opened the loading gate, pulled the hammer to half cock, and rotated the cylinder, dropping the brass cartridges one by one onto the dirt.

"What are you doing?" Tommy cried out.

When the Colt was empty, the circuit rider lowered the hammer and knelt to pick up the bullets, which he then took to the saddlebags and dropped inside.

"Those are my bullets!" Tommy shouted.

"And your revolver needs cleaning. Sand and dead grass stuck to all that hog grease."

He was walking back now, face calm, eyes seeing everything, and kneeling beside Tommy. But he also reached over and picked up the canteen. "A small swallow," he cautioned and let Tommy drink.

"You wouldn't happen to have anything stronger, would you, Parson Taylor?" Tommy asked when the canteen was removed and corked again.

"Callahan," the stranger said. "Taylor's my first name. Don't worry. I hear that more than I hear 'Rock of Ages.' But you can drop the Parson. Taylor's fine. My pa's ma's maiden name."

Tommy started thinking. He didn't know who he was named after, if he had been named after anyone. His pa certainly never told him, and his pa hardly ever even called him Tommy. It was usually, "Boy," "Bub," "You There," "Jackass," "Fool Kid," "Idiot," or something along those lines, often with profanity coming before and after.

The parson, this Callahan, now wadded up a handkerchief he withdrew from his britches pocket and held that out for Tommy, who took it with a question in his eyes.

"I'd have you bite down on your Colt's barrel," the man said, "but you'd break off your teeth, I expect, and I'll need it for a splint. Wood's scarce in these parts."

"Everything's scarce in these parts," Tommy told him, "except B Cross longhorns, Meskins, and, these days, sodbusters."

The circuit rider made no comment about that but moved toward Tommy's busted ankle.

Now Tommy felt the fear in his gut and everywhere else. "What are you gonna do?"

"I'm gonna have to cut this boot off."

"Noooo." That would be something else Ol' Vernon Browne could take out of Tommy's pay and his hide. He had paid twenty-five dollars for those boots, just last Christmas, over in Goliad. Almost a month's pay.

But Callahan's massive knife was already at work, and Tommy's busted bones in his leg let him know. "Please."

"Buster," the man said, jaw and eyes set, knife slicing leather. "You could've had a nice ride in the back of a cart. You think this hurts, wait till I boost you up on Job."

Tears welled in Tommy's eyes as he quickly stuck the stranger's cotton handkerchief into his mouth and bit down as hard as he could. A Colt's barrel breaking his teeth? Not hardly, Tommy thought. He could have cut down that seven-and-a-half-inch barrel into a sawed-off shopkeeper's special.

When he felt the boot and sock slide free, and heard them land somewhere a few yards away, Tommy spit out the rag as far as he could, then pulled the rest out with his trembling fingers. It took a million hours for him to catch his breath, to dare lift his head, just as high as he could, and find the circuit rider staring down.

"Preacher . . ." Tommy had to pause before he could continue, but this wasn't because of pain, but fear. "How . . . bad . . . is . . . it?" Tommy thought he said it, but wasn't sure the stranger heard.

The circuit rider turned slowly, but the man's face had changed. This Taylor Callahan now looked as if he were somewhere else.

Chapter 5

"Preacher," Billy Joe McTavish whispered, "how bad is it?"

Taylor Callahan, one-time reverend, now bushwhacking guerilla, finished filling a cup with what passed for liquor, and slowly turned toward the teenager and held out the dented piece of tin.

"I ain't . . . no drinkin' man."

You're not even a man, Bub. Callahan held that thought, but other bushwhackers camped in the thicket sniggered at the gangly boy. The rotgut in his left hand made Callahan's eyes water, but he made himself smile while ignoring his fellow Confederates. "You mean to tell me, pardner, that you never sneaked a sip of your daddy's corn liquor?"

"No, sir." The kid's eyes flamed earnestly such as nothing Callahan had seen since this infernal war had commenced.

"Not even once?"

The kid's head shook solemnly.

"Billy Joe, your ol' pap was knowed all the way up to the Ioway border, clear 'cross the Sni-A-Bar, far down to

Cape Girardeau, and at least as far east as Louisville, Kentucky, for brewin' the best corn liquor this side of Sodom and Gomorrah."

"Ma woulda slapped me silly, Preacher."

The smile that creased the beard stubble came honestly. "Your ma was known for a strong backhand, but . . ." Callahan sloshed the liquor and brought it to his nose. The stench almost made him gag, and Callahan wondered how he had managed to drink such foulness as this before he had entered the seminary. "This is medicine, and it's a type of medicine you need, sonny, so we can patch that leg of yourn up and get to some place cooler than these hinges of Hades."

The potent brew would have made Callahan gag, but the pungency came as a blessing compared to the stink and rot rising from McTavish's left foot. "You gotta drink some, Billy Joe."

Despite the sweat cascading down his pale face like creek water after a thunderstorm, McTavish shivered. August in these thickets proved hot enough, but the flames from the fire singed Callahan's braces and moth-eaten bushwhacker's shirt.

"Get on with it, Parson," Carbine Logan said from the fire. "Saw's ready."

Callahan's lips tightened into a hard frown, and he moved from his crouched position and sidled up next to the teenage Missourian who leaned against the rotting hardwood log. Rotting, just like McTavish's foot, courtesy of a Yankee ball.

Putting his right arm around the youngster's shoulders, Callahan eased the cup in his left hand to the boy's lips. McTavish's eyes opened, closed, opened again. It took a while before the boy's blue eyes focused, and then he whispered.

"Must I drinken it, Preacher?"

"It'll make you better, laddie."

"But I promised Mama."

"She'll understand." Callahan made himself smile. "Why, I reckon even your dearest mama, hard-shell that she was, likely sneaked a nip of your daddy's brew from time to time. That's how good his stuff came out. And this here nectar, it ain't quite your daddy's, but it'll sure do the job."

"It'll do a job on'm," Arkansas Plug said as he tamped tobacco into his corncob pipe.

Callahan ignored the interruption, and McTavish apparently did not hear. "And like I done tol' you . . ." Callahan put more warmth into his voice. ". . . it's medicine."

"Where's Buster?" McTavish asked.

"You need to drink this." Callahan spoke firmly. Buster Nicholas was dead. So were three other of Carbine Logan's Irregulars. That was a fitting name for this ramshackle group of misfits. Guerillas fighting for the Southern cause, or, rather, the Western Missouri cause. They weren't known as well as Quantrill's boys or those that rode now with Bloody Bill Anderson, but they were just as mean, just as wild, just as deadly. McTavish, the way Callahan remembered, had probably joined up before he had shed all his baby teeth. It sure felt that way. McTavish had been with them since . . . well . . . Callahan tried not to think about that. Actually, he tried not to think about anything lately, except staying alive. And right now, he wanted to keep Billy Joe McTavish alive. He was the one kid in this bunch who might have a future, a real life, if this unholy war ever ended.

So he held the tin cup at the kid's mouth. When the lips parted, Cutthroat Charly, who had eased up behind the rotting treefall, grabbed McTavish's head and pulled it back hard. The boy's mouth opened, and Callahan poured the rancid brew down the throat. Part of it spilled out of the weak mouth's corner, but much of it went down. Sure, some of the rotgut went down the wrong pipes, but that was to be expected. The boy coughed, and Cutthroat Charly let go of McTavish's shoulders. Callahan jerked the cup away and held it out toward the fire without looking away from the teenager.

"More!" Callahan barked.

The sound of whiskey filling the cup was the only answer he got.

McTavish leaned forward, coughing and spitting, but Cutthroat Charly's hands grabbed the youngster's shoulders and jerked the boy back, just as Callahan returned with a fresh round of snake-oil. Again, the whiskey filled the kid's mouth, but Callahan used his other hand to push the jaw shut, and he held it there until the Adam's apple bobbed twice. Those young blue eyes burned with fright, and the boy's face paled to an even lighter shade of white. When the heavily bearded Cutthroat Charly let the kid up again, Billy Joe McTavish vomited over Callahan's left hand.

"Gawd!" cried one of their compatriots.

Ignoring the filth on his arm—like anything could clean his shirt after all the carnage it had been through—

Callahan brought back the cup, never turning away, not even bothering to try to shake off the vomit on his shirtsleeve.

"More!" he barked.

"Seems a waste of good likker," Monty Howard said.

But again, liquor cascaded down the boy's throat. He bent over, puked between his right leg and his rotting foot, and when he raised his head, his wild eyes found Callahan as the boy wailed, "Please, lordy, please Preacher, don't make me drink no more."

Taylor Callahan dropped the tin cup and landed a haymaker against the kid's jaw. It was a punch like he had thrown before the ministry. Before Kansas redlegs and burned farmsteads. Before peace left Missouri and war— an inhumane, bitter war, as though any war could be benevolent or cordial. Cutthroat Charly caught the boy before his head hit the rotting wood.

Callahan moved fast, grabbing the unconscious kid at the knees and carrying him, with Cutthroat Charly's help, closer to the fire. They eased McTavish to the ground.

By then, Callahan was kneeling, cutting away the boy's left-side britches, grabbing the duck cloth, and jerking up to his knee. Then he removed what remained of the boy's sock, pitching the filth into the fire.

Cutthroat Charly unsheathed the Arkansas toothpick and held it over the flames.

"I'll take that," Callahan said, holding out his right hand a few minutes later. The bearded bushwhacker nodded, laid the knife handle on a rock, and Callahan spun around, grabbed the elkhorn handle and turned back toward the unconscious teen.

Arkansas Plug started whispering a prayer.

Another bushwhacker gagged.

"Grab his arms." Callahan ordered two raiders, before spotting two other bushwhackers. "You two. The legs. Hold him tight. Sit on his knee. You, grab his good leg and don't let go. Put your weight on him. All your weight. I don't want him kicking me. I don't want him to move nary an inch. Sit down on him. Put all your weight into this. Only chance we got to save his life."

"He's out cold," Arkansas Plug said, having regained some strength.

"Conscious or not," Callahan said, already turning and walking on his knees toward the knocked-out youth, "he'll kick harder than one of Barnard's Crooked River mules."

Callahan looked down at the ill-colored foot. He forced down the bile that had started to crest. Carbine Logan came into Callahan's peripheral vision and poured clear whiskey from the jar onto the ugly wound.

Taylor Callahan slashed deep and long.

Billy Joe McTavish's eyes and mouth opened and he tried kicking, but the nurses for the job were good at what they had to do. The boy tried thrashing, screaming, but the ankle and the foot below it never moved. Callahan looked at the flesh he had cut into, and, not liking the look of skin or muscle, had to draw in a deep breath.

"It's no good," he said and inched forward. The next pass of the blade cut into the kid's calf. He moved up to just below the knee, and cut again.

Unconscious, the boy still yelled like a coyote, and fell into a slump, no longer moving.

"He's de-ad," some Missourian said, drawing out the syllable, but Callahan saw the boy was still breathing. The blood ran redder, cleaner, and the muscles and fat weren't a stinking, putrefying wretchedness. Callahan drew a thin cut above his last slash, handed the knife that was taken from his hand by some unseen bushwhacker, before Callahan moved his legs over the boy. He wiped his sweaty palms on his filthy pants legs and held out his hand.

The saw was too big for the job at hand, but it was the only saw the boys had been able to find. The teeth sure would do the job, just as they had on the hardwoods in this thick forest. Cutthroat Charly grabbed the far handle of the cross-cut saw, and the blade sat on the thin, bleeding line of the knife's cut.

No one gave any order. This was no time for orders. Cutthroat Charly simply pulled back on the handle, and Callahan let the saw slide. Blood flowed freely, and Carbine Logan said, "Neil, Harry, get ready. When that lower leg comes off, Joey, you pull it away, and you two buckos burn that stump good and clean, before the boy'll bleeds out like a stuck pig."

The boy screamed as the saw cut deeper, but it was the shriek of someone in a nightmare. His head turned left, right, and fell still, until the teeth of the saw hit bone.

His birthing pa had owned a sawmill up on the Shoal. The man's hands were as hard as flowering dogwood. That name never seemed right to Taylor Callahan. Flowering dogwood. It just didn't fit for wood that wasn't worth anything but using for mallets or fence posts or handles for tools. That's why they called it ironwood, and that's what they called Taylor Callahan's pa. Ironwood Callahan. Well, he sure was a hard man who had lived a hard but mostly honest life. And had raised a son bound for Hell's hottest fires, or so folks thought. So thought Taylor Callahan, but not his ma. No, not Ma. Well, mothers tended to see goodness in their children, even the most-rotten ones. And rotten had been Taylor Callahan from the time he was twelve until he reached seventeen.

Folks figured he was bound for the gallows—if he lived that long—but more likely, he'd be bled out in some alley behind some Kansas City bucket of blood, from knife wound or pistol shot.

It was a Clay County miracle. That's what folks called it. Young Taylor Callahan had seen the light and heard the call and had taken off to the Logan's Knob Seminary down south of Sparta in the Ozark hills. Married a fine girl from Springfield, of good stock, and with a whale of a soprano voice that lured many a sinner into the log-cabin church that got started outside of Liberty.

It had been a good time, but the Lord had to test his servants, and the Border Wars failed many a man. Kansas Redlegs. John Brown's boys. Not that Missourians remembered the teachings and that turning the other cheek was the way to go, the way to redemption, salvation, and a swollen cheek.

The flames reminded Taylor Callahan of those trying times, times that had yet to end. So did the blood that soaked into the ground where once Billy Joe McTavish's lower left leg had been before some of the boys went to carry it off.

Liquor, maybe not quite as robust or lethal as the corn fire they had poured into Billy Joe McTavish's belly but that would surely strip the bark off a tree, splashed into a cup, and the cup appeared under Callahan's jaw.

His eyes raised.

"I'd say you earnt it, Preacher," Captain Carbine Logan said.

Chapter 6

"I haven't been a preacher in years, Captain." Callahan heard the words, knew he had said them, and he shook his head at the cup of dark whiskey.

"You ain't no doctor, neither," the leader of the irregulars said, "but you done a right good job on the kid."

Callahan looked at the one-legged teen. Captain Carbine Logan handed the cup of liquor to Cutthroat Charly, who thanked his commander and guzzled down the brew.

"We'll see," Callahan said, feeling as though he had aged ten years in ten minutes. And how much older was he now, after riding with Captain Carbine Logan's Confederate Irregulars? Methuselah would be a youngster compared to Taylor Callahan.

"Can he travel?"

Callahan's head shook. "Not for a day or two. If he lives that long."

"Yeah." Logan reached out behind him, and a moment later squatted, holding a tin cup of whiskey for himself. He sipped it like brandy, reminding Callahan of the days before the war, when Carbine Logan was known in Harrisburg as Carlton Logan, schoolmaster and poet, a man who knew good brandy and kept fine company. The toast of Harrisburg. Why, a newspaper reporter had traveled all the way from St. Louis to talk to Mister Logan about Lord Byron and John Milton and what he and Charles Dickens had talked about when the English writer toured across the United States and lighted in St. Louis back in '42.

"Well, this thicket's safe as anywheres, I reckon," Logan said. "Plenty of ticks and skeeters to keep you comp'ny."

"Better'n Yanks," Arkansas Plug said.

Both Callahan and Logan ignored the ruffian.

"Me and the boys'll be takin' off for The Holler. We'll lay low there for a week or ten days, let the bluebellies feel like they've done somethin' worth celebratin'."

Callahan looked at the boy's chest, timing the breaths. "I reckon I'll know about McTavish before then," he said without much feeling one way or the other. "If you ain't at The Holler . . ."

"You'll find us." A slight crease appeared on Logan's face, about as close to a smile as he ever got. "Just be careful who you ask."

"I'm a careful man."

"I'll leave one man with you. Way we've been gettin' shot up of late, that's all I can spare." He looked again at McTavish. "Sure hate losin' him. He was a mite wet behind the ears, but he was game." He sipped whiskey and called out a command, but kept looking at the missing leg, the wrapped stump bandaged with moss and other Missouri cure-alls. "Mount up!"

Another gulp finished the liquor. "You got any requests for a pardner?"

Callahan's head shook. "Someone who isn't pepperin' me with questions all the time."

"Shakespeare!" Carbine Logan barked. He did not wait for a reply. "Cut out two hosses who ain't got no riders no more. And yourn and the preacher's mounts. You'll be stayin' here."

No answer came. None was needed. Folks who rode with Carbine Logan's Irregulars knew what was expected and what wasn't.

He sighed, and Logan wasn't the sighing type. "Reckon we'll leave a shovel and pick. But hoping you won't have no need for 'em." His face turned back to the unconscious teen. "Game as a bantam cock, he was. He *is*." He smiled without any feeling and held out his hand. "So be you, Preacher."

"And you, Capt'n."

His knees popped as he rose, and he tossed the empty cup to the nearest man, Cutthroat Charly, who held the reins to the captain's gelding.

The right hand came down, and Callahan grasped the firm grip.

"I'll be seeing you soon, Brother."

"I look forward to it, Captain."

Carbine Logan spun around, pulled his hat down tighter on his head, and swung into the saddle. He did not look back at the preacher or the one-legged cripple, but spurred the bay slightly, and led the column of what had once totaled more than one hundred and seventy-five men to the deer trail that would lead them out of the forest and to a woods road.

And Taylor Callahan knew he would never see Carl Logan again. At least, not in this world.

* * *

For the rest of the day, and all the next, Shakespeare—a former schoolmaster, like Carbine Logan, only Shakespeare hailed from the prairie country down south and closer to the Kansas border—kept his nose buried in Sir Thomas Malory.

McTavish came to briefly the next morning, then consciousness became fleeting, but the fever broke after noon, and his sleep turned more relaxing, less fleeting.

The second day was worse. That's when the kid realized his left leg was gone below the knee, and the tears flowed like sweat in a forest that trapped heat like one of Ol' Badger's catfish traps that held twenty-pounders in the Missouri River bottoms.

Shakespeare peeked over the leatherbound book he had been reading. "Hey, Billy Joe," he called out. "Does it itch?"

The kid looked over, face pale, eyes red from crying so hard.

"Huh?"

Callahan's eyes rose above the fire where he was boiling soup, but the look on his face burned with a mixture of anger and disgust.

"Your missing leg, kid." Shakespeare grinned harder. "I've always heard that you'll feel an itch just like the leg wasn't buried over beyond the clearing where the picket line is."

McTavish's face turned blank, before a new paleness made him look like a corpse.

"Mister," Callahan said, his voice low but firm. "I liked

you a lot better when you kept your nose in *Le Morte d'Arthur* and your trap shut."

The bushwhacker laughed and opened another book.

Callahan filled a wooden bowl with a bland soup and brought it over to the boy.

"I ain't hungry, Preacher," he whispered.

"You need to eat," Callahan said. "Get some strength up so we can get back to Capt'n Logan and our pards."

The head shook. "Won't be able to help you-all no more. Not bein' crippled."

"You ain't crippled, son," Callahan said, setting the bowl on a rock near the rotting treefall and pulling a spoon from the pocket in his trimmed bushwhacker shirt. "You just got one leg. Actually, one and a half legs. You'll be fine. We'll have a wooden leg on you in no time, and you'll be ridin' with the boys and dancin' with all the pretty girls betwixt Hannibal and Nevada."

"I still ain't hungry."

"Well, I am. I'm hungry for something to see other than trees, leaves, and branch water. I'd like to see the sky again, and a sunrise. And I bet you'd like to see that pretty ga . . . what was her name?"

"Beth."

"Beth. That's right. Bet she'd like to see you, too."

"No." The head shook firmly. "She deserves a whole man."

"You're a lot more whole than most men I've known." He brought the spoon up. "Too full growed to be fed like an infant. So you eat. And I'll check our doctorin'."

To Callahan's surprise, the boy ate, though his hand was unsteady, and he paid more attention to what Callahan was doing than trying to get soup, which wasn't much more than heated broth, from the wooden bowl to his mouth.

Callahan pulled away the burlap sack, then lifted the bandages. The boys had done a fine job cauterizing the stump. It smelled like burned meat, but that was a much better aroma than the rot they had smelled before.

"How is it?" Billy Joe McTavish asked.

Callahan nodded, and dipped his hand in a jar of Arkansas Plug's salve, slathered it on, then brought up the burlap that held the moss and other healing powers—or so some folks swore—and tied the rawhide string around what was left of the boy's left leg.

"Don't look bad, Billy Joe. Not bad at all. We'll let you rest another day or two, then start out."

"I don't reckon I can fork a saddle, Preacher."

"Sure, you will. You got a thigh, and that's what keeps you on a hoss. Till we get that wooden leg fitted for you, at least. But Shakespeare and me'll fix you up a travois. Haul you back to The Holler." He grinned. "Lessen you want to stop off and see Beth first."

The boy smiled.

The kid talked a lot the next day, while Shakespeare read and did a couple of scouting jobs back toward the main pike. Callahan tended the horses, rubbing them down, feeding them, and letting them drink from the branch. He also started on the travois they'd need to get the boy out of the woods.

"What'll you tell the Yanks iffen we come acrost a patrol?" McTavish asked that evening after finishing a bowl of soup.

"That a tree fell on you, crushed your leg, had to cut it off."

"You reckon you and Shakespeare can pass yourself off as lumberjacks?"

Callahan, and even Shakespeare, now cleaning his pair of Navy Colts, laughed at that.

Callahan held out his hands, palms facing the boy. "See these hands," he said. "They didn't always hold the Good Book."

And then he dropped his gaze and looked at the hard hands himself. His next words came out in a whisper. "They haven't held a Good Book in some time."

"What made you come to ride with the Capt'n?" McTavish asked.

Callahan shrugged. "Felt like the thing to do."

"You reckon we done right?"

"I don't know."

"Bible says killin' ain't right."

"But the Book's also filled with a lot of killin'. Bad men gettin' planted, same as good men gettin' killed." He pointed his chin at the bowl. "You ain't finished your soup, Billy Joe."

"Kinda off my feed, I reckon."

Callahan placed the back of his hand on the boy's forehead. "You feel warm?"

The boy smiled. "Preacher, this ain't exactly December."

"Reckon you're right."

As he poured the last of the coffee into tin cups the next day, the boy slept, and Shakespeare knelt by the fire. Callahan handed one cup to the bushwhacker.

"Reckon we can pull out today?" Shakespeare asked.

"I don't know." He tried to sip coffee but blew on the hot black brew instead.

"They tell me you were hard on horses, women, and men back in the day." Shakespeare tried to cool his coffee, too.

Callahan did not look at the bushwhacker. "Folks say lots of things."

"I hear you were riding straight for the gallows."

"I was."

"What changed your ways?"

Callahan grinned and sipped the coffee. "Ever seen a gallows, Shakespeare?"

The killer laughed.

"So, you go from mad-dog rapscallion to choir boy." Shakespeare blew on the cup again, then took another sip. "Then you're preaching the Word and the Truth, even when Jim Lane's Kansas scum were burning Osceola and murdering good men. A year later . . . I read, anyway, that you and a handful of our boys even joined Quantrill when he left Lawrence in ashes."

Callahan's head tilted toward Shakespeare's bedroll. "I didn't know the Bard mentioned that in *The Most Lamentable Tragedy of Titus Andronicus*."

Shakespeare's laugh sounded almost musical, like there was a human being beneath the callousness and coldness. "See, you're an educated man. Not like most of the scum we ride with. But I notice you'll switch to that Missouri drawl. Educated one minute, sounding like a hick the next."

A long silence held them, but Shakespeare had to hear himself opine on something. "You're more than welcome to borrow Malory if you'd like. Or *Titus Andronicus*."

"I prefer Shakespeare's comedies," Callahan said.

"See what I mean. You're a man of contradictions. Preaching against violence, but riding with the coldest killers on the border."

"I wouldn't call 'em scum. The capt'n, he's smarter than a dozen newspaper editors and college perfessers."

Shakespeare smiled. "There's that drawl, again."

They sipped coffee. "Well, we can't stay here much longer," Shakespeare said. "Food's running out, and it's not like there's much game in this furnace to be found. Besides, this coffee is weaker than that boy's heart."

"Why don't you go back to reading?"

"That's another thing about you that mystifies me, Callahan. You're a preacher, and I've never seen you open a Bible once."

Callahan rose, drank the rest of his coffee, and said, "I like *All's Well That Ends Well.*"

"Yeah." Shakespeare leaned back, set the empty cup by one of his holstered Navy Colts, picked up a pine needle, and stuck it in his mouth. "There's another one of your contradictions. You know as well as I do that all's well that ends well—men like you and me, even that gimp boy now—all's well that ends well . . . that's not for the likes of us."

Chapter 7

"Eat your soup, Billy Joe," Callahan said.

Soup. His head shook. It wasn't much more than heated branch water, though Shakespeare had managed to empty his flask of the last of his brandy. Speaking of a man of contradictions, Shakespeare was certainly one.

"Don't reckon I'm hungry, Preacher."

"You want to look your best when you see that sweetheart of yourn, so you need to eat up. Otherwise, I'll think you're insulting the cook."

"I don't think you'd mind."

"I wouldn't, Billy Joe, but Shakespeare." Callahan tilted his head toward the bushwhacker who again was reading Sir Thomas Malory, having finished *Titus Andronicus* a few times the day before. "This morn was Shakespeare's turn to cook up your breakfast."

"Soup . . . for breakfast." The kid sighed.

"Well, I bet your sweetheart'll fry up a pound of bacon and a dozen eggs, maybe some flapjacks with maple syrup, and fresh milk."

He lowered the burlap and breathed a sigh of relief.

He smelled no rot. He placed his hand against the kid's forehead, and it didn't feel hot.

"Preacher?"

Callahan looked at Billy Joe McTavish, smiling as he pulled up the burlap, not bothering with the last of the salve, and quickly tightened the rawhide thongs.

"Looking fine, Billy Joe," Callahan said.

Shakespeare came over, holding a jug. He pulled out the cork, and filled the coffee cup with clear liquor.

"I don't want you wastin' good brandy on me, Shakespeare," the kid said.

"I'm not." The bushwhacker smiled. "This was left by Arkansas Plug. You drank all my good brandy tuther day. But this'll cure what ails you." He handed the liquor to the boy, who took it in a trembling hand.

"Y'all ain't gonna let me drink alone, is you?"

Shakespeare looked around for another cup, but those were by the hot coals of the fire, so he brought up the clay jug, and tapped the side of the tin cup. The kid drank, coughed, while Shakespeare took a long pull, then handed the jug to Callahan.

"No thanks."

"You ain't gonna drink with me?" the kid wailed.

"You don't want me even touching communion wine, son."

"Drink!" Shakespeare ordered.

"No," Callahan answered, but looked only at the boy.

"That's all right. I savvy what you're saying, Preacher." McTavish laughed so hard he spilled the rest of the liquor on his filthy shirt. "Ma and Pa wouldn't want me to lead a preacher down the wrong path."

When McTavish was asleep, Shakespeare came up to Callahan.

"I've been staying around this stinking cesspool for what feels like forever. I'm not sticking around waiting days for the boy to croak."

"Nobody's keeping you. Ride out. You can find The Holler, I'm sure." He walked few rods, stopped, and looked. Shakespeare hadn't moved. The man's thin lips moved, but he spoke not a word.

Realization hit Callahan, and he almost laughed. "You don't know your way out, do you?"

When the bushwhacker didn't answer, Callahan tilted his head toward the northwest. "There's a deer trail. Same one we followed in. Just follow it out to the pike. A man of letters like you can figure that out."

Callahan still stood like a statue.

"It's all right. By grab, Shakespeare, I'm surprised you haven't lit a shuck long before now."

"I'm not used to this country," the bushwhacker said. "The trail . . . well . . . there are forks."

"And the way out is the trail with plenty of hoofprints."

"No. The captain said stay. I'll stay."

"Suit yourself."

The man was scared. Well, a place like this, it could unnerve many a man. Callahan had learned something after all those months riding around with Shakespeare. The man was human like all the rest of the boys.

"Preacher."

"What is it, Billy Joe?"

The gloaming had settled over the thicket, not that it

cooled down the air. The air here never moved, and the heat remained constant, trapped by the thick woods and the August leaves. No wind. Not much light.

"You ain't gonna bury me here, will you?"

Callahan put his hand again on the boy's forehead. "I got some hard news for you, boy, and that's you ain't gonna die. At least, not from rot or that Yankee ball in your foot."

The boy's face brightened.

"Honest?"

"As the day is long."

"But I had a dream last night."

Callahan's head tilted slightly.

"It was my grannie's funeral. I mean, before we took her out of the house and to the graveyard. I walk outside, and I'm lookin' at the sky, and there's not even thunder, jus' lightnin', but like nothin' I ever seed before. They's little . . . well . . . like little suns, or meteors, or somethin', shootin' 'cross the sky. Hunnerds of 'em."

"Ball lightning," Callahan said.

"Is that what it was?"

"If it's what I think you're describing . . ." Callahan nodded.

"Well, I don't know what it was. Ball lightnin'. Reckon it makes sense. But I knowed what it meant."

Callahan leaned closer. "What did it mean, Billy Joe?"

"It was . . . well . . . Grannie was dead, and we was mournin' her . . . I mean . . . Well . . . she was tellin' me, through the ball lightnin' to have faith. That all that lightnin', it was all the angels in Heaven and they was welcomin' her to the fold. That's what it meant."

The kid smiled. Callahan saw that until the tears in his own eyes blinded his vision.

"That's a fine dream."

"Weren't no dream, though, Preacher," the boy said. "I saw it. Saw it when Grannie was called to Glory. I just dreamed it like I saw it. What does it mean, Preacher?"

"I've never seen ball lightning myself, Billy Joe," Callahan told him. "In person or in a dream. Just read about it. But, like I say, it's a fine dream."

"You can use it in a sermon sometime."

Callahan looked at the wood chips and weeds. "Well . . ." *Like he'd ever be allowed in a church again.*

He looked down at the billowy, embroidered collarless shirt with the big pockets that he had flung to the dead coals in the fire ring. A milliner from Independence had made him that shirt. A good-looking woman from a well-to-do family, and folks said her papa was a lawyer for the Union. Then he grabbed another shirt, walked a few paces, and tossed a clean calico shirt onto Shakespeare's book. "Best put this on," Callahan said.

Looking up with annoyance at the preacher, Shakespeare glanced at the shirt, then turned to see Billy Joe McTavish struggling to pull off his embroidered shirt.

"You quitting the captain?" Shakespeare asked.

"I'm not going to risk the three of us running into a Yankee patrol and explaining how come we wear shirts they find on the bodies of dead guerrillas. You want to do that?"

The book's cover slammed shut, and Shakespeare began removing his shirt.

* * *

Shakespeare came to help, without even being asked. Probably, Callahan figured, because he really wanted to get out of this thicket.

"Ready?" Callahan asked. He was speaking to McTavish, but it was the older bushwhacker who answered.

"Let's do it."

They boosted the kid into the saddle. He grasped for the reins, but it took a while before he found them. The horse danced a bit but eventually settled down.

"How's it feel?" Callahan asked.

"Diff'rent."

"Can you stay in the saddle?" Shakespeare asked.

"Reckon we'll find out."

Callahan liked the boy's grit.

"Just hold steady," the preacher said, and walked to the picket line to get the other horses. Shakespeare had saddled two and put the packs on the extra horse. They had expected to be carting a body out of the thicket, but that boy might live to see another birthday.

If the Yanks didn't ambush them.

"Well?" Shakespeare said as he took the reins to his horse.

"We'll take him to a church. First one we come to."

"Why?"

"You want to take him all the way to The Holler?"

"Ask a stupid question . . ." Shakespeare swung into the saddle.

Callahan pulled the Remington revolvers from his own waistband, and stuck them in the saddlebags, too, but he found a hideaway gun, and slipped it inside his right boot top.

"Lose one of your Navies," he told the bushwhacker. "One gun'll pass. Two will give you away as a border man."

"What's our story?" Shakespeare asked, but he did remove one of the Colts and drop it in his war bag.

"Loggers. Tree fell on the boy. Busted his leg. The rest of the story's true. Gangrene set in. Had to take off part of his leg. Now we're taking him to his folks."

"Where's our logs? Our tools?"

"We left them in the thicket. Plan to come back when we've seen to our young pard."

"What about our long hair? That'll give us away as Missourians."

Callahan shook his head. "Ain't like there are many barbers in these thickets."

After swinging into the saddle, Shakespeare pushed back his hat. "You think this'll work?"

"I'm hoping we don't have to find out." He stepped easily into the stirrup. "You take the packhorse," he told Shakespeare. He wasn't sure he trusted the bushwhacker with two free hands and a handy Navy Colt.

The horses started out skittery, having not been ridden in several days, but Callahan kicked his mount and led the way through the clearing to the deer trail.

There was no wind, no noise except cicadas, horse hooves and the occasional blowing from one of their horses. Three hours, they roamed down the trails, into one ravine, climbing out of the saddles to lead the animals up the other side. Sweating more as the day wore on.

The trail was rough, but easy enough to follow, just as Callahan had told Shakespeare. Hooves marked the way, hooves and horse apples, and Callahan's mount needed little guidance with the reins. Animals were smart.

Later, when the woods thinned, and a few birds called out in the distance, Callahan reined up, swung to the ground, and motioned Shakespeare to ride up. The bushwhacker handed the lead rope to the pack horse to McTavish, rode and stopped his horse near Callahan.

"Wait here till I give you the signal," Callahan said. He held out the reins to his horse for Shakespeare. "I'll take a look-see."

Afoot, Callahan eased off the trail some thirty yards, then pushed through the brambles, down another ravine, out of it, and came to the pike, where he slipped into the bar ditch, and waited, looking, listening, guessing. Birds sang, crickets chirped, and the road remained unoccupied. Convinced at last, he stood up, climbed out of the ditch, and walked to the trail, where he waved at Shakespeare and the kid. When both emerged from the woods, the bushwhacker stopped. Callahan took the reins and mounted his horse.

He nodded down the pike.

"The Holler's that-away," Shakespeare said.

"There's a church down this way. Billy Joe. We'll leave you there. They'll get you back home or get word to your folks." He smiled. "When you're all healed up, get word to the captain and we'll come fetch you to finish our job."

Knowing, of course, that all the guerillas in this part of Missouri would be finished. There were just way too many Yankees, and the war hadn't been going well for the South in better than a year.

"There's also a Yankee camp five miles or so in that direction," Shakespeare said.

"So I've heard." Callahan pushed back his black slouch hat. "But loggers have no need to fear bluecoats." Yet now he twisted in his saddle, and untied the frock coat of black broadcloth and slipped it on.

"It seems a mite warm for that, Preacher," Shakespeare said. "Even these nights are hotter than the fiery pit."

"Not so. Not so. You've never felt the fires of Hell, Shakespeare. But I warrant, one day not far away, you will."

Chapter 8

The riders were barely visible in the gloaming, but Callahan knew they were Federals. So did Shakespeare, who eared back the hammer on his Navy.

"Leave it be," Callahan said, and he reined up.

"They're bluebellies."

"It ain't that dark, and I ain't that blind. I also know that if you start the ball, they'll be burying all of us—unless they leave us to rot. Just follow my lead. If we have to shoot our way out, we'll die game. But I ain't all jo-fired about dying game right now, so let's see what a palaver will get us."

"I'd rather die by lead than by hemp."

"Just follow my lead." Callahan held up his right hand in a friendly wave.

There had to be forty of them, Yankees. Regular troops, not Redlegs or other vermin, and even in the darkening skies, Callahan knew these were battle-hardened troops who had likely seen the elephant from Wilson's Creek to Pea Ridge.

And they weren't going to be taken by surprise. Carbines were jacked from scabbards, pistols drawn. Half of the men stayed behind, out of pistol range, while the rest spread out. Two riders took their mounts into the woods on one side of the road, and two others went into the forest on the other side, flushing out game or taking cover. The commander of this troop had been in Missouri long enough to know how irregulars played the game.

"Evening," the captain said as he reined up. Even he held a Remington revolver in his right hand, though, for the time being, the barrel was aimed at the pike behind the black stallion's right front leg. "You appear to have had some trouble."

He motioned with his head at the lieutenant behind him, and the redheaded soldier dismounted, and called out for a sergeant and another Yank.

"Tree fell on the poor lad," Callahan said. "Busted his leg. We were far back in the woods. Had to amputate, the leg was so bad off."

The lieutenant and his entourage had made for Mc-Tavish, who gripped the horn on his saddle and shook as though he had a bad chill.

The captain introduced himself and his unit, then demanded their names.

With a flourish, Callahan removed his black hat, letting the long locks fly in the wind, and he bowed. "I am Taylor Callahan," he said. "And this is . . ." All those months of riding and raiding with Carbine Logan and he had never known Shakespeare by any other name. ". . . Tom Malory."

"I've heard that name," said a soldier a few horses back.

"Malory?" Callahan smiled.

"No. Yourn."

"By chance are you from Liberty, sir?"

"He's not a sir," said the captain, "but a trooper. And we're all from Indiana."

"A fine state, or so I've heard." Callahan pointed off in a northwesterly direction. "There's a log cabin about four miles from Liberty on road to Excelsior Springs. I preached there. Did, at least, till Kansans burned me out."

"Why did they do that?" the captain asked.

"I didn't ask. I just ran to keep from burning with the pews and pulpit."

Some of the boys laughed, but not the captain.

"So you're no Yankee-lover."

"I love all men. Even those that wish to do ill upon me." He drew in a deep breath, held it, and let it go. "War brings out the worst in men, and we are in a time of war. I'll rebuild my church one day. Maybe those that poured coal oil on the roof and tossed torches to the church will help rebuild it."

"I think you're a lousy coward," said the sergeant who held the horse carrying McTavish's remains.

"Coward?" Callahan shrugged. "Perhaps. I cannot say. ed? Bound for Purgatory? That, brother, will be up to the Almighty."

"Who's the boy?" the lieutenant said.

Callahan opened his mouth, but the commander said, "Let's hear it from the kid. Unless you cut out his tongue when you cut off his lower leg."

"My name," the boy said, "is Peg Leg Luke."

He smiled. And even a few of the Yankees chuckled.

"You don't have a peg leg yet, boy," the Yankee leader said.

"But I aim to," the boy said. "From the tree that knocked this one off."

"You know, Captain," said one of the Yanks, too far back for Callahan to make out the face, "these woodpeckers' hair is fairly long. Like them Reb butchers we've been killin' like flies of late."

Callahan was expecting that comment, and he was ready, and spoke quickly before Billy Joe or even Shakespeare panicked and started a ball that would end with their deaths. "The paintings I see of men from the Testaments, Old and New, from Moses and Noah to Paul and Matthew, show that they wore their hair long, too. Perhaps because the Philistines ran off all the barbers like Unionists and Secesh have done across Missouri of late."

"Can you quote us some Scripture, Parson?" another sergeant asked.

"Old or New?" Callahan smiled.

"How about Philemon?" the captain said. "Chapter Two. Verse Fifteen."

Callahan grinned, but this time with pleasure. "I'm glad you asked me for that specific passage, Capt'n, for it is among my favorites." He removed his hat with his left hand. "A man who wishes to hear that bit of scripture is a man who knows exactly what he wants. No wonder you have risen to your esteemed rank, sir."

"Just quote the passage, Reverend," the Yank said.

Callahan nodded, bowed, and looked toward the blackening sky. "'When I was a child,'" he said, "'I spake as a child, I understood as a child, I thought as a child: but when I became a man, I put away childish things.'"

The hat returned to his head. "Of course," he said as he watched the major grinning and while unfastening the flap of his holster, "that's actually from First Corinthians.

Because, good Capt'n, I think you know as well as I do that Paul's Epistle to Philemon is quite short. Just one book, only twenty-five verses."

The officer's hand came away from the holster, and he touched the brim of his hat. *"Touché."*

Chapter 9

"By the saints, Captain," another officer called out from the woods to Callahan's right. "We'll be here all night."

"I'm still in command," the officer roared, startling his horse, which spooked the others, leaving the Yankees cursing and trying to control the animals.

"Light a match," the captain ordered. "I want a better look at the faces of these . . . woodcutters. I've been fightin' bushwhackers so long, I can tell one by the look of his eyes."

"Here," Callahan said, and he slid out of the saddle. "I've got not only lucifers but also a few candles in my saddle-bags."

To his surprise, not one Yankee aimed a weapon and no one demanded that he stop. Callahan slid to the saddle bags, and unfastened the buckles. Maybe these troopers weren't so battle-savvy after all. He flipped up the cover, and reached inside. The revolver's butt was cold to the touch. He dared not look at Shakespeare. That would be a dead giveaway.

And this was how it would end. The captain would be

dead. Shakespeare was so good, he'd likely take three or four, even in the darkness, before they plugged him. Billy Joe McTavish might even have enough sand to kill one. The Yanks might even chop off Callahan's head and stick it on a pike as a warning to all bushwhackers.

"My Lord," said one of the soldiers. "Look at that."

Callahan turned, his right hand still touching the revolver, and he saw the fire in the sky, well off to the rest.

"Is it artillery?" asked a young Federal.

"Gosh," whispered the sergeant. "It's beautiful."

"It's like Grandma's funeral . . ." Billy Joe McTavish's sentence came out like the lyric to a song.

"St. Elmo's fire," suggested one Yankee.

Another said: "Ball lightning."

No. No Yankee said that. It was Taylor Callahan. Then he heard Billy Joe McTavish's words.

. . . *she was tellin' me, through the ball lightnin' to have faith. That all that lightnin', it was all the angels in Heaven and they was welcomin' her to the fold. That's what it meant.*

A lantern flared. "Don't bother with your candles, Preacher," said a Yankee. "We got this."

"I ain't never seen the likes," whispered a bluecoat.

"Ball lightning," said a Yankee. "What does it mean?"

But Taylor Callahan knew what it meant. Thought he did anyway. He pulled his hand out of the saddlebag, walked around the horse, and stepped up to the captain's side. Using both hands, he raised the leather-bound Bible, dried and still smelling of smoke from the cabin fire, the top right corner ripped, the pages brittle, and sometimes it felt as though it weighed more than an anvil, but on this evening, it was light as a feather.

"Perhaps you'd like to touch up on your Testaments, Major."

"Captain," the Yankee corrected.

Callahan turned to look at the fireworks in the sky.

He expected the Yank to put a ball in the back of his head, but if this was where Taylor Callahan's life ended, he'd be looking at something wonderful, something beautiful, something different than all he had been through the last few years.

"We have to get to New Jerusalem," the officer spoke. "Reverend, you will ride with us. Your colleague can take your gimp kid to that church or wherever. But we have need of your services in New Jerusalem."

Slowly, Callahan turned around. "Mount up," the captain barked, and called to the men still in the woods. "Lieutenant Jameson, Corporal Weatherby, fall into formation with your men." He fuddled with the leather covering of his holster, cleared his throat, spat, and stared at Callahan. "If you will oblige us, Reverend." He sighed. "Please."

Callahan nodded and stepped closer to Shakespeare and the kid. Suddenly, he shook his head and laughed softly. "Don't that beat all?"

Shakespeare seemed at a loss for words.

"You find the church," he said. "They'll take care of Billy Joe."

"You can't go with 'em, Preacher," Billy Joe McTavish said. His voice dropped into a whisper. "Someone might recognize you, tell 'em who you been ridin' with."

"I don't know why they need you in New Jerusalem," Shakespeare said.

Callahan winked. "Reckon I'll tell you next time I see you."

Shakespeare turned human. "I reckon I owe you."

"Forget it." He held out his hand. They shook, and Callahan slipped past the horse and held out his hand toward the kid.

"Billy Joe," he said. "You get stronger. And remember. Farmin' ain't all that excitin', but it makes for a better life than fightin'."

They shook, and Callahan turned around, took the reins to his horse, and eased into the saddle.

He did not look back, as Shakespeare guided the packhorse he pulled behind him to the right of the road, followed by Billy Joe. They eased through the darkness down the narrow lane.

"I hope you can ride like the devil," the sergeant said as he passed Callahan and swung onto his horse.

"I've been told," Callahan said, "that I ride like a Missouri bushwhacker."

Chapter 10

They rode hard all night, following the Yankee cavalry practice of galloping at ten miles an hour, trotting at seven-and-a-half miles an hour, and walking at three-and-three-fourths miles an hour, stopping to rest, and eating hardtack that would break a man's teeth if he didn't soak it in water first. Coffee would have been better, but the supper break was a cold camp.

At dawn, they arrived at New Jerusalem.

Or what was left of the Missouri town.

The church was the one building the raiders had spared, Callahan thought, until he realized they had torched it, too. Only the well was closer to the church than the one-street town, so the bucket brigade had managed to put out the flames before the inferno consumed more than the preacher's office.

"Preacher . . ." the Yank in charge called out.

But Callahan handed him the reins to his horse. "I know what to do," he said. He had pulled his Bible out of the saddlebags. Now he tugged the black slouch hat tight on his head and ran to the first Yankee soldier.

There was nothing to do for this poor soul but fold his

arms over his chest, close the eyes, and whisper a short prayer.

He ripped off his shirtsleeve to use as a tourniquet for a civilian's arm.

Then he came to the girl, ten, maybe eleven years old. Finding a bucket of water nearby, he hurried to it, loosening the bandanna around his neck, soaking the dirty piece of red silk, then hurrying back to the child. He scrubbed the blood off the face as best he could, had to go back to the bucket to clean the rag and clean some more. By then, as he used his fingers to comb the hair, and then cleanse the face more, he rolled up the wet bandanna and tied it around the girl's head, like a headband. Something to hide the bullet hole in the center of her forehead.

"That's Patsy Quinn, ain't it?" a voice said.

"I think it is. Poor child. It'll break her pa's poor heart."

"They're walkin' the Streets of Gold, Harry. Together. He was one of those they killed on the square."

Callahan turned his head and looked up at the townsmen. The potbellied one with the bald pate still wore his nightshirt. The younger, thinner, uglier one was covered with soot and ash, and held a firefighter's hat in his left hand.

Callahan's mouth moved, but no words came out. Not the first time anyway. Both men stared down at him, afraid to speak.

"What . . . what happened here?" Callahan finally heard his own voice, though he hardly recognized it as his own, as anything even remotely human.

"Rebel bushwhackers," the fat man answered.

"But . . ." He started to say that New Jerusalem was filled with Southern sympathizers.

"Why?" he asked.

"Because the whole state's turned plumb loco," the fireman said. "Don't nothin' matter no more. Ol' Preston Baker decides to print in his paper that the Southern irregulars ain't no better than Kansas Redlegs, and that these atrocities . . ." He stopped, and looked at the fat man in the nightshirt. "Ain't that the word?"

The fat man's jowly head bobbed.

"*Atrocities*. That's what Preston called it. They've got to stop." He turned his head and spit tobacco juice down the body-lined lane. "That's what Preston Baker wrote in the *Tribune and Leader*."

"They killed him for it," the fat man said.

"Have they fished him out of the well yet?" the thin man asked.

"Don't know," the fat man answered.

Callahan made himself swallow. He gestured at Patsy Quinn. "And her?"

The fat man bowed his head. The firefighter shrugged. "I don't reckon they mistaken her for a Yankee. Likely she just stepped in front of a lead ball. Poor kid. My niece and her were good friends." His eyes widened. "Oh, my Lordy, I gots to see about Jimmy, my brother, and his family."

He moved between two dead Federals, and raced to the charred ruins of the town's business section.

The bald man in the nightshirt watched the fireman until he was lost in the smoke and crowd, and then looked at the two dead Federals. "They say they lined up ten boys in blue," the fat man said. "In a row. Then one of the men took an Enfield rifle and fired a shot. Just to see how many men an Enfield slug would go through." He sighed, shook his head, and then walked down the path in a daze, glancing at one body, then the next. Was he looking for someone? Would he recognize anyone if he saw them?

"The world's gone mad," the fat man whispered as he walked and looked, walked and looked. "This was a nice, friendly town."

At noon, someone brought him a cup of hot coffee, and he drank it down like water. He looked into the face of a man of color, and then he asked, "I've been told bush-whackers did this."

The man's head nodded.

"Which outfit?"

A Federal captain overheard, stepped over the body of a silver-headed old man, and extended his cup toward the man of color, who refilled it, then leaned forward and re-filled Callahan's cup.

"Quantrill? Logan? George Todd? Bloody Bill?" He drank a sip, shook his head, spit. "Does it matter? Likely they'll all take credit for it. Till they're captured. Then they'll say they've never heard of New Jerusalem."

They buried the dead that afternoon. One funeral for all, but the local ministers preached and prayed, and the people sang and cried. Callahan was one of the men pass-ing around the collection plate. There wasn't much coin or paper money when he brought it to the front, so he fished out what little money he had, and added it, then walked down the center aisle and waited for the service to end.

Men, women, and even a few kids thanked him as they walked out the big doors. Most of them just walked out.

"Will you be staying?" one of the pastors asked as they

walked down the steps. Graves were still being covered in the cemetery.

"I guess not," Callahan said. He shook the hands of the men whose names he had already forgotten and went looking for his horse.

He found the Federal captain waiting, smoking a cigar. The officer did not thank Callahan for his help, not that Callahan had done anything helpful. Not that anyone could help the people of New Jerusalem.

"Does any verse in your Bible have an answer, a reason, for this?" The Yankee crushed out the cigar with his boot heel.

He had not been able to see him, even after the lantern had been lighted, the previous night. But Callahan had pictured the captain in his mind. A fat, brutal man, wearing a Hardee hat with a purple ostrich plume flapping in the breeze, brass buttons spotless, boots shined so hard they reflected like a mirror. He was a martinet, a ruthless butcher, a low-down Yank who spoke with the forked tongue and killed men like others stepped on cockroaches. Now he saw the man for what he truly was.

A boy. Probably just a few years older than Billy Joe McTavish. A boy who had but a few hairs on his cheeks, who had yet to taste lather from a shave or the sting of water or tonic after a good shave by a fine barber in Kansas City or up in Saint Joe. A kid. A kid who had joined the Federals likely for the chance of glory, to escape the doldrums of—where had he said they came from? Illinois? No, Indiana? Indiana. Wherever that was.

War. It could change a man. The captain's face looked young, innocent, fresh. But his eyes . . . those were different. Lost. Hardened. Disgusted. In a sense, lifeless.

Like the dozens of Missouri citizens, young and old, who had been slaughtered in this town that now was blackened forever.

Callahan did not try to form a response.

"They burned the newspaper office," the Yankee said.

"They burned everything they could." Callahan tightened the cinch.

"Some old papers survived. Including a big book of one of the Liberty newspapers, maybe Liberty's only newspaper. I wouldn't know. You're from Indiana?"

Callahan found his canteen, uncorked it, and drank.

"I'm from Missouri," Callahan continued when he had finished. "And I don't even know how many newspapers Liberty has. But I'd guess just one. Missourians ain't that big when it comes to reading newspapers. Just the Good Book. Well, some of them. Once. Before . . ."

"God works in mysterious ways," the captain said. "There was a copy from the Liberty paper from a few years back. About a church burning to the ground."

Callahan turned and inched toward the saddlebags. "Is that what you did all day, Major? Read old newspapers?"

"No, Reverend. I talked to mothers and orphans and widows. I wrote down what they said. I talked to widowers. I talked to schoolchildren who witnessed a barbarity even I have never seen—in seventeen months stationed in Missouri and Kansas. And then . . . I read. And it's still *Captain*. Not major."

Callahan's head lowered. He was changing. He didn't know how. Maybe the ball lightning. Maybe . . . well, that didn't matter.

"That article mentioned that a woman perished in the fire. A fire set by Kansas . . . trash."

Callahan looked at the saddlebags, then walked around the horse, gathering the reins, and swinging into the saddle. He stared down at the Yankee.

"The article said the dead woman was the preacher's wife."

Callahan said nothing.

"I suppose you have your reasons." His head shook, and his left hand disappeared behind his back. "I suppose I would feel the same as you did. Had that happened to my church—if I had a church—and especially had that happened to my wife." He turned and stared at the smoke, and heard the bells ringing again. "Reverend Callahan." He drew in a deep breath, then exhaled. Still not looking at the bushwhacker, the young man from Indiana said, "And I suppose the men who did this had reasons, too." The Yankee brought out the pistol Callahan had dropped into the saddlebags. Now he turned to face Taylor Callahan.

"You'll need this, Preacher." The captain extended the revolver butt-forward.

"No," Callahan said. "I won't."

Nodding at the major, Callahan clucked his tongue and eased the horse back a few feet. He then turned the gelding and rode west.

Chapter 11

"Preacher . . . How . . . bad . . . is . . . it?"

Taylor Callahan stared at Tommy Browne for another moment, snapping himself back to the present, and quickly picked up the boot he had just cut off the young cowhand's left foot. Now he saw the small hole just above the ankle, near where his Arkansas toothpick, honed to a razor edge, had carved down the worn leather tops. His pointer finger entered the hole, then came out, and he used thumb and index finger to wipe away the grime.

"What did you say happened, son?" he asked, still holding the ruined boot.

"Dumb colt started buckin', and I tasted travel. Ain't the first time I've been bucked off. It could happen—"

Callahan raised his other hand, and the kid caught on. He quit talking. The boy was telling the truth. Or maybe the sun had addled his brain.

"Son, I was bucked off horses before you were born." But he held out the left boot. "But you got a bullet in your ankle."

The kid's face told everything Callahan wanted to know. The boy had been struck dumb. He had absolutely no idea that someone had put a rifle ball into him.

"You . . . ain't . . . joshin'?"

Callahan's head shook. "You didn't hear a gunshot?"

"I dunno." He fell back onto the Prince Albert pillow the circuit rider had made for him. "I just recollect that widow-makin' cayuse start pitchin'. Then I hit the ground, the hoss rolled over my legs—left one catchin' the worser of it—and . . ." He raised his head slightly. "You sure you ain't funnin' me?"

Callahan shook his head and turned his attention to the bloody sock. "You laying still so long, not moving around, and how tight that boot fit, not to mention how thick your sock is . . . that might have kept you from bleeding to death." His hands moved, and he stopped, turning his head to Tommy. "Stick that rag back in your mouth. I expect this'll hurt. Blood's dried to your sock."

He took hold of the top of the wool. "Scream as loud as you want. That piece of glue bait that I ride won't run off."

He fingered the flattened bit of lead, shook his head, and leaned over toward Tommy Browne, dropping the ball into the boy's trembling hand.

"Fifty caliber," Callahan said, "be my guess."

"Shoulda blowed my foot off and kilt that chucklehead I was ridin'." The boy stared, shook his head, and sighed.

"Smoothbore," Callahan said. "Old gun would be my thinking, and it likely traveled a far piece. But still punched through your boot, broke the calf bone above your ankle, but I don't think it splintered any. The bone, I mean. The horse rolling over you, breaking your shinbone, that might have helped you out some. That and you not moving around much. The horse mashed your leg down into the dirt, your boots were tight fits—you must be still sprouting . . ." He waited for Tommy to smile, and, to Callahan's surprise, the boy let his lips turn just a little bit. "Sock was tight, too, so that effectively stanched the bleeding. I'm going to let it bleed some more, clean out the dirt and any bits of lead. Then I'll bandage you up, splint your busted leg, get you on ol' Job, and get you to . . . what did you say the name of that town is?"

"Falstaff," Tommy answered. "But everybody calls it False Hope."

"That's right." His joints cracked as he rose. "Don't move around too much. I'm going to take me a bit of a look-see. Need to find something I can use for splints. And I'll see if I can find out where that .50-caliber chunk come from."

"Can I have some water?"

"No." Callahan let that sink in before he explained. "My plan is to wash your wound before I bandage it. Then I've got to get you into my saddle. And Job has to walk us six or seven or however many miles it is back to Falstaff. Job gets the last of the water from the canteen, though I reckon I'll suck out what's left of the moisture. That's on account that I have to walk. You get to ride."

The boy wet his lips, and his head tilted ever so slightly. "I understand," he said, and Callahan smiled. The kid was growing up. But getting shot sometimes helped a boy do that.

* * *

The wind had wiped out most of the hoofprints of the runaway horse, but Callahan found a few here and there while he searched for wood in a woodless expanse. He also came to an ancient buffalo wallow and sank onto his buttocks and fingered the soil.

Yep, this was the spot. He rolled over, sank into the depression and aimed a make-believe rifle at the caliche road. Two hundred yards, two hundred twenty-five maybe. An old smoothbore. There was a chance that Tommy Browne, with his horse at a lope, might not have heard the gunshot. The wind might have been blowing, too. And the weapon was a relic, not like the cannons they started making during and after the War Between the States.

Callahan sat up. No butts from smokes. No dried chaw of tobacco spat out, and not much sign in the depression. He couldn't make out any boot prints or moccasins, anything. There would be no brass casing. This had been an old weapon, with the ball rammed down the muzzle, atop powder, and a percussion cap had set the .50-caliber ball.

On a galloping horse. At that distance. That meant a heck of a gunshot.

Or dumb luck.

He left the wallow and found a small heel print that took off to the northwest, and he could have followed longer, farther, but decided against that. That would be a job for the county sheriff, and Callahan had found what he needed. He picked up the dried-out spines of a cholla. Not ideal, but they might last for six or seven miles. He also looked back toward where he had left Tommy Browne.

As flat as this country was, whoever had shot Tommy had walked a right far piece because a horse would have been spotted. Even if the kid rider hadn't seen the picketed horse, Tommy's mount would have spotted it. So the assassin had left his horse a far piece away or had walked a right long ways. Or it was an Apache. That thought caused Callahan to straighten and rub the back of his neck with one of the cactus spines.

He shook his head, spit in the wallow, and walked around its edge, then started for Tommy Browne and Job, but stopped after only covering a few yards.

Dust was rising down the pike, off toward Falstaff or False Hope or wherever.

When he reached Tommy, he dropped the sticks beside the boy and next walked to Job, grabbed the reins, and led the horse off the road and past Tommy. He hobbled the white gelding, grabbed the canteen, and walked over to Tommy, then squatted.

"Riders." Tommy pointed without raising his right arm.

"Stagecoach?" Callahan asked.

The kid grunted and smiled. "Out of False Hope? You sure are green."

Callahan grinned back. "Well, I don't reckon it's an empty cart being pulled by a donkey."

The smile died quickly. "Reckon not." He sighed heavily. "I bet I know who it is."

He jostled the canteen, and handed it to Tommy. "Here. Take a couple of swallows. Then I'm going to wash your wound."

"What about that long walk you was talkin' 'bout?"

"I have faith in my fellow man," Callahan said. "Faith

that those riders will stop by and share some precious water with us—enough to get you back to Falstaff."

"False Hope," Tommy corrected.

"I don't believe in false hope."

"You will." But he took the water anyway.

Callahan had finished splinting the leg, tying the last knot, when the riders reined up. Six of them, led by a short, squat man with a dark mustache and sunburned, sun-dried face wearing one of those high crowned Texas hats and boots resembling the one Taylor Callahan had cut off Tommy's left foot. Only this fellow had big-roweled spurs, and the sides of his dun horse told the circuit rider that he liked using on them.

He got down to business right quick.

"Where the devil's my colt? What in tarnation happened to you?" The cold eyes glanced scarcely a second at Callahan, then drilled through Tommy Browne. "And who the Sam Hill is this?"

One of the riders, a lean, leathery chap in a brown hat and cowskin vest, had drawn his revolver and held it sort of pointing at Callahan, but not straight at him. Not threatening, perhaps, but certainly not friendly.

Since the short man had put his questions to Tommy, Callahan looked back at the ankle and leg and admired his handiwork, then tightened the knots just a tad.

"I got bushwhacked, Pa," Tommy said, trying not to whine, but not quite succeeding.

"I asked about that colt first, boy."

The kid wet his lips.

"I paid forty dollars," the lad's pa barked, "for that colt."

Tommy Browne's face paled, and not from the loss of blood, heat stroke, busted leg, and from laying on the hot, hard earth for a day or two.

"Sorry, Pa," he said, barely audible.

"And my saddle cost a hundred and fifty bucks."

"It . . ." the kid started, Callahan figured, to tell him that the saddle might have fallen loose and was lying out in the wasteland somewhere. But he decided against it.

"Which way did my colt run off to, boy?"

Tommy pointed north.

The man twisted in the saddle. "Skeeter, Sourdough . . . ride out eight to ten miles and see what you can find. Pick up the tracks if you can. Maybe that colt tired. Or maybe you can guess where he might head off to. If you think there's a chance, one of you can keep on riding, but one of you come back and give me a report. There ain't no bonus for finding that colt. Because I'll be taking the price of the horse and the saddle and the tack and the time out of this idiot's pay."

The riders loped out, and Callahan figured they were glad to be shun of their ramrod-backed tyrant of a boss for a few hours, maybe even a day or two.

"You got shot?" Vernon—that, Callahan recalled, was what Tommy said his pa was named—asked as he looked back, face not even trying to mask his disgust, at the crippled lad.

"Yes, sir." He pointed at his leg.

Callahan accurately guessed the tyrant's next sentence.

"I hope that the slug didn't go through and hit that black colt in the belly."

"No," Tommy said, adding quickly, "sir. The preacher here . . ." He nodded with his chin. "He dug it out."

"Preacher?"

Now Vernon Browne studied Callahan, who stood, coatless, holding an empty canteen, not saying a word.

"I asked you a question, buster," the rancher said.

"My pardon," Callahan said, and bowed slightly, mockingly. "I just heard you say *preacher*."

"Is that what you are?"

"I ride the ranges and deliver the Word," he said. "And I am ordained."

"Got a name?"

Out West, you never asked a stranger his name. It wasn't considered sociable. But nothing about Vernon Browne seemed sociable.

"Callahan. Taylor Callahan."

"We don't need no more sky pilots in False Hope," the man let him know.

Callahan smiled. "I'm just passing through."

This time, to the circuit rider's surprise, the rancher actually smiled. He pushed back his big, ugly Texas hat and said, "That's one thing I do like, Preacher. Folks who pass through. You ain't planning on working all those worthless nesters into going up against me and my ranch? Are you?"

"I try not to incite violence, sir."

"But you look like a man who has seen some of that."

"In these days"—Callahan let the canteen strap slide up his forearm and held out his palms, upward—"who hasn't?"

"Terry."

The one word from the rancher caused the man who

had been easily holding his six-shooter to slip out of the saddle with angelic grace, hand the reins to the closest rider, and cross the road. He holstered the revolver and nodded a greeting as he passed Callahan and walked straight to Job. The man unfastened the straps to the nearest saddle bag, tugged on the leather, and reached inside.

"Book," he called out. "Not a Bible. Not much of anything but . . ." He turned back, letting the covering fall into place. "A handful of ca'tridges, and a box of .45s."

He kept his hand on the gelding as he eased around the rear of Job and came to the other saddlebag. The man named Terry looked inside, cleared his throat, and said, "This book's bigger, and it is a Bible. Right next to a Peacemaker." He held out the late deputy sheriff's long-barreled Colt. Terry sniffed the barrel, and dropped it back inside the bag.

"Clean he said. Hasn't been fired recently."

He walked around the front of Job, patted his head, and stepped back closer to the road.

"I don't know many preachers that pack iron," Terry said.

"You should come hear my sermon, 'The Peacemaker and the Sky Pilot,'" Callahan said. He turned back to the rest of the crew. "You all should. And if the words move you, a slight donation would be appreciated."

"Len," the rancher said. "You and Terry get this knucklehead onto your horse. You'll ride double with Tatum. Tatum, you and Monty help. That kid of mine is likely to be as skittish and bawling like a frightened barn cat. Terry, what do you make of this . . . *parson*?"

"I don't make anything of him," the cowhand said. "Or the poor animal he rides."

Vernon Browne turned his glare back on the circuit rider. "How'd you happen upon my boy?"

"Just riding down the road and there he was," Callahan said.

"Maybe you figured on saving his hide, instead of letting his leg rot off and his bones bleach, and get a little reward for your troubles."

"Can't say that crossed my mind, since I don't know you from my Aunt Mildred's tom cat."

"Maybe you shot my boy."

Callahan let his eyes twinkle. "Well, as I've often heard and have occasionally preached, 'The Lord works in mysterious ways.' Why He could have changed my .45 cartridge into a .50-caliber ball fired by a smoothbore rifle. And He could have made it so that your top hand here . . . Mister Terry"—He bowed graciously—"would swear to you, Mr. Browne, that my Colt had not been fired recently."

Tommy Browne wasn't skittish, but he cried in agony as the rough cowhands carried him to the horse, somehow got him into the saddle, and the kid leaned forward, grasping firmly on the horn, and swayed a moment before steadying himself. Kid had guts, Callahan decided. He might grow into a fine man, despite his pa's efforts to steer him otherwise.

"All right." Vernon Browne glared at Callahan. "If I was you, Preacher, I'd find another place to preach at. Stay out of False Hope. If you know what's good for you."

"Pa . . ." Tommy croaked.

"What?" his father snapped.

"He's out of water. Gave most of it to me." The boy wet

his lips? "He could use a pint of water right now. Can you spare him some? It's a long ways to nowhere on that road."

"Shut up. I'm gonna tan your hide as soon as you can walk." He pulled his hat down hard on his head, gathered his reins, and spurred his horse. He galloped a few yards, circled the horse, and turned it back toward the way back home. He led the way. A man like Vernon Browne didn't know any other way. Some cowboys rode alongside Tommy, helping him along. It would be hard on that boy and that boy's leg. Seven miles or so. At the pace his pa was setting. Callahan wondered if the men riding double would be walking the last two miles into town.

Then he looked up and saw the foreman mounted on his horse, which wanted to take after the rest of the riders. The cowhand nudged his animal closer to Callahan. Then he held out his left hand.

"I'll take your canteen," the cowhand said.

Callahan held it out, and the man named Terry took it, then dropped his reins over his horse's neck, and used his free hand to lift his own canteen, which he offered to the circuit rider.

Callahan took it. "Thanks," he said.

"Could have forty-rod rotgut in it instead of water, which might suit your horse, but not you."

"I figure it's got water," Callahan told the cowpuncher.

"What makes you sure I wouldn't play a joke on a preacher?"

"Because I preach faith. Faith in that Major General in the Heavens. Faith in my fellow man—even after I met your boss."

The cowhand's head leaned back and he let out a raucous laugh. "There's a cistern in town," the cowboy drawled after he had recovered. "I'll leave your canteen by it. You can leave mine there when you get into False Hope."

"Your boss said I shouldn't go there," Callahan said.

"Your eyes told me you wasn't listening to Vernon Browne."

Both men offered grins as salutes.

"Thank you, Mister Terry."

"Page," the man said. "It's Terry Page." He wrapped the canvas strap of Callahan's canteen over his horn and turned his horse around. "I'll be seeing you, Parson Taylor."

"Callahan," the circuit rider corrected. "Taylor Callahan."

"The boss said False Hope don't need no more sky pilots, Preacher," Terry Page said as he kicked his horse and trotted it a ways down the pike. "But he's wrong. You follow this trail, though, and you'll be preaching a mess of funerals." The horse picked up the pace into a trot. The cowboy pulled his hat down tighter. He looked back and called out. "And someone might have to preach over yourn. Just a friendly warnin'."

The horse exploded into a gallop and carried Terry Page toward his compadres.

Chapter 12

Some towns had an excitement to them. Some reminded Taylor Callahan of those drawings of Rome and Paris and San Francisco and Florence and London and that lovely village on one of the Sandwich Islands, all that he had seen in those picture periodicals. Some looked new; others appeared to have been around during the Old Testament. And every now and then, the circuit rider drifted into a town that seemed best described by one word.

Falstaff, Texas, was such a town.

But the citizens—or someone—added a touch of realization and comedy. About a hundred yards from the main part, which took up much of the town because there just wasn't much to it, a sign was placed in the middle of the road.

WELCOME TO FALSTAFF

Of course, the town's official name had been scratched through and pulverated with bullet holes. Painted over and around the knife marks, splinters, scratches and holes made by assorted caliber were the town's new handle:

FALSE HOPE

And below that:

150 MILES
TO THE NEAREST POST OFFICE
100 MILES TO WOOD
20 MILES TO WATER
6 INCHES TO HELL

He let Job carry him the next hundred yards, and reined in. The sun had started to sink, but sunsets in this part of the country took a long time, torturing the souls here, the dry grass, the parched soil, the waterless ditches and arroyos, for as long as it could. But it gave Taylor Callahan a good study of the town where he figured he'd be staying a day or two, maybe a week or month, because he sensed he was needed in a town that had no real hope.

And he enjoyed the idea of becoming a burr under Vernon Browne's saddle.

No signs, as far as Callahan could tell, advertised the few buildings in Falstaff. Oh, the Catholic church was recognizable. It was the only building whitewashed. The bell-tower was empty, but from the looks of the tower, that might have been a good thing. The adobe needed some serious patching, and the ladder that led to the tower appeared unlikely to support the weight of the little Mexican kid running from a privy to a dirt home.

Three dirt homes. A livery stable, with only a jackass and a nag that looked worse than Job, standing still. A stone building that might have been a general store. Three other nondescript businesses, or maybe they were homes. He figured out which one was the saloon, but those were always easy. It's the one with the open windows, laughter coming from them, too, and clinking of glass, four horses hitched to the rail in front of it, and two men standing in the open doorway. Watching Taylor Callahan.

He recognized the hats on the two men's heads. The horses had to be branded with Vernon Browne's irons. But in the center of the town—there was nothing that resembled a square—he saw the cistern. He gave Job a nudge, and let the horse head to the water.

Terry Page might work for a loathsome heel, but he was a man of his word. Callahan's canteen leaned against the eastern side of the makeshift watering hole. The foreman of Browne's spread had put it there so the water might be tepid, might taste like dirt, but it would be a shade cooler than had he left it where it would have been baking in the sinking sun.

Callahan swung out of the saddle, decided that Job hadn't worked himself too much, like he ever did, and could drink from the cistern. He squatted, grabbed the canvas strap and brought the heavy canteen up. Filled to the brim. He sat on the edge of the dirt mound that held the water in, removed the stopper, brought the canteen to his lips.

And stopped.

The stench alone burned his eyes.

Behind him came the laughter.

Slowly, letting the cowboys have their joke, Callahan stood, returned the stopper, and looked over his shoulder at the two cowboys, giggling like schoolgirls laughing at some poor boy.

"Why don't you have a drink, Preacher?" the rail-thin one said. That one would be Len.

"It's better than the water in this pig pen," said the other one, Tatum.

"I appreciate the offer, Len," he said, enjoying the startled expression on the waddie who was more bones and mean. He looked at the other cowhand. "You too, Tatum."

The latter dropped his right hand to the butt of his holstered revolver.

"You know us?" Tatum said, his lips barely moving.

"We just met a few hours ago. On the road out of town. You remember." He looked at Len. "Surely you do, too, Len."

They shot each other a cautious glance.

"You a mind reader?" Tatum asked.

They were fools. Browne had called their names, and they had been the ones who had to ride double after broken-legged Tommy took one of their mounts. And remembering names was something they taught pretty well at the Logan's Knob Seminary. He remembered one of the instructor's warnings.

"You don't want to mistake Missus Monahans for Missus Farnum. Or Colonel Gilley for Major Carr. Figure out something to associate and differentiate. Burn their faces into your minds."

"You got papers on us?" Len asked.

Tatum drew and cocked his revolver. "You gonna drink, mistah. And drink it all."

Callahan grinned and brought up the canteen. "Boys,

you don't want me to drink this. All of this, especially. Why the last thing in the world, even in this forlorn place, anybody wants to see is Taylor Callahan when he's roostered." He shook his head. "A bad man he can be. You'd much rather see me sober and straight. Besides, it would make a bad impression on the holy man over there." He tilted his hat at the crumbling whitewashed church.

Len glanced at the priest who stood in his robe by the open door, but Tatum did not look away or lower the barrel of his Colt, one of those Civil War models, an Army, that had been converted from a cap-and-ball to take brass cartridges.

The pair began circling the cistern, Tatum coming the shorter course, to Callahan's left, and Len rounding the other way, past Job, still slurping up water, on the circuit rider's right.

"Drink," Tatum said as he walked.

Callahan withdrew the stopper and turned the canteen over, hearing the gurgling as the foul whiskey cascaded to the ground. Even the dried earth tried to reject the potent brew.

"Hey!" Len snapped, and started to run, but slowed quickly, when Tatum barked out, "Leave him for me. I'm gonna stove in his thick skull."

Canteen empty, Callahan turned around and bent toward the water. He scooped off the dust that covered the water, submerged the canteen, let it gurgle a moment, pulled it out, and emptied the water atop the wet mark where the earth had finally soaked up the rotgut.

The canteen went back under the water, and this time Callahan let it fill. He brought it out, liking the coolness of the water on his hands and forearms, returned the stopper, and turned around. Both men had their guns now trained on Callahan's chest. Callahan licked his fingers.

"You know, the water tastes a lot better than I thought it would." He held the canteen out toward Tatum. "Thank Terry for the loan of the canteen."

"I'm gonna fill your gut with lead," Tatum said.

"In front of a priest?" Callahan said.

The cowhand looked at the church, frowned, slowly released the hammer and slid the Colt into the holster.

"Then I'm a-gonna beat you within an inch of your life."

"Now, gentlemen, I think we can settle this is a civil, and charitable, manner. I'll even treat you to refreshments of your choosing at that watering hole that you favor over this cistern—filled with water from a long ways off, I suspect. You should thank those hard-working men who keep this town with some water."

He turned to Len. "How deep do you have to go to hit water in a well?"

Tatum's fingers dug into Callahan's shoulders and spun him back around.

"Don't you never turn your back on me when I's speakin' at ya."

"No insult intended, kind sir."

He slapped Callahan savagely with a backhand, a stinging blow, quite powerful, that cut his bottom lip and came close to knocking him into the water supply. Which, after a hot few days, Callahan might have appreciated. The canteen slipped from his grasp and landed at his feet.

When Callahan straightened, he thought he could hear Len, behind him, swallowing.

Tatum's hands were clenched into fists that displayed, even in the fading light, scars of many a brawl. The man was shaking with rage. He'd blow a boiler if he kept this up.

"Friend," Callahan said. "I want you to know that that saying . . . 'Turn the other cheek' . . . well, it's one I put quite a store in."

The left fist flew up, but Callahan blocked it deftly, then landed a haymaker that slammed the cowpuncher's right cheek and sent him sailing into the dust.

"I believe," Callahan said as he turned to face Len, "that I just turned Tatum's cheek black and purple. Shall I turn your cheek, too?"

Len's hand darted for the Smith & Wesson he had holstered. Callahan's fist slammed straight into the cowboy's nose. He heard the crunch of cartilage and the gushing of blood. Len forgot about his revolver and clasped his face with both hands, unable to stanch the pouring burgundy, and dropped to his knees.

"Your mistake," Callahan said. "A bruised cheek heals quicker than a ruined nose."

He leaned over, jerked the revolver from Len's holster, and pitched the .38 into the cistern. Then he walked toward Tatum, who was trying to sit up. When he saw the tall, lean man walking toward him, he reached for his Colt.

"Don't make Satan happy to get a new idiot to torture in his fiery pits."

The man paused, his face paled, and Callahan stopped, and held out his left hand, palm up.

Without speaking, Tatum knew what the circuit rider

wanted. He slowly started lowering his right hand toward the holster, then thought better of it, and raised that hand and moved his left across his body. The weapon came out, was carefully laid into Callahan's hand. Callahan nodded, even whispered, "Thank you, sir," and threw the iron behind him, hearing it splash in the cistern.

"Now get up," Callahan ordered.

Tatum struggled to his feet.

"Let's go."

He followed the weaving cowhand to his pard, who was sobbing between coughs, still holding his busted nose.

"You, too," Callahan said. "Up. On your feet."

The man's head lifted, his eyes teary and filled with fright.

"Do you hear out of your nose?" Callahan barked.

The man used his left hand to find support on the earthen dam, and pushed himself to feet that didn't want to cooperate.

"Let's go," Callahan said.

"Where?" Tatum asked. "There ain't no jail in False Hope."

"Who said anything about jail? I told you boys I'd buy you a drink. Now let's mosey over to that watering hole."

The bleeding man and the bruised one eyed each other, frowned, but finally started. Callahan watched as the crowd—a bartender, a soiled dove, and another rider for the Browne ranch made a crowd in a town like Falstaff— quickly backed from what passed as a boardwalk, with dirt instead of pine planks, outside the door and into the dimly lit hovel.

Len entered first, then Tatum, and they bellied up to

the rough bar, where the balding man in sleeve garters tugged on his waxed mustache.

Callahan slapped a greenback on the bar. "Give these two boys whatever they please. It's on me, the Reverend Taylor Callahan, and I'll be in this fine town to offer comfort, guidance, and prayers to all who need." He nodded, turned, tipped his hat to the dove and headed for the exit, but stopped at the doorway, and turned back to the bartender.

"Oh, yes. And give Len that bar rag to stop his nose from bleeding. And if you got a thin slice of raw steak, that might take away the shiner Tatum's gonna be sporting."

Chapter 13

The squeaking of the cell door awakened Johnnie Harris with a sharp gasp. His eyes saw the darkness from the window in the empty cell across from his own bunk. The only light came from the opening to the jailer's office. Harris recognized the clopping of the county sheriff's boots. When the keys jangled and jammed into the lock, Johnnie rolled off his bunk and tossed the ticky blanket off, which caused him to gasp from the pain that paralyzed his right hand—at least what was left of his hand after the sawbones in Bonham finished working on it.

At least he still had a hand. He had begged the doctor not to take it off, because his brothers, his ma, and his pa had always said that you wanted to be buried with every part you come into the world with. Two missing digits might be tolerable, but the hand still hurt, and he had the fingers that mattered most: thumb, pinky, and trigger finger.

"What is it?" he asked urgently.

"Grab your hat, boy," the sheriff drawled.

"I ain't supposed to hang till Friday." He gasped. Had he lost track of time? "It . . . ain't it . . . Tuesday?" The question came out like a plea, which is exactly what it was.

"Let us sleep!" cried out Wolf from a neighboring cell.

"Don't make me come in there, boy," the sheriff warned.

Nervously, Johnnie Harris stood, trying to get his heart to stop racing, trying to remember that he was a man, and recalling how his big brother, Boss Harris, always said that a man had to die game, never show yellow, all that dime-novel stuff. Johnnie sucked in a deep breath now, let it out, and headed for the silhouetted figure of the lawman by the open door.

"Yer hat, boy," the sheriff said.

He twisted, stepped back, found the hat, using his left hand, the one with all the digits, and moved toward the open door.

"You ain't lynchin' me, are you, Sheriff?"

"Get out," the lawman barked.

Johnnie figured what his brothers would do were one of them locked up in this dungeon. Boss, Everett, or Digger would step into the narrow hallway, then throw the full force of his body against the door, pinning the county lawman against the iron bars. Johnnie even visualized himself doing that, grabbing the bars of the door, pulling the door away, then ramming it again against the man. Hearing the man scream, beg for mercy. Seeing Wolf and Bigham leaping off their cots, coming into the dim glow of light from the office, eyes wide in wonder, watching Johnnie batter the lawman into unconsciousness.

It seemed so easy in his imagination.

But he heard voices and footsteps in the office. And the vision ended right then and there. The sheriff nodded toward the office, and Johnnie moved forward. He didn't even glance at the cell where Bigham and Wolf bunked together, where both men hadn't even risen from their bunks.

The door to Johnnie's cell slammed shut, the keys jangled again, and the sheriff said, "Move it, boy."

Johnnie had to shield his eyes as he stepped into the tiny office.

"Kid," a familiar voice rang out.

Johnnie squinted, heard the door to the cellblock close, and the sheriff's boots clatter toward the potbelly stove and the coffeepot. Remembering his hat, Johnnie put it on his head and pulled down the brim. Slowly, his eyes opened, and the man before him came into blurred view, but the voice was clear and concise.

"They say you let a preacher cripple you," Boss Harris said.

Now Johnnie could see his big brother.

Boss Harris took after their pa, while Johnnie had many of his mother's features, a fact Everett and Digger, and especially Boss, never let the kid forget. Boss was big, dark-haired, dark-tempered, with eyes most folks said were like looking into Satan's own. He wore black all the time—to match his soul and his heart, he liked to say—even in a hot summer, and Texas summers were never on the chilly side.

Those evil eyes flared, and Johnnie tried to get enough moisture in his throat to swallow.

"Get your gun rig," Boss said, "not that it'll do you any good."

Blinking, Johnnie tried to figure out just what was going on. The sheriff cleared his throat, and when the youngest of the Harris boys looked at the desk, the sheriff, tugging on his mustache while recrossing his legs at the ankles on the rolltop desk, tilted his head toward Johnny's holstered Remingtons.

"You . . . ? What? I don't . . ." The stunned, frightened lad glanced at Boss, then at Everett, but didn't bother looking at Digger because Boss said, "We posted bail."

Johnnie blinked. He wet his lips, then remembered the gunbelt and the Remingtons, so he moved to the sheriff's desk, shaking his head, and muttering, "But I . . . they . . . we got convicted of murder. You can't bail out nobody after the jury's done handed down the verdict, and the judge has passed sentence." He was talking to himself. Finished, he looked up at the sheriff, who yawned.

"Ain't that right?"

The sheriff released the ends of his gray mustache and let himself smile. "It's what you might call . . . a *private* bail." He let his right hand wipe his mouth and drop to an envelope that was mighty thick to be just a letter. And Johnnie Harris was young and with a throbbing hand, but he wasn't the complete idiot his older brothers took him for. He turned quickly and tried to match Boss Harris's stare, but that was a mistake. He immediately looked at his scuffed boots.

"Buckle on that rig, boy," Boss Harris said. "We ain't got all day."

"You bribed him?" Johnnie finally managed.

"Not that you're worth it, kid, but you are our brother." That came from Everett, who didn't look up as he rolled himself a smoke.

"What about Bigham and Wolf?" Johnnie asked.

The spittoon rang as Digger sent tobacco juice into it. Wiping his mouth, the long-haired brother sighed and said, "We shoulda let him swing, Boss."

"You want to keep that date with the hangman, boy," Boss said, "go back to your cell. But it ain't like you killed that deputy or anyone in that holdup. The way me and the sheriff here figure it, you held the hosses. Those two *men* . . ." he started, gesturing at the closed door to the cells. "They's the ones who did the killin', and probably did the plannin' and just took you along 'cause the name Harris means something in this part of the country when it comes to outlawry."

"Now . . ." Johnnie started to defend himself but he knew everything said was true.

"They're my pards," he said.

"Somebody's gotta swing, kid." This came from the sheriff. "Y'all killed a fine deputy. And some good folks during your shenanigans. I can let you go. But not all of you all. I wouldn't win re-election if that was the way we said things happened. But if Boss Harris broke his kid brother out of jail whilst I was out chasing a hoss thief, well, ain't nobody gonna get bent out of shape for not having a run-in with Boss and his two brothers."

Reluctantly, Johnnie moved over to the gun rig, but cringed when he tried to lift the heavy leather, made heavier with twin Remington .44s.

"Here," Everett said, and he walked over and helped Johnnie get the gunbelt buckled across his waist.

Meanwhile, Boss Harris crossed the room and stood in front of the sheriff's desk.

"Now what about the preacher who crippled my kid brother?"

The sheriff removed his feet from the desk and pushed back the chair, taking the envelope that held his greenbacks with him. "Stranger in these parts. Taylor Callahan was his name. Nice enough gent. 'Bout your height, but much thinner."

"He say where he was preachin'?"

"Said he went where the spirit leads. Nah." The old man's face knotted, relaxed, and he smiled. "Nah, he said he goes where the Major General in the Heavens sends him."

"What's that mean?" Digger asked.

"Means he's country folk, hill folk. And I'm thinking that he likely saw some service during the War of Northern Aggression."

"Which side?" Boss asked.

"Don't matter. Accent suggests Missouri. But that could be North or South, as well you know."

"Where was he going?" Boss demanded.

"Like I done told you," the sheriff said. "He didn't have any place in mind, but he rode out south. And I think it was Ma Parker . . . you know Ma. Runs the boarding house over on Honey Street. You oughta know Ma Parker anyhow, seeing how you cut down her middle son, Jasper, down in Dallas two-three years back. Anyhow, Ma said he said something about seeing the ocean. So that's why he rode south."

"He still on that white horse?" Johnnie said, just to show his brothers that he could be of some help.

"I reckon so. Though if that preacher had a lick of sense, he'd get rid of that worthless nag for a horse with some sense and some stamina."

Everett came up off his knees and moved to the door, pulling back the curtain and looking at the night sky.

"What's it look like?" Digger asked.

"Dark." Everett chuckled at his wit.

"South, eh?" Boss told the sheriff. "Galveston? Indianola? Corpus?"

"That I can't say," the sheriff answered. "He's got better than two weeks' head start on you boys, but, like I told you, his horse and the preacher, they both travel like they ain't in any particular hurry to get anywhere. But you shouldn't have no trouble finding him."

"Because he moves slow?" Digger asked.

"Nah," the sheriff said. "Gait ain't got nothin' to do with it. There's something about that man, boys, that circuit rider, Taylor Callahan. He's slow and deliberate, acts a wee bit gullible and speaks like he's got a mouth full of molasses. But he also has a presence. And well, we had a lightning rod salesman pass through town right after the trial—the trial that doomed your kid brother and his two low-life pards—and that reminds me of the preacher."

"The salesman?" asked Everett.

"Nah. Them lightnin' rods. They's like the preacher. He ain't afraid of getting struck by lightnin'. Figgers it be part of his job." He picked up his envelope and started to put it in the inside pocket of his vest. "I figger he's been struck by lightnin' before. So you just look for some lightnin', and you'll find the preacher. Or look where there's something about to explode."

"Before you put that money away," Boss Harris said coldly and slowly pulled the .45 short-barreled Colt from the holster.

"Nah, Boss, you ain't gonna plug me to get your money back," the sheriff said, calm as a sleeping babe.

"Why not? Look better if someone put up a fight, and made that ultimate sacrifice, to keep a condemned murderer from swinging from the gallows." Boss brought up the revolver and put his thumb on the hammer.

"Because you'd never get out of Bonham alive, boys. I

ain't as foolish as that circuit rider. I got six armed men on the rooftops. And you'll noticed that the street lamps are turned up pretty bright for this time of night. Yes, sir. The boys got instructions that if there's one shot inside this jail, they's to cut down on every poor sucker that makes a break for the horses tied out front. Good shots, those boys. And they ain't gonna miss their aim knowin' what be in it for them." He patted the envelope, grinned underneath that thick, gray mustache, and let the envelope disappear inside his vest.

"You're bluffing," Boss told him.

"You are entitled to your opinion, my friend," the sheriff said.

"I could kill you anyway."

"Yep. That's why I didn't bring my gun when I came over and sent Horace home." Horace was the usual jail-keeper; Johnnie thought how sorry he would have felt had Boss, Everett, or Digger had shot down that thin little rummy with the wooden foot.

"They might get us, but you'd still be dead," Boss said.

The sheriff laughed. "Boys, I'm sixty-seven years old, turn sixty-eight if I make it to November the eleventh. But you four . . . y'all got your whole lives left ahead of you. So if you want to live to see the break of dawn, I'd be lightin' out right now. Folks in Bonham can be early risers. We ain't no big city like San Antone or Austin. If I was y'all—which I ain't—I'd be out of my county by daybreak. Which comes up quick this time of year."

He sighed, put his hands behind the back of his head, and propped both feet on the rolltop desk again. Grinning up at Boss Harris, calling the killer's bluff. And it worked.

"Come on." Boss grabbed Johnnie's left shoulder, spun him around, and shoved him to the door.

"Where we going?" Everett asked.

"To find that preacher," Boss said.

"There ain't no money in that," Digger whined.

"It's family honor," Boss said. "Nobody cripples a Harris and gets away with it."

"I tell you I ain't crippled . . ." But a hard punch into his kidneys ended any further dispute from the youngest of the Harris boys.

For now, anyway.

The door opened. It felt hot and sticky, and the sky had yet to start showing any gray off to the east. Johnnie knew his brother would work off the shame he had felt by the old but wily sheriff whenever they stopped to rest their horses. Boss Harris didn't like to lose anything, and now he was out whatever bribe he had paid to the sheriff to get Johnnie out of jail, and away from the gallows, and Boss would give Johnnie a good beating.

Johnnie went out first, followed by Everett, and then Digger.

Before Boss stepped out, he looked back at the sheriff. "That preacher, you sure he rode south."

"Yep. Probably stop in Dallas. Then pick a path to San Antone. From there . . . like you say . . . Galveston, Indianola, Corpus Christi. It'll be warm in those black duds you fancy, Boss." As Johnnie stepped into a stirrup and swung into the saddle, he heard the sheriff's laugh as he said, "Course, y'all should get used to it, seeing where you'll be settling down in the hereafter."

Chapter 14

The priest still waited in front of the whitewashed building, a robed silhouette with the lanterns and candles glowing from inside the tiny chapel. Callahan glanced over his shoulder to make sure nobody seemed intent on following him, then walked to his horse, took the reins and led Job toward a hitching post in front of the Catholic church. Removing his hat, he stepped up to the man, whose face he could not see beneath the hood.

"Father," he said, "my name's Taylor Callahan."

"Buenos noches," the man said evenly.

Callahan stared at him blankly.

"Good evening," the priest said, his accent thick.

"Forgive me, Father," Callahan said. "I'm not much good with your lingo." He smiled. "Fact is, lots of schoolmarms and right educated Americans say that I ain't much good at the English language." He shook his head. "My seminary instructors had a he . . . a right hard time with me. You shoulda heard how I spoke before they beat something close to sense and education into this thick head of mine."

"I believe the *vaqueros* of Señor Vernon will have no

need of a translator when you speak to them again." The priest raised his slender hands and pushed back the hood, and then turned and gestured. "Please, come inside."

Callahan let his black hat hang by his legs and followed the padre into the tiny building. He saw the small candles burning to his right and left, and more in front of the pulpit. Lanterns hung from the vigas that served as some sort of rafters. It was a small church, but comfortable, the pews well used, and small benches on the floor that Callahan figured probably helped some of the older members of the congregation when it came time for kneeling.

The priest was younger than Callahan expected. In a town that looked as old and run-down as Falstaff, Callahan expected to see a wizened, white-beard with a face as wrinkled as much of the wood and adobe he had seen. But this man looked barely out of his teens, black hair gleaming like a wet crow, eyes like midnight, and a face that spoke of none of the suffering or wisdom one earned with years.

"Pardon me," the young man said, as he held out his right hand. "I am Father Pedro Sebastià Fernández de Calderón y Borbón."

"Long handle." Callahan grinned, but he admired the firmness of the kid's grip, and felt the callouses on the priest's palms and fingers. He might be young, but he had worked mighty hard with those hands, and a priest didn't get those from making the sign of the cross.

The young man shrugged. "Most people here call me Padre Pedro, or Father Pete."

"I'm . . ."

"Taylor Callahan," the priest said. "You are welcome

here." He waved his hands to show off his church, but added, "The *villa* of Falda welcomes you."

Callahan grinned. "I ain't rightly sure the whole villa welcomes me. But . . . *Falda*? That ain't what's on the sign."

Father Pete nodded. "Falda was the name of this town before it became part of Texas. Before I was born, of course. When this was Mexico. I, of course, am Tejano. A native of Texas though . . ." He drew in a deep breath and let it out slowly. Callahan figured that needed no explanation. He had seen and heard how many Anglo Texans felt about Mexicans since crossing the Red River.

"What's Falda mean in Mexican?" Callahan asked.

"Spanish," the young priest said.

"Forgive me. Like I said, I'm more ignorant than intelligent."

The man smiled, revealing white teeth, straight, unlike Callahan's crooked, yellow-stained number—which were short a few in the back from a few brawls back in those wilder days.

"It means 'Skirt.'"

"Skirt?" Callahan raised his eyebrows.

Father Pete smiled. "I was not here when my forefathers named it." He waited and whispered conspiratorially, "But it does make one imagine . . ."

They laughed together, and the priest turned, beckoning Callahan, and leading him past the confessional and through a narrow door into the rear of the chapel. This room was much darker, with one candle burning, and Callahan could make out two chairs, a table, and a bedroll on the dirt floor—not even a cot. The priest pulled out one of the chairs, motioned to it, then moved to a corner with some shelves and clothes. He returned with two cups and a bottle.

"Communion wine?" Father Pete held out the bottle.

"I'd better not, Father," Callahan said.

The priest was not insulted. "I have coffee, but it is cold."

"Cold coffee would hit the spot."

Moments later, they sat, the priest having a small taste of red wine, and Callahan sipping coffee that tasted more like what he had had in Missouri during the last days of the war, when they had to burn grain to pass for coffee. But it helped settle his belly.

"What brings you to our poor little village?" Father Pete asked.

"Just passing through," Callahan replied.

"No one just passes through what has become known as False Hope."

"I don't believe in false hope," Callahan said, and noticed the young man's head tilt, as though he were trying to figure out just who he had invited into his private room.

Father Pete's head straightened, and he slid his empty glass—he had poured not more than two fingers—and nodded.

"We are being tested," he said after a long silence. "There has been no rain in more than a year and a half."

Taylor Callahan was a Missouri boy, so a drought of that length of time was unheard of. "Nary a drop?" he asked.

"Oh, it rains, rarely," Father Pete said. "Drops here and there. Sometimes a pleasant shower. But not the rain we need. Not enough for crops or cattle, or, the longer this test lasts, human beings. And a lot of people grow angrier, more frustrated, and they lose their will and their hope."

Callahan pushed his stoneware cup away. "A lot of people?" He wanted to figure out what Father Pete considered a crowd. From what little he had seen, there wasn't many folks who lived in Falstaff, and the Vernon ranch wouldn't have that many riders.

"Ah," the priest said wisely, "but you have just seen what we call our city limits. This community is much wider than what you have seen in False Hope. There is, of course, Vermin Browne."

"Vermin?"

"Ah." The priest dropped his head. "A slip of the tongue. *Señor* Vernon Browne. I should not drink so much wine."

Smiling, Callahan had to agree with the youngster on that account. If two fingers of wine could cause him to let a derogatory nickname slip out, Father Pete shouldn't drink anything stronger than this bad coffee. But he laughed anyway because Vermin Browne was a cracker-jack nickname for that old hard rock.

"It's a good one, Father," Callahan let him know. "Fits that old-timer to a T."

The young man was silent, so Callahan did some talking to help him forget the embarrassment. "Way I figure, it being dry and all, Browne can't run that many head of cattle, so he can't have that many men working for him."

"He is a greedy man," Father Pete said. "You are right in that he has had to move some of his cattle—as far west as the Territory of New Mexico—and has sold some in Kingsville and Corpus Christi. But he still has a herd of some size. The problem is, with grass so short, there is not enough to feed his longhorns."

"I've seen a lot of land. Empty land." Callahan sipped the last of the coffee.

"And that is what brought Señor Milton Clarke to this area."

"Milton Clarke? Don't reckon I've made his acquaintance."

"You will. If you stay. Three years ago, he brought in a number of men to farm."

Callahan raised his eyes.

"You are familiar with the Homestead Act?" Father Pete asked.

Callahan nodded. "I can't quote it accurately, but I get the gist of it."

"Señor Clarke is what is known as a land agent, a land developer, something along those lines," the young priest said. "So three years ago, he brought in several families, even some men who have no wives, no children. I know the rules have changed since the late President Lincoln signed the Homestead Act into law, and that Texas has its own laws and ways of dealing with this, but all of the land that Vernon"—He paused, just to make sure he had not let another Vermin slip out—"all that land that Señor Browne had used to keep his cattle fat was not deeded. Was not leased. Was open for homesteaders, and thus the farmers have pushed the cattle off what is, for the time being, theirs."

"Time being?"

"My understanding, though it might not be completely accurate, is that they can own their land when three years are up. And that will be in three months, I believe."

"I thought they had to prove up the place in five years."

"Again, that is something I do not know. We have no newspaper in False Hope. We have no lawyer, unless you count Señor Clarke."

"So, if those farmers get the land deeded to them, that's a hundred and sixty acres of land per farmer that's no longer grazing pasture for Browne."

"I believe it is more than that, but . . ." He shrugged again.

Father Pete put his elbows on the table and cradled his head in his hands as he leaned forward and whispered. "There has been talk, *mi amigo,* that Señor Browne is bringing in men who are not so skilled with reata and branding iron, but more familiar with revolvers." The voice got even looser. *"Asesinos."*

Taylor Callahan didn't savvy much Spanish, but it didn't take a bishop or a professor to figure out the meaning of that word.

Assassins. Hired gunmen. Browne was planning on a bona fide range war.

"No jail," Callahan said, "so I reckon that means no constable, marshal, sheriff?"

"Sí. But we have a mayor."

"A mayor." That wasn't quite the same as a U.S. marshal or, from what Callahan had heard, a Texas Ranger.

"He is *norteamericano,* a good man, a decent man, a friendly man. Wallace Scurry. I would be delighted to introduce you to him tomorrow."

"I'd be delighted," Callahan lied. The name alone— Wallace Scurry—made Callahan already dislike the gent, which was a character trait that a circuit rider ought to avoid, but, well, Callahan was human, after all. Wallace Scurry. What kind of name was that?

"I didn't see too many farmers this evening," Callahan said.

"Farmers sleep at night," the priest reminded him. "Some might come in for supplies or to see if any mail arrived. Tomorrow. Usually in the afternoon. Most of the Anglos come to False Hope to shop. There is another village, three kilometers away to the northeast, that is where most of the families of my heritage live. Arroyo Verde. Another poor name. Nothing has been green here for years."

"Why don't you live there?"

"The church is here."

Callahan had to laugh at that. How did that saying go? *Ask a foolish question, get a foolish answer.*

"Well." Callahan started to rise. "For the conversation and the coffee and a most enlightening evening, I thank you, Father Pedro Sebastià Fernández de Calderón y Borbón. But I should be on my way."

Both men rose and bowed, and the priest said, "You remembered my name."

"Names are one thing I'm good at."

"But where is your way?"

It took a moment before Callahan figured out the question. "Oh," he said, "I'm used to sleeping on the ground and all. I'll just take Job and find some . . . undeeded land . . . and stretch out there. Been doing it for some time."

"There is a stable behind this church," Father Pete said. "Better than the one owned by Diego. He is a nice man, but not clean, and his stalls are filthy. My stable, it is not much, but the straw is fresh . . . delivered just three days ago . . . and the burro, Dagoberto Diminuto, he does not snore as much as I do. You are more than welcome to spend the night, and as long as you wish to stay in False Hope . . . Falstaff . . . I can make you coffee and fry some eggs for breakfast. Then it would be my honor and my privilege to take you to the *casita* of our honorable mayor, Wallace Scurry, who can tell you all that I have not, and correct all the falsities that might have come from my ignorance."

Callahan just stood there.

"You are a man of faith, as am I. We must look after one another even if what you preach and what I preach may be different in some ways. We all wish for the same thing."

"I don't want to inconvenience you," Callahan said.

"And you shall not. I can also introduce you to the land agent, Milton Clarke. But I really would like you to talk to our mayor. He has a plan that might end all our troubles."

"What sort of plan would that be?"

"Oh." Father Pete shook his head. "I cannot tell it as well as our mayor. He knows all of the details and the man who he is bringing in."

A gunman? Callahan thought. Maybe a marshal. Or one of those newfangled Texas Rangers. Those might be able to stop what Callahan figured was about to make most of the residents of Falstaff and Arroyo Verde forget all about a three-year-long drought.

"Please," the young priest said. "Por favor. It would be an honor, and a treat, to have you as my guest."

"Many folks who have said that lived to regret the offer," Callahan said.

The priest laughed, as though Callahan had said a joke instead of stated a fact, and put his arm around his shoulder. He opened the back door, and grabbed a nearby candle and walked Callahan back to the front of the church, where Callahan gathered the reins to Job and followed the priest to the stable and rickety corral.

"By what name does your horse answer to?" Father Pete asked.

"Job," Callahan said. "A few others, but Job's the most polite."

"A fine name. My burro is named Dagoberto Diminuto. They shall be fine friends."

The candle didn't reveal much of the stable, and Dagoberto Diminuto showed no interest in his new bunkmates. Father Pete showed Callahan a woolen blanket and the hay fork for freshening the straw, then stifled a yawn, took his candle, and left Callahan to unsaddle and stable Job in the dark.

"Oh!" the priest called out about twenty paces later. "I should warn you. Watch out for rattlesnakes."

"Rattlesnakes?" Callahan barked.

"Sí. They have never bitten Dagoberto Diminuto, but often they come for my chickens and my eggs. Just watch where you step. And don't roll over too much in your sleep."

"Rattlesnakes?" Callahan called out, but he heard the priest closing the door to his chambers.

Chapter 15

He used index and middle fingers to pull the skin on his cheek closer to his nose, then let the keen edge scratch through the stubble, shook the straight razor, and moved to his upper lip. The cheeks were one thing, but this required a certain amount of delicacy. Just like his throat had.

Hearing he footsteps behind him, Taylor Callahan adjusted the mirror to see Father Pete coming toward him with, mercy, a steaming cup of coffee. Callahan studied his face, and went back to touching up his face.

The priest stopped, then said, "I have never seen a man shave without lather."

Callahan scratched at the underlip, then wiped the razor on his towel, and folded the blade into the ivory handle.

"Figure water's precious," Callahan said, "so I decided to give it a try. And it's already hot enough, so I had some sweat dampening my cheeks. But . . ." He toweled off his face. "Not exactly the best shave I ever had."

"Your conservation of water is commendable, but I do not think I would be able to do that."

Callahan grinned, found his hat, and walked to the priest, thinking, *Like that young pup has even peach fuzz to shave.* He took the cup.

Yep, the coffee tasted as bad hot as it had tasted cold. But it was coffee.

He rubbed his face, which burned from the dry shave. As a Missouri boy, he had often shaved with cold water, and riding with the irregulars, had learned to shave without lather, but with no water at all, that's not something he wanted to make a habit. He glanced skyward, and saw a blue that was practically white, and not a cloud to hide the hot white orb that kept slowly creeping above the eastern plains.

"Did you have any trouble with snakes?" Father Pete asked.

"Nope."

"*Muy bien.* Very good. I said a prayer that you would not be tormented by anything."

"Slept like a baby," Callahan fibbed. Job and that burro kept him awake half the night.

"Well, when you are ready, come to my vestibule and I shall feed you eggs and hominy and tortillas. And more coffee."

"Sounds delightful. Let me feed Job and finish dressing and I'll see you in a jiffy."

After breakfast—Father Pete's grub was, at least, better than his coffee—they walked to what passed for city hall in a town like Falstaff, a room over the saloon. The mayor, Wallace Scurry, was having his morning bracer, and did not appear embarrassed in the least. He even offered the priest and Callahan a drink. The young priest appeared to blush, but Callahan merely shook his head.

After the introductions, Wallace Scurry nodded at the chairs, and told them to pull them up to the desk and they could have a fine confab, that it was fine to have another man of the cloth in False Hope—even the mayor was calling the burg that—and that he would spread word to the fine souls living in town and even some of the ranches.

"There's more than Vernon Browne's spread?" Callahan asked as he dragged two chairs across the creaking floorboards, motioned at the one for Father Pete, and studied the mayor.

Wallace Scurry had a big belly, puffy cheeks, and long Dundreary whiskers that were starting to gray at the bushy ends. His face was damp with sweat, but that was on account that they were upstairs in a room with just one window and it was sealed shut. Fat cheeks, fat lips, and now that Callahan had a chance to think on it, he might be the ugliest man the circuit rider had ever laid eyes on—and Missouri was not known for producing many men who had the looks of Adonis, though Callahan had known a couple of men who had the luck of that Greek god, meaning they had been killed by wild hogs.

Which made Callahan realize that Wallace Scurry had the face of a fat, mean boar. The nasal congestion didn't help that image as the mayor kept snorting, too, or at least trying to clear his throat.

"You're welcome . . . snort . . . to pray for rain as much . . . snort . . . as you can, Preacher. Snort. I figure." This time, Scurry turned sideways, drew in a mouthful of grotesqueness and deposited it in the spittoon. "I figure we can use all the prayers we can get. But I've arranged for . . . snort . . . Professor Jessup Hungate to come to our fine community and bring us rain."

"This Hungate," Callahan drawled, "he carries rain in his grip, does he?"

The mayor stared long and hard, swallowed, and leaned forward. "I know what you're thinking, Preacher, and I've heard some of our citizens express sentiments that are similar, but this professor . . . snort . . . he's legit as you are. I read about him in *Dustin Guinan's Illustrated Weekly*."

Which Callahan figured was about as reputable as the *National Police Gazette*.

"My understanding is that he blows up bombs in the air, and that causes rain?"

Scully spat again.

"The professor'll be here in a day or two, Preacher, so I'll just let him explain the process. It's sci-en-teefic. Maybe you won't find it in any of the gospels, but it works. And Professor Hungate, he's got faith in this, what he calls producing rainfall by concussions. And I'm putting my faith in him."

Callahan smiled without any effort. "I'm a big believer in faith, Mayor. I look forward to meeting Professor Hungate."

"Well, Preacher . . . snort . . . I'll waive the usual fee for setting up a tent or bringing in a medicine wagon— usually charge six bits a day—since you're a man of the cloth and all."

Callahan chuckled. "I have neither tent nor medicine wagon. Got a horse. Well, some folks doubt Job's lineage, but he gets me from place to place."

The major turned, cleared his throat, and let it ring against the side of the spittoon again. "You ain't gonna give us no revival? No healin'?"

"Well, Mayor, with a solid priest like Father Pedro Sebastià Fernández de Calderón y Borbón here, I reckon y'all have no need of reviving."

He caught Father Pete bow his head slightly in embarrassment.

"For the Meskins, maybe," the mayor said. "But some of our new farmers, they ain't of that faith."

"Well, I'd be honored to preach to them," he said. "And you, as well."

"Preachin's fine, Preacher . . . Snort. But rain'd be a whole lot better."

"I wonder if Noah heard similar sentiments."

"How's that?"

Callahan shrugged.

Scurry topped off his drink, took another sip, and looked at a half-dime novel on some of his papers. Callahan figured he was about to be dismissed so the mayor could get back to his mayoral duties, so he turned the conversation in another direction.

"Drought's not your only problem here, is it, Mayor?"

The mayor snorted, swallowed, took another drink. "How do you mean?"

"Vernon Browne?"

The mayor's jowly face hardened, quite the accomplishment. "Vern is the biggest taxpayer in the county."

"One man. One vote. And since he doesn't live in the city proper, he shouldn't even get a . . . *snort* . . . vote. Legally." Callahan winked.

"That's right." The mayor stiffened. He started to suck up that mucus, but stopped. Those eyes turned hard on the wild boar's face, making Scurry even uglier, but Callahan had no regrets for his faux snort. "And you might be surprised at how far the town limits of False Hope extend."

"I might be." Callahan grinned. "Would those city limits extend to the farmers outside of town? And how about the Mexicans in the Arroyo Verde section?"

"You know, Preacher," the mayor said, "I'm gonna have to re-sign that executive order and charge you the regular fee for preaching here in our fine town."

"Rescind," Callahan corrected.

"Huh?"

"It doesn't matter." He found a gold piece in his pocket, and pitched it onto the desk, enjoying the look on Scurry's face as the coin spin hit the spine of the half-dime novel and wobbled before the mayor's beefy hoof slapped down the coin down. He picked it up, studied it, then bit it to see if it were real.

Which it wasn't. It was actually a five-cent piece painted gold. The generous donation from a patron in that San Antonio watering hole.

The mayor casually slid the bogus five-dollar piece into his vest pocket, and not the cash box on the desk. Callahan rose, nodded, and smiled wanly at the fat old thief.

"Not that you need any preaching, but I sure hope you'll come to one of my gatherings, Mayor," Callahan said.

The old boar did not even look up, but muttered, "Where do you plan on holding your revival?"

"Best place in Falstaff," Callahan said. "Downstairs. In the saloon."

When they shut the door and stood on the staircase's platform, Father Pete asked, "Surely, my friend, you do not intend on preaching in the saloon."

"Surely, I do, my friend." Callahan chuckled. "I've made a habit of preaching in such places. Biggest crowd, I expect, in a town like this." He winked at the young priest. "Except for your place during Mass."

Father Pete smiled.

"This professor," the priest said, "he sounds like an interesting man. Does he not?"

Callahan was admiring the day. Well, it was going to be another hot one, but up here, on the platform at the second story of the saloon, a breeze came as close as possible to cooling a man off in this sweat box. A man could see a right far piece, not that the scenery amounted to much that Callahan had not spotted from ground level, but the sky went on forever. Now this wasn't Missouri, but it was something to appreciate. Land. Lots of land. Dry land, getting parched by every second the sun shined on it, but land had a power, a draw, and all land was worth something.

"Sorry, Father Pete," Callahan said. "What's that you said?"

"I said this professor sounds like an interesting person."

"Indeed. I relish the thought of getting to know him, and more about this experiment he has."

"It will be a blessing."

"Rain's always a blessing."

Again, he admired the view, till he caught the rising of dust in the corner of an eye.

Callahan turned to the sound of hooves and saw the dust before the riders showed.

"You reckon that land agent's in his office by now?" Callahan asked.

"Señor Clarke? We shall see. He usually . . ." The words trailed off as the riders slowed their horses. One man in a high-crowned, big-brimmed hat pointed at the top of the stairs, and the riders looked up, turned their horses, and eased into a semicircle at the foot of the stairs.

More of Vernon Browne's waddies, Callahan noticed, recognizing a couple of them from last night. He tugged his Boss of the Plains on and leisurely descended the staircase, Father Pete trailing him.

"Morning," Callahan said when his boots planted on the sod. "Up and about early, I see."

"Lookin' fer a stray," the one who had pointed said.

"Figure to find it in town?" Callahan asked.

"Ya never know," said the cowboy.

A younger man, redheaded and freckle-faced, reached over for his lariat. Another pulled out the makings from his vest and began rolling a cigarette.

"Visitin' our mayor?" the leader of the group said.

"Paying the price of the permit to preach," answered Callahan, admiring his alliteration.

"Uh-huh." That came from one of the faces Callahan recognized, the cowhand called Tatum. He was the only one of the six who looked uncomfortable, and, apparently, he had not taken Callahan's advice and put some raw beef on that ugly bruise underneath his eye, which was almost swollen shut. Callahan didn't see the other cowhand he had been forced to rough up. What was that one's name? Len. That's right. He remembered the one who was shaking out a loop now on his lariat, but did not get that teen's name.

Turning toward Father Pete, Callahan whispered, "Stay here on the steps, Father. I don't think this'll take too long."

Once he faced the Browne riders again, he nodded, broadened his smile, and said, "Church'll be tomorrow evening, starting at six, in the saloon. Bring your booming voices and we'll sing some fine songs that'll please the Major General in the Heavens and all the angels walking those streets of golden caliche."

He gave the Browne men another smile and nod, and started walking, between the rider on the zebra dun and Tatum, on a brown mustang. He walked toward the water tank, casually, in no particular hurry, and then he heard the whistle of a rope sailing in the air, the chuckling of cowboys, and the squeaking of leather as some of the men twisted in their saddles to watch the show.

He caught the shadow of the lariat, but kept walking, bracing himself. The cowboy might have been on the green side, but he sure knew how to throw a loop. The rope came right over Callahan's head, hit the left shoulder, then dropped quickly to his feet, and the boy was fast, too.

The loop shrank before it even hit the bottom, catching Callahan's boots between the ankles and the knees, and just as he expected, Callahan was jerked to the ground, hitting with a thud that jarred him but did not come close to drowning out the uproarious laughter from most of the Browne cowboys.

Callahan's hat went rolling off to the left on the brim, gathering dust. Father Pete shouted something in Spanish, but one of the riders barked back, "Stay put, greaser, or you'll get the same treatment."

"Nobody roughs up one of Vernon Browne's riders, Preacher," growled the leader. "Let's take him for a ride, boys. Through some prickly pear."

Chapter 16

"Didn't I tell you boys that I was the best heeler in Texas?"

That had to come from the roper, Callahan thought as he rolled over, and sure enough the greenhorn kid was looking over at the older riders of Vernon Browne's brand. The boy gripped the rope, right hand tightly near the horn, left hand holding the slack. Problem was, the boy should have started to make his dallies around the horn. Then Callahan would've found himself in a pickle—a pickle about to be dragged through prickly pear.

By then, the young cowhand figured out his mistake, and he started to wrap a few loops around the horn. But that lapse in judgment, that need for just a wee bit of Texas cowpoke braggadocio, enough to make the older hands give him some credit, was about to cost the kid dearly. He tightened his grip on the lariat and began desperately trying to make those dallies, but Callahan had plenty of experience and at least forty pounds on the boy.

He jerked his legs up, bending his knees. That caught the boy unawares, and it was the boy who was losing his seat in the saddle. He let out a shriek—sounding more like a girl than a Texas waddie.

"Aiiyeeeeeee!"

The kid dropped the lariat and put out his hands to break his fall while his horse whinnied and began twisting, caught in tight quarters between his riding pals' mounts and the shoddily built saloon. The commotion the frightened cow pony caused left most of the other cowboys trying to control their mounts. All except Tatum. As Callahan rocked forward into a seated position, he saw the black-eyed cowpoke merely leap off his horse and move underneath the awning of the saloon.

Which proved to be a wise move because two other horses tangled, and Callahan briefly lost sight of them because of the dust.

That gave him enough time to shake loose the lariat's loop around his legs. He pressed his palms against the dirt and pushed himself to his feet. Four of the six horses were now riderless, and one of the Browne waddies had his hands full as his brown Texas cowpony started bucking hard and mean, twisting, spinning, and kicking those rear legs high, one hoof splintering one of the half-baked column posts that held up one end of an even cruder awning.

That caused Tatum to sidle over to his right.

Callahan was on his feet now, and saw the leader of the bunch, face hardened into nothing but savage fury, spurring his mount and charging out of the carnage and straight for Callahan.

The circuit rider did what he remembered from riding with Carbine Logan's Irregulars all those long years ago. He stepped forward, raised his hands over his head, contorted his face to try to match that ugly look on the

Falstaff, Texas, mayor's unpleasant countenance and let out with:

"Yip-yip-yip-ahhhhh-eeeeeeeeeeeeeeeeee!"

The oldest of the six riders was Tatum. The way Callahan had figured things, only Tatum was old enough to have fought during the War of the Rebellion, War of Northern Aggression, War for Southern Independence, War Between the States, Civil War, actually, a mostly *un*-civil war, or whatever anyone wanted to call it, even the "recent unpleasantness." Tatum had decided to deal himself out of this hand, which earned the old cowpoke a wee bit of respect from Callahan.

The other five, well, they all appeared to be too young to have fought in that late war, so none of them had ever heard of a Rebel yell. And what Taylor Callahan yelled wasn't exactly what any Texan would have sang out, cried out, belted out during a battle. This came from the mouth and belly and heart and soul of a Missouri bushwhacker, part scream of terror, part scream of rage, part scream to strike fear into those chicken-livered bluebellies who knew that would happen if they were captured.

He raised his hands and wiggled his arms.

The horse reared, the rider let out a yelp and a few words that might not make the old Major General in the Heavens all that happy when this young whippersnapper stood before him several years from now at those Pearly Gates.

Callahan ducked beneath the flailing hooves and moved to his left. The cowboy hit the dirt with yet another *oof,* and his horse managed to set all four feet on the ground and then light out for parts unknown.

As the cowboy came up, he shook his head, and saw the charging preacher. He reached for his gun and managed to jerk the .44 perhaps halfway out of the holster, before the toe of Callahan's boot caught him right on the hard part of the jaw. Teeth cracked, and maybe the jawbone, too, and the man went backward as hard as a felled pine in the Missouri woods. His head smacked against the caliche, and Callahan figured this old boy was out of the fight and maybe the rest of the bright and toasty Texas morning.

The bucking horse moved over toward the Catholic church, with the cowboy holding on like the professional he was. Callahan admired the young Texan for that. The circuit rider would have bailed off a whole lot earlier. Other horses scattered. Tatum relaxed and began to find the makings for a cigarette. The cowboy who had roped Callahan to start this old fandango was pushing himself up, so Callahan made a beeline for him, the boy being the closest.

The kid's eyes widened as Callahan raised his right foot and kicked the boy, catching him in the chin and driving him up and over. His head smacked hard on the dirt, and his eyes rolled into the back of his head.

Two down now, Tatum still paying scant attention to the free-for-all, and the rider on the angry mustang still bouncing up and down, and grunting every time a muscle in the bronc twitched. And a horse like that had a passel of twitching muscles.

By now, the brawlers had an audience. Father Pete had brought his rosary to his lips, the mayor of Falstaff now stood on the platform outside of his office, hands on the stair's balustrade, the muscles on his face completely limp, intensifying that hangdog appearance. Other men, and even a few women, had come out of their hiding places to watch the show.

One of the waddies pushed himself into a seated position, his back pressing against a trash barrel, and he clawed for the pistol in a holster on the right hip. The other one had pulled himself to his knees and elbows and was vomiting. Callahan moved for the one with the hog leg.

There was just too much ground to cover between where Callahan started out and where the cowhand with the gun was sitting. No chance at all to reach him before the cowpoke would have that Smith & Wesson out and filling Callahan's belly with bullet holes. So Callahan shouted, using his voice saved for fire and brimstone sermons: "Don't twitch a muscle."

And the cowboy, struck dumb, left his right hand on the butt of the .38, thumb against the hammer, and the barrel and most of the rest of the long-barreled revolver in the holster. He didn't realize he wasn't moving at all until the circuit rider was right in front of him.

Then he let loose with an oath, and jerked the rest of the .38 from the holster.

But he had waited way too long.

Callahan was a mighty fine kicker. And again, his boot connected, the cowboy's lips turned into a pulverized mess of blood and pulp, the back of his head slammed against the trash barrel, and the poor boy's eyes rolled back into his head. He slipped over to his left and caught up on some sleep he probably needed.

Spinning on his right boot heel, Callahan glanced at the young Browne hired hand who was still losing his breakfast. Through the dust, he saw a horse galloping between the church and the jacal next to it, probably startling Father Pete's burro and that mostly worthless Job in the back of the whitewashed building.

Callahan spun, found the cowboy who had finally wound up tasting gravel—caliche, to be correct. The man's hat was gone, but he was game as a bantam, and he reached up toward a hitching rail with one hand, and pulled himself to a seated position.

Another game rooster. One thing he would have to give Vernon Browne credit for. He hired men with grit and determination and not much quit in them. Callahan figured that the late Captain Carbine Logan would not have minded letting these men, had they been older and Missourians instead of Texans, ride with the Irregulars. With boys of this ilk, the Captain might have been able to stretch the war on for another six or seven months. Not that anything would have changed in the long run, just a lot more dead men on both sides.

Probably things worked out for the better, he thought.

Then he bolted across the square of Falstaff, Texas, that wasn't exactly a square but far from a corral.

The cowhand was on his feet, tilting to his right, then staggering a few paces before bracing his right foot against a giant mound of horse apples. Steadying himself, he brought his right hand down and jerked the revolver from the holster.

"Touch that gun and you'll be facing a grinning Lucifer!" Callahan barked.

Once again, the inexperienced cowhand stopped. That gave Callahan all the time he needed. His left hand found the soft part of the waddie's belly, and the man doubled over as Callahan brought up his left knee.

Callahan felt a twinge in his knee. Came from years and miles. Hard years, harder miles, both a lot harder than the poor old boy's nose. The man flipped backward, and joined a few of his riding pards in a deep, miserable slumber.

"Hold it, Preacher, or your next sermon will be with your own Maker!"

Callahan stopped just long enough to catch his breath. Well, he had given these boys a run for their money, had whupped most of them pretty good, but six against one. That was long odds.

Wiping the saliva dripping off his chin, his freshly, if not all that well-shaved, chin and saw the formerly vomiting cowboy with a Colt drawn and aimed, more or less, in Callahan's general direction.

"On second thought," the waddie said, "go ahead and meet your Maker."

"Put that pistol down, Marco."

Callahan thought the words came from Tatum, but as he turned slightly to the left, he saw a new rider on a fine black gelding, pushing the hat back on his forehead and eying, with unmasked disgust, the Browne riders scattered about in the center of what passed for Falstaff, Texas.

Terry Page. Callahan remembered this gent from yesterday, too. Foreman of the Browne spread.

Page drew in a deep breath, turned and spit into the dust, and waited until the cowboy lowered the pistol's hammer and struggled a few times before he finally jammed the old hogleg back into the holster. Then Vernon Browne's top hand twisted in the saddle and eyed Tatum, now enjoying his smoke.

"You too good to get your knuckles skinned?" Page asked.

"Did my fightin' yesterday," Tatum said. "Wanted to see how these roosters made out." He took another pull on the smoke, pitched it away and ground it out with the toe of his boot. "Reckon it's 'bout like I expected."

Page let out a long sigh. "Well, find a horse and gather the ones that ran off. Then get out of this pigsty and get these boys, the ones still worth a day's pay, and get back to work. Work. Ranch work. Cowboy work. No more of this hooliganism."

Hooliganism. This Terry Page had something of an education. Might have made it through a few of the *McGuffey's Readers.*

A door slammed and Callahan looked up. Mayor Wallace Scurry had disappeared from the platform at the top of the stairs and went back inside his stifling office. Lowering his eyes to the bottom of the steps, Callahan let his sore jaws and lips work until they formed something that resembled a smile.

Father Pete crossed himself, nodded, and grinned back.

Once Tatum had found a horse that hadn't bolted, swung into the saddle, and went off at a lope following the disappearing dust left by a few of the riderless mounts, Terry Page moved his horses toward the riders, who slowly began picking their bodies up off the ground, dusting their chaps and sleeves, finding their hats, battering the dirt and dust off them by flailing the beat-up old lids against their chaps.

"You boys are paid to be cowhands," Page barked at

them. "Not amateur pugilists. No, that's not what you are. That's an insult to any fighter. Mr. Browne pays you for work. You want to keep this job, you better get to work. Next man to show up at the bunkhouse with a bruised face, split lip, or busted nose, he's drawing his time and riding out of this country forever."

He pulled his hat low down on his face.

"You boys understand me?"

The defeated men mumbled something that no one could understand.

"Then get yourselves a bracer in the saloon—it's coming out of this month's pay—and when Tatum's back with your horses, get to work."

He kicked his horse and rode up toward Callahan. For a moment, it appeared Terry Page planned to ride over the circuit rider, slowly, and the gelding, a good sixteen hands, had some muscle on him, with thick feet. Callahan didn't move an inch, though.

The big horse stopped on a dime, just a few inches from Callahan.

Page leaned forward and said in a tight whisper: "And, Preacher, you lay a hand on a Browne rider again, and I'll be coming to collect from you. And man of the cloth or not, you'll find that when it comes to fighting, I ain't an amateur like these pathetic fools. Am I clear?"

"Clear as the dust in this town," Callahan said with a grin.

"Just don't you forget it."

Terry Page turned and spurred his mount and raised more dust on his way out of town.

Callahan looked down at the hoofprints in the dirt, shook his head, smiled, and walked to find his hat, dusting it off on his pants legs and carrying it with him as he made his way to the water tank. He laid the hat, crown up, on the top of the earthen walls, and again blew the dust off the water's surface, cupped a handful, and splashed his face, letting most of the water drip back into the tank. The next handful went down his throat. The water burned the cuts in his fingers and knuckles. He soaked his bandanna, wrung it out until it was just moderately wet, and wrapped it around his neck.

Father Pete stood beside him.

"You are not like most men of God," the priest said.

"I'm not like most men," Callahan said. "Period."

"I must agree. Where did you learn to fight?"

Callahan smiled, which hurt his lips and his jaw. "Missouri seminaries teach all sorts of fire and brimstone."

"Well. We should go. I will make a poultice that my grandmother passed down to me. It will ease the pain you must be feeling."

"My pains can wait, Padre. We haven't finished our morning chores."

Father Pete cocked his head.

Callahan explained. "We had our chat with the mayor. I still want to hear from this land agent. What's his name? Clarke?"

"Sí. Milton Clarke. Are you sure you are up for an interview?"

"Shucks, Father Pete. This here little episode wasn't nothing. Just getting the boys' attention. I ain't hurting a bit."

All of that was a lie. But the Major General in the Heavens didn't mind an occasional stretch of the truth. Especially when one was in Texas.

Chapter 17

The land office was a rock building, stones hauled in from a quarry about fifteen miles southeast of town. At least, that's what Milton Clarke said, and Taylor Callahan had no reason to believe a land agent would lie about something like that. It was cool inside the office, which wasn't big at all, maybe ten feet by eight feet, with a couple of windows that allowed for a draft, especially with the door open. What Callahan admired most about the building was the screen door. He just stood inside the office, at the door, running his fingers of the thin screen.

"You like that, Reverend?" Milton Clarke said as he filled three coffee cups with a pitcher of water.

"Brenda Parsons's daddy had a nice home back in Missouri," Callahan said. "I always fancied that gal, red-headed she was, and eyes as green as Ireland. They were probably the wealthiest family in the county. My ma and my pa at that time—Ma went through husbands like the Grim Reaper went through families in the Black Plague—we lived in a log cabin, like most folks in the hills. But Brenda went to school with us, and she'd invite us to stand on the porch door and just look at that screen door. Kept out flies and mosquitoes, made the candles flicker a bit when a gust of wind would blow up." He shook his head in awe and wonder. "Never thought I'd see a screen door in Texas."

"I'm an Alabama man myself." Clarke handed one cup to Father Pete and brought the other to Callahan, who accepted it with a nod and a thanks. "I ordered this one from New Orleans. Otherwise, I'd suffocate trying to read through all the documents I have to pore over. From the chimney of my lantern. Or sweat to death without a draft of wind coming through."

"You're a wise man." Callahan took a sip of tepid water.

"You'll get some debate about that." He motioned to a bench against the wall, and Callahan moved away, with some reluctance, from the screen door and the pleasant memories and sat closest to the table. Father Pete walked over and sat on the other side, and Milton Clarke made his way behind his desk, moved a few papers to his left, and sat in a small chair with leather pads for the hindquarters and the back.

"That was quite a show you put on, Reverend," Clarke said. "I don't know of many pugilist preachers."

Smiling still hurt a wee bit, but Callahan made himself acknowledge the statement, only he offered a slight correction. "Preacher pugilist. The preaching comes first. Punching comes only when I'm provoked."

More alliteration. Good one, too. Now how come, he thought, *I never think to say something like that during a sermon, marriage, or funeral?*

"Terry Page is a tough customer, though," Clarke said. "You made an enemy."

"I don't think so." He sipped more water, bringing it

around his teeth to make sure they were still all in his mouth, excepting a couple he had lost back in his wilder days. Nothing burned. No new holes. He had done pretty good.

"I do believe I heard a threat."

"Threatening his men. That's the boss man in him. I figure he's a good man. Knows his business."

"I'm not so sure about that."

"Well, Mr. Clarke, I look at it this way. I could be laying spread-eagled on the dirt out yonder, waiting on Father Pete here to give me a kind send-off and I'd hope a deep enough grave."

Father Pete crossed himself and kissed his rosary.

"What can I do for you, Reverend?" Clarke asked. "Other than give you a screen door to remind you of an old girl-friend?"

Callahan emptied his cup. Fighting, he recalled, worked up a man's thirst. After setting the tin cup on the edge of Clarke's desk, he said, "I don't rightly know if nine-year-old boys have ten-year-old girlfriends. It's just that growing up in a log cabin, without the soundest of doors, we just admired something fancy."

"I'm not sure screen doors would be called fancy. You should see the thick and studded door at Vernon Browne's adobe fortress that he calls a house."

That surprised Callahan. "Vermin Browne invited you to his place?"

Clarke grinned at Callahan's intentional slip of Vermin.

"He needed me. At that point in time."

"I'd admire to hear that story."

"I'd admire to know why."

Callahan nodded. "I'm preaching in these parts for a while. Need to know what I need to preach about."

"I thought you'd be praying for rain."

"From listening to the mayor talk earlier this fine morn, I figure he's got that end covered with this professor he's bringing in."

"Let's hope the professor has good connections with the Almighty."

"You believe this professor can actually produce rain?"

Clarke opened a drawer, pulled out a small bottle, and spiked his cup of water with a bit of an eye opener. "At this point in time, Reverend," he said as he returned the green bottle with clear liquor to the drawer, shut it, and concluded, "I'm up for believing in anything. At least giving it a chance."

"Well, like I've been saying since they told me to go out and preach the Word, my second-favorite subject of preaching is about faith."

"And your favorite?" Clarke took a nice swallow.

"Common sense."

He drank again, but then put the cup on the desk. "Those can be contradictions, can't they?"

"Which makes religion interesting. Wouldn't you agree?"

Clarke laughed. It was an Alabama laugh. Good and soulful. The land agent drew in a deep breath, let it out slowly, and leaned back in his chair, placing his legs on the desktop and rocking on the chair's rear legs.

"Browne brought me in after the late war. Helped me set up this office—no screen door then—that didn't come about till two years ago."

"I thought it looked rather new."

The land agent nodded.

"When Vermin Browne got here, there wasn't nothing but rocks and grass and Arroyo Verde, which some folks say was pretty green in those years," Clarke said. "The Mexicans had some farms, maybe a dozen at best. Rest of the land wasn't claimed. Browne claimed it. Had to fight off Comanches and Kiowas and Apaches. When the War Between the States came, he sold beef to the Texas government, Confederate army, and even some Indians on some reservations over in the Territory of New Mexico. It was after the war when things started to change. Falstaff grew. A lot of that was Browne's doing. He had made a decent fortune—smart enough to demand payment from the Confederate and state government in gold or silver, not Texas or Southern script. Federal Army running the reservations paid him in gold, too. But once the war ended, and when the Yankees set up shop in Austin, he learned that ranching and power isn't just hooves and horns and even gold."

Clarke stared, and Callahan nodded, understanding now. "It's land."

"Right. Deeded land."

"He hadn't filed on it."

Clarke stopped rocking and sat up straight. "He didn't see any need. He had done his ranching by sheer will. Words and legal documents meant nothing to him. But farmers started setting up here, taking advantage of the Homestead Act."

Callahan nodded. He thought he understood. "Lincoln's act," he said. "A hundred and sixty acres. Prove it up in five years, pay a fee, the land's yours."

With a grin, Clarke sipped his drink, set the cup down, and shook his head. "War's been over ten years, but Lincoln's a name best not used in these parts, Reverend. Besides, you're thinking federal land. That doesn't apply to Texas. We've been a state for thirty years or so. And you know we were a sovereign nation before that after licking the Mexicans and avenging the Alamo and Goliad."

Clarke, an Alabaman, had adopted Texas, it seemed. Or vice versa.

"Texas had its own homestead laws. Even before the United States put theirs together during the war. It was three hundred and twenty acres to begin with. Wouldn't that have been something? But years back, when I was but a young whippersnapper in Alabama, they cut the acres down to a hundred and sixty, just like the Yankees did. A man needed to prove up the land, and he had three years to do it, but then he had to pay two dollars an acre to get clear title. Three hundred and twenty times two is . . ."

"Six hundred and forty dollars," said Father Pete.

Both men looked at the young priest. Callahan smiled. "You did that in your head, didn't you?"

"Sí." The priest looked embarrassed.

"Boy, if you'd done that in the school back in Missouri, our teacher would have whupped you for cheating. Or showing him up." Callahan patted the young priest's shoulder to let him know that was just a joke, though it was also likely true.

"The state government reduced the acres to a hundred and sixty in '54, repealed the law two years later, but in 1866, the law came back onto the books. That's when folks started coming into Falstaff. Farmers. Taking land that

Vernon Browne had figured would be his and his alone till Judgment Day."

"So he brought you in," Callahan said.

"Yes, sir, he did. And I had his men file on land, usually near the water holes, creeks. He'd buy them out once they gained title to it. But once he figured he had all the good land, the land with water—usually, though you might have to dig a mighty deep well to get to it—or land that he thought had water that wouldn't run dry, I was out of work."

"But you're still here."

"I was about to pull out. Five years ago. But then Texas changed its homestead act again."

Before 1870, Clarke explained, public land could be claimed by heads of families, single men, even single women. The 1870 act limited new claims to the head of a family who had yet to earn a homestead and all single men twenty-one years or older.

"Just men?"

Clarke shrugged. "There's some debate to the legal definition of 'man,' but talk is that this new constitutional convention will sort all that out. Or the attorney general will at some point."

"How much money?"

"Just a filing fee." Clarke shook his head. "Browne could have filed claims on most of this county. There were few restrictions at first. But he's always been a miser."

"And that's when you brought in your farmers," Callahan surmised. "Right?"

The land agent grinned, leaned forward, and rested his chin and interlocked fingers, elbows on the desk. "There was land for the filing. All it needed was some farmers to file. No waiting period. No demands to put up a house, make improvements. Just file and it's yours. I just set up an office, keep my plats and my maps up to date. Tell them what's available. Handle the filings, just charge them a little bit. And . . . well, now, you know Alabama, or at least you've heard about it. It's farming country. I figured we could grow some cotton, get this state back on track. Texas still hasn't recovered completely from the war and all that Reconstruction."

"The difference between Alabama and this part of Texas," Callahan said, "is that it rains a lot in Alabama."

"Browne can still make out," the land agent said. "If it doesn't rain, these farmers will quit, and they can sell their land to Browne. Even the skinflint that he is, surely he can pay something that'll get these sodbusters back to a wetter, friendlier climate."

Callahan figured out the rest. Then Browne would pay Clarke to file the new deeds, register the transfer of land, and both rancher and land agent would make a bit of money. Honest? Well . . . that would depend on a body's point of view. Legal? Maybe. Most likely. Compassionate? Not to Callahan's way of thinking. But in this part of the country, compassion was hard to grow and harvest.

He rose, shook the land man's hand, thanked him for his time and the information. "And, particularly," he added, "for your fine screen door."

Once he and Father Pete were outside, feeling the heat of the day, they noticed that all of the Browne hands had departed, and Falstaff or False Hope was back to its sweltering boredom.

"I am sorry," Father Pete said.

"For what?" Callahan looked at the young man.

"My information that I told you was not correct," the

priest explained. "I thought they had to stay on their land for three years, and I thought they could file on much more than the one hundred and sixty acres. It was three hundred and twenty, as Señor Clarke said, but that has changed."

"That's the thing about laws," Callahan said. "They always change. To keep men thinking. There's no need to apologize. And that's a good thing. If they had three years to prove up, and those three years were just about up, I fear our Vermin Browne would be ready to do just about anything to make sure those poor farmers didn't get a chance to own that land. Now we got time. Hold on for one moment, Father. I got one more question for Mister Clarke."

He walked back, opened the screen door, smiling at its squeaking hinges, and stuck his head inside the cool office.

"If I might ask you one more question, sir . . . ?" Callahan queried.

The land agent was sucking on that green bottle in his top drawer again, not bothering to cut it down with Texas water from a cistern.

"By all means," Clarke said after a cough and a not-quite-discreet slipping of the bottle behind the desk.

"Who ramrods the farmers?"

Clarke looked puzzled. "This isn't a ranch, Reverend. They are independent . . ."

"I know that, sir. But who's the leader? Who is the bull of the herd, so to speak?"

The land agent grinned. "That's easy enough. Logan Lamerick. He's about as muleheaded as Vermin Browne."

Callahan started to ask another question, but Clarke headed him off.

"A mile and a half west, dry wash, little trail turns north. You can't miss it. He brought in some of Glidden's fencing. Which is another thing that really riles Browne and his cowboys. He can be meaner than the devil. I ought to warn you."

"Thanks. Course, you might have noticed that I can be a bit mean myself."

The screen door slammed shut. What a beautiful sound.

Chapter 18

He had seen wire like this before, not exactly, up in Missouri, years before that Illinois farmer named Glidden got a patent on this . . . Devil's wire, he had heard a Pleasanton, Texas, cowboy call it.

Barbed wire, they called it. Two strands of thin wire that had been twisted into something resembling a braid that held sharp metal spurs spaced apart. Split-rail fences. That's what Taylor Callahan had grown up with, but to fence in a hundred and sixty acres with split rails, that would have taken a lifetime. By thunder, it would have taken ten lifetimes just to find enough trees in this barren country. Instead, all Farmer Logan Lamerick needed was a post-hole digger and a bevy of posts. And the strength and determination to secure the barbed wire to the posts. Hard work. Long work. But this wire wasn't going anywhere for a long time. Maybe a post would rot or be broken somehow, but a post could be replaced.

Job snorted, grazing off on the other side of the road, while Callahan tried to figure out how to get past the wire fence. He saw the hoofprints in the dirt, and if he read sign correctly, the horse walked right through the barbed wire.

He could see the drag marks of a post that had to be the one that hooked a wire loop at the top of another post at the corner. So this was a gate. But there was no latch, no lock, just a loop that bit into the cedar post.

"This is a mystery for sure," Callahan said. He took off his hat, wiped his brow, and eyed the barren blue-white sky to see if the Major General up there might send him an idea, but that old boy must have been preoccupied with someone else's needs, and Callahan didn't press for any more help.

He worked on the loop and the post, trying to wiggle it loose or free, without any luck. The wire here was flimsy, but firm. There had to be a way to get this gate open, but Callahan gave up. He looked again at the dirt, the hoof prints, and then he knelt and examined the tracks closer.

"Well I'll be da . . . daisies," he said, and raised his head, staring between two strands of barbed wire at the pike that ran to the Lamerick house beyond the rows of plowed land that showed no green buds of the crops to be. Just dirt being blown by the occasional breeze.

"Huh." Callahan even touched the hoofprint to make sure he wasn't suffering from heat stroke or seeing some sort of mirage. Nope, the print was there, all right, complete with the snakelike mark on the front right shoe. His finger wiped out the mark, but the one past the closed gate was the exact same. No mirage. Same print. Same horse. One that Taylor Callahan had seen in town.

Sighing, Callahan reached up and grabbed the highest wire, carefully avoiding the spurs that looked sharper than his straight razor. He pulled himself up, and didn't pull down the fence. There was a way to open this gate, but

Callahan figured he'd be here till Judgment Day and never guess the right combination.

He crossed the road, grabbed the reins, and pulled himself into the saddle. Job snorted and blew out his nostrils, before Callahan kicked him into a walk on the farmland across the road. He covered maybe fifty yards before stopping and turning around. Now a farmer might object to having some rider, even a preacher, mess up his plowed earth, but there wasn't any sign of crops growing here, either.

"Do this for me, Job," Callahan whispered, "and I'll double your grain for supper."

He kicked hard, and then harder, set his teeth, held the reins, and felt with surprised pleasure as Job went into a lope. Callahan found the right rhythm, tried to guess just how high that fence was. With his luck, Callahan figured, Job would stop at the last second, duck his head, and send the preacher into the barbed wire. He might be wrapped in that mess, bleeding profusely, till he had bled himself empty.

This, he began to feel, *might be the dumbest thing I ever done since the time I set off that Roman candle down my pants leg.*

But suddenly, Job became the winged Pegasus, Callahan held his breath, felt the wind in his face, reached up to hold onto his Boss of the Plains, heard one of the gelding's rear hooves clip the top wire, and then they were coming down.

It wasn't a graceful landing, but Job kept his feet, and Callahan remained in the saddle, but it would take a few minutes before his crotch settled from halfway up his windpipe to where it belonged. And another several minutes before he realized he wasn't going to throw up all that chow he had eaten or the water and bad coffee he had been drinking.

Job snorted. Callahan leaned forward, once he felt he could lean any which way and not lose his breakfast. He rubbed the gelding's neck, gave it a couple of pats, and said, "Gidyap."

He kept the horse at a walk. A very slow walk, perhaps not quite a quarter mile till he saw corral, privy, and a house, not a soddy, but a stone house, with a matching barn. Stone that probably came from the same quarry where Milton Clarke had gone to put up his land office in Falstaff.

Deep wagon tracks led to the barn, arousing Callahan's curiosity. He hadn't noticed the tracks on the path that led to the main road, but now he saw they led from the east, back toward Falstaff. But as far as Callahan knew, there was no road in that direction.

He shrugged it off. Maybe he had hauled stones from a quarry. Or supplies. Plenty of supplies, from the depths of those tracks. And now he realized there must have been two wagons. Well, in a drought, a smart man would stock up on tons of potatoes to get through the summer and the winter, and carrots and beets.

He frowned.

How he detested beets.

Again, he looked at the house and then at the barn.

Callahan expected to find a sod house, and not much more. But the stone house explained why Milton Clarke had singled out Logan Lamerick as the man who led the farmers. But that did not explain the horse tied up short at the back of the house, near an open window.

Callahan had a pretty good view of that as he rode up. Which made him look again at the wagon tracks. A horse tied behind the house wouldn't be noticed by someone riding in from the east. But from the way Callahan came up to the homestead, it was clear as a really good man's conscience.

Chickens squawked, but not too loudly, and most of them remained inside the barn where the shadows kept things cooler.

"Hallooo, the house!" Callahan called out, and shifted a little forward in the saddle, just a wee bit that would not remind his crotch of how a person is not supposed to sit when he has his horse jumping a three-rail, or four-strand, fence. "The Reverend Taylor Callahan, come a-calling."

He sat there for a few long minutes, wondering if anyone intended to answer. Callahan knew what was expected in this country. A visitor did not dismount, walk to the door, and knock. He waited till he was invited to step down and visit a spell. Eventually, the front door cracked open, just a bit, then maybe six inches farther. Someone behind the door moved a bit, likely making sure no one else was here.

"I'm alone," Callahan said in an easy voice. "I'm a circuit rider. Gonna be preaching in Falstaff for a spell. Mr. Milton Clarke at the land office in town told me that Logan Lamerick was the man to see. I figured he might help get word to all the other farmers."

"You Irish?" It was, to Callahan's surprise, a woman's voice. Not an old woman, either, by the sound.

"Well, yes and no, I reckon," Callahan answered. "Way back when, some relatives crossed the ocean and left Ireland. But I'm from Missouri."

"Pa come from Northern Ireland. We ain't Catholic."

"I'm not either. Ordained by the good folks running Logan's Knob Seminary."

"Logan!" the girl said. "That's Pa's name."

Callahan hadn't even thought about that. "It's in the Ozarks. Down Sparta way."

"Never been to Missouri. We come from Indiana."

"Then we're even." Callahan smiled. "I never been to Indiana."

"I don't reckon y'all named that church school after my pa, though." She giggled, the door opened, and a young woman stepped out. She wore a calico dress, blue and white, and was barefooted. She busily tried to straighten her hair, and even from this distance, twenty feet away from the porch, Callahan could see that she had missed a button on her dress. She figured that out, too, turned after she had tied the ribbon in her hair, and worked on righting that mistake.

While that was happening, Callahan heard the hooves of a pony galloping away. On a path, he figured, that separated a couple of fields. He saw the dust begin to rise. The rider was heading away from the main road, the road he had taken from town to that confounded gate, a gate he knew how to open. The trail the man was taking was off toward . . . Callahan grinned . . . Vermin Browne's spread.

"I reckon not," Callahan said.

The woman turned. Woman. Girl. Maybe seventeen or thereabouts. Sweet and lovely. Ah, to be young and in love, even in a place dubbed False Hope. She looked confused.

"That the seminary was named after your Pa. You know. Logan. A joke."

"Oh."

The Earth spun. Hoofbeats faded.

"Pa ain't here," the girl said after a long quietness. "He went off to a meetin' with some of the others. Should be back in an hour or so."

"I see." Callahan looked away from the trailing dust.

"I ain't supposed to let nobody come inside whilst Pa's gone."

"Good advice." Callahan faked a cough that might hide the smile he could not control. Maybe this lovely young lady figured you could not let a man come inside through the front door, but the window of a boudoir, well, that could be proper. Sort of. He wiped his mouth with his bandana.

"My name's Lorena."

"A lovely name, and a lovely song."

"There's a song?"

Gosh, now here was something to behold. A woman in her teens who had never even heard the song "Lorena." Callahan could not recall how often he had heard it in camps with Carbine Logan's boys. Ol' Harp could pick a banjo to pieces and had such a soulful tenor voice.

"I'd sing it to you, child," Callahan said, "but then your chickens might never lay again and your cow might quit giving you milk."

She smiled.

"Your voice don't sound that bad."

"'Cause I'm just runnin' my trap. Speakin' I can do. Singin', that's something not many folks want to hear. And very few have heard. Is your mother around, Miss Lorena?"

She was slow in answering, and Callahan felt like a heel because he knew the reply.

"Ma died."

He removed his hat and bowed slightly. "I am sorry to have brought up bad memories."

"Oh, the memories ain't bad, Preacher. Memories be nice. All I got now are memories."

She ought to be a preacher. Callahan wished he had a pencil and paper where he could jot down those words and use them sometime. That would be something.

"Well . . ." He stopped. How stupid was he getting in his old age? Asking a teenage girl if her mother were home when she had been entertaining a secret male visitor who had come into the house from the window? *Of course, nobody is here, you confounded idiot, so don't bother asking about any brothers or sisters.*

"Well, I reckon I shouldn't trouble you anymore, Miss Lorena. Tell your father I'll pay him a visit next time I'm out this way."

"He'll be plowing come first light," she said.

Now that was faith. Callahan already admired this farmer. Plowing. Plowing earth so dry it wouldn't even sprout weeds.

"And if you'd tell him about the revivals I intend to be holding. In town." He decided not to mention that the preaching and singing and soul-searching and possibly soul-saving would be handled in a saloon. "But I was hopin'"—he went back to his Missouri twang, developing a plan off the top of his head while he spoke, liking the plan, too—"that maybe he would allow us to hold a revival for the farmers in this masterful barn he has built."

She looked at the barn, as though noticing it for the first time.

"Huh?" she said, staring at the barn for maybe half a minute, before she looked back at him. Or starting to turn toward him. She stopped. And stared at the path Callahan had ridden down.

A horse whinnied, causing Job to turn his head. Callahan looked, too, and saw a man on a mule, riding bareback, and raising his own mess of dust, whipping at the mule's hindquarters with a switch.

Callahan looked the opposite way, glad that the dust Lorena's secret admirer had been raising on his getaway was no longer in sight.

"That's Pa," she said. "I best get inside."

"My ple . . ." He didn't finish. The door closed. Well, she did have some things to attend to, he figured. Like closing the bedroom window and maybe straightening up some things.

Grabbing the reins, Callahan turned Job to face the mule.

Logan Lamerick had trouble stopping the mule, which was lathered considerably, and his red face and burning eyes let Callahan know that the farmer might have designs on beating him with that stick. So Callahan did his explaining.

"My name's . . ." he started.

The switch rose. "I know who you are," Lamerick spat out. "You're that gunman Vermin Browne's hired to run us out of town. Well, we aren't going nowhere, Gunman. But you are. You're getting off my quarter section, or I'm whipping you till you look like you've gone through a reaper."

"My name," Callahan said casually, "is Callahan. Taylor Callahan. Circuit rider."

The man stopped. "That preacher folks been talking about?"

"Well, I haven't heard much talk, but I guess some folks in Falstaff might be talking about me." He let the reins fall over Job's neck, and then spread open his coat. "I don't wear iron on my person," he said and let the black coat fall back into place, "but there is a Colt in one saddle bag and a box of cartridges in the opposite one. Balance. Balance is needed in a man's life."

"And a Colt's revolver?"

"In this Western country . . ." Callahan smiled. "You never know."

Chapter 19

"You're the circuit rider," Logan Lamerick said, the eyes softening just a mite, and the bulging veins in his neck slowing down. "Who whupped up on a couple of Browne's gunmen last night."

"Cowboys," Callahan corrected. "Not gunmen. There's a big difference."

"They carry guns."

Callahan smiled. "Well, so do I." His head tilted to the saddle bag. "Not on my person. But there are snakes and other dangersome critters in this part of the country." He remembered the rattlesnake that pointed him in this direction.

"Some of them snakes and a passel of them critters are the two-legged kind. And I hear tell that Vermin Browne is bringing some of them in." The farmer glanced at his house, then to the barn again, and finally let his eyes settle on Callahan. "What kind of preaching do you preach, Preacher?"

"What kind of preaching do you like?"

"An eye for an eye, tooth for a tooth."

"Well . . ." Callahan touched his face just below the left

eye. "I've given some men a shiner or two in my day." He let the fingers fall to his jaw. "And I've had some teeth loosened and a couple lost."

"How to you stand on killing?"

Callahan shook his head. "Mr. Lamerick, I've seen enough killings in my time. Missouri, Kansas. During the war. I figure this land's hard enough to make a living on. Maybe men ought not to make it harder to live on."

The farmer dismounted, slapped the mule's hind-quarters, and watched it trot to the water trough near the well in front of the barn.

"How deep did you have to go to get water?" Callahan asked.

The farmer looked surprised at the question. "I didn't put no yardstick to it, Preacher. Two months' digging. I'll tell you that. Maybe a hundred fifty. Maybe two hundred. Feet. I don't know. I just dug till I found water." He laughed. "Folks called me a fool. And my hands sure agreed with them that did, blisters that I got. But we got water."

"You are a determined man."

"I'm a man with a will."

"And a well."

Callahan smiled. The farmer didn't.

"Well, here's why I came to visit, Mr. Lamerick," Callahan said. "I'll be preaching in town for a few days, as long as I feel the need and the folks in the area feel like listening. But my venue is not what most folks would call consecrated grounds, maybe not even fitting for hymns to be sung and scripture to be quoted. Though I feel that the Word is good enough and strong enough to be heard anywhere and anytime. Would you agree?"

He didn't wait for Lamerick to answer.

"I have been seeking out a place that farmers might feel more at ease with. More at home. A saloon, I fear, which is where I am to preach tonight, would not bring many farmers, and their families, to hear hymns and words of comfort, words of love, words that are good for the soul."

"Especially," Lamerick said, his face souring, "when there's a bunch of Vermin Browne's boys bellying up to the bar, and every one of them packing iron. You're right there, Preacher. We won't be going to listen to you run your mouth in that dram shop in False Hope. That'd be like asking us to go listen to that Mex priest speak his stuff, speaking Mexican instead of English."

"I believe it's mostly Latin," Callahan said.

If the farmer heard the correction, he did not bother to acknowledge, just went on spraying his fertilizer on his sentiments about the brown-skinned residents of False Hope. Eventually, Lamerick had to stop to catch his breath, and that is when Callahan turned in the saddle and pointed at the magnificent stone barn.

"That, sir," Callahan said, "is what I consider a temple. A temple for farmers, one they would feel at home in, and a temple to hear the Good Word from the Good Book. Wouldn't you agree?"

Callahan grinned with pure pleasure. He felt as if he were witnessing a miracle. Logan Lamerick had been struck mute.

"My . . ." the big man started after Callahan had counted of twenty-eight seconds. The farmer swallowed.

Another eight seconds.

"My . . ." Only five seconds this time.

Callahan enjoyed this immensely.

"Barn?"

"Indeed, sir." He turned back to the big rock structure, noticed the mule finished with its drinking wandering through the open door and causing the chickens to start raising their protest. "It's one of the finest barns I have seen in Texas, sir. But that is to be expected from a man that will dig for two months to get a well."

He turned back to the stunned behemoth. "Have you given any consideration to trying to irrigate your farm through your well?"

"What?" At least that didn't take him practically a minute to ask a question.

"Irrigation. Dig channels to your fields. Use the well to water when the Major General in the Heavens does not seem to feel any urgency to bless us with some rain."

The big man kept staring at the barn. At length, his head shook and he walked over and drew two rails through the fence, closing the gate. When he looked back at Callahan, his eyes had narrowed. The man sure had one suspicious nature.

"I couldn't do that," he said. "Just can't be done."

"Irrigate?" Callahan tilted his head to one side. "Perhaps not. Wells can run dry. And I'm no farmer or an engineer. Perhaps . . ."

"No." The big man's head shook. "Ain't what I mean. Well, it is, I reckon, since I ain't gonna dig no ditches. I got a hundred and sixty acres here. A hundred and twenty or thereabouts cleared for fields. Might be up to a hundred and forty before next season. That's too much ground to irrigate with no ditches."

"Perhaps dig another well. Two. Three."

The man's eyes narrowed to slits. "Way too much digging, Preacher. And my barn is for my chickens and my stock. And my plows. And my reapers. It ain't fit for no preaching, no hymn-singing, no Scripture reading."

"Well, it was just a thought. Maybe I can find another farmer with a barn not quite as busy as yours."

"Maybe. Old Burke's got a good one. Five miles north." He pointed.

"I'll give him a visit."

"I'd invite you in, Preacher," the farmer said, with no intention of inviting him in ever, Callahan knew. "But I suspect you ought to be catching Old Burke. He ought to be home by the time you could cover five miles. Finished his plowing and such."

"I suspect you are right."

Lamerick nodded, then turned toward the house. When Callahan made no effort to get Job walking back toward the road, the big man stopped, turned, and stared.

"Something else on your mind?"

"Yes, there is," Callahan said. "Your gate."

"Huh?"

"I'm embarrassed to say, but your gate at the road left me puzzled."

"You mean the wire trap."

"Wire trap." Callahan's face lighted up like a beacon. "So that's what that was. Well, it didn't trap me, but it sure perplexed me."

"How'd you get here if you didn't get the trap opened?" He swallowed, then asked, "A miracle?"

Callahan laughed. "I suppose one might look at it that way." He patted Job's neck. "We leaped over it."

"You leaped over my fence?" The farmer shook his head and reconsidered Job. "On that hoss?"

"Yes, sir." Callahan pushed back his hat. "I was surprised myself."

"You got something of a will yourself, Preacher."

"Well, I don't know if it was a will or just a wild streak. But I don't think I'd like to try that jump again."

"And I don't reckon I'd want to have you knocking down my fence, or having to patch you and that nag of yourn up after untwisting you out of a bunch of Glidden's patent wire." He started walking toward the fence.

"Would you like me to fetch your mule?"

"No," the man said without answering. "I'd rather walk than ride."

Callahan glanced at the barn once more time, pulled his hat down, and nudged Job into a walk.

There was no conversation. By then, it was too hot to talk, Callahan figured, and he glanced at the sky in hopes of finding a dark cloud, but knew he would be disappointed.

When they reached the road, he halted Job and asked if he could help. Lamerick just shook his head, and Callahan watched the man work a wire loop that latched the post. Brute strength, that iron will, and angling the post just right. "It's the cheater-bar," the farmer said. "That's the trick."

He caught the gate post, and dragged the fence away, just enough so that Callahan and Job could ride to the road. As he turned in the saddle, Lamerick closed the gate, the loop dug into the post, and the fence looked rock solid, practically impenetrable.

"Nothing to it," Lamerick said. "Once you get the hang of it."

"I see." Callahan nodded. "Well, I surely thank you for your kindness and hospitality."

"I ain't kind. And I ain't hospitable. I just don't want nobody ruining my fence. Glidden's wire ain't cheap, you understand. And it's hard work keeping this fence up."

He pointed north.

"Old Burke's straight down that little squirrel trail," the farmer said. "Like I say, five miles, no more than that. His barn's made of adobe bricks. Like some of them buildings in False Hope. He had some Mexicans build it for him. Ain't as good as mine. Rocks last longer than dirt. But it might suit your purposes."

"Thanks again."

He snorted and spit and fished a morsel of jerky out of his trousers pocket. He bit into it and started chewing.

"You know," Callahan said. "I understand that you don't like Vernon Browne. And I've always heard that cowboys don't care much for farmers, and farmers don't care much for cowboys. Or ranchers. But if you're neighbors, you got to get used to one another. And you need each other."

"I don't need no cowboy. And no rancher."

Callahan smiled. "That's beef jerky you're eating."

The man swallowed.

"Beef comes from cattle," Callahan said. "Cowboys wear cotton shirts. Farmers grow cotton. And cattle and horses need grain or corn. Especially when the grass is dying."

Callahan pushed back his Boss of the Plains. "Seems to me, farmers need cowboys, and cowboys need farmers. We ought to be able to reach some mutual understanding."

"Mister, I ain't selling nothing I grow to no rancher, no

cowboy. On account that it was a cowboy who killed my only son."

Well, Callahan thought, *there's the rub.* And it was something that rubbed raw, tore the skin, got into the soul.

"Killed in a stampede."

Callahan's eyes narrowed. "A stampede? At your farm?"

"No. Ryan run off, that's what happened. Got some notion that he wanted to cowboy, not farm. Farming was too hard work. That's what he said. And he's right. It's hard work. Sometimes, it's brutal work. But it's work for a man, not a boy. Any dumb fool can sit in a saddle. You're doing a right good job of it right now. So he run off when we got here. Signed on with Browne. Didn't make it three nights up the trail before the cattle spooked. Ryan got caught in the mix. Horse spooked, threw him, and fifteen hundred of Vermin Browne's mossy horns run over my boy."

He was yelling now, in full fury, his eyes reddening from a mix of tears and heartbreak. But now Callahan understood the farmer's hatred. And once you understood something, solving the problem came a bit easier.

"Browne could've sent word back, spared a rider. It took them days to round up all the cattle that scattered. Instead, he waited till they reached San Antone. Sent a letter. Took three weeks to get here. But he told me where they had buried my boy. Even drawed a map. And I went there with a wagon." He pointed back toward the farm. "Brought Ryan home. Buried him next to Lois, his ma." Callahan now recalled a small fence that Callahan had barely noticed, so preoccupied with the stone home and stone barn—and the farmer's daughter and her cowboy paramour. Barbed-wire fence, of course, and that must be the Lamerick family cemetery, with two graves. A mother and a son. Lost in Texas. So now Callahan understood the man's bitterness.

"Found the grave. They'd wrapped him in his bedroll. No coffin. I had to order a coffin, but, well, there wasn't much left of Ryan. Not after all the hooves done their work on my boy. Fourteen years old. You want to know what fifteen hundred longhorns can do to a fourteen-year-old boy?"

He spit, whirled, and stormed away.

Callahan sat in the saddle, baking in the sun, until the big man was nothing but a small shadow and finally nothing.

Job snorted. Callahan gathered up the slack in the reins. His heart ached for the farmer's loss, and he decided to think of a prayer for the suffering farmer. He wouldn't visit old Burke. Not today. He'd ride back to Falstaff and consider his accomplishments.

The visit to the Lamerick farm might have ended poorly, but Callahan had learned a few things.

He knew why the old man hated Vernon Browne and cowboys.

He knew why Lorena Lamerick didn't want to introduce her beau to her pa.

Even more important, Callahan now understood what it took to open a wire trap.

He looked off to the southeast, recalling the direction those deep wagon tracks had come from. But he wouldn't ride that way just yet. He wanted to think on a few items. And he wanted to talk to Lorena Lamerick's beau.

So he let Job pick his own pace as they returned to Falstaff.

Chapter 20

And here was another miracle, right before Taylor Callahan's eyes.

Falstaff, Texas, was overflowing with living, breathing, human beings. Mexicans, farmers, cowboys, women, children, young, old, middle-aged, Mayor Wallace Scurry, land agent Milton Clarke, even Father Pedro Sebastià Fernández de Calderón y Borbón crowded the streets.

It was understandable, Callahan reasoned, when he saw the fancy rig parked at the cistern, the lead horses slaking their thirst with the dusty water, the two wheelers, alas, having to wait their turn, maybe if the livery man got around to unharnessing them rather than leaving them standing underneath a broiling sun in the middle of the day.

The horses appeared to be Cleveland Bays, close to sixteen hands tall, with deep girths and short but powerful legs. Old Bertram Brett, an Englishman, used to raise them up near Toller Creek in Clay County. He said they were the classiest draft horses a man would find anywhere. Smart, too. Big bay horses—not a mark of white to be found on them except when they opened their mouths—with big heads, and long necks. They sure made a horse like Job look right puny and poorer.

But the four draft horses weren't getting any attention or admiration from anybody in Falstaff other than the Reverend Taylor Callahan. Most of the kids, and many of the men and women, were pointing at the wagon the team was harnessed to.

It was painted blue, with wide yellow trim, and a lightning bolt of orange streaking down at an angle. In big, bold black letters at the top read:

PROFESSOR
JESSUP HUNGATE

And below that:

PRODUCING RAINFALL BY

Which is exactly where the artist that painted this rig got his money's worth. The painter had copied from every artist's rendition of cannon fire he had ever seen. Shades of orange and red and black, with gray to black smoke spelling out the word:

CONCUSSION!

On the back of the wagon was a small door—the professor couldn't be a fat man to fit through that—with more artistry, thunder clouds with lightning, vibrant water running through brooks and a lake between two lame-looking mountains, smiling faces on children, and a verdant pasture that almost blinded an unprotected eye.

There was also a warning painted in black and gold on the door.

DANGER: EXPLOSIVES INSIDE

Callahan turned to a farmer who was as curious as the circuit rider.

"You might want to put out that cigar, sir," Callahan said.

The bearded man puffed and frowned. "What fer?"

Callahan pointed to the warning.

"I don't read, mister," the man said.

"Keep puffin' on that stogie, you won't be farmin', either." He tapped the door, and stopped, staring at his knuckles.

"He's got explosives inside," Callahan said and pressed his palm against the wood. His next words came out as a whisper. "You don't want to blow Falstaff off the map of Texas, do you?"

The man snorted, threw the cigar into the cistern, and walked toward the land office.

"I'd be doing False Hope a favor if I'd blow it and all of us to Kingdom Come," the grouch said.

Callahan pressed against the wagon. He tapped it again, but not so hard this time.

"Iron," he said. "Not wood."

Which meant maybe Hungate wasn't any run-of-the-mill idiot. An iron wagon wouldn't be likely to burn and blow up if he were hauling black powder or dynamite or some other kind of explosives. He looked at the crosses cut into the iron. Two in the back. Two on each side, as he moved around the wagon. Windows. That allowed a draft and some air and some light inside. But also a spark or two.

And that got Callahan thinking about another wagon, or two, but ones he had not seen. The tracks at the Lamerick farm, leading from the east to the big stone barn. Could it be?

He looked down at the wagon's wheels.

No, it could not be. The rear wheels were sunk three to four inches into the ground, and the front, smaller wheels looked about two inches deep. Granted, the land here, this close to the cistern, was on the damp side, compared to the farmland, but these wheels didn't fit what Callahan had seen, even if he also accounted the time that had elapsed since the wagon, or wagons, left those prints at the farm. But, no, this wagon was heavier. Much heavier.

That's when Callahan noticed another wagon, off in empty land. That wagon was huge, and men and children from Falstaff gathered around it, too. Oxen pulled that wagon, and he saw men bringing a giant basket out of the back.

A man in a Yankee shell jacket was directing the men to lower the big basket to the ground, then he barked at them. "We'll need wood. As much wood, coal, anything that burns brought here. Do you understand?" Someone translated the orders into Spanish. And Callahan realized that the basket was part of the balloon. He had never seen one except in illustrated magazines.

Callahan dodged between four children running around, screaming their young heads off, and spotted a familiar face. He circled the cistern to the far side, and held out his hand toward Father Pete.

"Buenos tardes," the priest said. "Good afternoon," he then translated.

"Quite the fandango," Callahan said.

"I have never seen such excitement in this town in . . ." The young priest shrugged.

"Makes a man wonder," Callahan said and waited for Father Pete to stop looking at the commotion and turn back and stare up at the circuit rider.

"You and me, Padre." Callahan grinned. "We've been selling what our fathers, grandfathers, and great-great-great-how many greats whatever we can count to have been selling. Selling what most folks seem to need or want. What men, women, young and old want to have, must have, or are just curious about. Now here comes some young whippersnapper selling something new, some promise that seems more like a bet than gospel. And folks come flocking to hear what he has to say. And what he says don't start with, 'In the beginning . . .'"

"He promises hope," Father Pete said.

"When you get right down to it, Father, that's all we can promise, too. Hope. You gotta hope what we're selling is good and right and lives up to what we've written on the label. There ain't no guarantee what we're selling is right, you know."

"I believe," the priest said with young indignance.

"So do I. But I'm curious . . ." A horse caught Callahan's attention.

"This professor," Father Pete said. "He desires to meet you. He is in . . ." The priest turned to point, but Callahan laughed.

"No need. You ain't got to be Jim Bridger or Kit Carson to figure out where the erudite Professor Jessup Hungate is selling his wares this afternoon. And I'd be delighted to hear what he has to say. But I need to speak to someone else first."

Callahan made a beeline for the saloon, but he went through the open doors on the ground floor. Didn't pay any attention to the stairs that led to Mayor Wallace Scurry's office. Besides, the bottom of the stairs were filled with people, and the crowd at the platform had to be ten to twelve folks thick.

The saloon wasn't exactly spartan.

Callahan looked at the crowded bar, then glanced at a few tables. At the window, he got his first true surprise, but then realized how seeing young Tommy Browne leaning on a crutch at the window with a beer stein in his right hand should have been expected. This was, after all, Vermin Browne's boy. The boy had just slid a paper note to the bartender, who took it and handed the kid some coins in change, which went into the boy's vest pocket.

He walked to the kid, who looked at him, nodded, stared out the window, then whipped around his face.

"What are *you* doing?" Tommy practically sprayed Callahan's shirtfront with beer. "In *here*?"

"I might ask you the same question. Did the doctor say you ought to be up and about after busting your ankle so? How far is it to your ranch from Falstaff anyway?"

"Falstaff? Oh . . . False Hope." The youngster shook his head and smiled. "You're about the only body I've heard who has called this blight Falstaff in a coon's age."

"False Hope is not in my vocabulary, son. How far?"

"I came in a buckboard."

"How's the leg?"

He sighed. "It hurts."

"Which is why you should be at home. In bed. Maybe elevating that leg."

"Pa . . ." He stopped. "I'll be all right."

Well, the boy was old enough to punch cows. Of course, so was Logan Lamerick's son.

"Where's your segundo? I saw him walk in here."

"My what?"

"Segundo. Your boss. Foreman. For a boy who uses 'blight' in a sentence, I figured you knew what *segundo* means. I just learned it myself. My Spanish vocabulary is growing every day."

Which reminded him that he needed to ask Father Pete about *Vaya con Dios*.

"Well." He started to bring the stein to his lips, but blushed, and lowered the beer. "Honest. Some drummer called this bucket of sin a blight when he come through town two months ago. Me and the boys started calling it that, too. It's better than just the saloon, we figured."

Callahan's grin was honest again.

"Terry Page? I saw him step through the batwing doors."

"Oh, Terry." The boy turned, first at the bar, focusing harder as he studied the tables. "I don't know. I heard Fletch call out his name just a minute or two ago. So, yeah, he had to come in here. I wasn't really in no sociable mood. Just drinking. Waiting to see what happens. We was wondering if they might start blowing up dynamite in the air tonight. That'd be something to see."

"I imagine it would be." This wasn't getting Callahan anywhere.

"Well." The kid pointed to a rear door. "Privy. That's the most logical place, I reckon."

Callahan smiled. "I reckon you're right." He patted the boy's crutch. "You figured out how to walk with this thing. They've been known to be tougher than some of the rankest widowmakers in a cowboy's string."

The kid laughed. "It has a certain temperament."

"You'll figure it out." He smiled warmly. "You're a

bright young man. But bright young men don't usually hop about when they just got a chunk of lead pulled out of their leg."

The boy's face hardened. "And Pa and me aim to find out which Meskin bushwhacked me."

"That sounds more like your pa talking than you, Tommy."

Callahan turned and headed toward that back door, dodging one frilly dressed old hag carrying a tray of maybe a dozen beers, avoiding a drunk on his knees, and moving with caution between a poker game and a faro layout.

Finally, he was through the door, back into the sunshine and the stink of the privies.

Perfect timing, too, he thought, because Terry Page had just stepped out of one of six one-seaters.

The cowhand stopped and stiffened.

"Afternoon," Callahan said, and moved to the outhouse farthest from where Page stood. The preacher opened the door, shut it, and then moved to the next one. It was empty, too. So were the next three. He didn't bother looking at the one Page had just vacated, since there wasn't a two-seater in sight.

"I reckon we're alone," Callahan said with a grin.

"You're good at reading sign."

"Better than you think," Callahan said. "That prancing little gelding of yours. You got a bit of a snake-like-looking thing on one of your shoes."

"Reckon I'll have the smithy at the ranch take a look at it."

"Well, it doesn't appear to be harming how fast your horse can gallop."

"He's got a good trot, too," Page said. "Feels as smooth as a canter."

"That's a good hoss."

"I like him."

"Don't blame you." Callahan grinned. "Job. That's my horse. The white gelding. You know. He crawls pretty good. But that's about it." Callahan's head shook. "No, no, I'd be remiss if I didn't point out that old Job can leap a right-high fence. Course, that could be that barbed wire scares him into jumping higher."

"If you'll excuse me, Preacher." Page started to back for the saloon. "I've got some drinking to do."

Callahan let the cowboy get five steps away, but cowboys didn't have long gaits, not after riding horses all day for weeks on end.

"Do you reckon Miss Lorena knew where her pa was today?"

The man stopped. His entire body tensed. Slowly, he turned around.

"Who?" The question was spoken through tight lips, and the anger began boiling in the cowboy's eyes.

"Miss Lorena Lamerick. Daughter of Logan Lamerick. Funny, I've known a passel of Logans. Rode with a Logan during the war. Before that, I learned all about the Good Book and more at a seminary named after a Logan. And now there's a farmer. Do you think she knew where her pa was this afternoon?"

"Why would I know that?" His hands balled into trembling fists.

"Well, your horse was tied up on the west side of town. Good hiding spot if her pa was working his east pastures. But he wasn't. He came home from the north. Same way

I rode up to his house. And knowing farmers, knowing how good their eyes are at distances, unlike mine after reading so much small print to figure out how to preach, well, I imagine he could see that hoss a lot better than I could. And I saw the gelding real well. And if her pappy could have seen it . . ."

He didn't finish. Didn't have to. But he expected the charge and the uppercut, which Callahan deflected easily, then stuck out one leg, twisted the cowboy's arm and pushed him right into the outhouse he had just left. The door was opened, and he fell onto the wooden floor.

Page started to rise. That told Callahan something. He wasn't a gunman. A killer would have gone for the revolver on his hip. Page just wanted to beat the ever-loving tar out of the preacher.

"What would Miss Lorena say?" Callahan said.

Page came up like grapeshot, but once again, Callahan did a spin, slight punch, twist and push, and Terry Page was tasting gravel one more time. The cowboy rolled over, wiped his mouth with his shirtsleeve, and pointed a finger.

"You mention her name again, and it'll take a month of Sundays till you can see straight."

Callahan let out a sigh, and took off his hat, slapping it against his thighs.

"Well, that's good to hear. I reckon I ain't got to ask you the next question."

Page was pushing himself to his feet, but now he stopped. His brow knotted, and his head twisted slightly to the left. The eyes burned, but not so much with rage. It was a sign that Taylor Callahan knew pretty well.

"Huh?" Page asked with complete confusion.

"Sonny boy," Callahan said, returned his hat to his

head, and stepped over, then extended his right hand toward the sitting cowhand.

"You're all right in my book, Terry. Don't mind if I call you Terry, do you? You can drop the 'Preacher' and 'Parson' and 'Reverend' and what-not if you want to. My name's Taylor. Named after daddy's ma. Her maiden name, not her Christian name. That was my birthing daddy. I had lots of daddies in my day. But that don't rightly matter."

The Browne ranch foreman ignored the extended hand.

"What the Sam Hill are you getting at?" he demanded.

The rear door to the saloon started to open, so Callahan reached down, grabbed the confused cowhand's arm, and hoisted him up, then turned him around and whispered. "Let's go. Folks in need of the privies here might want a bit of privacy. And there ain't nothing more private than a noisy saloon when a rainmaker just rode into town."

They let two waddies make their way to the facilities, and when Callahan held the rear door to the saloon open for Page, he finally answered the foreman's question.

"What I wanted to know, Terry, for certain, is this: Do you love Lorena Lamerick? Because if you was just using her, well, it would be a month of Sundays before you could sit a saddle."

"I didn't tell you nothing," Page said back inside the noisy building.

"Not in words. That's a fact. But circuit riders know all sorts of languages."

Chapter 21

Taylor Callahan had never cared much for sardines, but now he knew how one of those itsy-bitsy salty things that looked more like bait than any fish felt. He sucked in his belly, which wasn't anywhere near pudgy, and squeezed between cowboys and merchants, gamblers and farmers, even a few boys of school age who had managed to sneak inside.

Fat chance they had of making it all the way to the bar. The kids knew that too. Callahan saw the sadness in their eyes.

It took him three minutes to get through the batwing doors, which never banged shut or open, just stood, one pointing inward, the other outward, letting the throngs move in or out.

Outside wasn't much better. Callahan had to blink sweat from his eyelids. The arrival of the professor had turned Falstaff into a boomtown. All the Mexicans had come in from Arroyo Verde, and Callahan figured most of the farmers had gotten word. He stood on his tiptoes to see if he could spot Logan Lamerick, but couldn't see over a couple of bowlers and an Abe Lincoln silk hat. He heard a woman's voice, and turned to his left.

He saw her, but that wasn't Lorena Lamerick. It had to be another farmer's wife, and that one was older and fatter, and one with the vocabulary of a prison guard.

When Callahan finally got to a place where he didn't have to hold his breath, and could actually lower his arms without hitting someone, he paused to wipe his face with the bandanna.

Over the commotion, a voice called out from the heavens:

"Reeee-veerrrrr-annnnnd!"

Callahan looked up, not at the cloudless sky, but the top platform on the stairs outside the saloon.

Wallace Scurry stood outside his office. Father Pedro Sebastià Fernández de Calderón y Borbón stood beside him, and behind the young priest, Callahan saw an older Mexican, in the thick woolen robes of a priest or a monk or someone who wanted to torture himself on earth so he'd have a nicer street of gold in heaven. Wearing wool that heavy on a day this hot. Now that was a man who believed in suffering on earth. Had to be the priest from Arroyo Verde. Another man stood in the doorway, fanning himself with a flat-brimmed, flat-crowned straw hat. Callahan thought he might be the professor, but no, the face was one Callahan had seen around Falstaff.

"Can we have a moment of your time, Reverend?" the mayor called down.

Callahan started to shout out his answer, decided that would be pointless, and he made himself smile and began squeezing between more men, more women, more children, all ages, all sizes, all sweating.

Heading up the stairs proved even tougher, but the crowded stairs stopped about halfway up, and Callahan saw why. Two guards, wearing two holstered Remingtons in crisscrossed shellbelts, the red mustached one clutching a double-barreled Greener, thumbs on the cocked hammers; the bald one with a brown patch over his right eye, using his Winchester Yellow Boy as a barricade, blocked the way. And they weren't letting anyone through—without the mayor's permission.

Or maybe . . . the professor's approval.

The two guards were strangers to him, and they were still dressed in linen dusters. Dusters were worn by traveling men. And the faces on these men told Callahan that they had done some hard traveling of late.

Say by way of the Missouri state pen in Jefferson . . . or Yuma over in Arizona Territory . . . and, this being the Lone Star State, perhaps Huntsville.

They let him through without argument, though a few of the townsmen and farmers behind him swore and cussed and complained that this wasn't right, that they'd been here waiting for too long.

"You got to be Godlike to see the professor?" one shouted.

Callahan turned, and found the man who had said that. It was easy enough. His face paled when he saw Callahan's eyes.

"We're all Godlike, Mister," Callahan said. "We were all created in His, or Her, image. Remember that. Remember that."

Removing his hat, he turned back and, able to breathe without being reminded of how farmers and cowboys and sweating men smelled, he took the steps two at a time, and warmly greeted Father Pete with a handshake.

"You said, 'Remember that,' twice, Reverend," Mayor Scurry said.

"A lesson one of my iron-willed daddies told me," Callahan explained. "Say it once, a man might forget. Put it to him twice, he's twice as likely to remember. Or . . ." Callahan winked. "Twice as likely to forget."

Callahan was introduced to the priest from Arroyo Verde, and to Troy Fell, a minister and farmer who had a quarter section four miles south of town.

"Come inside," the mayor said, showing the way, as if Callahan needed any directions, with his fat cigar.

Professor Jessup Hungate sat at the mayor's desk, in the mayor's chair, sipping from a fine coffee cup that Callahan figured did not belong to the mayor while bending over and using a spyglass to read over a contract that must have been fifteen or twenty pages.

"Profess—" the mayor began, but stopped when Hungate raised his left hand and continued to read. The magnifying glass moved like a sloth. This Hungate was a careful man. A silk top hat lay to the professor's left, crown down. His cravat, silk of a deep and rich crimson, had been loosened, and the paper collar unbuttoned. His suit was white, the vest a silvery brocade. His hair was long, blond, curly and to the shoulders, and he wore a well-groomed blond mustache, twisted and turned up at the corners. If it weren't so hot in this stuffy office, Callahan might not have noticed that the mustache was secured with theatrical paste, which was sweating, and there was just enough sweat on the man's forehead to let Callahan in on Hungate's secret that the long hair was a wig.

Finally, the magnifying glass was lowered, and laid atop the thick papers, and the professor straightened and found his cup. He drank, nodded, and looked directly at Callahan.

"So you are the fighting parson," he said in a booming, theatrical voice.

"Callahan," was the answer, neither confirming nor denying the label. "Taylor Callahan." He stepped forward and held out his right hand.

The man's grip wasn't firm, but the hand was far from pasty. Long fingers on this gent, reminding him of what his favorite pa had said once. *Long fingers are good for nothing but playing pianos or gouging out someone's eyeballs.* This professor did not just read contracts. He had done some hard work with his hands, and his arms were hairy, dark hair, not blond like the wig and fake mustache, except around the wrists. Which could have meant a number of things, but the only thing that came to Callahan's mind was *manacles*.

"I mean no offense," Hungate said, "but I shall be clear with you as I have been clear with the other men of cloth in this dry wasteland." He rose, buttoned his collar and began retying the cravat. His fingers worked fast. Limber fingers. Callahan wondered how he dealt a hand of stud poker, but his favorite pa had never said anything about that all those years back. And Callahan had met some real good sharpers with stubby fingers, not to mention that fellow in Kansas City who didn't have his middle finger or his pinky on his left hand, and he had dealt good, from top or bottom, till Millard Clepper gunned him down back in March of '60.

"I am not a man of God, but a man of science. That's where I put my faith. And science can bring rain. That I have proved in Georgia, Kentucky, Oregon, Florida, Pittsburgh, and France."

"You get around." Callahan smiled.

"During the late unpleasantness, I had the distinction and the honor to be an observer for *Dustin Guinan's Illustrated Weekly*."

"I was a *Frank Leslie's* reader myself."

Callahan grinned. The professor did not.

"What I noticed, while following Robert E. Lee's army all across Northern Virginia was that whenever artillery was used copiously in battle, thunderstorms followed. Torrents of rain. It seemed obvious, to me, that the concussion of the cannon fire, the explosives used, resulted in a chemical reaction caused by the nuclei. The multiple explosions led to a reaction. A concussion caused the atmospheric pressure to adjust, reacting to the buoyancy of the gases from the explosives, and the heat from those explosions forced a wind current up. Explosions generate not only electricity, but friction. The sky and the earth thus polarize."

He drew in a deep breath. The man wasn't big, but he sure could talk a heap before needing to fill his lungs.

"Do you have any idea what I'm saying, Reverend?"

"That the cannon fire rattled up the sky and caused a frog strangler."

The man stared as though Callahan had spoken to him in Greek.

"Frog strangler?" the professor asked.

Callahan tried a different expression. "Turd float?"

Disgust showed on Hungate's face. He looked at the mayor for help, got nothing, and so he concluded. "You can produce rainfall by concussion." He smoothed the lapels on his coat. "That's all there is to it. Balloons and bombs."

"In Georgia, Kentucky, Oregon, Florida, Pittsburgh, and France?"

Hungate stopped fidgeting with his coat. Callahan's memory surprised him.

"That's correct."

"Kind of humid in those states, and I reckon France. Never been there. Actually, I've never been to Georgia, Oregon, Florida or Pittsburgh—which is a city in Pennsylvania, I do believe—and not a state. Ma and one or two of my daddies hailed from Kentucky, though, and spoke of it often. I do believe those places get more rain than we typically get out west."

"Which is why I have brought my experiments here. To prove that we can produce rainfall by concussions anywhere." He looked at the mayor. "Your contract will work fine, and I shall sign it after consulting with my colleagues."

"Mr. Vernon Browne will handle payment," the mayor said.

"Per my specifications?" the professor inquired.

"As stipulated in the contract."

The professor's head nodded.

"Browne's forking up his own money for this experiment?" Callahan asked.

"Yes," the mayor said with irritation.

"So how does this work?" Callahan asked.

When Hungate stared, Callahan fashioned a guess.

"You fly up in some balloon and drop bombs? Or shoot Roman candles into the sky?"

"Don't be silly and do not mock science!"

"I'm not being silly, and I'd never mock science. Not as much as science seems to mock religion, I reckon."

Callahan liked how the men of faith reacted to the last sentence.

"We send bombs into the sky. And we also use dynamite and other devices on the ground. The cannons at Antietam were fired from ground level, as you might know."

"Well, I wasn't there, so it certainly makes sense. I never read anything about Yankees or Rebels flying up in balloons and dropping mortars from them onto camps below." He grinned. "Though wouldn't that have been an interesting way to fight a war? From the air. Dropping bombs on the enemy. Gosh, just think of the possibilities. A country could have an army to fight on the land, and a navy to fight on the sea, and an . . . an . . . an . . ."

"Air army," Father Pete suggested.

"Yeah. The United States Air Army. Fighting from the sky."

"Are you mocking me, sir?" Hungate asked.

"No. I'm interested to see if this plan works." He sighed and shook his head. "These folks have been hurting, Professor Hungate. I'm a newcomer to these parts, and I'm just passing through. I'll do my preaching and maybe lead a few hymns, and then I'll be on my way. To another town. Another county. Another state or territory. Another set of folks with a whole different set of problems. I got no stake here. No claim. I just try to help people out. Get 'em straight."

"The only thing that will help this town and these people is rain."

Callahan grinned again. "Yeah, and I've said this before. I wonder if it was dry back when Noah was building that boat of his. Maybe all those nasty folks that angered the Major General in the Heavens was mocking and mean because it was so hot. Maybe they was praying for rain. Look what it got them."

"Stop this nonsense. I can produce rain. If I do not produce rain, we do not get paid." He turned directly to the mayor. "Advise any spectators to keep their distance. We will begin setting up tomorrow. My assistants, Fitzjohn and Lowrie, are veteran balloonists."

Those would be the ones unloading the balloon. Callahan asked: "And what do the men with the pairs of Remingtons do? Fire off shots from the ground to replicate the artillery from the late war?"

"Do not mock me, sir," the professor said.

Scurry cleared his throat and said, "Vernon Browne has also agreed to put you up at his ranch. His accommodations are much . . . well . . . more civilized than anything we have here in False Ho . . . in Falstaff, Professor."

"Does that mean the ranch gets the rain first?" the farmers' preacher asked.

"No," the professor said. "But we have no control as to where the rain falls. It could be right here, in town, and it could be in the surrounding area. But it will rain. That is our guarantee. And when it rains, as the saying goes, it pours. It pours when you have hired Professor Jessup Hungate." He shook the mayor's hand first, then the hands of the men of faith.

Callahan's hand was shaken last, and the professor gave him a strong, hard stare.

"You appear to be the biggest doubter," Hungate said.

"No doubt," Callahan said, in a tone that could have been taken as a denial or a confirmation. "We all have doubts. It's human nature. I'm just curious. But I'll pray for you, Professor. And I'll pray that you bless this country with rain. A good, nice rain. Lots of rain. One rainstorm, you understand, does not end a drought."

"But it would be a blessing," Wallace Scurry said.

When the professor stood at the door, Callahan called out to him.

"I'll be holding my first revival this evening, Professor. At the saloon. You're welcome, you and your associates, to drop in. No donations demanded. Just whatever the spirit makes you feel like doing. Sing some good songs. Tell some stories. And pray for rain."

"I am sad to say that I, and my associates, will be far too busy to attend those festivities, Reverend. But we wish you all the luck, and we appreciate the prayers. We must work on this together."

Hungate departed, and the crowd below began yelling questions. The professor tried to answer, and he said something that left the men and women cheering. Looking out the door, the priest from Arroyo Verde whispered, "That crowd parted like the Red Sea."

"What did he tell 'em?" the farming preacher asked.

"Couldn't hear," the Arroyo Verde man said.

Probably, Callahan thought but did not say, *he's buying drinks downstairs.*

Chapter 22

His sermon in the saloon had not been well attended because it was tough to bring in a big crowd when a balloon was in town. He should have preached in the camp with the two balloonists.

After sundown, when the temperature might have dipped below ninety, and a wind kicked in, Callahan left the shade of his boudoir in Father Pete's barn and walked around town. A horsefly could hardly find room to fit between the crowded hitching rails, and boisterous song, ribald laughter, and loud clinking of glasses rang out under and over the batwing doors.

Six o'clock, he told himself, is too early to preach in saloons. Make it later next time.

The professor had to be at Browne's ranch by now, so the cowboys were buying their own drinks. The farmers had gone home, but that was typical of farmers. Early to bed, early to rise.

Continuing on toward the eastern road that had brought him to this town, he stopped again at the bullet-riddled sign.

Welcome to Falstaff

Of course, the town's official name had been scratched through and pulverated with bullet holes. Painted over and around the knife marks, splinters, scratches and holes made by assorted caliber were the town's new handle:

False hope
150 miles
to the nearest post office
100 miles to wood
20 miles to water
6 inches to hell

Farther down the trail he found another sign in front of a deep arroyo, the bank higher on the eastern side leveling off to basically nothing as one came into the outskirts of Falstaff, but an easy climb down for wagons or horses. Job had made it with hardly any effort.

The first words were older, rougher, but carved and painted, though the black paint had begun to peel and fade into just a few gray streaks.

Peligro
no cruzar

The next words he could not make out, but the final word was still legible.

Inundado

The three planks below, Callahan figures, were the English translation.

Danger

Do Not Cross

When Flooded

These boards had been used for target practice, too.

Callahan walked into the arroyo, away from the road, dug his heel into the sandy soil here and there, then shook his head.

Like I could dig a well here.

How deep had Logan Lamerick had to go? A hundred and fifty to two hundred feet or more. A flat stone caught his eye near the embankment, and he moved there, picked it up, blew the dust off the stop, and turned the burning stone over. He brushed off grains of sand with his thumb, and stepped back toward town, turned so that the setting sun shined on the flat rock and he marveled at what he saw.

What was it they called these things? He had read about it, and not in *Dustin Guinan's Illustrated Weekly,* but a New York City newspaper he had found in a stagecoach station near a Kansas railroad.

Artifacts? No, that wasn't it. *Fossil.*

By thunder, Taylor Callahan had just walked up and picked up an honest-to-goodness fossil. It was . . .

Callahan shook his head.

"A miracle?" he whispered and looked at the darkening sky.

It wasn't anything spectacular, he figured, just a dark patch that rose from the sandstone, broken in places, but even in the gloaming he could make out what appeared to be scales. It wasn't a whole fish, though, just the tail.

From the great flood? Callahan wondered and heard the sound of a horse's hooves. Job snorted and looked at the approaching figure, silhouetted by the sun, but Callahan knew he had company.

He walked back toward the road as Terry Page reined in his horse, threw a leg over the horn, and fished out the makings for a cigarette.

"Evening," Callahan said, still holding the sandstone.

Page did not say a thing, just worked methodically on getting the proper amount of tobacco in his paper.

The cigarette went between his lips, his right hand struck a match and brought the flame to the end till it glowed orange and began to smoke. The match was shook out and sent into the sand, and Page stared down at the circuit rider.

Callahan gestured with the flat stone at the sign, then to the dry wash.

"You ever see water running here?"

"No." He blew out blue smoke, and spit a tobacco flake into the wind. "Most of the boys figure this was put up here as a joke."

Smiling, Callahan walked closer to the horse and rider, holding up the sandstone.

"There was water here once."

Page blew smoke out of his nose, removed the cigarette and studied the fossil.

"Looks like an arrowhead to me," the cowboy said. "Maybe a spear."

"Fish's tail," Callahan said, "back when water covered this whole country, I suspect."

Page put the cigarette back in his mouth and looked at the sandstone again. "What happened to the rest of him?"

"Don't know." He turned and looked at the dry sand. "We could start digging, maybe find another piece to the puzzle, but from what I've read and heard, it's hard to find a complete fossil. Usually just fragments. Like this."

"Or maybe a bigger fish came by and ate him, spit out the tail. Tails ain't much good for eating anyway."

"I don't know about that. We fried up bream up in Missouri, fried 'em good and hard, with lots of batter and salt, and they were crunchy and delicious."

"I'll have to take your word for that." He took another pull on the smoke, holding it in, and flipped the cigarette on the other side of the horse. "But I didn't come here to talk about fish or . . . whatever it is you call that?"

"Fossils."

Page wet his lips with his tongue, thinking of what words to use. Finally, he just asked, "What do you plan on doing about me and . . . me and . . . Miss . . . Lorena?"

Callahan admired his fossil for another second or two before sliding the sandstone into the pocket of his Prince Albert. "Well," he said, looking up again at Page. "Unless you or Miss Lorena come up to me and ask me about marrying y'all, I don't reckon there's much for me to do."

Page looked like he had been struck dumb.

"You're both old enough, it appears to me, to make up your own minds about things. And I can sense that y'all have strong feelings for each other. She must see something special in you to do something behind her pa's back." He laughed. "That wasn't like me at all, though, with most of my daddies. Some of them was all right, and I wanted to please 'em something fierce, but quite a few I didn't care what they thought, and they didn't care what

I done. I'd hope . . ." He smiled up at the cowhand. "I'd surely hope I've got y'all pegged right."

"We haven't talked about getting hitched."

"Good," Callahan thundered, so much that the horse's ears went alert, and Job, standing bored a few yards away, turned and snorted. "A bunch of young whippersnappers rush into these sorts of things. Meet one day, court another, marry in a hurry, and don't know hardly nothin' 'bout one another. And then they start learnin' things that just annoys both of them something terrible."

"I just don't want no talk spreading."

"I preach," Callahan said. "I don't gossip."

"All right." The leg came down from the horn, and Page looked about ten years younger.

"What do you think of Professor Hungate?" Callahan asked.

A weary smile creased the foreman's face. "He sure bought a lot of whiskey and beer tonight."

"Pay in cash?"

Page straightened. "I wouldn't know."

"Does your boss think he can deliver this . . . rainfall from concussions?"

"You'd have to ask Mr. Browne."

"I might do that." Callahan faked a yawn, said it was getting night bedtime, even though the sun was still slowly sinking, stretching out the day as long as it could.

"Be nice if we could get a good gully-washer here," Callahan said.

"Yep."

"You know anybody who ever saw water running through this wash?" Callahan asked.

The cowboy's head shook. "Maybe some old Mexicans might recollect, but I've been working for the old man for six years, last two and a half as foreman." He pointed to the flat side on the northern edge of the road. "Used to be sand bags stacked up yonder. When the farmers started coming in, they taken the bags, dumped out the sand. I guess they figured the bags was better suited for putting taters or carrots in."

Callahan remembered the Lamerick house. "Or curtains for windows."

Page shrugged. "I reckon."

"You like working for Mr. Browne?"

Another shrug. "He pays me a good wage. I give him an honest day's work."

"What do you call honest work?"

The face aged again.

"Listen, the farmers come here, and at first, that was fine," Page said, his voice not with as much edge as Callahan expected, talking as though he had said this before a few times. And maybe he had. To Miss Lorena. To maybe some other cowboys who weren't as easily riled as Vermin Browne. "There weren't many of 'em, and they didn't take up too much land. But then this Clarke comes in—"

"He came in to help Vernon Browne, I do believe," Callahan interjected.

"That's right. But that was different."

Callahan could not hide his grin. It was different, all right. Different when Vernon Browne was letting his hired men claim a hundred and sixty acres, then selling the deed to Browne so he could own more property.

"Did you claim a section?" Callahan asked.

"Quarter-section," the cowboy answered. "All that was allowed."

"Ever wish you had kept that land for yourself?"

Page stared hard again. His lips did not move from that straight, hard, flat line. He didn't answer, but Callahan figured the cowboy didn't have to. His face told the whole story.

"Those farmers," Page said. "This ain't farm country."

"Not right now," Callahan said, "but it's not cattle country either. Not without rain. And let's get down to what really matters. Your boss could have had as much land as he wanted, had he not been such a skinflint. He claimed land that wasn't his, but land that could have been his. He could have had three hundred and twenty acres, got that, and gotten more. And he could have paid for other homesteads instead of just picking out the best spots. Those farmers have a right to be here. Maybe they'll make it. Maybe they won't, but they deserve a chance. Don't you reckon? Like you and Miss Lorena deserve a chance."

"I ain't paid to reckon."

Callahan patted his Prince Albert pocket. "Well, there was water here once. Might be water will be here again. That's up to the Major General in the Heavens."

"I hope you're right." The cowboy turned his horse, and Callahan started for Job. But he turned when Page called out his name.

"Did you notice anything peculiar about that professor this afternoon?"

Callahan walked away from Job and returned to where the cowboy and horse stood.

"Such as?" He wondered if Page had seen the same thing as Callahan.

The young man hesitated, wet his lips, probably wanted to roll another smoke. Finally, he answered. "His . . . hair."

Callahan exhaled with relief. So he had not imagined that.

"He wears a blond wig," Callahan said.

"That ain't all."

"The mustache isn't real, either."

The cowboy's face brightened. "I knowed you was something more than just a preacher. You're a detective."

"No." Callahan laughed with good humor. "I am far from a detective, but when you are called to preach, you have to notice things. All I noticed was that he wore a wig, and he had a mustache pasted on his face."

"But why would he do that? Don't seem like something a professor would do, not that I've knowed many professors or even schoolmasters. I got my learnin' from Ma and those McGuffey books."

"So why do you think he wears a wig?" Callahan asked.

"I ain't sure. I don't reckon he wants to be like some of them long-haired scouts and all, you know, men like Wild Bill Hickok and Buffalo Bill Cody—you see 'em in those dime novels now and then. They always have long hair. So do the mountain men."

"You read dime novels?"

"Well, sometimes I see 'em in the bunkhouse, and I'll pick 'em up. Especially in the winter when there ain't much work to be done, and we ain't runnin' a full crew at the ranch."

Callahan nodded. "Yes, I suppose that could be why Professor Hungate wears a wig. Perhaps it makes him feel more heroic. That's a good selling point, you know, when you're billing yourself as a rainmaker. I haven't known many professors, but I always pictured them as bespectacled men with poor eyesight, smoking pipes, puny cusses, their shoulders in permanent slumps from carrying tons of books around."

"And with girlie voices."

Callahan laughed. "But I fear we discredit professors. They must be like cowboys. Good and bad."

"Reckon so. Might say the same of preachers."

Callahan laughed again. "Indeed. I believe the jury has yet to reach a verdict on myself. Good. Or bad. Or somewhere in between."

"You ain't like no preacher I ever met."

"I take that as a high compliment."

A long silence followed until Callahan said, "But there could be another reason for the wig."

"What's that?"

"He's a vain man. I got that from listening to him."

"He ain't just vain," Page said. "He thinks a whole lot of hisself."

Callahan had to choke back his laugh. "Yes, yes, he does that, too."

"And the wig?"

"He might wear the wig because he's bald."

Page was shaking his head before Callahan even completed the sentence. "No, no, Preacher, he ain't bald. I seen him. That's how I figured out he wasn't no long-haired blond scouting type of hombre. He's got short dark hair. Darker than yours even."

"The mustache I noticed because of the theatrical paste," Callahan said. "Probably wouldn't have noticed it had it not been for the heat, and the sweat on his face."

"I wouldn't have figured out he wore no wig if Harvey

and me wasn't toying around with this spyglass Harv won in a poker game at the bunkhouse. Peered through them cross windows that's in that fancy wagon, and there he was. Reckon he had a mirror on that side of the wall and all, because he was just putting on that wig. I told Harv, but when I give him his spyglass, the professor had the wig on and all, and Harv said I was just funning him. But I weren't."

Short dark hair, more black than brown. Callahan decided to remember that.

"Well, people do strange things sometimes."

"That's a fact," Page said. "Reckon I ought to get going."

He kicked the horse into a walk, and Callahan strode to Job, but as soon as he grabbed the reins to the white gelding, he turned back and called out Page's name.

The cowboy looked, and Callahan swung into the saddle and rode up to Page.

"I do have a question for you, Terry," he said, using the young man's Christian name. "But it's of a personal nature, maybe even more personal than about you and Miss Lorena."

Page waited.

"Were you with Miss Lorena's brother when he got killed?"

Chapter 23

The memories came rushing back to Terry Page, so vivid, things he had tried to push into the deepest parts of his brain, that he hoped he would never recall. But that was impossible. He never stopped thinking about that. He even recalled when the kid first showed up at the roundup . . .

"Well, lookey here," Tatum said as he squatted, tipping over the massive coffeepot and filling a cup, first for Page, then himself.

Page looked across the camp at the sodbuster, duck pants, linsey-woolsey shirt, straw hat and the biggest pair of work boots—something you might expect to see on the feet of a giant. The kid wasn't small, broad chested, thick-necked, with a right fat head and arms that looked like they could hoist one of those McCormick Reapers over his head without even needing to grunt.

"Probably wants to eat," Ol' Cookie said, and spit tobacco juice against the coffeepot, setting off a sizzle and steam and stink. "Never yet found a farm boy who wasn't hungry."

"He'd eat you out of a week's grub," Tatum said.

"Run him off, Terry," Ol' Cookie said.

And Terry Page probably would have done just that if Ol' Cookie hadn't told him to do it. Instead, just to torment that old belly cheater and to see just how big this boy was and how much chuck he could eat in one sitting, Page straightened, and motioned the kid in by waving his hand that didn't hold the cup of steaming black coffee.

"Come on in, boy! We don't bite!"

"No." Tatum rose with his own cup of coffee. "But we shoot real fine."

"Let's see what the boy wants," Page whispered. "We can shoot him later."

The boy looked west, then back at the cook fire and the crew surrounding it. His fingers flexed and he drew in a deep breath, thinking it over, trying to make himself do something.

"Come on, kid!" Page yelled. He made a general gesture at the food and the chuckwagon. "We got more grub than we can eat. Come on. It'll just go to waste."

Cookie spit again, but this time just into the fire. "We might got more grub that we can eat, but I ain't rightly certain we got more than that Goliath can put into his big belly."

Which caused a snort of a laugh from Tatum.

Bronco Bart said: "You best hope the big boss man don't ride up here and see us feedin' one of 'em tater pushers."

"Browne's down at the county seat," Page reminded them, "getting his road brand registered."

A few other cowboys came over, checking the cartridges in their pistols.

"First man to shoot that boy who ain't me," Page said, "buries him. Deep."

That might stop them. Digging a hole six feet deep was work no self-respecting cowhand would do, especially as hard as the ground was here. And like people said about spring in South Texas: Hades in the summer is about the only thing cooler, whilst only thing hotter is summer in Texas.

If he had time to place a wager, Page would have bet that the kid would turn and hightail it for home. And the boy glanced again in that direction, but finally drew in a deep breath, let it out, and started walking for the cook fire and the cowboy crew.

"I'll be a suck-egg mule," Bronco Bart said.

"I better fry about ten pounds more of bacon," Ol' Cookie said.

The kid stopped in front of the fire. Wet his lips. Breathed in and out. Swallowed. Glanced at the coffee and the pot of beans. Finally looked at Page and said, "Thanks."

"You're welcome," Page said, and held out the coffee cup. "We're short on tinware. But I've drunk enough to keep me going till supper."

The big kid stared at the coffee for a bit, finally took it, and drank without even wiping the lip. "I been walkin' all morn."

Page asked, "You one of those farmers Clarke brought in?"

He nodded, but corrected himself and shook his head. "Well, my pa is. I don't wanna farm."

"I run off myself first chance I got," Ol' Cookie said, bringing over a tin plate filled with beans and his rock-hard, bad-tasting biscuits. He looked at the cowhands staring at him. "Only regret is tellin' folks I could cook and drive a team."

"You lied twice," Tatum said, which got a laugh from the cowhands, and a rash of cusses from Ol' Cookie and even the slightest grin from the farm boy.

"I'll bring ya some bacon, boy," Ol' Cookie said.

"That's one thing he can cook," Bronco Bart said.

"You mean burn," Tatum said.

"Nah," said Pete Oakley. "He burns ever'thing."

When the boy finished eating two helpings of chow, he asked if he could wash the dishes. Which got a "Glory Hallelujah!" from Ol' Cookie. The rest of the crew went back to work, but Page stayed around—they had plenty of men to take care of the branding and culling—and he wanted to see what the kid was doing this far from home. Though he had a pretty good notion.

"You . . . needin' any . . . extra help?" the boy said when he had dried the last dish.

Ol' Cookie walked over to inspect the work, and Page rolled a cigarette.

"You got any experience?"

"Just farmin'."

"Can you ride a horse?"

"I think so. Ride a mule. No saddle, though."

"Well . . ." He was trying to figure out a gentle way to let the boy down, which sort of surprised Terry Page because he had little use for farmers.

"I jus' ain't cut out to be no farmer," he said. And Terry Page remembered saying those same words, only he had said those to his own father, and his own father had told him, "Ain't nothin' keepin' you here, boy."

The boy kept right on talking. "I'm a hard worker. I don't know nothin' else but how to work hard. That's one thing Pa made sure I've done."

"Your pa might need you helping him," Page said.

"He don't even notice me. Gets me up, tells me to dig this well, then he goes about trying to plow this infernal ground. He's got a mule helpin' him plow. I dig and this is all I get . . ." He held out the heavily calloused hands, blisters forming from the lower palm to the fingertips.

"You oughta wear gloves," Page told him.

"Pa says only girls wear gloves. But he don't even let my sister wear 'em."

Page was still trying to figure out a way to get the kid out of camp, when hooves sounded. Turning, he feared he would find Milton Browne. It was worse. It was his son, Tommy, who slid his horse into a stop and leaped out of the saddle.

"Tatum said that Goliath of a plow pusher was here. I thought he was joshing. But, well, it got me out of castrating calves. Worth the dollar we bet." He ran up to the kid and held out his hand, even swept off his hat.

"Ain't you the farmer . . . with the funny Irish name?"

"Lamerick," the boy said. "I'm Ryan Lamerick."

"And you got a sister, ain't you?" Browne said. "Goes around barefoot."

"Lorena." Ryan Lamerick nodded. "Pa says he'll get her shoes when the first crop comes in." The farm kid kicked the sand, and held his head down. "I thought . . . if I made enough money . . . I might get her some shoes. Ain't right goin' 'round on this hot ground with nothin' on your feet."

Page pictured that pretty farm girl who walked about False Hope with no shoes. She had to be the prettiest girl he had ever seen in these parts, and, once he put his mind to it, anywhere else he'd ever been.

"Cowboying ain't much of a life, kid," Page told him.

"Yeah," Tommy Browne agreed. "But if you introduce me to your sister, you can take my place on the drive to Wichita."

"Really?"

"Hold on!" Page sang out. "Tommy, get back to work. And pay the money you owe Tatum."

"Now wait a minute—"

Page gave him the look, and the boss's son swallowed, cursed, and headed back to his horse. When he had departed, Page said, "Your mama might not—"

"Ma's dead," he said, hanging his head. "Died last year, wasn't here but six months." He looked at his hands. "Dug that grave, too. All I'm good for is diggin' graves."

"So," Page said, "Lorena's your sister?"

He nodded. "You know her?"

"Oh, I said, 'Howdy' to her in False Hope. Y'all must have been shopping."

"She don't go to town," the boy said. "Pa don't let nobody go to town. Wouldn't even let Ma come when she was ailin', but, well, it ain't like there's no doctor in town."

Page wasn't interested in doctors or the kid's mother. He said, "Dark hair, blue eyes, she was wearing a calico dress."

"Blue and white checks?"

"Yes."

"Well, that looks like Lorena. But Pa ain't never let us go to town."

Page remembered stopping, sweeping off his hat and saying, "Ma'am, if you need an escort, my name's Terry Page and I'd be honored."

Gosh, she blushed so cherry-colored, but how those eyes sparkled.

"I don't reckon I should."

"But this is a rough town, Miss . . . ?"

"Lorena," he told the boy, but hearing how she had said her name.

"That's right. Lorena Lamerick. And I'm Ryan Lamerick. And I sure would like a job, Mister . . ."

"Page," he said. "But you can call me Terry." He held out his hand, then called out to Ol' Cookie: "You got yourself a louse."

"I ain't gonna turn down no help," the cook sang out from the chuckwagon. "But you gotta explain this hire of yourn to Vermin."

"What's a louse?" the circuit rider asked after Page finished telling him that much.

"Cook's helper. Don't pay much. He chops wood when there's wood to be had or gathers buffalo chips. Does whatever the cook tells him to do. Not a job men take, but boys . . ." He laughed. "I hated it when I was a cook's louse."

The preacher smiled. It was a pleasant smile, inviting, warm.

"So," Callahan said, his voice as friendly as his eyes. "Y'all hire Ryan. He's on the drive. Did the cattle stampede through camp? Is that how the boy got killed?"

"No." Page breathed in deeply, shaking his head after he exhaled.

"We push cattle hard the first days on the trail. Wear them out. And this was a mixed herd. Cows and steers. They can be harder to manage, which is why we only ran fifteen hundred, instead of two thousand. There just come up a storm. Wind was blowing, but no rain. Didn't hear no thunder, didn't see a flash of lighting. Right before dawn . . . the cattle . . . they just ran."

He was coming in, having spent the past four hours circling the herd, singing, cooing, doing anything to keep the longhorns' minds off the storm, which now appeared to be blowing off to the southeast. There was no point in going to sleep, since Ol' Cookie would be rousing the boys in less than an hour.

They had made it through the night, Page thought, and swung down from the saddle. Ryan Lamerick was coming over—Ol' Cookie probably never let the boy sleep—smiling, and holding a steaming cup of coffee.

As soon as Page's right foot hit the ground, the earth rumbled.

He was swinging back into the saddle before the unholy roar of a night herder rang out.

"STAMPEDE!"

Page galloped out of the camp, seeing men jumping out of their bedrolls. Most of them grabbed hats and boots, trying to put them on, before giving up and running for the picket line in their stockings. Veteran cowboys, men like Tatum, Bronco Bart and even young Tommy, knew on nights like these to sleep with their boots on.

He didn't see Ryan Lamerick. Figured Ol' Cookie would have him help hitch the team, get the chuckwagon to safe ground–in case that frightened mass of hooves, horns, and muscle came into the camp. The one thing you couldn't afford to lose on a cattle drive was the chuckwagon.

But he did hear Vermin Browne, trail boss on this drive, roar: "Everyone! In a saddle! Now!"

He saw the herd running, away from camp. Good for Ol' Cookie and everyone, but not so good for the work that would be needed. They were running south, back to home, with the wind at their backs. He knew he had to head them off, try to turn them. He also knew the dun he rode was tired. But this is what he had.

The gelding had a heart. And a mighty good gait. And horses, Page always thought, saw better than longhorns, certainly better than men.

He let the dun pick its path, and when he was ahead of the herd, he turned in, drawing his gun, ready to fire, into a few beeves if he needed to. Get them turned toward the tree-lined hills. There they'd have to slow to a crawl, calm down. Runs like these usually didn't last long.

That's what he was thinking. And then he was thinking: *I'm a dead man.*

The dun stumbled in a gopher hole. Even with the roar of hooves echoing in his head, Page swore he heard that awful sound of a leg breaking. He thought it was the dun's. Till he tried to stand.

He'd have to crawl.

Like he would have a chance.

And then, he felt incredibly strong hands grabbing him, dragging him while he screamed in agony.

"I'm sorry, Terry." The voice he could just make out. It sounded like the kid, the cook's louse, Lorena Lamerick's brother, but that couldn't be.

The next thing he saw was the outline of a . . . mule. Without a saddle. One of the john mules that pulled Ol' Cookie's chuckwagon. Still yelling and feeling the ground moving, Page tried to turn, but he was pushed up over the mule's back, dangling, sweating, and if he had thought about it, he might have started praying.

He managed to regain something that came close to sanity, and yelled, "Ryan!"

But the kid must have smacked the mule's rump, because then Page was screaming, bouncing up and down, knowing he'd get tossed up and land right back on the ground in front of six thousand hooves.

He landed on his back. And let the blackness slip over him.

Chapter 24

"When I woke," Page said. He was off the horse now, holding the reins, squatting near the sign that he had shot at a few times.

WELCOME TO FALSTAFF
FALSE HOPE

"When I woke," he tried again, "I was in camp. Ol' Cookie looked at me, and that's when I knew. But I had to ask."

Taylor Callahan nodded. He could tell that the cowhand's leg hurt. The pain likely became more pronounced when Terry Page thought about that early morning on a cattle drive two years ago. Even though Ol' Cookie had set it good. Callahan knew that for a fact because he had never seen Page favor the leg.

They had loaded him into the wagon and took him straight to the first town they came to, Page said, picking up the story. A town that happened to have a mighty fine doctor.

Callahan listened as he moved to the cowboy's saddlebags and began digging. He didn't find what he was looking for until he moved around the horse and opened the other bag. Page had stopped talking, and Callahan grinned when he saw the cowboy's suspicious eyes.

"I figured you might have something like this," Callahan said excitedly, and turned around holding the flask that Page, he figured, rarely used. Callahan untwisted the cap, sniffed and said, "Smells like aged bourbon."

Page smiled without much emotion. "Aged so long I can't remember the last time I had a drink."

The flask was put in the cowboy's hand. "Now seems like a good time."

Page drank, and must have figured that Callahan spoke truly, for the cowboy took another sip, and held the pewter container up toward Callahan, who smiled and shook his head.

Two sips was enough. That impressed Callahan, as well, because many men would have emptied the flask to try to forget those nightmares. Instead, Page screwed the lid back on and tossed the flask to the circuit rider, who returned it and fastened the saddlebag.

They sat in silence for a minute. The sun had disappeared, but full dark was a ways off.

"I don't talk about this much," Page said, and punctuated that with a snort. "Don't reckon I never really talked about it."

"Not even to Miss Lorena?" Callahan asked.

The cowhand eyed him with suspicion.

"Sometimes it's a comfort."

"Not for me."

"I don't mean for you." Callahan patted the man's thigh. "But it might be a comfort for her."

"I don't know," Page whispered.

"So the boy didn't make it out," Callahan prompted.

Likely, now Terry Page regretted not having the bourbon. His head shook. "I guess he ran to get my horse." Another long sigh. "But that dun had played out, and was too frightened, I guess. I mean. I don't know. I didn't see anything except, and maybe I was imaging that, that john mule's back as I bounced up and down. Then I didn't see nothing."

"Miss Lorena's pa said Vernon Browne wrote a letter. But didn't post it till San Antonio. Guess nobody thought to send someone back to the farm."

Page turned to spit. "I thought about it. And I would have. But I didn't get out of bed for three weeks. And didn't get out of that worthless little town called Catclaw for two months."

"I don't reckon Catclaw was completely worthless."

Page's eyes met Callahan's. "They had a good sawbones."

"I wish . . ." He didn't finish, but Callahan knew what the young cowhand was thinking. He wished it wasn't Ryan Lamerick wrapped in a bedroll and buried on the side of a cattle trail, but Terry Page.

"Did you ever learn how the kid came to fetch you out of harm's way?" Callahan asked. "I mean, he was supposed to be with the cook, wasn't he?"

"Yeah. But Ol' Cookie said when Vermin . . . Vernon . . . Browne yelled for everyone to grab a horse, Ryan just swung onto the back of one of the mules that was supposed to be harnessed to the chuckwagon. And that was the last they saw of him."

Page let out a short laugh, and shook his head. "Boy could stick on a mule's back like he was born on the back of one. Bareback. I bet he would have made a crackerjack cowboy. He would've been something to see on a horse, especially a real mean bronc. Bet he could ride the rough off the meanest horse in all of Texas."

"When did you start seeing Miss Lorena?"

Page sighed. "As soon as I could sit in a saddle." His head shook. "First three times, he pa run me off. Third time he fired a shotgun over my head."

"He's a bit on the ill-tempered side."

"Just a bit." Page shook his head. "I learned to go there whenever he was gone. It taken a while. She didn't trust me. I was just one of them cowboys, low down and shift-less, with no honorable intentions. But eventually she started to trust me. I don't know if she'd care nothing for me if I was to tell her that her brother died and could've, would've been alive, if not for me. So we just don't talk about that. Course, every time I ride over there, I see that grave—grave wired in with the devil's rope—and I think and ache all for that good ol' boy."

He sighed, reached up and wiped both eyes.

"Lorena . . . she might shoot over my head if she was to know I was responsible for Ryan's death. She might not even be as generous as her pa. Instead of aiming over my head, she might try to blow it off." He turned again and started massaging his leg. "Couldn't blame her for that, neither."

"I don't reckon Miss Lorena would want to do that, Terry."

He looked again at Callahan, and the circuit rider waited for the question people always asked him.

"Why did he do it, Preacher? Why?"

"You were his friend."

"I don't know about that. I mean, well, I guess I was starting to like him, but the only reason I give him the job as a cook's louse—and that ain't no job to have—"

Callahan interrupted him. "You had a job just like it."

"Yeah, and I knowed it wasn't a decent job."

"But like you said, it's a way for youngsters to get into the cowboying business."

The young man's head shook, and then he went back to his original thought. "I wouldn't have give him that job if I didn't want the chance to meet his sister."

"You had no way of knowing what would happen, Terry. Tell me: Were you ever involved in a stampede when you worked as a cook's louse?"

"Nah. But I only had that job for two trail drives. Then they let me ride drag." The head shook again. "Never ate so much dirt in all my life. Started thinking that working for a miserable old bellycheater wasn't that bad after all."

"How many stampedes have you been in?"

"Three. Four. But one of them wasn't much. Three were scary. The worst, though, well . . ."

"Only stampede where you ever lost a hand."

"How'd you know?"

Callahan smiled. "Just guessing. Sometimes I guess right."

"It should have been me."

"But it wasn't." He shook his head, and let out his own sigh. "Want to know a secret about this circuit-riding minister?" There was no need to wait for an answer, because dusk was fading into full night, and snakes came out at night, and Callahan wanted to be back behind Father Pete's church before he stepped on something slithery that rattled and bit and sometimes killed. "During what the genteel ladies keep calling the 'recent unpleasantness,' I rode in one of the valiant armies on one of the sides. Don't matter which one."

"I hope it was for Texas."

"Spoken like a Texan. But like I say, the side don't matter. The reason don't matter, either. I can't tell you how many scrapes we had, or how many brothers in arms I saw fall. Or how many of what we figured were our enemies fall. It was years and miles of gore and blood and the wickedest savagery known to man. Yet here I am, alive and well and hardly have nightmares about those dark times no more. And all of those comrades that I saw fall, more than a few who died in front of me, or right beside me, or those who died in my arms back in camp. But I give up on thinking and trying to find a reason about why they died and how come I didn't. Because when it comes to war, there ain't no reason for anything." He shrugged. "It happens. Men die. Boys die. The whys and the what fors don't matter at all. What matters is living."

He waited a moment, breathed in and out, listened for any rattles, and said, "We live. And maybe because we know we could have, perhaps should have, been killed. Maybe we ought to live right. And try to make things right."

"I don't know," Page said. "I just don't know why he died and I didn't."

"You didn't die because young Ryan Lamerick saw fit to save your life. I don't reckon the boy figured he was going to die. He just figured you needed saving. I sure don't think he wanted to die. Nobody really wants to die. I sure don't."

"I do," Page said.

"No, you don't. And you know you don't. You want to live for Miss Lorena's sake. And your own sake."

He stood, turned to make sure Job hadn't walked back to Father Pete's on his own.

"Look, I can tell you stuff you've likely heard and read before. I can tell you that"—he pointed up at the dark sky, still without stars or the moon—"there's a plan for you, and that's why Ryan got killed and why a mule somehow managed to get you out of harm's way bouncing up and down on a frightened beast of burden's back.

"I can tell you that young Ryan Lamerick died that early morning because it was his time, and it wasn't your time, and that the Major General in the Heavens knowed what he was doing and that's why he did it and you just can't question what He is thinking. His *Will* be done. That kind of thing."

Job came up behind him and snorted. Likely he was hungry. Callahan didn't figure the gelding wanted to get closer and hang on to every word he was preaching to that dazed and lovestruck cowboy.

"But the thing is, Terry, we don't know nothing. We don't know what the plan is, if there even is a plan. We don't know if the Major General in the Heavens even knows what he's doing. All we know is that we are here. Maybe for a reason. Maybe for nothing. But we gotta have faith. That's what keeps us going. That's what makes us who we is."

He reached down, extended his hand, and waited for the cowboy to take his offering. When Page did, Callahan pulled him to his feet, then came up to him, and patted his back.

"No one ever saved my life in the war, Terry. Not the way the kid saved yours. I likely saved my hide myself a time or two. No, there ain't no likely to that. I saved my hide more times than I deserved. And maybe I saved my hide just so I could come down here and try to help some folks, some of them cowboys, some of them farmers, some priests, some . . . calling themselves professors. Or maybe I just come down here because I'm lazy and wanted to see the ocean or gulf or bay or big mud puddle and got turned around by a slithery serpent that might have been the very one that tempted Eve in the garden."

He kicked a stone.

"Like anyone ever thought of this chunk of land as a garden. But I'm here. And I'm gonna do my job. And you're here. And you're gonna figure things out and do what you think's right. And that's right by me."

He could barely see the cowhand's face now, but he saw the teeth as the mouth opened, and he heard the words.

"Preacher, I don't know what the Sam Hill you're talking about."

"Good." Callahan laughed and slapped Page's shoulder. "I've done my job. I've confused my congregation so they leave more confused than when they come in. Have faith, Brother Terry. For a man has to be confused before he can solve the problem. I'll see you around."

He grabbed the reins to the gelding and swung into the saddle. Then he waited until Page was on his horse. They left the arroyo, the signs, and eased their way back into Falstaff, where business continued to boom inside the saloon.

"Is Hungate staying at the ranch?" Callahan asked Page.

Saddle leather squeaked as the cowboy turned. "Yeah. There ain't no hotel. Nobody wants to stay here. Most people get out as quick as they can."

"How about the professor's two-gunned . . . guards . . . I reckon that's what they are?"

"They're at the ranch, too."

Callahan pointed at the camp of the balloonists. "Does it strike you, as it does me, that, if your livelihood depended on a balloon to take dynamite into the sky and blow it up and bring rain, that maybe you'd leave armed guards around to protect your balloon?"

The foreman shrugged. "One of them boys wears a Yankee shell jacket. I reckon he can handle himself."

"Maybe."

He held out his hand, which Page somehow saw and accepted.

"Terry," Callahan whispered as they shook. "What we got to talking about earlier, meaning how Professor Hungate wears a wig and an actor's mustache. I think that's something that we ought to let other folks figure out for themselves."

"You mean keep my big mouth shut."

Callahan laughed good-naturedly. "Both of us ought to keep our big mouths shut. But I can't make you."

"You don't trust him?"

"Why, son, as a circuit rider, I ought to take a man's word till he proves me wrong."

"A man who wears a wig and a fake mustache makes me tend to think he's wrong."

"Likewise." Callahan released the cowboy's hand and nodded at the church. "But I'd like to figure out how wrong he is, and if folks learn that he's got real dark hair, close-cropped, and is clean shaven, he might run off before we can . . . say . . . scalp him?"

Chapter 25

He wondered what Father Pete might have cooked up for supper, but then he saw the light shining from inside the old adobe church and figured the priest might be busy with confessions and the like, because since a large percentage of the county and the villages had come to Falstaff this day for the show. And, truth be told, Taylor Callahan wasn't that hungry anyway.

So he led Job into the stall, striking a match on a rough board and lighting a candle, then looking for snakes or black widows—did they have those nasty spiders in this part of Texas?—and used the candle to fire up a lantern and another candle.

That gave him enough light to unsaddle the white gelding and rub him down, then feed him some grain and hay.

"You never ate this good, boy," he said, and rubbed the horse's neck. Glancing down, he noticed a footprint in the sandy path between the straw and hay. Taking a candle in his hand, he squatted and traced the footprint with his fingers.

"Seems we had a visitor," he told Job, who expressed no concern or curiosity and went right on eating.

He looked up, but knew the visitor had not spent much time here, and certainly wasn't hiding in the hay intent on doing him any harm. He wondered if he would be called upon again.

Then a more pressing thought occupied his mind.

What he needed was a map. The land agent likely had one in the office, but the office would be closed, meaning he would have to go see the gent in the morning. Problem being, he wasn't sure how many secrets land agents would keep. No, his best bet would be to ask Father Pete for some directions, and hope the fine, young padre had wandered about this desert enough to know how a stranger might get to the county seat.

Footsteps sounded outside, and Callahan smiled, leaving the horse to finish his supper, and stepping from underneath the structure's rickety roof.

"Good evening, Father," Callahan greeted the priest.

"How did you know it was me?" the priest said.

Callahan pointed. "Your sandals. No spurs jingling. No boot heels grinding. And you're a soft walker. Man learns to recognize how a person comes up on somebody. Talent like that can come in handy. Don't want to be surprised, you see."

The priest didn't see at all, but then this young man had lived a different kind of life than Taylor Callahan had.

"That is a unique trick. Perhaps you can teach me how this is done."

Callahan let out a soft chuckle. "Just open your ears, Father. You'll pick things up real fast. Just make sure to keep wax out of your ears. Don't want your hearing to get all clogged up and all, you see."

The padre didn't see, and Callahan didn't let him in on the joke, for the priest quickly changed the subject.

"You have a visitor," the priest said, and held his candle toward the old whitewashed church.

"For me?" Callahan said.

"Sí. I did not . . . well . . . she is not Catholic, but I thought, well, it is late and . . . it would be better for her to wait for you in the church than . . ." He looked at the stable.

Callahan smiled. "I agree with you. Thank you, Father. I will see what I can do for Miss Lamerick."

The priest took a step back. "How did you know it was the daughter of Señor Lamerick who asked to see you?"

Callahan let his smile widen and he pointed at the dirt. "Reading sign is something else that comes in handy. And it's a mite easier to figure out than listening to how folks walk."

"But she . . ."

". . . Is the only gal I know in these parts who goes about barefoot." Callahan slapped the young priest's shoulder as he walked past him and headed to the church. He stopped when Father Pete called out his name.

"I must go visit my cousin in Arroyo Verde," the priest said. "Her son is . . . sick . . . for two days or so now."

"Nothing serious, I hope," Callahan said.

"I hope so, too," Father Pete said.

"Kids are tough," Callahan told him. "Don't fret too much, but let me know if there's anything I can do."

"*Gracias*. And if there's anything I can do for the *señorita*."

* * *

The heavy door creaked as Callahan pushed it open and slipped through, hat in hand, and let his eyes adjust to the lights from the candles and the candelabras. He first looked at the confessionals, but quickly figured out that Lorena Lamerick would not be there. He saw her bowed head on one of the front rows, and made his boots sound louder than necessary so she would hear him coming up to her. Her head turned briefly, then bowed again, and Callahan continued. He slid in the pew behind her, sat his hat down beside him, and leaned forward, his forearms folding on the back of the pews to the farm girl's left.

He heard her whispers as she finished her prayers, and then she leaned back, inhaled deeply, and let out a weary sigh.

"Miss Lorena," Callahan said softly. "Father Pedro Sebastià Fernández de Calderón y Borbón says you wanted to have a word with me."

"I reckon that's right."

He waited, then pushed himself back. "This is a right pretty church."

She turned, wet her lips, and glanced around the chapel.

"Don't look like much from the outside," he said. "Well, I mean, it's a lot more handsome than the log buildings we had for houses of worship up Missouri way, and I've preached in all sorts of places not as becoming. I guess adobe is something you have to get used to."

"It is pretty in here," she said. "I mean, the whitewash on the outside makes you notice it."

"Probably could stand a new whitewashing."

"Probably."

"Pretty belltower."

"Ain't no bell, though."

"I noticed that. Wonder what happened to it."

She shrugged.

"Could be, during the recent unpleasantness, they had to melt it down for cannonballs."

"That don't sound right."

"Not much about war ever sounds right, especially when all the shooting's done and all the treaties have been signed. Course, it could be that they just never got around to putting a bell in the tower."

"It's a right poor church."

"Right poor country."

"Yes, sir."

He moved back to rest his arms on the back of the pew. "But not poor in spirit."

Her lips flattened.

He let the silence pass for a minute or two, then asked, "You didn't want to talk to Father Pete?"

"I ain't Catholic. Don't reckon he'd want to hear me."

"Maybe. But Father Pete don't strike me quite that way. Fact is, he told me if there's anything he can do for you. He's a good man."

"Well. I didn't want to trouble him."

He smiled again. "And I'm used to troubles."

"No." Her face blanched. "I didn't mean that."

"I know. What's troubling you?"

She inhaled, exhaled, looked at the crucifixes and retablos on the walls, frowned, and perhaps began trying to pick the quickest route of escape. Callahan remained a statue, smiling, trying to look like a peacekeeper.

"You ain't never told me what faith you is?"

"It's not Catholic," he said.

"Figgered that. But . . . ?"

"Does it matter?"

She chewed on that thought for a right long spell. "I reckon not. We're Lutherans. I think."

He waited, wondered if Job had finished eating and drinking his supper. Wondered if any venomous serpents had slithered their way into the stall where he had been bunking. He shifted his shoulders, recrossed his legs, and tried to guess if Lorena Lamerick would ever get around to telling Callahan what was on her mind.

"Did you really want to hold a revival in our barn?" she blurted out.

That took a firm grip on his curiosity. He had to do some quick recollections to make sure that was indeed what she had asked, but his mind did not appear to be playing tricks on him and he hadn't been sipping any intoxicating spirits that he could recall, so she had asked about her pappy's barn.

"Well," he said, recrossing his legs. "It's a mighty impressive structure."

Her head bobbed, and then she bit her lower lip.

"I expect it would be right cool inside, too."

"Iffen you leave the door cracked, it draws in a nice, cooling breeze."

"I expect so." He waited, saw she didn't know where she wanted to lead the conversation, so he put a conclusion to this part of the talk. "But your pa seemed to be right firm in his opinion that he did not want me preaching or singing or even nosing around in his barn. And y'all have your own preacher, I do believe."

"I don't think he's Lutheran. But he might be. It's just . . .

confusing." She stopped staring at her dirty, bare feet and looked Callahan in the eye. "Pa's with him now."

"In your barn?"

Her head shook. "No . . . no, they . . ." But she did not say any more.

"Miss Lorena?" he said after two minutes of hearing nothing more than flickering candles.

"Yes, sir?"

He let his head tilt to the left just a little and tried his most charming smile. "We can go about this till the new century sweeps right past us, maybe the millennia, or you might tell me what's troubling you. I don't think it has much to do with my preaching in your pappy's barn. Or whether your preacher is Lutheran or Baptist, pagan or Presbyterian."

"Pa don't want you in that barn."

"That's what I gathered."

"It is a good barn."

"Finest I've seen since I've been in Texas," he said, and he wasn't kidding.

"Pa's a better stonemason than he is a farmer."

"Well." Now Callahan began to figure out why Catholics knelt so much during services. This pew had to be the most bone-crunching, muscle-aching bench he had set on since those forty-eight hours he spent in that squirrel cage monstrosity of a jail in Liberty, Missouri, back during his high-spirited days. He tried to find something a mite easier on his rump and lower and upper spine and neck and shoulders. He even considered kneeling.

"You understand, child," he said, "that what you say to me stays with me. Don't you?"

"Pa ain't much of a farmer," she said.

He breathed in and out. "Well, from what I've gathered, he really hasn't had much of a chance to prove how good of a farmer he might be. Making a stone barn is one thing. All you have to do is spend a whole lot of backbreaking hours and have some rocks and mortar. Farming requires some cooperation from the Almighty and the weather and about fifteen thousand other things."

"It was Ma's doing," she said.

"How's that?" Callahan asked.

"Ma made him quit building. She's how come we come out here."

He waited, and she sailed into the story.

Her father had been working as a stonemason in San Isabel, Lamerick Brothers Construction. Folks said the two brothers built half of the town, and then one day while they were putting up a new church for the Presbyterians, a drunken soldier at the nearby fort tried to light his pipe while he was next to the arsenal. A keg of powder was touched off, and the poor drunk was blown to pieces. But the explosion shook the whole town, and down came a right big chunk of granite.

"Uncle Sean pushed Pa out of the way. The rock hit him, instead of Pa." The girl dabbed her eye with the hem of her dress.

"Ma got so scared, she begged Pa to quit. Said next time there wouldn't be no Sean to save Pa's life. So Pa . . . well . . . here we are."

"With a barn, though," Callahan said.

She dabbed away another tear.

"Yes, sir. But that went up after . . . after . . . Well, you know."

Callahan could add up enough to get relatively close,

which was better than most of the kids had done at the subscription school.

"I still don't think your pa would want me to be leading any services in his barn," he said.

"You'd be right, Preacher."

"That barn's built like an arsenal." He just tested the sentence, and looked at the girl's hard eyes as she met his.

"Don't you think you ought to be getting back home?" Callahan said. "Your father is going to be worried."

"He ain't home. He's meeting with the preacher and some of the other farmers."

"All night?"

"When they meet, he don't come home till nigh day-break. And they'll be meeting good and long now that the rainmaker's here." She rose to her feet, but her eyes remained locked on Callahan.

"I don't reckon I got much else to say, Preacher."

He stood, bowing slightly. "Should I walk you back home?"

"Too far for you to walk, Preacher," she said.

"I'd say it's too far for you to walk, too. Snakes," he suggested. "And you could use some shoes, I might add."

"Balderdash. Snakes keep away from me, and my feet is tougher than them ol' boots of yourn. I'll be fine."

He debated, but knew she would not hear of him escorting her back to the farm, and he figured she was right. She could sneak in, but Callahan would have ridden Job, and horses weren't always quiet. Sound traveled a good ways in this country, especially at night.

"Any idea when that next confab will be with your father, the preacher, and your neighbors?"

She nodded. "They've been meeting every other night.

Not much chance they'll change that till it's time to . . . clean out the barn."

"When do you reckon they'll want to do that?"

She reached into her blouse pocket and withdrew a receipt, and held it out for him to read.

FLETCHER'S HARDWARE

Sold to L Lmrck, Falstaff, Texas

2nd Order

Army Surplus

Spencer Repeating Rifle Co.

.56-56 Spencer Rimfire Caliber

2,000 rounds .55-56 cartridges

PAID IN FULL

Estimated Delivery from St. Louis . . .

He sighed when he read the date, and handed the yellow sheet of paper back to her.

She shook her head, but Callahan did not bring the receipt back.

"I thought you might be able to do something with it," she said.

Callahan sighed and shook his head. "I don't reckon I could pass for your daddy, child, and it's not like this Franklin gent will mistake me for him, either. Besides, if your pa doesn't find the receipt where he left it, he might be upset at you." He let out a breath. "I wouldn't like that. You're a good young woman."

"And Pa ain't a bad man, Preacher. He's just had some bad times. But he's blaming the wrong person for my brother's death and this drought. And I don't want no harm to come to . . . well . . . any . . . ummm . . ."

He nodded with complete understanding. "This is your father's second order," he said, not asking a question, and knowing from the deep wagon tracks that he had seen when he visited the farm that the first order had already been delivered.

"It's God who he ought to blame, Preacher," she said. "Don't you reckon?"

Taylor Callahan had no answer for that. "The first order of your father's?"

"It ain't just Pa, Preacher. He's got plenty of . . . what's the word?"

"Co-conspirators?"

"Well, that ain't what I was thinking."

"What was the first order?"

But she was already walking away. He watched her go, until he realized she had one important bit of information he needed, and she might answer this question. He could find out the answer to his second question, and he figured he had better do that quickly. But he needed one bit of information from her.

"Miss Lamerick," he said and breathed easier when she stopped at the door. She didn't turn around, but she did not pull the heavy door open.

"Where is this hardware store?" he asked. "It's not in Falstaff, and I don't think I'd find it in Arroyo Verde."

"County seat," she said.

He grinned and slipped the receipt into his pocket. "And, ummm, would you by chance happen to know how I might get there? How long it would take me to ride there and back? Keeping in mind that Job isn't known for winning many races."

Chapter 26

For a county seat, Jubilee, Texas, didn't have any air of superiority. Taylor Callahan could see that the town wasn't that much larger than Falstaff, though it did have appearances of civilization such as the telegraph wires that stretched off to the south and then to the west.

There had to be at least five, maybe six, streets in this town running north-south, and from the looks of the chimneys, maybe two or three running east-west. That was a fair size compared to the one street that ran through Falstaff. But one expected such bigness in a county seat, especially in a county seat in the great state of Texas. Chimneys puffed smoke, and the wind brought forth scents of bacon and ham, all reminding Taylor Callahan that he had left Falstaff before daybreak, before breakfast, and now people were preparing their noon meals, and his stomach was growling and old Job was grunting and probably longing for even a drink from the dust-covered cistern in Falstaff.

With luck, the county seat would have a bevy of wells, and maybe a kindly café proprietor might offer a free meal to a man who spread the Word and faith and tried to convey goodness wherever he happened to travel.

Although Taylor Callahan had come to Jubilee, Texas, with something other than just goodness in his heart. Part of it was curiosity. Most of it would be something known as . . . well . . . conspiracy.

But the Major General in the Heavens was generally a forgiving sort, especially when one's heart had the best of intentions.

The sign at the edge of town read:

> Welcom to Jubilee
> Justice County Seet
> Populayshun . . . Two Early to Count
> But We Sure Keep Growning

And below that:

> See Marvin Newman,
> Real Estate
> 101 Wst. Main Street
> We Am to Pleeze

"And not spell," Callahan whispered to Job, who did not respond, just kept plodding on into the county seat of Justice County, Texas.

The buildings were a mix of adobe and wooden structures with the false fronts, and there was a towering steeple with shingles and a fine white cross atop, meaning the Major General in the Heavens had a presence in the county seat, and the county seat had at least a real good carpenter who could put up a church that dominated the city. If you could call Jubilee a city. Callahan figured he would introduce himself to the parson of that fine church, and maybe get a right nice confab going so he could find out this and that and maybe figure out what he planned to do at Fletcher's Mercantile and with the county sheriff. He saw the fence off on the northwestern edge of town that had to be the local cemetery, and it pleased Callahan that only a dozen or so crosses and monuments had been set. But then he saw the other cemetery, the pauper's field, the boot hill, and Callahan understood why Jubilee's population was never settled upon. People kept getting killed here.

It wasn't until Callahan rounded the livery stable and turned onto the main street that he realized the town was bigger than it looked.

Job snorted as Callahan reined up, and stood in his stirrups.

The street was blocked by dozens of people, all pointing and talking urgently at one another. Even the blacksmith at the livery had stepped away from his forge and was studying the commotion.

Callahan sat down, mopped the sweat off his brow with his sleeve, and slid out of the saddle. He led Job to the water trough next to where the smithy stood with his hammer in his hand and about fifteen acres of tobacco crammed into his cheek.

"Howdy," Callahan said to the bearded, burly smithy.

The big man grunted.

"Mind if I water my horse?"

"Cost you a nickel."

Callahan found a coin in his pants pocket and set it in the big man's free hand. After dropping the reins, he watched Job mosey over to the water and start sucking some up.

"Come far?" the smith asked.

"Falstaff," Callahan answered.

"Huh?"

Callahan tried again. "False Hope." He pointed with his head in the general direction.

"Oh."

Callahan hooked his thumb toward the crowded street.

"What's all the excitement?" he asked.

The man spit into the dust. "I ain't rightly certain. Heard some screamin'. Then some cussin'. At least one gunshot. Then more shouts, and by the time I got out here, half of Jubilee had come to see the show."

Callahan turned to study the crowd.

"Where's . . . ?" He had to fish the receipt out of the pocket of his Prince Albert as he could not recollect the name of the hardware store. "Fletcher's?"

Callahan hoped the store might be easier to access from another street.

The man worked his giant chaw of tobacco, spit again, and wiped his mouth with his sleeve. "Appears to be where everyone's lookin' at," the smithy said.

"I see." So much for finding a road that wasn't blocked.

"I'll be back for my horse," he said, and pitched the smithy another nickel.

"Want me to board him?"

"Nah." Callahan walked to the crowd.

"What if he wanders away?"

"That horse?" Callahan laughed and found a saloon dancer leaning against a post holding up an awning to a dance hall. He looked at the sun, wondered what a dance-hall girl was doing up this early in the afternoon.

"What's all the ruckus about?" he asked her.

"Injun Periwinkle has been drinkin'," the redhead said.

Callahan tried to look over hats and bonnets but couldn't see much but the roofs of buildings.

"I reckon they're gonna blow his brains out."

Callahan looked at the woman, who pulled a prerolled cigarette out of a garter on her calf and stuck it in her mouth.

"That's a bit extreme," he said. "Ain't it?"

"You don't know what Injun Periwinkle's capable of when he's had a snoot full."

"Marshal!" a woman's voice said from beyond the wall of Jubilee's residents. "You cannot do this!"

"Missus Mason, I ain't got no choice."

Someone a few feet in front of Callahan and the redhead yelled, "Blow his brains out, Taft!"

"Marshal!" the woman said.

The crowd took up a chant.

"Kill the injun! Kill Injun Periwinkle! Kill Injun Periwinkle! Kill the injun!" Loud enough to be heard halfway to Falstaff.

Callahan tried to squeeze between a drummer and a butcher, but the butcher snarled and said, "Stranger, I ain't giving up this spot. You shoulda got here sooner."

The drummer turned and said, "This is gonna be something to see."

"Marshal!" the woman's voice cried out in pure terror. "My daughter!"

"That's who we're tryin' to save, Missus Mason."

"But—"

The crowd drowned out her words with cheers.

"That'll be Thompson Taft," the redhead said and coughed out smoke from her cigarette.

"Best shot in the county," the drummer said.

"Which ain't sayin' a whole lot," the butcher opined.

"Marshal!" the woman cried out. "Please."

Callahan turned on his heels and moved quickly back to the livery, where the big smithy was staring at Job. When Callahan reached the saddlebags, the big man asked, "When's the last time you watered this nag of yourn?"

Callahan withdrew the Bible. For a second, he studied the Colt .45, but left it. He looked over the saddlebag at the smithy and found another coin. It was a whole quarter, but Callahan didn't want to count out five pennies, so he pitched it over Job's back.

"Drinking's the one thing he's good at," Callahan explained.

"Same can be said about Injun Periwinkle," the smithy said before biting the quarter to make sure it did not bend.

When Callahan was back at the wall of people, he cleared his throat, and lowered his shoulder, "Make way for the preacher!" he shouted, and heads turned.

"Coming through," he said, holding out the Bible. "Coming through."

"How do we know he's a preacher?" someone said, and the wall of men and women began to teeter.

"Only a preacher or a fool would be dressed in black broadcloth on a scorcher like today," the redhead said, and pitched her cigarette onto the boardwalk.

He slid this way and that, apologizing when he brushed up against a woman, shoving one recalcitrant cowboy into a potbellied barber, and finally inched between some kids with marbles and one with a horned toad.

"Marshal," said a woman in a straw hat. "It's a man of God."

The marshal was a small, balding fat man who was talking to a lean dude in tan britches who held a Sharps rifle in his left hand.

"Preacher!" a young woman said. "Don't let them do this, for the love of God."

"Missus Mason," the sheriff said. "Will you be quiet?"

The woman ran up to him. "Preacher," she said, and she pointed at a long, rectangular building across the street. "My daughter is in there. She went in to get some cans of tomatoes. I'm making tomato soup for the church social this Saturday. You can't grow tomatoes in this county. I never would have sent Patricia Anne in there had I known Injun Periwinkle was in town."

Callahan stared at the woman. The heat and the tenseness of the situation must have addled her brain. "Tomatoes?" he said. "At a hardware store?"

She blinked. "Patricia Anne said . . ." But the rest of the sentence trailed off and her eyes glazed over and she stared at the advertisements on the window panes, not one announcing prices on any type of food stuffs. Yep, Callahan noticed, every pane was decorated with advertisements for the price of nails by the pound, coal by the bucket, horseshoes by the dozens, and all sorts of ammunition for various rifle and pistol calibers.

Pointing at the Sharps rifle in the waddie's hands, Callahan asked, "What do you plan on doing with that?"

"Ain't no plan," the cowboy said and spit between his teeth into the street. "I'm gonna blow that red devil's head off."

"Marshal," the woman said, stopped, and turned toward

Callahan. "Preacher, they can't do that. Patricia Anne's inside. They might hit her."

The cowboy pointed the Sharps barrel from his hip. "I'm gonna shoot right through that window when I get a clear shot."

"How do you know you'll be shooting at the Indian?" Callahan asked. "And not this lady's daughter?"

"I ain't blind."

"You stare at the glare coming off that window," Callahan said, "and you will be. And you can't see through those advertisements anyhow."

He turned to the lawman. "Marshal, there's got to be a better way."

"Injun Periwinkle's already killed my clerk." This came from a firmer voice, and Callahan looked at a tall man wearing sleeve garters and a bowler hat. "My name's Maurice Fletcher."

Callahan sized the man up. "Your store," he said.

"That's right. And that's my clerk." He pointed.

Looking back at the hardware store, Callahan saw a pair of city shoes sticking out on the boardwalk from behind a water trough.

"Injun Periwinkle's been raising Cain far too long, Preacher," the store owner said. "Now he's committed murder. Cold-blooded, senseless killing most foul. That was a mighty fine clerk."

"The injun didn't kill that Manfred," called out a fat man with beer suds hanging from his handlebar mustache. "The marshal sent a round when that injun started whooping and hollerin' and everybody run out of the store—including you, Fletcher."

"Shut up, you walkin' whiskey vat," snapped a fat woman with a parasol.

Callahan studied the shoes, then examined the rectangular building. He found the open front door, but couldn't make out anything inside. His eyes went back to the tan and black shoes.

"I don't think that clerk is dead," Callahan said one or two heartbeats later. "His left foot just moved."

All eyes went to the boardwalk.

"Must've been the wind."

"Or rigor mortis," offered a man sipping from a bottle of Irish whiskey.

"Rigor mortis?" said the redheaded dance-hall girl from way back in the crowd.

"By thunder," said a man with half his face shaved. "That foot did move. That ol' boy might not be bound for Boot Hill after all."

"He will be," said another voice, "if somebody don't do somethin' real smart and real quick."

"That's what I'm aimin' to do," said the cowboy, and he brought the stock of the Sharps rifle to his shoulder.

"Preacher," said the mother. "Please."

"How do we know he's a preacher?" the cowboy said, and he eared back the heavy hammer. "And don't say it's because of his black duds, you dern fool."

"Name's Callahan," he said and saw the alley between the far right of Fletcher's store and a café. "Taylor Callahan. Circuit rider. Been preaching the Word and helping folks at Falstaff."

"Where?"

"False Hope," somebody corrected.

"They sure could use some heavenly help over that way," another woman commented.

"Hey!" yelled one of the schoolboys. "Look at that dude's feet now!"

Faces, including Callahan's, turned. Sure enough, only one black and tan shoe remained sticking out from behind the water trough. But torn burgundy and tan britches appeared just above the rim of the trough. The clerk's knee, Callahan figured.

"Manfred!" Fletcher yelled. "Are you all right?"

No answer.

"Manfred!" the lawman called out. "How bad are you hit, son? How bad did the injun hurt you?"

The profanity that came from behind the water trough caused many of the fair ladies of Jubilee, Texas, to gasp.

"I'm sorry you had to hear that, Preacher," the store owner said.

Callahan chuckled despite himself.

"Marshal!" the voice called from behind the water trough, not loud, but a long ways from dead. "If I can ever see straight again, I'm gonna shove that Remington pistol up your—"

A man in a collarless shirt caught the fainting milliner and looked for help.

"Manfred," the lawman said, "I'm gonna fine you five dollars for using that kind of language in my town."

The kneecap disappeared, and the black and tan city shoe joined the other beyond the trough.

"Manfred?" Fletcher called out.

A groan, then a whimper, came from the boardwalk.

"Marshal," the mother of the child inside cried out.

"Preacher. We've got to help that poor man . . . and my daughter."

"Injun Periwinkle!" called out the barber. "Give yourself up."

No answer.

"Show yourself, you red vermin!" said the cowboy with the Sharps. "And I'll show you what a Big Fifty can do to a redskin's face."

"Marshal!" the mother pleaded. "Preacher." Her voice kept getting more and more desperate with the passing of every second, and Callahan could not fault her. He was sweating himself.

"Let me kill him," the sharpshooter said.

Callahan looked at the alley again.

"Marshal," he asked softly. "How many men do you have watching the back of the mercantile?"

The lawman suddenly became aware that every eye on the main street had trained upon him.

His Adam's apple stuttered and finally bobbed.

"Back of the mercantile?" the Jubilee city marshal whispered.

Chapter 27

A few hissed at the lawman, while others called him all sorts of filthy names, but when the marshal started to order several volunteers to go around the back, Callahan stopped him.

"We don't want to be doing that," Callahan said.

"He might escape with my daughter!" the mother cried.

"If he wanted to leave, he'd be gone by now. And if he sees a bunch of you men heading for the alleys, well . . ." He took in another lungful of hot Texas oxygen. "Let me see if I can get around there, sneak in, maybe get this situation defused."

"I don't know," the lawman said, and the mother's face revealed similar doubts.

But Callahan wasn't going to let this turn into a debate. He wanted to get inside that hardware store, and this was a golden opportunity. Holding out the Bible to the sharpshooter, he commanded, "Here, hold this."

When the man dumbly took the Bible, Callahan took the Sharps rifle.

"Hey," the man said, "what's the meaning of this?"

"I'm not going in there unarmed," Callahan said. "And

I'm not going to risk you blowing my head off with some errant shot."

The man opened his mouth, but Callahan was already moving down the street, calling to the sheriff. "Just keep an eye out on the place. Especially the front door. If I open it, I'll wave a white flag on the barrel of this Big Fifty."

He refused to allow any protest, and took off at a trot down the street. All of the residents of Jubilee had to be on this main street by now. Yes, Callahan determined, this was indeed the county seat. When he reached the tonsorial parlor, he figured he was likely out of view of Injun Periwinkle, if anyone remained inside Fletcher's store. So he cut across the street and didn't stop until he was in the alley.

There were no windows in the hardware store facing onto the alley. Callahan had not expected to find any, or even a door. He moved to the Fletcher side of the alley, leaned the Sharps against the wood, and peered down the boardwalk on the main street. The unconscious man remained behind the water trough, his head moving from side to side, slowly, and his chest rising and falling, rapidly. Which meant the lucky son of a gun was still alive, and he might stay that way.

As best as Callahan could tell, there was not too much blood leaking from that city slicker's head, though the knot on the side of his noggin appeared to be about the size of a Missouri crabapple.

Callahan gave a short wave to the lawman, grabbed the Sharps and moved quickly down the alley, enjoying the shade for the moment. Texas wanted to do everything big, including the length of alleys, and Mr. Fletcher wanted to have the largest hardware store in the county. He saw a sign nailed to a post on the next street.

Second Avenue

He found what appeared to be a boarding house across the street, along with a café—the door still open—and a butcher shop, where the owner had hung a sign on the closed door that said he would be back "pert soon." There was an adobe building that claimed to be a gunsmith. Some towns had stores backing up against one another, and undoubtedly Jubilee had some of those, but Fletcher's Hardware store covered both the main street and Second Avenue.

Callahan stepped onto the empty street, seeing a few horses tied to hitching posts, and a buggy in front of a lawyer's office. There were no windows in the hardware store on the Second Avenue side, but a big barn-style door, probably for deliveries, and a smaller door.

With a wagon, the team still hitched, near the big door. When Callahan got closer, he saw the brand burned into the side of the wagon. Vernon Browne's brand.

He tried to remember the faces of the men on the street in front of the hardware store. Not that he could have seen a quarter of the people. He hadn't recognized any of Browne's men.

It doesn't matter if any Browne cowpoke is here or not, he told himself. *You better get in that store before that sharpshooter talks his way into putting holes in the store and maybe some innocent girl.*

He moved to the delivery door first. It opened from the inside. But it wouldn't budge. That didn't surprise him. A town with as many people as he had seen in Jubilee likely had problems with the criminal element—Injun Periwinkle appeared to be proof of that—so Fletcher did his part to keep anyone from breaking into his store. He stepped onto the boardwalk that ran the length of the store and came to the rear entrance. His free hand grabbed the knob and turned it, then he pushed.

He almost let out an oath that would leave the Major General in the Heavens frowning, but stopped himself, and stepped back from the locked door. He considered rubbing his shoulder, but kept the Sharps in his hand.

Maybe, he thought, he had made a long run on a hot day for nothing. Maybe he'd have to go back to the main street and come in through the front door. But if Injun Periwinkle were still inside, that could prove deadly. Not just for Callahan, but the girl inside.

He stepped off the boardwalk, moving toward the café, where the aroma of bacon made his stomach growl. There was a temptation to keep walking into the empty eatery and fill his stomach, at least find a cup of coffee, but in the middle of the empty street, he turned around, and looked up.

There was the window, a lace curtain fluttering. An open window. Probably an office. And he might be able to reach it from the awning.

He had to move a trash can to the edge of the boardwalk, and somehow managed to pull himself to the rim. He slid the Sharps rifle onto the awing, then whispered a short prayer, and reached up. He wasn't exactly catlike, and he kicked the barrel over, cringing at the sound it made as it rolled toward the butcher's shop and fearing he might fall on his back and knock the breath out of him. But his left hand found a piece of wood that didn't break. He felt the shingles and thatch and dust sifting through, and he almost sneezed when his right hand found a large nail that had stuck out of the side of the building. He hoped it wasn't rusty, and that he wouldn't cut himself.

Again, the Major General in the Heavens was kind to him, and his waist found the edge of the awning. He lunged, and dragged his legs onto the top.

Callahan had hired good carpenters, too. The awning groaned, but Callahan managed to stand, holding the Sharps again, and he inched his way close to the wall, toward the open window.

A minute or two later, and he was inside, breathing heavily, sweating like a pig, and in a dark office. Slowly, his eyes grew accustomed to the darkness, and the window offered just enough sunlight so that he could make out the light shining from the crack of what had to be the bottom of another door. There was a desk, and plenty of barrister bookcases, a keg of what appeared to say JAMAICAN RUM, and a Seth Thomas clock on the wall, the ticking sounding like a blacksmith's hammer.

He waited till his face no longer felt like a waterfall of sweat, and, when his chest wasn't heaving too much, he put his right foot out and let it ease onto the floor.

So far, so good.

But when he lifted his left foot, he heard the annoying and, to his ears, deafening squeak of the floor.

He cut off the oath he was about to whisper.

What seemed like weeks later, he continued moving his left foot and put it in the darkness ahead of his right, touching the floor like a moth landing on a bush.

He nodded at the lawman, the redhead, the gunman holding Callahan's Bible.

The next movement of Callahan's boots did not wake the dead, nor was the noise as soft as a mouth's padded feet.

This, he told himself, *was not the smartest move you ever made.*

The toe of his left boot touched something soft, and Callahan slid the rest of his boot onto what felt like a fine Persian rug.

When his right foot joined the left on the rug, Callahan breathed easier. He took another step, and this time heard nothing but his own breathing and his heart hammering away. Callahan covered the rest of the rug in a hurry, then he bumped into a chair that some idiot had put in the middle of a floor. It was a nice chair, though, leather with studs, and he fingered his way around it, and stepped back onto the wooden floor.

Which did not moan under his weight.

The light underneath the door remained his beacon, and he picked a direct path, moving softly but urgently, listening for the wood to moan, but hearing just his soft steps. He put out his free hand as he neared the door, and when the fingers touched the wood, he stopped, and waited till his breathing once again resembled the breath of a man without fear.

The hand found the doorknob, and the squeaking just audible, and he pushed to feel no movement at all.

"Idiot," he said in a whisper, and immediately stopped and inwardly cursed his stupidity for saying something out loud. Instead of pushing the door, this time he pulled it toward him. The hinges did not make a sound, and he looked at another wall.

That was a surprise that Callahan welcomed with a prayer of thanks. He thought he would be staring over a banister at the store below. Instead, he was in a hallway that was filled with crates, boxes and sacks. He looked down the left at no more doors, but shelves and more merchandise, then glanced at his right and saw two more office doors and then a length of maybe fifteen feet where the hallway ended and light shined, revealing a balustrade to the stairs that led to the first, gargantuan, floor.

He moved to the far wall, glanced again behind him, then began inching his way toward the opening. He wet his lips, studied the planks on the floor, looking for any board that might be loose, trying to move like a mouse. When he reached the first floor, he saw the name on the door.

FLETCHER
PRIVATE

There was a brief moment when he considered moving across the hall and trying that door, wondering if he might find some information about a certain gun shipment, but stopped. That would have to wait. He had a young girl being held captive by some gent called Injun Periwinkle. If he could save the girl, and even the Indian, his standing might raise substantially in the county seat. Perhaps he could get any information he needed from the county sheriff, although he had yet to see any county official— just a town lawman and a town mayor.

The second door had no name on it, just the "Private" designation, and now he covered the last few feet before the wall, his cover, his bit of safety ended. He waited a full two minutes before easing toward the edge.

His lips turned upward and his eyes brightened when he saw the giant mirror hanging on the wall facing him, about halfway up the wall below. Now he could see the bottom floor, the pickle barrels, the taffy on the counter, the peppermint sticks, the bolts of calico and duck cotton, hats, and kettles and even a fine display of assorted Bibles, big enough for a Baptist and small enough to fit in a man's trousers pocket. He saw the front door, the front windows with the back of the advertisements, the glare from the sun just as bad from this side as it was trying to stare inside from across the street.

He saw bracket saws and shaft tips, singletrees and doubletrees, wagon bows and stump pullers. He saw feather dusters and lathes, taper files and hammers, axes, hay forks, hay knives, spades, horse shoes, stone haulers, and every sort of bolt, nail, screw.

There were guns, too. Shotguns, single and double barreled, rifles—but no Sharps that he could see—Winchesters. And a mighty fine display of Bowie knives. He saw workers clothes and harness oil, a few catalogs and a cash register.

He wet his lips and studied the mirror again. He could see practically the whole store, but what he could not see any sign of was Injun Periwinkle or Patricia Anne. He also didn't see any cans of tomatoes, and he began to wonder why someone would come to a hardware store instead of a grocery for canned fruit.

Or is a tomato a vegetable?

He never could get that straight.

That's when Taylor Callahan heard the soft giggling of

what he recognized immediately, from his wilder days before Logan's Knob Seminary down south of Sparta in the Ozark hills.

He looked back at the door marked only "Private."

Yes, he told himself, that was the sound of a young girl in love.

Callahan made one final pass over the reflection from the mirror, and then moved to the other side of the hallway, to the door, and he put one ear near the crack.

"Oh, Thomas," a young woman said, "you shouldn't."

"Patricia Anne," a voice that sounded nothing like an Indian said, "you know I love you."

"Do you really?"

"You know I do."

"But I shouldn't."

"Oh, you must. We must. It's our only chance."

"But . . . Perry!" A slap of the wrist made Callahan shake his head.

Kids, Callahan mouthed, and he pushed the door open, stepped inside, and raised the Sharps to his shoulder.

"All right!" he barked. "I'm . . ."

Two lamps bathed the windowless office in fine light. It wasn't a big office, but what one might call cozy, with more of those barrister bookcases, and assorted boxes and sacks, a calendar from four years back, but one with a fine drawing of a Rocky Mountain vista and an advertisement for a stagecoach company that Callahan recalled went belly-up two years ago.

The girl was sitting on a desk, holding a book in her right hand. The boy was standing a few feet away, holding a similar book. The boy was leaning on something, and as they both lowered their books and looked at Callahan, the circuit rider remembered the face of the boy.

The boy was leaning on crutches.

That's when Taylor Callahan felt the cold muzzle of a revolver brushing gently behind his right ear.

"I don't reckon," the guttural voice said, "I've had the pleasure."

"The Reverend Taylor Callahan," he introduced himself, lowering the Sharps. "Circuit rider working out of Falstaff."

"Falstaff?" the voice asked.

"False Hope."

"Oh."

"All right, kids," the man with the gun against Callahan's head said. "You can put them five-penny dreadfuls down."

The paperbacks fluttered to the floor, and the girl rushed into the young cowboy's arms, almost knocking him off the crutches.

"Tommy Browne," Callahan said. "You're up and around pretty good."

The voice belonging to the gun against Callahan's head said: "I reckon you brought that buffalo gun to shoot me dead."

Callahan shook his head. "Not hardly, Injun Periwinkle. I'm a preacher."

Chapter 28

"Preacher!" The word came out like a snort, and the revolver barrel never moved off Callahan's skin. "The Reverend Taylor. Yeah. In a pig's eye."

"Callahan. The Reverend Taylor Callahan. Named after daddy's ma. Ma's maiden name, not her Christian name. That was my birthing daddy. I had lots of daddies in my day."

"And I suppose that's your Good Book."

He understood the man's meaning. "No, that belonged to a gent outside who wanted to use it to blow off your head. He's holding my big Bible now instead of sighting this inside the store."

"You talk a lot. Baptist?"

"I don't talk that much."

That caused a snort that was more laugh, and the gun barrel left Callahan's ear. "Girl," Injun Periwinkle said, "take this hombre's rifle, and try not to blow his guts out or your beau's or your own."

Slowly, Callahan shifted the grip of the rifle, and held it out to the young girl, who had been clutching Tommy

Browne's arm. "It's pretty heavy," he told her, "but it's not cocked, so don't worry yourself into a fit about it accidentally going off."

"Turn around," the man with the gun ordered Callahan after the girl had taken the rifle and stepped away, out of reach from her beau. Callahan assumed the rancher's son was wooing the girl, and he couldn't blame him for that, as she was pretty as a peach.

Slowly, Callahan turned, giving his after-services smile that he used in hopes of getting an extra nickel out of some of his flock. Well, the color was off, but Injun Periwinkle was Indian of some sort. Copper faced, short, squat, the black hair in braids that were streaked with white. The revolver now aimed at Callahan's middle was a Remington .44, the hammer at full cock, and a stubby finger pressing slightly against the trigger. He wore brogans, tan britches, and a calico shirt, with a necklace of pretty stones hanging all the way down to the third wooden button.

"You're quiet on your feet," Injun Periwinkle said. "Part Injun?"

"Not that I know of." Callahan shook his head. "And I'm not too quiet. You heard me."

"Luck." That came from the girl, and Callahan and the man holding him at gunpoint, looked at her.

"He brought us up here to try to find some whiskey. Otherwise, we'd be downstairs and never heard you come into Fletcher's office."

Well, that made Callahan feel a tad better. He wasn't noisy, he was just unlucky. He turned back to his captor. "Find any?" he asked.

"Any what?" The Indian stared at him hard with suspicion.

"Whiskey."

The big head shook. "Nothin'. Nothin' worth drinkin' in here."

"That's because this is a hardware store," Tommy Browne said, "you danged fool."

Callahan looked over at the busted-legged teen. "What brings you here?" he asked. "Other than this charming young lady."

"Pa sent me."

"With your busted leg?" Callahan shook his head. "You still shouldn't even be out of bed."

"Man's gotta earn his keep," Tommy Browne said, quoting, undoubtedly, his father. "Said I could take a wagon here and get all that dynamite and stuff."

Callahan's muscles tightened. "Dynamite?"

The kid's head bobbed. "For that rainmaker. What's his name?"

"Professor Jessup Hungate," Callahan said. "He didn't bring his own?"

The boy's head shook. "Also had to pick up the payroll for our hands."

"That's got to be a tidy sum. You don't have any guards with you?"

The boy's head shook once more. "Nobody's fool enough to rob my pa . . . not in these parts. Besides, the money's in the dangedest strong box you'd find this side of the Denver Mint. Take a ton of dynamite to blow it open."

"Which you happen to be carrying, too," Callahan pointed out.

"Well, ain't nobody crazy enough to rob my pa."

"Hey!"

The boy, the girl, and the circuit rider turned to study the man with the Remington .44, who apparently did not like being left out of the conversation. He squinted, bit his lip, snorted, and lowered the Remington's barrel from Callahan's heart to his waistline.

"Did you say . . . Hungate?" Injun Periwinkle asked.

"That's right," Callahan replied. "You heard of him?"

The revolver dropped toward Callahan's knee, and that's when the girl swung the Sharps up, braced it against her shoulder, thumbed back the hammer, and touched the set trigger, then moved her finger to the second trigger.

"You heard that click, Periwinkle!" she said sharply. "You know what happens when I touch the next trigger?"

Yeah, Callahan thought as he held his breath. The Indian's brains are plastered against the wall, and I'm crippled for the rest of my life if he touches the trigger on his .44.

But Injun Periwinkle just stared at the girl blankly, confused, perhaps in shock at how that tiny little kid could hold a heavy buffalo gun like it was a fly swatter. Callahan eased his way to the dumbfounded man, raised his hand, and took the barrel of the revolver, gently bringing it down till it pointed at the floor. Then he took the Remington from Injun Periwinkle's hand and lowered the hammer. "You can let down the hammer on that Big Fifty, Miss," Callahan said.

He held his breath until he heard the heavy hammer rest in a safe place.

Tommy Browne filled Callahan in as they left the office and headed down the stairs, Injun Periwinkle leading the way, though his shoulders sagged and his head was bent like a man bound for the gallows.

Tommy had arrived at Fletcher's hardware store. Patricia Anne was conveniently waiting for him, having talked her mother into sending her to Fletcher's store.

"For tomatoes," Callahan said.

They reached the ground floor.

"Oh." She understood her blunder.

"You might have some explaining to do to your ma."

Tommy Browne offered: "Try telling her that you come here to get one of them newfangled openers for the tin cans."

Callahan shook his head. "Try telling her the truth."

The rest of the story was simple. Injun Periwinkle came in looking for whiskey. The clerk ran outside. Periwinkle shot him as he stepped onto the boardwalk, and the rest of the time, they had been sitting on the steps, the Indian trying to figure out where he might find whiskey.

Whiskey and cans of tomatoes in a hardware store. In the county seat.

Callahan looked at the back of the advertisements on the window panes, and decided that he needed to stall for some time.

"Marshal!" he yelled.

"Yes," the voice called back.

"Is that red devil dead?" That sounded like the man now holding Callahan's Good Book.

"No!" Callahan looked around, saw a door that had to lead to one of the back rooms. "But the girl and Browne's son are all right. And if you give me fifteen minutes, I think I can talk Injun Periwinkle into surrendering."

Three faces stared at Callahan in complete confusion.

"I'll give you ten!" Yes, that was the man who wanted his Sharps rifle back. "Then we're storming that place just like we done at Gettysburg."

Callahan shook his head. "Remember what happened to y'all at Gettysburg!" he shouted. "Fifteen minutes." He looked at the clock on the wall.

Then, Injun Periwinkle said, "It ain't his real name, you know."

Three pairs of eyes now trained on the Indian, who sat on the bottom step, shaking his head.

"Who's that?" Callahan asked, but he had a pretty good idea who the man was talking about.

"Carl Del Russo," Periwinkle said. But frowned, shook his head, and tried again. "Nah, that ain't right. But it's somethin' like that. Russo. I think that's what he called himself. In Shaw Town. North a spell from El Paso."

"Where's your wagon?" Callahan asked the boy.

"Out back." The kid gestured.

"I was hoping that was yours. You haven't been to the bank yet, have you?"

Now the lad grinned. "I ain't that green, Parson. Pa would flog me something fierce was I to leave a month's pay in the back of the wagon while I was . . ." He glanced at Patricia Anne, and blushed. So did the girl.

"I believe the proper word is *courtin'*," Callahan said.

He moved toward the store rooms. "C'mon," he said. "You, too, Periwinkle."

He left the door to the storeroom open to bathe the giant room with some light. Since Callahan knew what he was looking for, he went down the first row, followed by three confused people, passing the barrels and the baskets, glancing at the crates of shovels, stopping briefly at another long box, till he saw Winchester Repeating Arms Co. stenciled into the wood, and moved on. He found what he was looking for on the third row, which made him happy. It also happened to be just fifteen feet from the back door. And if Callahan was guessing correctly, Tommy Browne's freight wagon was parked just outside the door.

On the other side of the aisle, he saw the boxes of Spencer ammunition. Enough to start a war. A war Taylor Callahan planned to prevent from ever seeing its Fort Sumter.

"Tommy," Callahan said in a deep whisper, "how much room will you have in that wagon after you've got your money for your pa and that dynamite for that professor?"

"I don't know. Won't fill up the wagon, but it's gonna be heavy with all that gold."

"Gold?"

The boy looked away from Callahan before answering. "Pa don't hold with paper money, Preacher. It's gold or silver or nothing."

"You think you can manage to haul these rifles?" He pointed at the ammunition. "And those bullets?"

The boy looked long and hard, not at the boxes, but at Callahan, probably worried that the circuit rider was testing him. "It's important," Callahan said.

"But these guns . . ." the kid started, and looked at the order receipt tacked to the top of one of the boxes of repeating carbines. "They're for . . ."

His head jerked up.

"You're smart enough to figure it out," Callahan told him.

"That dirty, low-down sodbuster."

"Grief affects men in different ways." Callahan put his hand on the boy's good shoulder. "I just want to keep this fuse from being lighted, son. Keep these guns out of Lamerick's hands till I can talk sense into him."

"You got as much chance of talking sense into that old man as . . ." Tommy Browne stopped, but just for a heartbeat. He made himself finish his thought. ". . . as you got of talking my pa out of doin' the same dad-burned thing."

"That's what I'm going to do." Callahan did not blink or change his stern countenance. "But I need your help."

"Tommy . . ." the girl said, but the boy did not look at her.

"I can't get these crates onto that wagon." He looked toward the rear door. "Not with this bad leg."

"They're not complete idiots in this town," Callahan said. "They're sure to have put men on those streets by now. And you've got that dynamite for Professor Hungate, too."

"Isn't that dangerous?" Patricia Anne asked.

"Only if he's careless with his cigarettes," Injun Periwinkle said. "And Hungate isn't his real name."

"How 'bout it, Tommy?" Callahan asked.

"I don't see how Mr. Fletcher will let us take somebody else's order," Tommy said. "He don't care what happens in False Hope."

"You leave that to me." Callahan nodded at Patricia Anne. "Come with me, miss. Your mother's sick to her stomach with worry. Tommy, you wait here. Periwinkle,

I'm afraid you're going to have to spend some time in jail. But as long as that clerk doesn't die, I think some time alone will be good for reflection."

"I guess I could use some time to myself . . . without the devil's whiskey."

"Bully for you, Periwinkle. Bully for you!" Callahan patted the Indian's back, though in the back of his head, the thought—*I could use a shot of Devil's whiskey right about now*—bounced around his brain. "You're on the right road, Periwinkle. And it's a good road to travel."

Callahan stopped at the cash register, opened it, found plenty of greenbacks, gold, and silver, and he figured fifty dollars would be plenty, even in a county seat, especially this particular county seat.

"Are you stealing that money, Reverend?" Patricia Anne asked.

"No, ma'am," he said. "I plan on giving it to Mr. Fletcher." He stuffed the notes into the inside pocket of his Prince Albert, took the Sharps, drew the Remington from his waistband, and led the girl and the Indian to the front door.

He didn't just walk outside—not after seeing how the men of Jubilee handled things. Stopping behind the advertisements blocking the window, he cupped his hands over his mouth and yelled, "Marshal!"

"You all right in there, Preacher?"

That wasn't the lawman's voice, but it wasn't the girl's mother or the fellow holding Callahan's Good Book, either. It was heavy Texan, though.

"This is Bert Elliott. Sergeant, Texas Rangers. I got ten privates out back, and my six top men out here with me.

Just give the word, Preacher, and we'll come in and get you all out. Dead or alive."

Callahan thought that, yes, he should have followed the rattlesnake instead of heading this way.

"I mean . . . get y'all out alive. And that red devil out dead."

A few seconds ticked off on the clock on the wall.

"It's the Texas way," the Texas Ranger drawled.

"Sarge," Callahan said, trying to sound like a good, ol' Texan. "Miss Patricia Anne is safe, and I have Vernon Browne's son, too. We have disarmed the poor, misguided Indian, drunk on white man's whiskey sold to him by the most treacherous vermin who slanders the reputation of this fine, grand, ol' Republic. Hold your fire. We're coming out now."

Callahan waited for some sort of assurance, which he got.

"Bert Elliott, you numbskull. My daughter's in there, and if you or one of your men even puts a finger on a trigger, I'll blow your head off. For goodness sake, let that good man—the only one who had the nerve to try to save some lives—bring out Patricia Anne and that poor, misguided Indian."

After a string of profanity, Sergeant Bert Elliott called out to his men. "Hold your fire, boys. Don't even shoot the injun. Dad gum it. This coulda got me writ up in 'em Austin newspapers."

Chapter 29

After breathing in and out deeply, Taylor Callahan shook his head, glanced skyward and hoped the Major General in the Heavens wasn't asleep on his golden rocking chair. He pushed the door farther open, saw the clerk's shoes still sticking out behind the water trough, and stepped onto the boardwalk.

He made out the Texas Ranger sergeant in the big tan hat, guns holstered on both hips, and a Winchester repeating rifle in his arms. The crowd had not thinned out. He glanced at the wounded clerk, waved for some volunteers to come.

"Let's get this gent to a doctor!" Callahan yelled.

"Or Dusty's Saloon," the clerk groaned.

Patricia Anne's mother raced forward, followed by a handful of Jubilee's most curious citizens, who wanted to get a closeup view of the wounded clerk. The sergeant of the Rangers strode forward, as did Maurice Fletcher and the man holding Callahan's Bible.

"I'll take my Sharps back, mister." The sharpshooter was the first to reach the boardwalk. The exchange went off without a fumble or an accidental gunshot, and the

Ranger took Injun Periwinkle by the shoulder and shoved him toward his men.

"Haul this red vermin to the calaboose," he ordered.

Mother and daughter were arm in arm, though the mother stared at Tommy Browne with not a whole lot of sympathy. Maurice Fletcher asked how much damage had been done to his store.

"Not as much as was done to your clerk's noggin," Callahan said as the volunteers carried him down the boardwalk to the nearest doctor's office. And seeing how red Patricia Anne's mother's neck and face kept getting, he added, "Thanks to the bravery of this kind, courageous cowboy. Why I haven't heard of anything like this happening since David faced down Goliath." He removed his hat with the hand that didn't carry the big Bible. "He kept his wits, and kept this young lady out of harm's way."

"Huh?" Tommy Browne said.

"Good job, son. Your pa will be mighty proud of you," Mr. Fletcher said and slapped the boy's shoulder.

"You men!" Callahan shouted, and waved a few stragglers over. "Vernon Browne's son here can't load all those supplies he has by himself. Nor should he do after this harrowing, but heroic, day in Jubilee. Help him get his wares on the back of the wagon." He pulled out a ten-dollar greenback and waved it. That brought several men forward.

"Here." He handed the note to the burliest of the men. "You're honest. Divide the money up after the work's been done."

Turning, he handed out the rest of the money he had taken from Fletcher's cash register, "This is for you. The profits you must have lost from not being able to sell screws and ax handles for what . . . three, four hours?"

"More like ninety-five minutes," said a man with a pretty gold pocket watch that chimed when he opened the cover.

"Well . . ." Fletcher stared at the money he now held.

"This is from Mr. Browne," Callahan whispered. "There's some things in your storeroom that Mr. Browne doesn't want to see in a certain farmer's hands. A farmer down Falstaff way. You understand?"

"Well . . . I can't . . ." But he looked at the money, and nodded ever so discretely, then slid the cash into a deep pocket in his pants. "You tell Vernon that those Spencers haven't gotten here yet." He grinned. "Don't understand it. That's what I'll tell that sodbuster."

Callahan smile broadly, and moved to Tommy Browne, guiding him into the store, whispering, "Get this wagon loaded, and covered with a tarp, get to the bank for your payroll, and get out of town in a hurry. You got a good idea for a place we can store what your pa don't need to see, neither?"

The boy's lips flattened as he thought.

"The quarry?" he suggested.

Callahan's head shook immediately. "Not if we're keeping them away from a certain stonemason turned farmer."

"Oh, right." He wet his lips and stared at a hand saw. "There's a bend in the river. Well, the river bed. Never been much water in it, and none for years. Maybe a mile and a half past the sign. As the crow flies. You know, the False Hope sign, 'Six inches to hell' . . ."

"Which direction?" Callahan asked.

"Thisaway."

Callahan nodded. "That'll have to do. I'll catch up with

you. Take it slow. They'll be loading Lamerick's goods onto your wagon, too."

"I understand." Tommy Browne inhaled and started sweating. "What if they can read?"

"They might be able to read," Callahan said, "but I doubt if they'll remember much after ten dollars of whiskey in this town."

Someone was calling his name, so Callahan smiled, nodded at the boy, and moved back to the crowd. Tommy Browne hobbled on his crutches to the storeroom, followed by a handful of big, thirsty men.

Patricia Anne and her mother were gone, but there were hands to shake, and a newspaper editor to entertain with a few choice quotes, and then he found the mayor, who wanted to tell the newspaper editor all that he had done to save the day, but Callahan had other business to attend to.

"Mayor," he asked, "might you direct me to your county sheriff's office?"

The silence was immediate.

"Did I say something wrong?" Callahan asked.

"Sheriff ain't here," the mayor said.

"I see." Though Callahan didn't see. "This is the county seat."

"For now," said the newspaper editor.

"Hush up, Charles," snapped the mayor.

Callahan figured it out. Another town, probably a larger town, wanted to take over as the county seat, and the sheriff likely preferred something other than Jubilee. Things like that happened across the West, but Callahan didn't need a lawman.

"Well, I don't need the sheriff. I just need access to . . . how do I put this . . . wanted dodgers?"

"You bounty-huntin'?" asked a man holding a post-hole digger.

"I'm looking for souls that need help. Like Mr. Periwinkle, you see."

He waited, then the Ranger sergeant's voice boomed, "Ten-shun!" And the sergeant and his men snapped into a sharp, rigid erectness. Even a few businessmen and two raggedy-looking hide hunters came to attention.

"Captain Lincoln, suh!" Sergeant Bert Elliott said, and a gentle-looking man with cold eyes stepped through the doorway.

He looked immediately at Callahan, and slowly withdrew a pipe from his mouth, and turned to the sergeant.

"Report, Sergeant," the captain ordered.

The sergeant stuttered a bit, but got the gist of the facts right, even if he embellished the part he and his Rangers played in the apprehension of the prisoner Periwinkle.

"And the visiting reverend?" Captain Lincoln's pipe stem pointed in the general direction of Callahan.

"He was a big help, too, Capt'n," Elliott allowed.

"I bet he was." Captain Lincoln turned to Callahan. "If you need to take a look at wanted posters, Preacher," Captain Lincoln said. "We have a cabinet full of them in my office. By all means, be my guest." He motioned at the doorway with his pipe. "Shall we?"

"Of course." Callahan carried his Bible toward the door. "Captain . . . Lincoln."

Headquarters for the company of Texas Rangers lay on Third Street, but an easy walk through the storeroom and out back and beyond, though Captain Lincoln stopped and watched the volunteers loading Tommy Browne's wagon. He had to notice the two crates of Spencers and boxes of ammunition being loaded, along with the dynamite, but his face never changed expression, the sardonic grin still chiseled on his sun-bronzed face.

The headquarters were a long stone structure—the stones perhaps coming from the same quarry Logan Lamerick used—and Captain Lincoln motioned at a chair, tossed his hat on a hook, and moved to the coffeepot resting on a potbellied stove in the back. The place seemed more bunkhouse than office, and no jail was to be found. That made Callahan relax a bit. He wasn't going to be locked up . . . at least, not here.

He removed his hat, setting it atop his lap after he sat in the proffered chair and crossed his legs. The captain handed him a cup of hot coffee and then sat in the leather chair behind his desk. He opened a drawer, withdrew a bottle of rye, and tossed a finger of amber whiskey into his cup, then held it out for Callahan.

"No thanks," Callahan said, smiled, and added, "Shakespeare."

Captain Lincoln let the rye bottle disappear, and he closed the door, took a sip, set the cup on a stack of papers and said, "It's Lincoln, these days, Parson. Rufus Lincoln."

"So I hear." The coffee, to Callahan's surprise, was the best he had tasted in months. "Lincoln. Good choice."

"I thought so," the Ranger captain said. "It's not very likely any federal lawmen would expect to find one of Carbine Logan's Irregulars using Lincoln as an alias. And I never cared much for the name Rufus. Such a silly name.

Rufus Lincoln. That had to be a fellow's real name, not some handle he took for the summer or so."

Callahan studied the bookcase behind the former bushwhacker's desk.

"Nothing by the Bard," he said, and sipped more coffee.

"Gave that up, too."

"What didn't you give up from Missouri?"

He knew the answer, and Shakespeare, now Texas Ranger Captain Rufus Lincoln, knew Callahan knew. "I'm a fair hand at killing." He grinned. "So were you."

"Nah," Callahan said, shaking his head. "I'm ain't nothin' but a poor ol' circuit rider."

"Yeah." Shakespeare set his coffee cup down. "Who can still switch his speakin' manner when it suits his purpose." He opened a drawer to his left. He didn't have to fumble, just pulled out a notice and laid it flat on the desk, found his spectacles in a vest pocket, settled them on his nose and ears, and read.

"Seems there was a bit of a set-to up on the Red River. Johnnie Harris, brother of three real hardcases, got himself crippled in a gun battle with a circuit-riding preacher. Who also took down two of Harris's gun pals."

"No one died."

"Excepting the lawman those bad boys killed. In Nathan, I mean. There was also a robbery and some blood spilled on the other side of the county."

Callahan spoke evenly. "But I didn't kill anyone."

"Well, you sure helped send Harris's pals to their Maker. Townsfolk didn't even wait for a fair trial. Strung up two gents—wanted to string up the sheriff for some reason."

Now it was Callahan's time to put his coffee aside, and

he reached over and asked with his eyes to read the notice. Smiling, Shakespeare, alias Captain Rufus Lincoln, obliged.

"The kid broke out of jail," Callahan said, after returning the notice to the bushwhacker turned Ranger. "Left his two pards to swing."

"Oh, knowing Harris's blood relatives, I'd think money had something to do with that. And, seeing how a bullet ruined Johnnie's gun hand, my reckoning is that the Harris boys will be coming after you for payback. You recall those family feuds up in Missouri. To the death." He pulled out another paper, but this was a wanted placard. "And the reward for Boss Harris and his two other lowlife brothers, Digger and Everett, that would set me up fine, just fine."

They returned to their coffee.

"What's it been, Taylor? Nine, ten years?"

"More like eleven."

Shakespeare shook his head. "I figured you got planted after we separated."

"Thought the same of you," Callahan said, and took another sip of the wonderful coffee. "What happened to McTavish?"

"Who?"

"Billy Joe. The kid we were . . ."

"Oh." He smiled. "You got a weakness for cripples, don't you?"

Callahan set the coffee on the edge of the desk. "If you mean that cowboy back in the hardware store, he's gonna be a fine young man."

"That's Vermin Browne's boy, right?"

The circuit rider nodded.

"There's gonna be war breaking out up near False Hope. That what brought you there?"

The head shook. "Just luck."

"Yeah. Bad luck follows you like a hound."

"What about McTavish?"

Shakespeare shrugged. "I let him off at some church. I think that's what I was supposed to do. And I started thinking that I really didn't want to die at such a right young age. You'd gone off with the Yanks. The gimp was in good hands. Carbine Logan, if he wasn't already driven mad, he was right close to it. So I drifted, dodged the Yankee patrols, made it into Arkansas, and started dealing poker in Little Rock. Moved down to New Orleans after the surrendering started. Drifted into Texas, and then the state government decided to bring back the Rangers, but give them star-packing authority. I volunteered. Thought they might, Texans being peculiar about Northern names same as Missourians, reject me outright. But they saw how good I was with revolvers, and here I am. Captain now, for the past four months."

"So why don't you and your Rangers ride to Falstaff? Your presence might be enough to stop this war."

Shakespeare finished his coffee, then refilled the mug with two fingers of rye. "Well, you have to understand, my orders come from Austin. Austin would rather me shoot down real outlaws, cutthroats." He found a book on his desk, and tossed it to Callahan. "That's a list of fugitives wanted in the real fine state of Texas. That's who I'm paid to bring in, dead mostly, sometimes alive." He yawned, shook his head, and grinned another malevolent look.

"There just isn't much profit in me stepping in between a muleheaded son of a gun like Vermin Browne and some sodbusters. But, don't you worry your soul too much on the matter. I'm sure once Austin hears that there's a range war, they'll send me and my boys in to clean up the mess and arrest, or shoot down, the winning side. Likely there will be bounties posted on the survivors by then. That's when I'll be up to save False Hope. You might be alive to see it, but I ain't so sure. You always had a habit of . . . well . . . getting in men's way."

"Well . . ." Callahan started to rise.

"What's your hurry?" Shakespeare finished his whiskey. "You wanted to see some wanted posters, I think. Or was it just about the Harris brothers?"

Callahan thought about the Harris gang, but shook his head. He thought about keeping Shakespeare, now a Texas Rangers captain, out of Falstaff, but then decided to be honest. A man like Jessup Hungate might be wanted, but there wouldn't be much of a reward on a confidence man, and a killer like Shakespeare, a professional gunman, he wanted something a bit more sporting than an easy arrest for a few bucks of reward.

"There's a gent claiming to be a rainmaker."

Shakespeare nodded. "So I hear. A professor."

The door opened without a knock and Shakespeare came out of his seat, his Colt in his right hand and cocked.

Chapter 30

Callahan turned as Injun Periwinkle came in, his hands and ankles clinking from the iron manacles and chains. A gray-bearded, bony Ranger stepped in behind him with a tobacco plug straining the right cheek so much it made Callahan's jaw ache.

"Capt'n," the old-timer said, "the injun here pleaded guilty, judge sentenced him to fourteen months in prison. Reckon some of us'll have to take him to Huntsville, though that ain't a trip I want to make. Not this time of year."

"Well, I'm not making it, either," Shakespeare said. "Get Mills, Calloway and . . . Pry . . . yeah, Pry, I'm sick of his face . . . have Newton provision them, and tell them to come get this drunk and hit the trail now. I'll expect them back in a month."

The old man saluted and closed the door.

"A month." Callahan whistled.

"In case you haven't noticed, it's a big state." The Ranger captain pointed at a bench against the wall. "Move some of that tack off and sit down, Injun," he ordered.

"And keep your mouth shut." Looking back at Callahan, he asked, "Where were we?"

"The rainmaker," Callahan answered. "Jessup Hungate."

"That doesn't ring a bell."

"Probably an alias anyway."

Shakespeare brought out a book and slid it across the desk. "This is what we call The Book. Attorney general puts it out once a year, around the first of January—meaning we don't see it till late spring or early summer—and it lists all the fugitives from justice. You can see why we have our work cut out for us."

It was, Callahan noted, a heavy tome.

He flipped through the pages till he got to the first county. The listings were alphabetical by county, but then any sense of order stopped. Names were not alphabetical, but by the date of the crime. Last name, first name, crime, date of crime, date of indictment. Some stopped there. Others had descriptions that might be detailed "red hair, blue eyes, scar across right cheek, about 5 feet, 8 inches, around 45 years old"; others were extremely vague—"tolerably fair Mexican."

He flipped to the end of the book, which was more than two hundred pages, including an index that listed the names and the pages on which the criminal could be found. Some names in the index had been scratched through with Shakespeare's inked closure: *Killed*.

Callahan went to the H's but found no Hungate between a Hughes and a Hussack.

"I don't think this is going to do me much good." He slid the book back toward Shakespeare.

"It's certainly not your Good Book . . . or *The Two Gentlemen of Verona*."

"How about an iron wagon?" It was a stab in the dark, but Callahan figured that might ring a bell. "Pulled by four draft horses. It's blue and . . . well, if the wagon was stolen, Hungate likely repainted it. Had to, anyway, since his name is all over the thing."

Shakespeare laughed. "You are fit to be tied. Iron wagon, eh. Well, that doesn't mean anything to me. Not many rewards offered for wagon thieves, and we have our hands filled with cutthroats, brigands, and veritable demons. And if you're bound and determined to save souls, I think you might have more luck riding with us." He slid a star in a circle across the desk. "Pays better than what you'll get out of a collection plate in this part of the country."

Callahan fingered the badge, looked into the captain's eyes to make sure he was serious, then pushed the star, which appeared to have been made out of some kind of Mexican coin, back to the former bushwhacker.

"You want my Bible or my gun?"

"Your gun'll come in handier. Something tells me you probably carry one somewhere."

Callahan nodded. "There's one in my saddlebag. Compliments of Johnnie Harris."

"He might come looking for it now that he's out. With his brothers in tow."

The door opened again, and three Rangers entered the room, saluted their captain, and walked toward the prisoner.

"Stay out of jail," Shakespeare warned the men. "And you ought to be back in a month."

"Aye, aye," said one of the Rangers as he pulled Injun Periwinkle to his feet and guided him toward the open door.

"Good luck, Periwinkle," Callahan said. "Watch yourself in that prison, but remember, when you're out, you'll have a new life ahead of you. Stay away from liquor."

The Indian stopped, nodded at Callahan and said, "You should stay away from Professor Jessup Hungate. He's a dangerous man."

The Ranger shoved Periwinkle toward the door.

"His real name," the Indian said from outside, raising his voice, "I just remembered. It's Carlin De Russy. See if that's in your book!"

The last Ranger slammed the door shut.

Callahan started to go after them, but stopped, sat back down, and reached for the list of fugitives. Laughing, Shakespeare slid the book back toward him.

He found De Russy in the index, and said, "He's wanted in three counties. Three listings for him." He flipped to the end of the book. "No. This is just a list of rewards offered by the governor."

That grabbed Shakespeare's interest. "How much of a reward?"

Callahan was already turning to find Jack County, but stopped, went back and said, "Fifty dollars."

The Ranger captain shook his head, and found his bottle of rye, which he drank straight, corked, and returned to the drawer. "That's not worth my time."

"Where's Jack County?" Callahan asked.

"Northwest somewhere of Fort Worth."

"Parker?"

The head shook. "No idea. Like I say, it's a big state."

Callahan frowned. "Wanted for graft. Fraud." His head shook and he slid the book back to Shakespeare. "Not even a description of him."

"You're also trusting that drunken Indian that this De Russy is the same fellow as your professor. And that the lawmen that arrested him spelled his name right. And you're also assuming that he doesn't use just one alias."

The captain grinned.

Callahan shook his head. "Now I know why they made you captain. You do have a head on your shoulders."

"I always had a head on my shoulders. And at least one gun on my hip. So did you." Shakespeare grinned. "The difference is . . . I want to keep my head right where it is. And I didn't hang up my guns."

"There's a Colt in my saddlebag," Callahan said.

"Which you still know how to use, according to this description of Johnnie Harris's hand and that gunfight in Nathan."

"Druther keep it in that ol' saddlebag, Capt'n." Callahan stood. "For balance. Man needs balance in his life." Tommy Browne would have the wagon loaded by now and would be making his way back to his father's ranch. "Well," he said. "I've wasted enough of your time, Captain."

The bushwhacker's eyes gleamed, perhaps more from the rye than anything else, and he stood, extending his hand.

As they shook, Callahan suggested, "I think Falstaff could use you and your men."

"You might be right." Shakespeare picked up the book that listed the Texas fugitives. "Here. You might want to read it—maybe just to see how our lives could have turned out." He considered that statement for a moment, and then added, "Maybe should have turned out."

Callahan shook his head. "You might need that."

"Nah," Shakespeare said. "I have my own. The Ranger who owned this one got cut down north of the Pecos. We're not likely to get a new recruit—unless you change your mind—before the next year comes about, if then."

Callahan suddenly found himself holding a big book as the Ranger sank back into his chair and propped his boots on the wood, already scarred from his spurs.

"You sure you don't want to drift over to Falstaff? Keep the peace?"

The head shook. "Vermin Browne is a big man in this state, and he probably has enough influence to have me removed from my lofty position. As you might say, 'A man's gotta look after hisself.' You know that, Preacher. But, like I've said, I'll have to ride up that way to clean up whatever's left. Hope to see you alive when that happens."

"Thanks." Callahan walked outside with the heavy book. He wondered how he would have to adjust his saddle bags to accommodate the size and the weight.

There was no wagon parked behind Fletcher's Hardware Store on Second Avenue, and the main street of Jubilee seemed to be back to normal, although several horses were tethered in front of the saloons—which, Callahan figured, might be normal even at this time of day in a Texas county seat in the middle of nowhere.

He stopped to help a woman with gray hair in a bun and needing a cane to walk as she left a grocery store. Callahan carried her eggs and flour, set the merchandise gently in the back of a wagon, and helped her up. She gave him a nod, muttered something that might have been a *thank you*, whipped the zebra dun, and took off down the street.

At the livery, he found Job standing in the shade and the livery man mopping his face with a rag.

"Owe you any more for what Job here drank?" Callahan asked.

The man tossed the rag onto an overturned barrel. "Iffen you do, we'll call it even. If you preach as good as you handle yourself, I might even be tempted to tithe generously."

"Maybe Jubilee will be my next stop on my circuit ride," Callahan said, smiling, and offering a shake.

Which he regretted for the next mile and a half. That big cuss had a grip like a vise, and Callahan had to keep shaking his hand to get the blood circulating again.

Three miles out of Jubilee, he caught up with Tommy Browne. After tethering his horse to the back of the wagon, Callahan climbed onto the bench beside the youngster, who did not speak more than a half-dozen words over the next few miles.

"Something bothering you, Tommy?" Callahan asked.

The kid shrugged.

"Want to talk about it?"

When no answer came, Callahan just watched the country slowly passing by. Two more miles stretched past, and the boy kept moving his jaw, but not distributing any actual words. That didn't happen till another three-quarters of a mile.

"Them guns," the boy said, and used his left hand, the one not holding the leather that kept the wagon and horses under control, to thumb to the back.

Callahan nodded. "I see," he said, and turned around, looking at the crates and the boxes of cartridges and then at the canvas tarp that covered the strong box. "Must've taken some big boys to get that box on this wagon."

Tommy shrugged.

"Your pa always pay in gold and silver?"

"That's what I told you in Jubilee," he said, focusing on the team pulling the wagon. "Ain't it?"

Callahan smiled. "Yep. And you didn't look me in the eye when you told me that back at Fletcher's, either."

The kid turned, staring hard. "You callin' me a liar, Preacher?"

"I saw you pay with United States currency in town, Tommy. Saw Terry Page use paper money, too. Handy, paper money. And it spends like silver or gold." He grinned. "Course, what I find usually when I get paid is copper. And often wood." His head shook. "Wooden nickels. Those things are older than Methuselah."

Tommy Browne flicked the leather to urge the team harder, and he made himself focus on the wheelers' rumps.

Callahan let him keep looking at the animals for another quarter of a mile. He recrossed his legs at the ankles, leaned back, and said, "You know one thing I've noticed about cowboys? Mind you, I ain't no expert. Ranches were small affairs where I come from. More mules than horses in Missouri anyhow, but they are some of the best you'll find anywhere. But ridin' through Kansas, Texas, even some leases in the Indian Nations, well, cowboys be . . . cowboys. They work cattle. They wear guns—like a six-shooter is part of their uniforms, so to speak."

"Need 'em," the boy said without looking up from the team. "Snakes. Coyotes. I had to put a horse out of its misery, too. Colt came in handy." But the kid's face revealed that was not a memory he enjoyed recalling.

"You might not believe this, Tommy, but I was a fair hand with a revolver during the war."

Now the kid looked at him, in the eye, just for a moment, but Callahan figured that was a promising start.

"Cowboys are workin' men," Callahan told him. "They ain't killers. You have to pay for killers." He turned and spit over the side of the wagon, wiping his mouth with the sleeve of his Prince Albert. "We were paid to kill in Missouri and Kansas. Paid in blood." His head shook. "It ain't pretty. But that was dif'rent. That was war."

"Maybe this is a war, too," the kid said.

"Nah." Callahan recrossed his legs. "But even if that was true, one thing I learned in Missouri is this: War ought to be avoided. Stopped before it ever starts. 'Cause once it starts, it gets real tough to stop."

Another quarter of a mile. The land started becoming familiar.

"Who's the money for, Tommy?" he asked without looking from the road that stretched ahead. He could make out the dried river bed now.

The boy sighed. "That professor," he said. "He's chargin' my pa a thousand dollars. Could be he's the one who don't trust paper money."

"I'd say rain is worth a thousand or more in this country. This year at least."

The boy's head nodded. They covered another two hundred yards. "But it *could be* that there's money for someone else in that box. And it *could be,* Tommy, that if the money was for the professor, you wouldn't have said, *could be.*" He grinned. "Lyin' don't suit you, son. You gotta be convincin' to be a real good liar."

Callahan let them cover another hundred yards. "That's what I thought, Tommy. Maybe some of that money's for the professor. But I think most of it's for some other fellers." He sighed, then shrugged. "Logan Lamerick spends money on rifles and ammunition. Your pa pays for men. I wonder which comes out cheaper."

"My pa's in the right," the boy said, but there wasn't much conviction in the sentence. "Don't forget." He had found a better argument, and pointed at his bandaged ankle. "Someone tried to bushwhack me."

Callahan's head shook. "Fighting for land?" he said. "That's one thing, I guess. Even this dry land. Fighting for revenge, like Logan Lamerick. That's another. Me? I don't see much sense in either. Not anymore. Would you kill the man who shot you, Tommy?"

"Dang right I would!"

"How sure would you have to be, Tommy? Would you ask him why he shot you?"

"You don't know nothing, Preacher. You don't know what it's like."

He reached inside his Prince Albert and pulled out a pocket Bible. "I use the big one," he said as he flipped through the pages. "For preachin' at revivals and gatherin's and reg'lar Sunday services. Wednesdays, sometimes, too. Impresses the folks. Bigger the Bible, bigger the collection plate gets. Sometimes. But the size of the Good Book don't matter. Words is still the same."

He found the commandments, wondered what Moses thought when he first heard them, and, reading the lines over and over again, not looking up, he said softly, "They murdered my wife, Tommy. Burned her alive in the church we built. Oh, I think I know all about how Lamerick feels, and how your pa feels. And I can tell you from first-hand experience . . ." He gestured with his thumb toward the back of the wagon. "Guns or gold . . ." His head shook. "They won't reap you nothin' but regret."

The next mile and a half was covered without a word. Then Tommy Browne pulled the team to a halt. He breathed in and out deeply several times and finally pointed off to his right.

"That bend I was telling you about," he said softly. "It's a couple hundred yards off that way. I ain't gonna be much help, though, with my busted leg and all. Ain't gonna be no help. I couldn't even get that professor's dynamite on the wagon. All I could do was watch."

Callahan reached over and squeezed the nearest shoulder. "Don't you worry none, Tommy. I'm stronger than I look. And we can push together."

It wasn't actually a hiding place. But no one would spot this from the road, and, as high as the arroyo banks were, Callahan didn't think anyone riding along below would see where they had pushed the boxes and crates out of the back of the wagon and partially down the slope. Not unless they were looking for them.

He wiped his brow with his shirtsleeve, and brushed off his hands on his trousers. Next, he studied the landscape, north toward Falstaff, noticing the landmarks—or what passed for landmarks out here: a trough carved by running water down the west side; a patch of prickly pear that must have covered twenty square feet; a sunken mound that might be a grave, the marker long carried away by years and wind. A dead yucca. He checked the time by his pocket watch, and memorized the position of the sun, surprised to find it so low on the horizon. But then this had been a pretty tough chore, and it had already been a long, hard day.

"What about the gold, Preacher?"

Callahan looked back at Tommy, and then studied the road, finding spots to remember.

"What about it?" he asked.

"You gonna bury it, too?"

He shook his head and pointed. "Sugar is a better trap than lead and iron. And I'm curious about how much dynamite the professor will need to bring about his monsoons." He moved to the wagon seat and picked up the Prince Albert he had removed for the hard work. Looking up at the kid driver, he said, "Turn the wagon around and get back to the road. You ride on home, Tommy." He was already moving to the rear of the wagon, where he loosened Job and began tightening the cinch.

"What exactly is your plan, Preacher," the boy asked.

Callahan snorted. "I haven't rightly come up with one yet," he answered in all honesty. "But I'm thinking on it. If you have any suggestions, I'm all ears."

The boy shook his head, dumbfounded, and then grinned. The wagon was turned around, and Browne guided the team back toward the road. Callahan followed, pulling Job behind him, brushing away the deep tracks made by the wheels and hooves with his feet.

That took time, too, because Callahan was thorough about this. He didn't want anyone to find any sign that a wagon had left the road. The wind would likely pick up and blow away all evidence, but Callahan was not one to take any chances.

The wagon was still on the road when he finished and darkness was beginning to settle over the country. Callahan swung into the saddle, and rode up to Tommy Browne.

"Did you hear that?" the boy asked.

Callahan straightened. He had been so preoccupied with hiding the tracks, he had drowned out everything around him—even Job's snorting and urinating.

But then he heard the noise in the gloaming, and he looked north toward Falstaff.

"That ain't thunder," Tommy Browne said in almost a whisper. "Is it?"

Chapter 31

"No," Callahan remembered telling the boy. "It ain't thunder."

He had a pretty good idea what it was, though. So did Tommy Browne. Before they had parted ways, the boy had said, "Pa had some dynamite. Give it to the professor yesterday."

Callahan remembered holding out his hand to the kid, and the kid's perplexed reaction before he finally accepted, and they shook. The kid had a good grip. He'd make a pretty fine man, Callahan figured, providing he didn't follow his father down the wrong path, but he didn't think the boy's pa was a bad man, just wrong-headed, and stubborn as Callahan's fourth and sixth daddies. The wagon had turned down the fork that would carry the boy, and the money, to his pa's ranch, and Callahan let the horse walk the rest of the way to Falstaff.

Now, he saw the flashes in the dark sky, and tightened his grip on the reins to the white gelding before the boom rang out, causing the horse to stutterstep and snort again.

There were no clouds. The flashes were certainly not streaks of lightning. Not Independence Day fireworks, either, but then not many Texans felt like celebrating the Fourth of July, even ten years after the war. Maybe that would change.

Job wheeled at the booming above, the orange, red, yellow, and white streaks that reflected off the smoke. How high was it? Five hundred feet. On the outskirts of town, Callahan heard singing, wretched singing, but they were singing songs from a hymnal. The white gelding kept acting up, and Callahan swung down, wrapping one rein three times around his right hand.

Torches lighted up much of Falstaff, and Callahan saw the Catholic church and walked Job toward the stable behind it. Even Father Pete's mule was skittish, so Callahan doubled the gelding's evening feed, made sure the horse had plenty of water, and put hobbles on Job's forefeet to keep him from running all the way to some quieter place, like California.

He didn't find the young priest in the church, so he went through the front door and looked at the burning torches, the singers over by the cistern. Again, the light showered above in various colors, followed by a deafening roar.

His mind flashed back to the cannon fire, the screams of men and horses whenever Carbine Logan's Irregulars rode up against artillery.

Callahan never cared much for artillery. Cavalry, especially Carbine Logan's men who fought with pistols—"Carbine" Logan had to be the greatest joke of a misnomer in the annals of military warfare—that was the way men should fight, face to face, pistols having such short range, and bouncing on a horse's saddle and hitting your mark took a great deal of skill and providence.

He counted till the next explosion—the professor was taking his time—and above the brilliant streaks of fire, he made out the balloon a fair distance above the fireball. Maybe a thousand feet for the balloon, six hundred or thereabouts for the explosions. He couldn't recall many thunderstorms anywhere in which a cloud had hung that low to the ground, but, well, he wasn't a scientist. That's for sure.

Kids and a few parents and possibly grandparents circled the dying flames of a bonfire in a field, and Callahan spotted the professor's iron wagon parked in front of the land office. The professor wasn't there, but the gunman in the black hat leaned against the side of the long box, smoking a cigar. Callahan turned to the saloon. That place was doing standout business. No one might have been inside the saloon except the bartender, Callahan figured, but beer and whiskey flowed. Most men outside, especially those watching from the front of the saloon, held glasses of beer or whiskey, and a couple had entire bottles.

He saw Logan Lamerick, too, standing with a couple of burly farmers, watching the show in stern silence. Most of the farmers, Callahan determined, were in the spur-of-the-moment choir, singing and praying and shouting "Praise God" and "Glory hallelujah," after each detonation of dynamite. But Lamerick wasn't singing or shouting. From the light of the torches and candles and lanterns and bonfires, Callahan decided that Lamerick wanted to be somewhere else.

Come to think on it, Callahan thought, *so do I.*

But first, Callahan walked to the professor's other wagon, not the iron one, but the one at the bonfire that carried the balloon.

The first man pitched a cigarette to the dirt and ground it out. Callahan gave this man his friendliest nod, then hooked a thumb toward the balloon he could only see when dynamite discharged.

"I thought y'all needed that special gas to get a balloon up in the air," Callahan said.

The gunman glared without a word, but the shorter gent, the one in a Yankee shell jacket, stepped out from behind the wagon and started talking like he had been hoping someone would ask him about ballooning all day.

"Hydrogen." The man's head bobbed. "No, sir. You don't need that gas when hot air will do the job." He pointed to the bonfire on the other side of Falstaff proper. "We had hydrogen inflation wagons when Harvey and I served with the U.S. Balloon Corps. But more than likely we would divert the gas from the city's pipes." He waved both arms around Falstaff. "I don't think you'll find any gas lines in False Hope. Am I right, sir?"

"Shut up," said the professor's gunman with the white hat.

But the gas man wanted to talk.

Callahan figured an answer to the gent's query would keep the professor's balloonist happy. "Streetlamps here are wax and wicker."

The man laughed with pure glee.

"So the professor's up there?" Callahan pointed.

"He and my associate, Mr. Fitzjohn. That's all the professor wishes to handle this mission. The risk of volatile explosives, you see. The professor and my associate are brave, brave men—all in the name of science."

Fitzjohn. Yes, that was one of the names the professor had mentioned. And the second?

"Yes," Callahan said with not an ounce of conviction. "Brave, brave men. But then, so were you, Mr. Lowrie."

The man turned. "You know me?"

"Just your name," Callahan said, smiling. "And," he added with a lie, "your reputation."

Lowrie beamed with delight. "It's as big as the *Intrepid*." He laughed. "Not my reputation." He pointed at the sky. "Our balloon. The *Intrepid* I helped operate during the late war. For the Union, of course. That wonderful vehicle of the skies could hold thirty-two thousand cubic feet of lifting gas. And this one—which, alas, we have never named—can hold an equal amount."

Callahan whistled like he actually cared.

But that pleased the professor's gentleman balloonist. "Hot air is much safer than the hydrogen gas. Especially considering . . ." He stuck his fingers in his ears as the explosion roared and caused the flames to reflect off his spectacles.

"I see," Callahan said with the echoes of the concussion and the screams of the excited Falstaff populace quieted. He turned and looked at the outline of the balloon, clearer now as the moon, maybe two or three days from being full, began to rise. "How high up are they?"

"A thousand feet, more or less."

"Dropping the dynamite?"

"We cut the fuses so they should detonate at five hundred feet above the ground."

Callahan turned. "And that produces rain?"

The man shrugged. "I am not the rain expert. Mr. Fitzjohn and I work only in balloons and dynamite."

"Shut up," the gunman said again.

Callahan whistled again. He looked at the horses in front of the saloon, and spied a man leaning against the wall, holding what probably was a beer stein in his right hand. "How long will they be up here tonight?"

"Shut up!" The gunman spoke sharper this time.

"Oh, you shut up, Mr. Black," Lowrie said. "We are making history here, and this man is a gentleman."

"A preacher, actually," Callahan said, thinking: *Black wears the white hat. I can remember that name easily.*

"Well," Lowrie told Callahan, "the professor is a man of science, alas, not of religion."

Callahan smiled. *I believe half of that.*

"They have, by my count, thirty more sticks of dynamite," Lowrie went on. "So to answer your question: At the rate of dropping one every two to three minutes, I would say seventy-five minutes at the least, ninety minutes more likely. But ballooning is not an exact science. There are all sorts of things to take into consideration. Why, I remember during the Rebellion when a tether rope snapped and sent a balloon drifting over Confederate lines. It was harrowing, sir, quite harrowing. The rebels took potshots at us—yes, I was in the balloon with Major Matthews. Quite the scare. Quite the scare. Till we drifted back to our lines and came down hard in the middle of the town's square."

The gunman kept telling him to shut up, but the little man was still talking as Callahan walked away and made a beeline to the saloon. He stepped under the saloon's awning as Terry Page lowered his beer.

"Get your horse," Callahan whispered. "And meet me behind Father Pete's church. We don't have much time."

He was glad he had kept Job to walks for most of the journey to the county seat and back, and Job was happy to be running away from the fires and thundering in the darkness. The near-full moon bathed the terrain in light, and the explosions being set off by Professor Hungate and his assistant slowly died. Callahan figured that Terry Page's horse could leave him in the dust, but Vernon Browne's foreman kept the bay just ahead of Job. Page knew the way to the Lamerick ranch quite well.

They made good time, and the cowhand handled the wire trap like a safecracker working a lock. Callahan had thought about trying it himself, but decided he should leave it to an expert on a mission as important as this.

Now they trotted to the house and the big stone barn, and Callahan saw the candle appear behind a window.

When they reached the well, they dismounted. Page handed Callahan the reins to his horse and stepped toward the flickering candle.

"Lorena!" he called out through cupped hands. "It's me." He swallowed, spit, and added, "Your peach dumplin'."

Callahan did not laugh, though he turned his head, smiling, and busied himself tying the horses up short to a post by the well.

"Terry?" Lorena's voice could not mask her shock.

"The circuit rider's with me, Lorena," Page said. "And we don't have much time."

As they walked toward the house, where Lorena waited for them by the front door wearing what looked to be an overcoat to cover her nightgown, Callahan whispered to Page, "You know, son, she might think you have brought a circuit rider for something other than . . . burglary."

"Shut up, Preacher."

"Terry?" the young woman asked in a tentative voice.

This time, Callahan, holding his hat in front of him, did the explaining.

Holding the lantern, Lorena led them into the barn. She would not hear their arguments to stay in her home.

Callahan saw the wagon that had been used to haul in the merchandise, and the mules and horses in their stalls. He had never seen a barn this clean or this big. He certainly had never seen a barn built like a church. The lantern made the shadows dance as they walked to an empty stall.

"How did your father get to town?" Callahan suddenly asked. Farmers usually did not own much in the way of horses or mules, and the stalls they had passed had been full.

"He walked, of course." The girl handed the lantern to Page, and moved to the gate at the last stall. "He'll ride a mule now and then, but not often. It reminds him of . . ." She could not mention her late brother.

Callahan, an old horse soldier, and Page, a cowboy, shook their heads at the thought of a man walking all that way to town when he had horses and mules that could carry him a whole lot quicker. Then Callahan looked down and smiled at Lorena Lamerick's bare feet.

She pulled the latch and started to drag the gate open. Since Page held the lantern, Callahan stepped up and helped. Callahan nodded, and Page walked closer, then the circuit rider held out his hand and took the lantern. He led the way and raised the lantern over his head.

All he saw was hay.

"Here," the girl said, and she walked to the wall of hay and began pulling the feed away.

"Aren't you a gentleman, Terry?" Callahan asked, and the cowboy didn't need any other encouragement, even though, from everything Callahan had heard since first setting foot in Texas, cowboys did not feel right doing any kind of work that could not be done from the back of a horse.

They cleared enough to reveal the first crate.

A curse started from Page's lips before he remembered he was in the presence of a lady. Callahan started forward, but Page held out his left hand. "Not too close with that lantern," the cowhand said.

Callahan stopped. He could read well enough. It was a keg. The top lettering read:

DANGER

Below that:

GUNPOWDER

"How many kegs?" Page asked his girl.

"Ten," she said with a sigh.

Page spun to face Callahan. "What's he gonna do with gunpowder? I figured he'd have rifles or six-shooters."

Callahan said, "He does. Well, he did. I kind of intercepted two crates of Spencer carbines and enough cartridges to win a battle or two."

The cowboy stared at Callahan, who lowered the lantern. "It's a long story."

"Pa don't believe in six-shooters," Lorena said. "He figures they're toys. He wanted Springfields. This fellow told him that repeaters are the future." She moved down a few feet, and began removing more hay. When Page joined her to help, they did not uncover a keg but a box, a box much bigger than the crates of Spencers that Callahan had left in the top of a bend south of town.

Callahan moved forward just a few feet. He didn't think the receipt Lorena Lamerick had shown him could be true, but this time Terry Page could not stop his curse, and he whirled at Callahan, pointing at the pine box.

"A Gatling gun. A Gatling gun! How can he get a Gatling gun?"

"You can buy anything for the right price," Callahan answered. "According to the receipt, which was conveniently labeled Gatling Enterprises Reaper—which I found nowhere in Fletcher's store—from Juarez, Mexico." He found Lorena. "Ammunition."

She pointed to another pile of hay. "Four boxes," she said.

"Gunpowder." Page spit into the hay. "A Gatling gun. And Spencer repeaters. Your old man wants to blow us up, then shoot us down like dogs."

"Well," Callahan said calmly, "your boss is bringing in his own way of killing."

The foreman stared at the preacher in disbelief. "What are you talking about? Mr. Browne, he—"

"Stop fooling yourself." Callahan lowered the lantern and moved out of the stall. "You know exactly what I mean. You just don't want to believe it. Well, believe it. And believe this: We got to get out of here now, so cover that stuff back up. Lorena, you get back to bed. Terry, we're riding out of here before her pa gets home from Falstaff."

Chapter 32

After Taylor Callahan explained everything that had happened and everything he had seen in the county seat and inside the Lamerick stone barn, Father Pedro Sebastià Fernández de Calderón y Borbón sat a long time in the church thinking. In fact, so much time passed, Callahan wondered if the priest would ever speak his mind.

It wasn't exactly a confession. Callahan and the priest sat on the front pews—not in a confessional booth—both of them sipping coffee. That caused Callahan to think back to all his time in churches as a kid. He had never seen anyone in Missouri drinking coffee inside a church. No one ever smoked a cigar or dipped snuff or chewed tobacco in one, either. Nobody drank water, and sometimes, especially if you got a preacher who loved to talk and shout, a sermon could go on for a long, long time in a scorching room. Women had passed out during some of those hottest July or August meetings, and Callahan himself figured he had sweated off a couple of pounds sometimes.

But they drank coffee here. And for some reason,

Father Pete's brew tasted a lot better in the cathedral than it did in his office or in the stable with the mule and Job.

Finally, the priest let out a long breath, and asked, "What is your plan?"

Callahan had to suppress the laugh that wanted to explode out of his throat. Did everyone think he was such a schemer?

"And since you stole the farmer's guns from the hardware store, why not steal the others from his barn?"

This time Callahan answered. "There was no time. I had to drag the guns out of the back of the wagon that young Browne helped me carry. The boy helped some. Tried to, anyhow. But a Gatling gun? And kegs of gunpowder? And ammunition for the Gatling? We would have had to hitch up Lamerick's wagon."

"You have a plan, though?" the priest inquired. "Is that not so?"

Callahan finished his coffee. "Let's just say that I'm working on something."

"Bad times," the priest said.

"Yeah." Callahan changed the subject. "How is your cousin's son?"

The young priest sighed. "I do not know what ails him. It is a new sickness. More of his heart, his soul."

"I'm sorry to hear that. If there's anything I can do . . ." Like Taylor Callahan didn't have enough to worry about right now.

Father Pete let out a long sigh and shook his head. He was about to say something else, when the door to the church was pushed open and a white-headed woman crossed herself, saw the priest, and said something in rapid Spanish, then turned, pointed, and hurried away.

Both men heard the shouts from outside. Both also understood the tone and the sense of trouble. And both were out of the church in a matter of seconds.

They walked past the crowd gathered at the cistern and toward where the big wagon that hauled the balloon the size of the Yankees' *Intrepid,* whatever that was, from way back during the war. The talkative balloon man from the other night was not around, but his partner, Harvey Fitzjohn, if Callahan recollected the name correctly—and he rarely got a name wrong—was backed up against the basket of the balloon, looking this way and that way for help, while a burly farmer kept jabbing a finger as thick as a dynamite stick into the little man's chest.

No wonder Professor Hungate took Fitzjohn up in the balloon. The little runt probably didn't top ninety pounds. The farmer, on the other hand, looked as big as a pregnant cow. And a pregnant cow was why the man looked to be about ready to break the puny balloonist into pieces of kindling.

"My cow abort," the leviathan barked in some European accent. Swedish maybe. Callahan wasn't certain. "You blame. Boom. Boom. Boom. All night. Cow lose calf. Because of you. Boom. Boom. Boom."

Callahan realized he had outpaced Father Pete and reached the scene first. Or maybe the priest, recognizing the size of the farmer, had slowed his gait to something resembling a sloth's crawl.

"Howdy!" Callahan called out, letting a smile crease his beard stubble, and waving like a clown at a circus. "What seems to be the problem?"

The farmer turned, reaching toward Callahan before stopping, frowning, and saying, "Professor. Not you."

"No." Callahan kept his smile, and kept his head tilted as he looked up at the farmer. The man had to be six-foot-nine at the least. "I'm not Professor Hungate."

The balloonist chimed in. "He's blaming the professor and me for his cow losing a calf, Preacher. That isn't our fault."

"No rain!" the farmer thundered.

"Confound it, man," Fitzjohn said, "we just started the experiment last night. These things take time."

"I bet they do," Callahan muttered under his breath.

A donkey hee-hawed, and Callahan watched a couple of Mexicans in dingy cotton clothes and straw sombreros bring two carts filled with wood into the camping site. They began unloading the wood near the pit.

"Y'all going up again today?" Callahan asked.

Fitzjohn nodded.

"Kill more baby cows," the farmer said.

"Listen," the balloonist said, "you don't know what killed that cow. Ask the preacher here. He'll tell you that it was God's will. Ain't that right, Preacher? God picks who dies when and where and how. It has nothing to do with us trying to end this infernal drought. It's up to God."

And, Callahan thought, *if you keep right on talking like this, the Major General in the Heavens might decide that your time has come.*

But the farmer, he noticed, was staring at him, long and hard.

Or is it my time?

"You . . . preacher," the man said, and pointed that dynamite stick of a finger at Callahan's chest.

"Yes," Callahan said, drawing out the word, turning to find the priest now helping the men unload the firewood for tonight's balloon launching and more of the professor's scientific, alleged that is, experiment. "I'm the circuit rider. Just passing through, mind you. That's what we do. Circuit riders. Preach here. Preach there."

He usually wasn't so tongue-tied.

"Why you no preach?" the farmer said.

"What!" Callahan stepped back, mocking his shock, wondering if he could have made a career as a thespian, drifting from town to town, much as he found himself doing these days, acting in plays or reciting poetry in some fancy opera house. "You haven't heard me preach? You didn't come to hear me at the saloon the other night?"

You, he thought, *and all but a handful of others*.

He looked at the saloon, decided against that, then swung around, pointing at the crossing.

"C'mon, folks!" he cried out, and started marching toward the dried-up bed of a river. He sang:

Shall we gather at the river?
Where bright angel feet have trod . . .

When he started the chorus, the big farmer joined in. And other voices, including one he recognized by the nasal tone of the balloonist, Fitzjohn.

Yes, we'll gather at the river
The beautiful, the beautiful river . . .

When he turned around, he stopped, and had to suck in a deep breath. Half the town, it appeared, had followed him to this dry bed of stone and sand—and a sign—a weather-beaten board that had been used for target practice, but on which one could still read. One in Spanish. And the other:

Danger
Do Not Cross
When Flooded

He saw Father Pete and the two wood-haulers and smiled, but that vanished when one of the saloon loafers, a rider for Vernon Browne's outfit, called out, "Where's your river, parson?"

"I'm standing knee-deep in it," Callahan said, turned to study the high-walled far bank. "Nope," he corrected as he turned back to the crowd. "More like chest-high."

The cowboy spit and laughed.

"You think I'm joking?" Callahan asked. "I didn't put this sign up." He raised his eyes and studied the old warning. The wood had to be older than the joke that stood closer to Falstaff proper. The paint on this old relic hadn't been refreshed in ages. Maybe for good reason. Maybe . . .

He glanced down the riverbed, before it turned, stalling, as he usually did when he had no prepared sermon, no list of songs to launch in to, not knowing exactly what he wanted to say. So he said:

"And maybe I am. But . . ."

He stopped, and for half a minute looked into the faces of the men, young and old, and children. Children had followed him, too, and these likely had not been dragged by the parents. But he wasn't thinking about the people who came to hear him preach. He was thinking about what he had seen above the banks of the river. He was thinking that either he had just seen his first mirage or his mind had been burned to a crisp by the sun, the heat, the events the other day in Jubilee. He wet his lips and slowly looked upstream at the pale blue sky.

A few people looked that way, too.

For the longest while, there was no sound. The wind had stopped blowing. The donkey had ceased making its racket. People might have been talking in town, those who had not come to hear a stranger give a sermon or just lead a bunch of struggling people in prayers and songs, but if they were, no one heard them down here.

It was a child who spoke the first words, a young girl, Callahan believed.

"Is that," she asked, "a cloud?"

The four horsemen stopped their horses in front of the telegraph office in the South Texas town of Verdun. Boss Harris said, "Digger, you keep an eye on the marshal's office. Everett, you ride over to that trough in front of the dance hall. Let him drink and if something happens, you cover us with your Winchester. Baby brother . . ." He turned and spit. "You fetch the telegram."

"Why me?"

"Because you're the cripple. You can't help us shoot our way out of this flea trap if trouble breaks out."

Everett was already riding off toward the dance hall when Johnnie Harris slid out of the saddle. His right hand, still bandaged, still hurt like blazes.

"Remember," Boss Harris called out. "It's under the name Oliver Twist."

"Didn't you think that alias would arouse suspicion?"

Johnnie said. On this day, like many others, he loathed being a Harris brother.

"Like anyone here reads," his brother said.

"Who's Oliver Twist?" Digger asked.

"See what I mean," Boss said, and Johnnie stepped inside the building by the railroad tracks.

He told the elderly clerk what he wanted, and the old man said. "Are you Mr. Twist?"

"I wouldn't ask for his telegram if I wasn't," Johnnie said.

"No offence," the old-timer said and he hobbled back to a bunch of cubby holes. "I just don't know you."

"'Cause I don't live here. Just passin' through."

"Here it is," the man said, and fished out the yellow piece of paper. "Oliver Twist. That name sounds like I ought to know it."

"The Twist ranch," Johnnie lied. "Up on the Brazos."

"Oh. Well, I know the name of the man who sent this to you, Mr. Twist." His head bobbed and he shuffled his feet at the pace of a snail. "Yes, a big rancher like you would certainly know a man like Vernon Browne."

Johnnie took the paper and tossed the old man a coin. He stepped outside and raised the paper to his oldest brother.

"Just read it to me," Boss said. "Then tear it up and toss it in that trash can at the corner."

Bending his head and bringing back the telegram, Johnnie sighed, read it twice, and looked up. "All it says is 'Terms agreeable.' And it's signed 'V.W. Browne, owner, B Cross Ranch.'"

"Let me see it." Sighing, Johnnie handed the telegram

back for his brother to inspect. That took a couple of seconds, and then the paper was handed back. "Now do like I told you. Tear it up. Throw it in the trash. And let's get out of this town." He backed his horse up, waved at Everett, and put his spurs to his mount before Johnnie reached the trash can.

"What's the job?" Digger asked when they stopped under a shade tree to cool off.

"Range war," Boss said with a smile.

"How much do it pay?" asked Everett, after he fished a bottle out of his saddlebag and removed the cork.

"Fifteen hundred," Boss answered, and held out his hand for the whiskey. "Gold and silver coin. No more of that paper money and these kinds of jobs."

"What are you talkin' 'bout?" Johnnie asked.

"Last bank we robbed was paper money," Digger said. "From the bank. Which wasn't no good no more. That paper money, I mean."

"Least, not after we robbed it," Everett said and happily accepted the bottle back from his older brother.

"But"—Johnnie's head shook—"I thought we were tracking down that preacher who—"

"Crippled you?" Boss turned to spit. "Yeah. That's what we're doin', you dunderhead. But didn't robbin' that bank up in Bonham teach you nothin'?"

Johnnie knew better than to answer.

"People get mad as the devil when someone takes their hard-earned money. You get sheriffs and bounty hunters and Texas Rangers and marshals and even detective agents chasin' after you. Hirin' out your guns . . . that's where the real money is."

Johnnie waited for the whiskey bottle to reach him, but it went from Everett to Digger and then back to Boss, who finished it and sent the empty bottle sailing into the sand.

"Are we givin' up the hunt for the preacher?" Johnnie asked.

"Of course, we ain't," Boss said. "But this is how we get paid. That preacher has been hard to find. We don't get a job that pays, we'd have to find honest work."

"Hey," Digger said, "range war . . . that's honest. Ain't it?"

"Don't matter," Everett said. "Fifteen hundred bucks in gold and silver."

"That'll pay our way to kill that cripplin' preacher," Boss said.

"Where's this ranch?" Digger asked.

Boss pointed. "Somewhere between this town called False Hope and Jubilee. We got some ridin' to do."

"Jubilee?" Everett whistled. "Hope it ain't too close to that burgh. There's a Texas Ranger who has set up shop, and he ain't nobody I want to tangle with."

"Then he best stay out of our way." Boss kicked his horse into a trot. Digger followed in behind him. Everett tugged down the brim of his hat and looked at Johnnie. "You comin'?" he asked and kicked his horse.

Reluctantly, Johnnie Harris let his mount trail his brothers.

"It was a fine sermon," Father Pete said as he refreshed Callahan's water in the priest's vestibule.

They weren't eating the young padre's cooking on this evening. The wife of the part-time barber had brought over posole; another fine, upstanding lady provided the tortillas; and there were beans, vinegar pie, and even wine that was not meant for communion, plus stewed carrots and an onion. A feast, for sure, even if the posole was hot enough to make Callahan's nose run.

"You think so?" Callahan wiped his face with a cloth napkin, also provided by one of Falstaff's finest.

"Sí. But it is not just I who think this. You must have shaken hands until your hand and elbow hurt."

Callahan laid the handkerchief aside and looked at his hand, grinned, and found the spoon to go at the posole again. No matter how hot it was, it was filling and tasted great.

When they finished and pushed away from the table, the priest reached inside his robe and withdrew a sheet of paper. "I have written this," he said, and slid the paper toward Callahan. "Salvador Blanco promises to take it to the newspaper editor in Jubilee. It says what all is happening, with your arrival, and, of course, the hopes for rain, the first sighting of the cloud, the glory of God, and the excitement."

Callahan wiped his fingers on the napkin and picked up the paper.

"Nothing about Gatling guns, kegs of gunpowder, stolen shipments of Spencer carbines and cartridges?" he asked.

"No, no, no," the young man said. "Of course not. That is not for . . . that . . . well, we pray it will work itself out so that no one ever needs to know that it almost happened."

"Amen," Callahan said and started to read, but stopped quickly.

"Is something wrong?" Father Pedro Sebastià Fernández de Calderón y Borbón said in fear. "Did I . . . ?"

"No, no," Callahan said. "It just struck me that I haven't heard any dynamite exploding."

"Ah." Father Pete's head bobbed a few times. "The man whose name is Fitzjohn says that the professor said no boom-boom tonight." He grinned. "I am sure the farmer whose cow lost its baby is pleased."

"I'm sure," Callahan said softly.

The priest looked at the closed door, too, and scratched his head. "I wonder why," he said softly and looked back at the circuit rider. "One would think that after having a cloud appear, though far from where we live, and moving in the opposite direction from us, but, still, with one night of . . ." He struggled to remember the phrase.

"Producing rainfall by concussion," Callahan said.

"Sí. *Gracias*. One would think they would want to . . . continue . . . after such a . . . good sign?" It was a question.

"One would think," Callahan answered.

"But we are not scientists."

"Neither are they." Callahan picked up the paper and continued to read.

The priest asked something in Spanish, but stopped and remained quiet.

"Two l's in Callahan," Callahan said and grinned. "Not that it matters."

"What?" the priest asked.

Callahan found a pencil and made the correction, and Father Pete rose from his chair and looked at the change.

"Ah. *Lo siento.* I am sorry."

"It's all right," Callahan assured him. "I don't rightly think I could come close to spelling Father Pedro Sebastià Fernández de Calderón y Borbón."

Now, the priest laughed.

"I suppose names have been spelled wrong many, many times. One might mistake one man's name for another's." He squinted. "Or . . . well . . ."

Callahan slid the paper back to the priest. "It's a fine article, Pete," he said. "Maybe it will get printed." He started to stand, stopped, and took back the paper. "If you don't mind, Padre, I'll look this over again."

"*Por favor.*" Father Pete's head bobbed with glee.

"Señor Majanor says he will take it to Jubilee in the morning. Please, make any corrections. Add anything you wish. Señor Majanor is stopping by in the morning. Around breakfast?" The last was a question.

"I'll be there." Callahan smiled. "Well, since there will be no dynamite exploding in the night, I ought to see how much sleep I can get."

The youngster nodded. "I should do the same!" he sang out with delight.

They shook hands, and Callahan hurried to the stable, found his reorganized saddlebags, opened the right one, and pulled out the list of Texas fugitives that Shakespeare had given him in Jubilee.

He remembered the Texas Ranger captain's words.

You're also trusting that . . . this De Russy is the same fellow as your professor . . . that the lawmen that arrested him spelled his name right . . . that he doesn't use just one alias.

Chapter 33

The circuit rider was surprised to find the balloon of Carlin De Russy, also known as, at least in Falstaff and Justice County, Texas, Professor Jessup Hungate, about to launch.

Walking from the stable to the front of the whitewashed adobe church, he saw the golden hair of the professor's wig flapping in the wind, and one of the associates, Fitzjohn or Lowrie, climbing into the basket, then taking a box of what had to be dynamite from one of the professor's two gunmen. The professor was chatting to the rancher, Browne, and the mayor and the land agent.

Señor Majanor rode over on his mule, and Callahan turned his attention from the field, and walked toward the approaching farmer. He reached inside his Prince Albert and withdrew the letters as the white-mustached Mexican reined to a stop.

"This," he said, holding out the first letter, "is for the newspaper. The one the padre told you about."

The old man nodded, so he must have understood English. That was a relief. "And this," he said, waving the second envelope, "goes to Captain Rufus Lincoln of the Texas Rangers in Jubilee."

The man's face tightened. *"¿Guardabosques?"* Majanor's voice was guarded. *"Asesinos."* Callahan recognized neither word, but he could read the hesitancy in the farmer's face.

"It's important," he said. "Very important." He reached inside his pants pocket for some money, but Majanor held up his hand and shook his head.

"No," he said, shaking his head firmly, and extending the callused hand for the two letters. "It will be done, amigo."

"Gracias," Callahan said, feeling the weight of Falstaff lifted off his shoulders, but thinking, *Now, if only Shakespeare isn't off chasing some cattle rustlers, isn't too lazy, or doesn't have something more meaningful to do.*

Those odds did not favor Callahan, so he was already developing alternative plans.

After the farmer stuck the letters in a pouch that hung over his shoulder, he looked at the sky. "A change," he said, "is coming."

"I sure hope so," Callahan said.

The old man smiled wearily and said, "Clouds." He turned back to Callahan and said, "I will see you when I return."

"Gracias," Callahan told him, but his attention was focused on the clouds. They weren't dark, not even gray, but they were big, and might block out the sun when it rose a wee bit higher.

"Vaya con Dios," the old man said, but Callahan remained focused on the clouds, and he did not realize what

Majanor had said until the rider was turning down the road and heading for the county seat.

That was almost as far as he got. The rider jerked hard on the reins, and got himself and his mule out of the way as several riders galloped down the road. Even Callahan had to use his hat to wave away the thick dust as the riders loped to the field and the balloon. When the dust cleared, Callahan saw that one of the riders was Vernon Browne.

Callahan was halfway to the cistern when he heard Father Pete call his name.

Turning toward the church, he gave up on trying to find out the rainmakers' plans for the day. The balloon was already rising with the balloonist and the professor in the basket, and Callahan figured what he could expect. A lot of deafening explosions that would rattle the few glass windows in Falstaff, probably upset a number of struggling farmers, and put Job and the priest's burro in foul moods. He noticed two tethers to the balloon on this day, perhaps because of the wind.

"Good morning," Callahan said when he reached the front of the church, but the priest's face said he was not thinking that today was so good. It was pretty early, Callahan thought, to be giving up on another day when you're healthy enough to be standing on your own two legs.

"Something the matter?" Callahan asked.

The priest was staring at the rising balloon. He sighed and looked at the circuit rider. Yep, Callahan figured, something was worrying this young gent, and not just the thought of more aborted cows and a few dozen explosions that will make it so that nobody could think straight.

"Oh." Father Pedro Sebastià Fernández de Calderón y

Borbón remembered that Callahan was here and that he had called for the preacher. "Pardon me." His eyes lifted again. "They are at this again, I see."

"Yep. If the farmers had some cotton, we could stick some in our ears. Won't drown out the noise, but it could deaden it a mite." The priest looked back at Callahan. "I handed your letter off to Señor Majanor. You just missed him."

"Señor Majanor. Oh, yes. *Gracias*. Thank you. I had forgotten."

Callahan pushed back the brim of his hat. "Something troubling you, Pedro?"

The young priest let out a sign, then jerked his head toward the inside, a signal. Callahan removed his Stetson and followed Father Pete inside. After closing the door behind them, Callahan walked past the lighted candles and the beautiful paintings, through the rear door and into the priest's living quarters. Callahan made himself smile when he smelled the coffee, and saw the priest finding the pot and filling two cups.

"I promised you breakfast, but I have been lazy this morning," Father Pete said. "Just coffee."

They sat, and drank for a few minutes in silence.

"How is your coffee?" Father Pete asked.

Callahan smiled and smacked his lips. "Just like always."

"Bueno." The man's head bobbed. "Good. Very good."

"That's what I'd call this coffee, Pete. Very good." The Major General in the Heavens would forgive him for this kind of lie.

"Lo siento," Father Pete said as he put his cup, hardly

touched, on the table. "My mind is distracted today. It is Juanito."

"Juanito?" Callahan said, holding his cup of wretched coffee.

"Sí. He is the son of my cousin."

"Right." Callahan managed to finish the coffee, and put the cup on the table. "Is he bad sick? You should have sent for a doctor in Jubilee. We could take—"

"He is sick, it is true," the priest interrupted, "but it is not a sickness like those doctors treat. That is what I believe. True, he will not eat. But also he will not talk to anyone. It is something in his soul."

"How old is the lad?"

"Twelve."

"Pretty young to be that kind of sick," Callahan said.

Father Pete just stared at the cluttered desk. "Sí," he said, nodding.

Callahan figured where the priest wanted to take this conversation, so he leaned forward, smiling, and tried to head things off. "You know, Pedro, one thing I've learned is that when something is ailing someone, particularly children, here." He tapped his heart. "Well, it can be easier for them to talk to a stranger than someone in their family." He realized he might need some help from that Major General in the Heavens, and quickly sang out, "Does Juanito speak English?"

"Sí." Father Pete's head nodded. "Yes. Most of our young children speak English. It is a shame that most of the other young children do not learn the language of Mexico."

Callahan smiled. "It's a right pretty language, that's for certain." He thought about asking the priest what *Vaya con*

Dios meant, but this didn't seem to be the appropriate time and place. "Well, if it's fine with you and your cousin, I'd be happy to have a palaver with little Juanito. Not that he'll say nothin', or not that I'll make him feel any better, but I'll sure give her a whirl."

Father Pete looked a million times better.

He wiped his boots and removed his hat before following Father Pete into the house. A *jacal,* the Mexicans called it, and Taylor Callahan had seen poverty in his years, but this? This seemed to be a whole lot worse than poor.

Until he saw the priest's cousin.

She bounced a dark-headed, dark-eyed infant on her side as she closed the door behind the two men and spoke in musical, rapid Spanish, her eyes beaming. And that little girl she held? Well, Callahan couldn't think of a prettier baby he had seen in years. And the mama, Father Pete's cousin, had to be an angel. The most beautiful woman he had seen in years. Yeah, the floors were dirt, there was only one room that housed the kitchen and the bedroom, but the place looked immaculate. Crucifixes and retablos decorated the walls, every candle had been lighted, and the woman kissed her cousin's cheek, bowed at Callahan, and handed the baby to Father Pete while she rushed toward the fireplace and pulled away a coffeepot.

"She asks if you would like some coffee," Father Pete translated. "I told her that, of course, you would." He made a funny face and noise at the baby, who fixed her eyes on Taylor Callahan.

"It is much better than my weak attempts," the priest added.

Callahan found the bedroll where Juanito had rolled over to face the dirt wall.

The coffee was hot. Callahan took the stoneware mug, thanked her, then sipped the brew. *Oh, yeah, thank you Major General and bless this angel. This is what coffee is supposed to taste like.*

The woman seemed upset and turned and spoke again in rapid, but musical Spanish, to her cousin, who kept bouncing the baby girl, and looked at Callahan.

"She begs your forgiveness, but she did not ask you if you would like milk, sugar, or honey in your coffee," Father Pete translated.

"Black is fine," Callahan said, bowing at the woman and turning back to Juanito.

"Then we shall go," Father Pete said. "My cousin wishes to show me how her onions are doing in the garden."

Callahan nodded, barely hearing, and slid his hat on a chair.

The way Father Pete had briefly explained on the walk over to Arroyo Verde, Juanito's father had gotten a job as a muleskinner for some freighting outfit that had passed through on the way from somewhere in New Mexico Territory to San Antonio. They never saw him again, but a letter came from the outfitter that said Juanito's pa had been taken with a fever and died. He had sent extra pay, the man's crucifix and some letters he had written, and the location of the church cemetery in a town called Rancho Blanco about twenty miles southwest of San Antone.

"How you doin', Juanito?" Callahan said as he sat on the hearth and sipped his coffee.

The boy rolled over, facing the bedroll of his mother and the crib of his sister.

Callahan stretched out his legs and crossed them at the ankles. They had left the door open, and that brought a breeze through the small dirt house, but Callahan saw the big rifle that hung over the doorway now and the Major General in the Heavens opened up his mind.

"So you went huntin' the other day, eh?" He drank more coffee, put the cup aside, and rose, crossing to the door, raising his arms, and lifting the rifle off the wooden pegs, and hefting it as he turned around.

"Ol' Betsy here must weigh more than you do, Juanito." He butted the stock on the ground and rubbed the barrel. "But you keep her clean."

"Put it back," the boy snapped, then bowed his head and whispered, *"por favor."*

Callahan nodded, and started to raise the rifle back, stopped, studied it again, and said, "Smoothbore. Haven't seen one of these in years." He returned the rifle to the wooden pegs. "What's that? Fifty-eight caliber?"

"Fifty," the boy said and rolled back to face the wall.

"Yeah. I figured. You had to be tired taking that huntin' the other day, I'd reckon. Five miles walkin'. There and back. Maybe even more than five miles. Six. But I'd say seven feels about right. Wouldn't you?"

The boy pulled the fine blanket over his head, and Callahan sat again on the hearth.

"My first rifle was a squirrel gun," he said and found the coffee cup. "One of my daddies give it to me, but he weren't no hand with a long gun or nothin' heavier than a full jug. Which he'd make lighter quicker than a hawk can grab a blind bunny rabbit. I remember when I went out huntin', probably younger than you be now, and I heard a squawkin' behind this bush, and I just shouldered that fine walnut stock, and hardly took aim at that bush afore I touched the trigger.

"And then come the most horrible screechin' I ever heard. And an ol' tomcat come dartin' right past me with only half his tail left. Scared me out of a year's growth, it did. It was our tomcat, too. A good mouser he was. Kept him in the barn. And I knowed that pappy I had for the time bein' would be madder than a hornet, and that be a long mile or two that I walked home. I guarantee you that."

He took another sip of coffee, and wondered if Pedro's cousin could teach him how it ought to be done.

"You know what happened, though?"

To his surprise, the boy rolled over. He didn't say yes or no, or ask to hear the rest of the story, but Callahan figured the kid at least had some interest in this stranger's story.

"The pappy—he'd be Number Four, if my recollections be right—he was tellin' my mama that Rex—that's what he called the cat—must've tangled with a wildcat or somethin' and lost part of his tail. Then he seen me and asked, 'You kill us any supper?' And I said, 'No, sir.' And he said, 'Well, go get some supper. Fried squirrel is what I want on my plate this evenin'.' And I walked away, right proud of myself, because no one knowed what I had done."

He finished the coffee, shook his head, and said, "We didn't have no fried squirrel for supper. I didn't shoot any. And truth be told, I couldn't have et a single bite—and fried squirrel, the way my Mama cooked 'em up, that was some good eatin'. I was just like you. Sick and grievin' and worryin'. Worryin' has got to be the worst kind of grievin' a boy, even a man, can do. It's a sickness like none other. Just wears you down to nothin'. Worryin' . . . and feelin' guilty. Know what I mean, Juanito?"

Tears streamed down the boy's cheeks or at least the cheek Callahan could see.

"Want to know what made me feel better?" He did not wait for an answer. "My mama. Pa was out plowin', and I crawled out of bed, come down from the loft—that's something that you ain't never seen, I reckon, but that don't matter. Truth be told, I'd prefer to have lived in a house like this—filled with love and religion, not bacon grease and forty-rod, skeeters an' ticks."

He finished the coffee, nodded at Juanito, and said, "I went to Mama. She was beatin' the dickens out of a rug. And I said, 'Ma, I gots to speak at you.' And she says, ''Bout time, boy.' So I told her that I'd shot off Rex's tail. Tweren't no coon or wildcat or nothin' like that."

"And she says to me, 'Know what you're shootin' at, Taylor, before you even put yer finger on a trigger.'" Callahan's head shook at the memory. "Best advice I ever got." He smiled down at the boy, who was showing both cheeks now, both of them stained by tears, and Callahan said. "I asked my mama if I ought to go tell that pa I had for the time, and she said, 'No need,' he knowed when the cat come runnin' in from the woods. We even heard the shot. He just wondered how long it would be till the guilt got you to confess.'"

Callahan laughed. "That ol' pa of mine was something, that particular pa, I mean. Sometimes I even wish we coulda kept'm."

He set the mug on the hearth and leaned forward. "You didn't kill nobody, Juanito."

"How . . . do you know?"

"I come along afterward. Found him. You hit him. But just in the ankle. You seen that cowboy that rides for Vernon Browne in town? Nah, I reckon you ain't seen nothin', bein' sick and all. Well, Tommy Browne's all right. The horse that you spooked, I reckon he's back home, too. Now, the boy got hurt, ain't no walkin' 'round that, but accidents happen. Especially with a young feller like you holdin' a gun I'd need a big fat walnut to brace 'er again' afore I'd squeeze that trigger."

"I thought it was a buffalo," Juanito said.

Callahan smiled. "I reckon I can see how that might happen. I bet you didn't bring no water with you, neither."

The kid's head shook.

"Thirsty, that's what you was. And I bet you didn't have much for breakfast, neither."

"I left before my mother awakened."

"Best time to hunt." Callahan's head bobbed. "Feelin' better now?"

The head shook.

"That's what I figured. It'll take time."

"I should confess to *mí padre*." The boy looked so solemn.

"Father Pedro?" Callahan asked, hoping the kid would confirm that, but knowing Arroyo Verde also had a priest.

"Sí. Yes. He is cousin to my mother."

"And a mighty good man and a real fine priest." Callahan nodded. "But you need to tell you mama what happened, too. There ain't no cure till that gets done. And then, after the confession to Father Pete, comes the hardest part."

Chapter 34

Callahan picked at his teeth with a toothpick, sitting on edge of the cistern, watching the clouds, some of them dark, and the balloon. He saw the sparkles of a lighted fuse as the stick of dynamite dropped from the basket, and he put hands over both ears a second before the explosion.

The water rippled, mules brayed, horses stomped their hooves, and a few men cursed.

"That's it!" called the balloonist in the Yankee shell jacket. "Bring them down." The pair of gunmen, one wearing a black hat and the other a white Stetson, and some strong locals began pulling on the tethers.

"Wait!" someone shouted. "Don't stop now. For the love of God, it's raining!"

Callahan shook his head, and removed his hat. Then, he felt it, too.

Sliding off the earthen mound, he looked up. Something wet hit his cheeks. *It's just water from the cistern,* he told himself. *The dynamite explosion had sent some water and . . .*

He was staring at the dust-covered water in the cistern, and saw the droplets. Small.

"It is raining!" someone else yelled.

"Glory be!"

And just like that, the rain stopped.

"I told you it ain't rainin', you dumb—"

"I swear I felt some drops."

"You're loco."

"I think I felt some, too."

"Listen . . ."

Another noise pulled Callahan's ears away from the scattered conversations and the balloon being lowered, and he turned and walked back to the Catholic church, where Father Pete, Juanito, and his mother, still carrying that cute, and quiet, baby girl emerged.

He stopped a few feet from the entrance. "How'd it go?" he asked.

The mother dabbed her eyes with a handkerchief. *"Gracias,"* she told Callahan.

"We owe you more than we could ever repay," Father Pete said.

"Balderdash," Callahan said and pointed at Juanito. "It was all his doings. He's gonna be a fine young man." He turned back, held out his hands, hoping to catch another drop.

"They stop their rainmaking?" Father Pete asked.

"Looks that way." He saw Vernon Browne mounting his horse and riding toward the saloon. Slowly, Callahan turned around. "Juanito, you ready for this?"

The boy was staring at the rancher and his cowboys, too.

"Yes," the twelve-year-old said. "I should have done this days ago."

"Juanito?" his mother asked.

The boy turned, spoke in rapid Spanish, words that made Father Pete step back, then walked straight, his back a ramrod, toward the saloon. Callahan smiled and followed.

"It ain't even noon yet," Callahan called out as Vernon Browne tethered his horse to the hitch rail in front of the saloon and began unfastening one of his saddle bags. "Now I don't condemn a man for drinkin', but when he starts chasin' his breakfast with whiskey . . ."

The rancher stepped away from the horse. Some of his riders—Callahan remembered those whose eyes he had blackened and teeth he had knocked loose—stepped off the boardwalk and moved on either side of their boss. Terry Page wasn't with them.

"Don't preach at me, Taylor."

"Callahan," the circuit rider corrected with a smile. "We ain't on a first-name basis yet, Mr. Browne."

"And we ain't likely to be, Callahan. Mind your own affairs."

"The boy has something to tell you, Browne." Callahan dropped the twang. "I expect you to listen to him till he's done."

The rancher saw Juanito, who stopped a few feet in front of the big man.

"He ain't heeled, Tatum," Callahan called out, returning to that Missouri accent, and staring hard at one of Browne's cowhands. "So why don't you take your hand off that handle."

It wasn't a question.

There was another interruption as a few townsmen ran

over to report feeling some raindrops. Faces lifted to the sky. And then the balloon man, Fitzjohn, ran over and said that they had felt some rain, too. Not much.

"Just a tease," Professor Hungate said, twirling a pencil in his fingers like some magic act. "A sample of what's to come."

"Rainclouds are often a tease, Professor," Browne said, but kept his eyes on Juanito and the preacher. "I ain't payin' for a mere sprinkle."

"And you shan't," the *faux* professor said. "Yes, I feel a change in the weather already. Today was a good day. Now, aren't we going to rinse out our throats with some of your fabulous varnish?"

"Speak your mind, boy," the rancher snapped at Juanito.

Callahan bit his lip. This could go well or it could turn right ugly in a hurry.

And that Colt .45 he had taken in Nathan was stuck in the saddlebag in the stable behind Father Pete's church. So he looked at the sky, where the clouds had moved southwest, and began a little prayer to the Major General in the Heavens.

Lorena Lamerick stared out the kitchen window as her hands kneaded the dough for biscuits. She could never make them as flaky as her mother could, but she kept trying. The clouds were something new, and some of them were dark. Not black. Not purple. But a bit of a gray, but that was enough of a change from the past weeks, months, even years, to stare at.

* * *

To wonder. And pray. Then the door slammed open, startling her, and Logan Lamerick stormed in, his face flushed—but not from the heat or the wind.

"Who come inside barn?" he shouted.

Heart pounding, she busied wiping her hands on the apron. She never should have shown that preacher and Terry the explosives. She tried to figure out what mistake she had made, how her father could have known she had let someone inside, had even led them directly to the gunpowder and, worse, the Gatling gun.

"Papa," she said, as he came through the house like some angry bull, "I didn't—"

Lorena never saw his right hand. One moment she was trying to think of a way to lie to her father, and the next she was down on the stone floor—skinning both palms to break her fall—staring at the blurry stones for a moment, then seeing the blood drops splatter between her hands. Above and behind her, Logan Lamerick called her all sorts of names.

She imagined the blood as rain. *Wasn't that what happened at Cana? Water turned into wine? Couldn't a miracle turn blood into rain?*

Those powerful hands grabbed her shoulders and Lorena was jerked to her feet and shoved against the cabinets.

"Who?" her father raged, but this time she saw the fist.

He swung over her but she felt the whoosh of the wind and the liquor on his breath as she ducked. The momentum carried him to the floor where she had fallen, and now it was Lorena who towered over her father. When he tried to stand, she shouted, "No!"

To her surprise, he sank back onto the stones he had

laid in, one by one, while Lorena, Ryan, and their mother had marveled at his thoroughness.

"You . . ." he said, "would not dare . . ."

She realized why he sat there. She held the rolling pin over her head. And she knew she would use it if he came at her again. Logan Lamerick knew it, too.

"You've turned mad as a hydrophoby dog," she said. "That rancher, he ain't to blame for Ryan's death. Or Ma's. And remember what Ma told you that time in San Isabel? When you and Uncle Sean had been drinking? You got mad. You hit her. Remember?"

He just blinked.

"She told you that if you ever done that again, she'd leave you."

"I never . . ." he managed to say.

"That's right. You never hit her again. And you ain't never gonna lay a hand on me, either. Because I'm not gonna give you the chance!"

She spun around, grabbed a bonnet, and walked out the door. Past the well. Past the graves of her mother and brother. She just walked toward False Hope. Yes, that name sure fit not just the town but this whole blasted country. Her father called her name from the doorway, but she did not answer. She just kept walking. A mile from the farm, she realized she still carried the rolling pin. She dropped it, too.

She would walk all the way back to San Isabel, she thought. No matter how long it took. She was good at walking. And not having any shoes would not be a problem. And Terry Page? Well, well . . . well, she'd send word to him once she got settled in San Isabel.

* * *

He watched her go. She'd come back, Logan Lamerick thought. "She has no shoes," he said, nodding, knowing that would force her to return, especially once she hit the caliche.

She has no shoes, he heard his late wife's voice tell him, *because you never bought her any.*

"Let her go!" he yelled at his mule, and moved angrily back to the barn, kicking at the chickens, heading to the stall that held the kegs of gunpowder and the box containing the Gatling gun. He kept a chicken feather on the latch. That was his security measure. If the chicken feather wasn't on the latch, someone had come inside. And the only person who knew where his cache was hidden was Lorena. But now, as he saw the chickens scurrying about, he realized that a chicken could have knocked the feather down. Or a mouse. A rat. Maybe just a breeze. But it did not matter. He moved into the stall, moved past the places where he had hidden the gunpowder and that fast-shooting gun that he did not know how to operate. He had not even opened the crate. He moved to the edge of the stall, and found the jug. He pulled out the stopper, sank into the hay, and drank.

"Lo siento," the boy said, hanging his head down. "I am sorry for what I have done."

Vernon Browne looked down at his hands, saw the fists clenched so hard that both hands looked to be white, trembling just below the hips, bouncing against his chaps.

"My boy could be crippled on account of you!" he shouted, and he turned around. He couldn't stand to look at the boy any longer, and saw some of his men. One word, and he could have the boy dragged around this pathetic little village. That'd teach anyone to go around and shoot a Browne, accident or not.

"If Tommy turns up crippled," he heard the preacher say in a deliberate tone, "you might share the blame. He ought to be in bed, not sent off to Jubilee to bring back all that silver and gold."

Browne spun around.

"You could at least have sent a couple of men to help Tommy," the man in black said. "It's not an easy ride to Jubilee and back."

"Don't you go preaching at me, Callahan."

"I haven't even started on you."

Browne made the mistake of looking into the circuit rider's eyes. Quickly, he looked past him, and drew in a deep breath as that beautiful Mexican woman, the young woman, carrying that daughter of hers, came up behind the Mexican waif who had shot Tommy—with a .50-caliber rifle—and the beautiful lass put her free arm on the Mexican boy's shoulder.

It took several seconds before Vernon Browne could get his mouth and vocal cords to work.

"Señora Iglesias." He swept the hat from his head.

"Señor Browne," she said, and smiled at him. She spoke again in rapid Spanish.

"She asks if everything is all right now between you and her son," the Mexican priest translated. "She knows he did wrong, and Juanito knows he did wrong, and she thanks all the angels who looked after your son, and thanks the Blessed Mother for sending this saint"—he pointed at the circuit rider—"to look after your son, and us all."

Browne wet his lips.

The preacher named Callahan shook his head and said, "I don't reckon I've reached sainthood, and it ain't likely that I ever will. But thank you, ma'am, for the sentiment. *Gracias*."

Another voice to Browne's left said, "Gold *and* silver?"

Browne turned to find that professor twirling one of his golden locks with a finger. The man smiled. "I don't believe I specified gold or silver, just a thousand dollars. Cash money. Script is fine. Just no checks." He smiled. "Checks . . . well . . . the ink could smear from all the rain I'll bring."

"Ya jus' give us a drizzle so fer," called a man from the saloon.

"I had to . . ." Browne looked back at Mrs. Iglesias. What a handsome woman. So kind and generous. She had a way of making him forget all about his wife, dead these past dozen years. "There was another agreement I made for another man. He demanded gold or silver. Just seemed easier to pay y'all both that way. Well, I also thought you might have . . . similar . . ." He lost his train of thought. Mrs. Iglesias did that to him all the time. One reason he never cared much for coming into False Hope. And, at the same time, the reason he always talked himself into coming to this wretched little place. She was so beautiful. He had even drifted into Arroyo Verde often, making sure he passed by her town, when heading to find a cook or a *caballero* or to buy some tequila.

"Well," said the professor, "our work is done for the

day, but we will be back here early in the morning. The rains are coming, ladies and gentlemen. We had a good round today. Now, I would like to retire to your lovely hacienda, sir. Come."

The two gunmen followed the professor to the buggy, and Browne looked again at the boy who had shot his son.

"Watch where you aim, son," he said. "Guns are dangerous."

"I would like to apologize to your son," the boy said. "Face to face. He might want to hit me, or even shoot me in my leg. But whatever he—"

Browne waved him off. "Tommy's the forgivin' kind. Takes after his mother. Maybe . . ." He stared at beautiful Mrs. Iglesias. "Well, I reckon I could learn from him. But I'll tell him what you said."

He kept his eyes on the boy's mother and bowed, "Ma'am, it is always a pleasure to see you."

"Y tu," she whispered and curtseyed.

When he spun around, he managed to get about five steps before that blowhard of a circuit rider called out his name. Browne stopped and turned around. He thought about making Callahan speak to his back, but decided against that. Turning around would give him another chance to look at the widow Iglesias.

"You got need for a new louse?" the preacher asked, and put his hand on Juanito's other shoulder. "Kid's a good worker and . . ."

His head tilted toward the boy's mother and baby sister.

"We ain't had nothin' but bad luck with louses of late," Browne said, letting his eyes find Juanito's mother.

"Luck changes," the circuit rider said.

Browne made himself look at the boy. "Come see me

this fall," he told Juanito. "When we start roundin' up and brandin' calves. If you can work for Ol' Cookie, you can work for anyone. This fall. Not before. If Ol' Cookie says you're worth your weight, we'll give you another job durin' the spring roundup. Then, maybe, on the drive to Kansas."

He whirled again and realized he was following his men to the saloon. Then he stopped and barked, "It ain't Saturday, by my way of figurin', and the day ain't hardly over. We got work to do. If you want to get paid for this month. And it ain't quite yet payday."

He moved for his horse. The cowboys followed him and kept their complaints to themselves.

Callahan spent the rest of the day feeling right proud of himself, and thanking that old Major General in the Heavens for being less Old Testament than he could get sometimes.

He even gave Job and the burro extra hay and grain before he wandered away from his comfortable quarters in the stable to see if anything was happening in town.

The land office was closed. The mayor's office did not appear to be open, either, and nary a horse, donkey or mule was tethered in front of the saloon. Callahan glanced at the sky but saw no clouds, and he walked slowly, humming one of his fifth pa's favorite hymns, to the cistern. Once again, he blew off the dust, stuck a cupped right hand in the water, and brought it up, feeling the coolness cleanse his lips and wash the dust from the stables off his tongue and down his throat. He used the remnants to soothe the back of his neck.

Then he saw the commotion at the crossing at the dry river.

It had gotten the attention of the two balloon flyers, Lowrie and Fitzjohn, who made a beeline to the crossing. The church door opened and out raced another Mexican—Callahan recalled seeing him in front of the blacksmith's shop in Arroyo Verde—and Father Pete followed him. Neither one was moving slowly, and this had turned out to be another blistering afternoon.

Callahan dismissed the thought of taking another drink of water, wiped his mouth, and walked after Father Pete, but they were running now, and Callahan wasn't running in his boots.

When he reached the river crossing, he saw another white-haired man in tan britches and a calico shirt, pointing at the empty expanse of dirt between the road and the low river bank. The man was pointing and shouting, but none of those words meant anything to Callahan. The two balloonists stood several yards back, probably fearing the man might be insane.

Finally, the old man fell to his knees and began scooping sand with his hands, shoveling the grains toward the river.

The mayor appeared.

"What is this all about?" Wallace Scurry demanded.

"Ladislao says we are in danger," Father Pete explained. "He asks what happened to the sandbags?"

"Sandbags?" Mayor Scurry asked. "He must be loco."

Callahan recalled the remnants of a canvas sack he had found here and his conversation with Terry Page.

"There were sacks of sand here many years ago," Father Pete explained.

"For what?" the balloonist named Fitzjohn said, the words coming out more like a laugh or snort.

Tears falling down his cheeks, the old man kept shoveling with his hands.

Another Mexican said something in Spanish. Father Pete answered him in the same language and told the mayor, "It has not flooded in years, but . . ."

The mayor cut him off. "It hasn't *seen* water in years."

Suddenly, a feeling struck Callahan, a feeling that that old Major General in the Heavens might have been generous today, but there was always another day coming.

He walked into the middle of the dry bed and looked upstream.

"Boys," he said as he turned and saw that warning sign.

PELIGRO

NO CRUZAR

INUNDADO

DANGER

DO NOT CROSS

WHEN FLOODED

"It surely would please me to learn that one of y'all has been buildin' an ark."

Chapter 35

Every man there, except the old gent shoveling sand, hurried to stand beside Callahan. The cloud was big, far in the distance, more black than blue, but some of that could be credited to the sinking sun. It was hard to tell just how big the cloud was, because a wall of a dark, demonic blue stretched from the cloud to the earth.

"Glory be," said Lowrie. "The professor—he's done it."

"That cloud's miles and miles from here, you idiots," the mayor said.

"Sí," said another Mexican. "It rains there. Not here. That professor—he give them rain. Not us."

Callahan turned to look at the crossing and how low the ground was all the way into Falstaff. "It may be raining over thataway, but that water's gonna be on us."

"Man, are you that daft?" the mayor shouted.

"No, no, no!" Father Pete called out. "He is right." He pointed at Callahan, then at the man still shoveling sand. "And he is right. Ask any of those who have been here for many, many years." He turned back and looked at the dismal village and his church. "That is why there were sandbags here. That is why this sign was put up. When this river floods, it floods with a vengeance."

The sun was sinking. And Callahan wondered if Falstaff would survive to see the sun rise again.

"Where do you think you're going?" Terry Page asked.

Tommy Browne had finished hitching a sorrel to the buckboard's harness. He worked pretty good for a kid leaning on crutches in the dark.

"To town." The boy made the last adjustments then limped on his crutch to the wagon.

"Your pa know?"

"He's asleep."

"Tommy . . ."

The boy whirled. "I got a right to go to town, don't I? Get drunk if I've a mind to. You gonna try to stop me?"

Page decided this was one fight he didn't want. Not tonight. It had been a long day, it was already dark, he was tired, and he hoped Ol' Cookie had left him some supper.

"Suit yourself," he said, and headed back to the bunkhouse.

Barefooted, Carlin De Russy crept down the hallway, past the bedroom where Vernon Browne snored logs, past the empty bedroom of the rancher's son—who had been forced to sleep in the bunkhouse where that mangy cook could tend to his bad leg—and put his hands on the doorknob. He turned it ever so quietly and then slipped into Browne's library. Only then did De Russy strike a match and light a wall lamp. Even with the door closed, he could still hear Vernon Browne's snores. Maybe that was another reason his son had taken to the bunkhouse.

Not to mention the fact that Vermin Browne was one despicable hard rock.

Pulling the stethoscope from his jacket pocket, De Russy made his way to the safe, there in plain view, and went to work. Over the years he had learned that conning greedy men out of money had its moments, and it gave him the chance to show off his thespian talents, but robbery got a man richer. He found the dial, and listened through the stethoscope as his long fingers worked their magic.

Why would any fool use dynamite to blow up a safe? Or rob a bank in the middle of the day at gunpoint? This was so much safer, relaxing, quiet, and very enjoyable. Just like pretending to be a scientist. And this safe was practically a toy.

He removed the stethoscope and pulled the handle. Vermin Browne kept snoring, and the safe's door barely squeaked as De Russy pulled it open.

The jingling of the bags sounded like a San Francisco symphony as he carried two toward the open window. The heat wave was a blessing. People kept their windows open all the time.

"Mr. Black," he called out in a whisper, and the gunman in the white hat stepped out of the shadows. De Russy handed him the money.

"Heavy," Mr. Black said.

"Yes."

"What does this do to our plans?" the gunman asked.

"The plan remains the same. We load the money into

the balloon. The wind will still carry us to the coast, near Corpus. We land. Catch the first schooner for Mexico."

"Even that big balloon can't carry us all. Not with gold and silver. I thought we were getting script."

"A change of plans, but still workable." De Russy held up his empty hands to silence any further protest. "There's script, too." He had to subdue the laughter rising in his throat. "We're a day before payday, so he has greenbacks for his men. We'll be taking that, too. And more gold than just our thousand dollars."

"Maybe we ought to just carry the script," the idiot suggested.

"Not as greedy as I am," De Russy said. He cut off any further argument. "We must hurry. Put these in the wagon. Then come back for the rest."

He watched Mr. Black carry the gold to Mr. White, standing by the iron wagon, then moved back to the safe. He'd tell them about the change in plans when they were in False Hope, tell them that the balloon could only carry him, the pilot, be it Mr. Lowrie or Mr. Fitzjohn, but they would still meet in Corpus Christi. He'd even give them some gold or greenbacks and send them on their way. Of course, an iron wagon would be easy for a posse to follow. But a balloon? Once out of sight, a balloon was mighty hard to track. And they would be flying out before daybreak. Even better, De Russy knew that the wind happened to be blowing toward Brownsville, not Corpus. Mexico was just a hop and a skip from Brownsville. And you didn't need a schooner to get there.

* * *

Torches lined the river bed and all across Falstaff. Callahan barked at the men carrying the backbar from the saloon toward the crossing. When he was certain they could get it to the river, he turned and yelled at Father Pedro.

"Are you sure Arroyo Verde is safe?"

"The floodwaters, I am told, have never reached that far," the priest said as he hurried Falstaff's less reputable female residents down the path that led to the Mexican village.

"Well, get them out of Arroyo Verde, too. As high as you can get," Callahan shouted. "We're not taking any chances. And make sure the men bring anything with them. Anything heavy and solid that we can use for a dam. And shovels and sacks. Feed sacks. Saddlebags. Anything."

The moon was rising. That would be a help. The fire in the field where the balloonists had made camp was beginning to roar. He swung into the saddle and urged Job to the fire, stopping a few yards from the flames, and found Mr. Lowrie.

"How soon can you get that thing up?" Callahan shouted.

"An hour," the man called back without ceasing his work. "Maybe two." Now he turned around. "Will that be enough time?"

Callahan shrugged. "I sure hope so."

The old-timer who had been shoveling sand had said it could take hours for the floodwaters to travel that distance, but it all depended on how hard the rain fell and how much water the ground could hold. Maybe dawn. Maybe afterward. Maybe a whole lot sooner.

"Just get it up as fast as you can and keep a lookout."

Lowrie went back to work, but his partner yelled, "That moon's gonna be a blessing! It'll shine like the sun."

A buckboard sped into town, the driver having a hard time stopping it in front of the saloon. Callahan almost let a few choice oaths slip past his tongue. Tommy Browne. But at least the kid was alone.

"We're gonna need a lot more than a blessed moon," Callahan said underneath his breath.

Lorena Lamerick stopped walking. Her feet hurt, and they'd never hurt before no matter how far she walked. Her lungs burned, too, and the night felt oddly cool. Nights did not cool down much at this time of year. Then she turned and saw the flash of lightning, way off in the distance. There were no stars in that direction. Just here and behind her, where clouds rarely appeared.

Another flash cracked the sky, and she remembered what her father had taught her. Start counting till you hear thunder, then divide by five. That number equals how many miles away the storm is.

She started counting, then quit.

"You've never run away from any storm," she said. "And what could you do in San Isabel?"

She thought of her father, realized he had never completely recovered from the deaths of Ryan and their mother. He was a good man. Deep down. And a good father. She couldn't hate him. Couldn't leave him. And she knew he wouldn't make the mistake of striking her again. So Lorena turned around and started walking back for home. She wouldn't use the road. The caliche was too sharp and painful. She'd find her way over the plains. The rising moon would light her way.

The sight of that balloon lifting above the church steeple startled Logan Lamerick and the mule he rode, so much that he had to swung off the bare back and grab a tight hold onto the hackamore. A lesser man would have given up, but mules could not match any Lamerick when it came to stubborn.

He pulled the beast behind him and stopped before he reached the cistern.

There was the preacher, barking at some men in a wagon. "Take lanterns with you. You know where the river bends, about a mile, mile and a half? There's a patch of prickly pear and a dead yucca. And . . ."

"That sounds like where we planted that cattle rustler we lynched six years back," said one of the men.

"That's right. Edge of the river bluff. You'll find two crates of Spencer repeaters and several boxes of cartridges. Load 'em quick as you can, and get 'em back here. Pronto."

Logan Lamerick forgot about everything. He dropped the hackamore and charged toward that black-clad preacher. "You!" he screamed. "You steal my guns! You drive Lorena away."

He raised his fist, then found himself sitting on his backside, blood pouring down his nose. His eyes seemed blurry, and the moon wasn't that bright, but he saw the man in black standing above him.

"I don't have any time for your nonsense, Lamerick!"

the preacher railed. "Those guns are going to be used to make us a dam. Because there's about to come a flood here you haven't seen in years. And if we don't have something to stop all that water, there won't be anything left of Falstaff, no False Hope. Nothing left. And maybe nothing left of Arroyo Verde either. So either you help or get out of my sight."

Lamerick looked around. Men and even women were at the crossing, working like ants, like farmers. Indeed, some of the Mexican farmers from Arroyo Verde were carrying boxes, bags. Others shoveled the sandy banks toward piles and piles of . . . everything.

Then he heard thunder.

And he knew that the circuit rider was right. That Lorena had been right. Even that Ryan had done the right thing.

"Reverend!" he yelled.

The man in black spun around, half expecting a fight. Lamerick pointed to Milton Clarke's land office.

"Take sledgehammers and chisels to that building!" Lamerick stood. "That is how you build dams. With stones. Not sacks."

Callahan turned and found some hearty-looking lads. "You heard the man," he said, pointing. "Get to it."

Lamerick continued. "Give me a wagon and four strong men. I will bring you back kegs, heavy kegs, boxes of cartridges. And a crate big enough to hold a . . . reaper."

Callahan turned. "Tommy!" he yelled. "We need your buckboard!"

The boy on crutches stopped and handed the sack of potatoes to the old priest from Arroyo Verde.

"Whatever you need, Preacher," the kid said. "But I'm drivin'."

Vernon Browne's eyes shot open, and he reached for the Smith & Wesson self-cocker under his pillow.

"It's me," the voice said.

The intruder had turned up the lamp, and that's the only reason Browne didn't blow his fool head off. Even though he recognized Terry Page, he still felt like shooting him. Just singeing his sideburns or maybe creasing his thigh.

"You better have a real good reason for waking me up at this hour, Page. What time is it?"

He didn't lower the hammer.

"Tommy left this evening," Page said. "For False Hope. He hasn't returned."

"Well, if he ain't back by daylight, he don't get today's wage or yesterday's when we pay off the men Saturday. That fool . . ."

"That professor and his two gunnies are gone, too. Took their iron wagon."

Now Browne really felt like shooting his foreman and not just creasing him.

"He said they was gonna fly up early this morn. Get that rain to comin'."

"Yes, sir. But Monty was visiting the privy and seen one of them walking from behind the house to the barn."

Browne held his tongue.

"Put something in that fancy wagon, then went back behind the house. Come back with something heavy, heading back to that crazy wagon."

Browne didn't put away the Smith & Wesson, but he

threw off the covers, not bothering to find his slippers, and headed out the door, down the hall, and into his library. Nothing looked amiss, though the lamp was turned up higher than he liked it. The safe looked fine, but he knelt anyway, worked the combination, and pulled the lever.

Then cut loose with every profane word he could recall at this time of night.

Tommy Browne pulled hard on the leather to slow the wagon down. The folks tearing apart the land agent's office had done a right fair job in the time it took him to get to that farmer's barn and back. The moon was high now, and between it and the torches and that bonfire in the field, False Hope was lighted up like noon. He let two Mexicans hauling a big log past, then clucked his tongue, flicked the reins, and brought the wagon to the edge of the crossing.

The mayor barked orders, and some men stopped what they had been doing and hurried to the buckboard. That big, mean old farmer was already down, carrying a keg of gunpowder. A burly Mexican and a strong teenage boy leaped out of the back of the wagon, the boy working on the knots on the lariats that had secured the crates and barrels. He recognized the smithy from Arroyo Verde leading five other men, Mexican and white, to the wagon. They grabbed the crate that held the Gatling gun. Tommy started to climb down to help, but the circuit rider stopped him.

"Don't get down," the preacher said, and pointed at the cistern. "I want you to park this rig there. Let the animals drink, but not too much. Then you just sit right where you are. And wait."

"Wait!" Tommy bellowed. "I can help as much—"

"You can help by staying right on that seat and with this rig." The man in black stepped aside to let some other men carry kegs to the makeshift dam. Then he pointed at the balloon. "Pretty soon." He stopped, stepped back, cupped his hands and yelled up at the balloonists. "How does it look?"

One of the aeronauts leaned over the edge of the basket and shouted, "No sign in the river beds! But that lightning! It's coming this way! And we can smell rain in the air!"

Tommy looked upstream. He couldn't see any stars in that direction, and not just because of the moon's brightness.

The circuit rider turned back to Tommy. "Tommy," he said. "Those gents up there are going to give us a warning. And when they do, people will be running for their lives." He jabbed a hand at the dam in progress. "'Cause there's a good chance that ain't gonna hold. You were born here. You know this country. And you can handle a team and a wagon. Every man jack of us will pile into the back of this wagon and then you're gonna giddyap and get out of here to the highest, safest place you can find. Savvy?"

Tommy nodded.

A cloud hid part of the moon.

No, Carlin De Russy realized, that wasn't a cloud. He almost stood in the driver's box on the iron wagon, pointed, and yelled, "What the devil is our balloon doing up there?"

"They're gettin' away!" Mr. Black said.

"From whom? And for what reason?" De Russy was so mad he almost threw one of the stolen double eagles at the rump of the closest Cleveland Bay.

Mr. White found the whip and urged the team to False Hope.

They rolled into town a few minutes later, and Mr. White had to use the brake and the reins to keep from trampling people, running toward the river crossing. Then he saw the crippled son of the rancher. "There!" he barked, and Mr. White steered the wagon toward the cistern.

Mr. Black yelled at the crippled cowpoke: "What in blazes is going on here?"

"There's been a frog strangler upstream," the boy said. "We're tryin' to put up a dam. If not, this whole village might be washed away."

"The dickens you say," the professor said.

"It's the gospel." The Browne kid pointed toward the balloon. "Your fellas is keepin' an eye out."

"Can't they come down?"

"Not on your life. Our lives!"

"Mr. White, get us out of here," De Russy said and felt the iron wagon crawl through men and women moving like ants, carrying rocks, boxes, bags instead of food.

He told himself that this plan would still work. They would get past the river bed. The Cleveland Bays would be strong enough to carry even the heavy wagon and its heavy load to the coast. He just needed to figure out how to get rid of Mr. Black and Mr. White so he could have all the money himself.

He almost relaxed.

Then he saw that little Mexican priest pointing from the sign that welcomed people to . . . *six inches from hell.*

"That wagon!" the priest yelled. "That iron wagon! That is what we need!"

By the time Taylor Callahan reached the wagon, the slaughter was complete. The professor, Hungate, De Russy, whatever his name was, had lost his wig and most of his dignity. The two gunmen, Mr. White and Mr. Black, were unconscious; their six-shooters had been thrown onto the pile that was a dam.

Father Pete was in the driver's seat, struggling to release the brake. "This can be part of our dam."

"Not at the dam." Callahan pointed. "See that narrow spot? Where the water's gonna come churning through? This contraption is just long enough to block most of it. Let's pray it's heavy enough to slow the rushing waters down a bit. So that when it hits the far bank, it might not bounce as far and as high and wipe out our . . . dam."

"It will be done." The priest flicked the reins, and Callahan stepped back and stared at the unconscious men.

He found the mayor and the land agent running by, worn out, but still game.

"Gents," he said, pointing at the gunmen. "Throw these boys into the back of Tommy Browne's wagon. They're useless to us for the time being." He looked at De Russy. "But you ain't."

"You don't know what you're doing," the confidence man and sneak thief said. "You don't know what's in my . . . my . . . my . . ."

Man looked like he was going to cry when Callahan jerked him to his feet.

"Bub. You go spell Perez from that shovel. And you start shovelin' sand onto our dam as fast as you can. Iffen you don't, I'm throwin' you over that barricade when your boys up there give us the warnin'."

One of Father Pete's altar boys helped the professor to the river crossing, and Callahan chased after the iron wagon.

He didn't know what all the professor was hauling in that contraption, but it sure weighed a ton. It took ten men to get the wagon turned on its side while Father Pete led the team away.

"Think it will work, Padre?" a voice asked.

Callahan tried to catch his breath, then turned to find the speaker was young Juanito. He started to bark, tell the boy to get out of here and up to higher ground.

That's when Mr. Lowrie yelled from the balloon: "It's coming. Heaven help us, it's coming!"

And Fitzjohn added: "Looks like a tidal wave!"

Chapter 36

If the Major General in the Heavens granted him an extremely long life, by Taylor Callahan's ciphering, he still wouldn't be able to sort out everything that happened till Judgment Day.

He was running in what certainly couldn't be called an organized retreat. The roar of the rushing water drowned out all the screams. Knowing they'd never reach high ground in time, most of the people were headed straight for Father Pete's church. Callahan carried Juanito. He headed that way, too, realizing his errors.

Had the balloon been higher, maybe the aeronauts could have seen the floodwaters earlier.

Abandoning the town and leaving its fate to higher powers also seemed a wiser course of action.

Somebody might have mentioned to me how fast water traveled.

Nobody ran for Tommy Browne's buckboard, and then the youngster whipped the team, and rolled away from the cistern. But not out of town. The fool kid was driving straight toward the river.

That's when Callahan tripped. Juanito went into the

dirt. Callahan pushed himself up and barked at the boy, "The church, boy! The church! That's your only chance!"

He rolled over and saw the water hit. Water sprayed over the crate marked Gatling Enterprises Reaper, which crashed to the ground, and a wall of black, ugly water came toward him while more water flowed down the river bed, rumbling like a tornado. The whole ground trembled. Then he saw Tommy Browne at the edge of the river bank, yelling.

That fool kid!

Callahan jumped to his feet.

That's when he saw Lorena Lamerick—clear as day in the brightness of the moon—standing on the high banks opposite Falstaff.

Till the ground gave way, and the girl was gone.

The next thing Callahan could recall was running past the balloonists' fire—toward the flood, not away from it—the earth trembling beneath his feet.

Standing in the back of the buckboard, Tommy Browne whirled a lariat that had been used to hold the materials from the dam. A horseman thundered past him. Then another. One reined up beside the buckboard. The rider jumped down, as his horse took off racing past Callahan and out of sight. The other rider began shaking out a loop as his horse galloped downstream where the raging water already rose above the banks and began covering caliche and prickly pear.

Callahan started toward them, not knowing why, or what he could do. He hardly comprehended everything that was happening. Until he tripped and fell flat on his face. He was trying to push himself up when the water hit him.

He expected to drown. Instead, he breathed air. And watched the water rolling back, toward the river.

When Callahan rose, he found that water reached all the way to the cistern, but no more than ankle deep, and now it was rushing back to join the roaring current that thundered down the bed. Men and women stood where the land office once was, by the church, on the trail to Arroyo Verde. A few began crossing themselves. Most just stood like pale statues, stunned into muteness.

Remembering the girl and Tommy Browne, Callahan spun around and ran with the receding water toward the empty buckboard.

"Tommy!" Vernon Browne yelled. "Tommy! Terry!"

That's when the moonlight vanished, and the world went black.

"What happened?" Callahan asked the rancher.

"I don't know."

He could barely see the rancher for only the torches lighted Falstaff now. The floodwaters had put out the fire for the balloon. He couldn't hear the sizzling coals because of the roaring from the riverbed. He could barely understand Vernon Browne.

"I saw my son roping something in that . . . that . . . that . . . !" The rancher appeared to be blubbering as he pointed a trembling hand toward the raging blackness that was a river. "And then he was gone." He clasped his hands.

Callahan understood, or thought he had. The girl had fallen with the crumbling earth into the rushing water. Tommy had lassoed her. How? Well, that's a question that could only be answered by the Major General in the Sky.

But the wild current had taken Tommy into the maelstrom. Callahan knew from floods back in Missouri that the chances of finding either body was well less than slim.

"Mr. Browne!"

Did he really hear that?

Tommy's father didn't appear to. He just sank into the water and started to cry.

"Mr. Browne!"

That wasn't his imagination. Turning, Callahan thought he was hallucinating. A vague shadow became clearer, and Callahan started praying. It was Terry Page, afoot. Behind him came Page's horse. When the apparitions were close enough to the flames from the torches, Callahan stared in awe.

Holding onto the horn, limping on the mount's right, was Tommy Browne. In the saddle, clothes drenched but looking angelic, sat Lorena Lamerick.

"Mr. Browne," Callahan whispered. When the rancher raised his head, Callahan pointed. "You got a couple fair hands with a lasso."

"To tell the truth," Terry Page told him as they stood on the damp boardwalk in front of the saloon, "I ain't sure I know exactly what happened myself."

Somehow, the current splashed Tommy onto the Falstaff bank, where the riverbed turned. All Page had to do was jump off his horse, run knee-deep into the water that had spilled out from the bed, grab that rope that somehow still held Lorena, keep from being drowned himself, and pull the girl to safety.

"Is that all?" Callahan asked, watching Mr. Browne

whip off his hat and talk to Juanito's mother by the cistern. All the while keeping his arm around Tommy Browne's shoulder, bragging about the champion roper in Justice County.

"Well," the foreman said, watching Lorena's pa practically crush his daughter to death with those stonemason arms. The big Irishman was bawling like a newborn sheep. "I got lucky."

"Maybe," Callahan said. "And maybe that's the reason you didn't die in that stampede. Maybe somebody knew you'd be needed for something. Something like what happened tonight."

He walked away as a lone rider drifted into town, feeling the rain on his hat, on his whole body. "Or," he called back without turning around. "Maybe you're just lucky." He stopped to stare at Lorena. Then he looked back. "Some men have all the luck, boy."

Laughing, enjoying the rain as dawn began to break, he walked up to a man he recognized.

"Captain Rufus Lincoln," he said, "I see you got my letter."

"You better hope you're right," Shakespeare told him. "I don't like riding at night in the rain."

"I thought you'd get here sooner."

"Had to catch a horse thief. Found your letter on my desk." He stared down with unfriendly eyes. "I'm waiting."

Callahan pointed at the professor, and the still unconscious gunmen. "That's Carlin De Russy, alias Jessup Hungate, the bad men wanted for just a pittance. But as Carl Russo, Tarrant County, he robbed two banks in one night. And in Galveston, there's a ship company that has put up a fifteen-hundred-dollar reward for his capture.

And, if what the professor told me is gospel, he stole a wagon used by some gold mine in New Mexico. But the reward was for the return of the wagon." He looked toward the river crossing and shook his head. "And that ain't likely to happen in the near future."

"I see." The Texas Ranger slid from his saddle, handed the reins to Milton Clarke, and walked toward De Russy, pulling a wanted poster from out of his slicker, and standing over the short-haired, trembling man. "My, my, my, this looks like a good day to be a Texas Ranger. Raining— a good steady, morning rain—and money for my retirement." He turned back to Callahan.

"How much you want?"

Callahan gestured at the whitewashed church. "Make a generous tithe."

He thought about breaking out into a song, secular or hymn, he wasn't sure. But then one of the Arroyo Verde boys came running from the river crossing, saying something in Spanish, something that Father Pete translated as, "Four men are on the other side of the river! They want to know how they can come to our village."

Chapter 37

He was saddling Job, listening to the music of raindrops dancing on the roof, when Shakespeare walked in, opened the saddlebag, and dropped in a handful of greenbacks and coin. Callahan finished cinching and stepped back as the Ranger opened the other bag and added some .45-caliber shells.

When Shakespeare turned around, he said, "For balance."

Callahan nodded. "You sure those boys were the Harris brothers?" he asked.

"Well, there definitely was a resemblance. Especially since one had a bandaged gun hand. Now, it's hard to see with the rain and all, and I couldn't get closer because of how far the water is from the usual riverbank." His lips turned upward in a slight smile. "And they were out of range for a six-shooter."

He pushed back his hat. "But they sounded quite disturbed to ascertain that no crossing can be reached for miles. And with it raining like this, the closest chance is the bridge at Valle Blanco."

"Which means?"

Shakespeare shrugged. "Three days? But if the bridge is washed out, that should buy you a day and a half more, maybe two full days." The Ranger captain shook his head. "The way the clouds are coming, the trail you leave might be long washed away before those boys get back up here."

He paused, and the face turned serious.

"This Harris family, they might be Texans, but they have the same code as we had in Missouri, Taylor. Blood feud. You hurt one, they come after you. You remember what that's like."

"That's why I'm ridin' out. No sense gettin' anybody here hurt on my account." Forcing a grin, he asked, "You don't want to tackle them?"

Shakespeare snorted. "Not alone. Now if you were to join the Rangers . . ."

Feeling a mite better, Callahan held out his hand. "I'm finished with that life."

"Young Johnnie's gun hand tells me otherwise. Not to mention some busted lips and noses and black eyes I've spotted in False Hope."

"Falstaff," Callahan corrected. "That bullet-riddled sign is one thing that got washed away that ain't nobody here's ever gonna miss."

Father Pedro Sebastià Fernández de Calderón y Borbón stopped as Taylor Callahan led Job out of the stall. Behind the circuit rider stood the Texas Ranger from Jubilee.

"You leave?" the priest asked. "In the rain?"

"Well . . ." The man in black used that drawl that had a way of soothing a man, even after a violent flood and near disaster. "Father Pedro Sebastià Fernández de Calderón y Borbón, you fine and noble servant, a circuit rider is like a thespian, I've come to learn. You leave to cheers. Or smiles. With folks wishin' you coulda given 'em another hour or two. Don't overstay your welcome, I gots to keep tellin' myself." He winked. "Besides, my work here is done. I leave the rest in solid hands."

He held out his hand, and the priest shook it.

"Don't look so forlorn, Father Pete." Callahan made a circle in the air with his right pointer finger. "Circuit rider . . . Circular. It's a path. August leaves, but August comes back. Just ain't no tellin', and only the Major General in the Heavens knows if and when, but there's always a chance I'll be ridin' back this way sometime. Sure hope to enjoy some of yer fine coffee when I do, Padre."

The priest grinned. "Until then," he said and bowed slightly.

Callahan swung into the saddle. "Keep the faith, Pete. And don't take no wooden nickels for the offerin'."

"Vaya con Dios," the priest told him.

The Reverend Taylor Callahan turned quickly, his eyes flashing with curiosity and a thirst for knowledge. "Padre, pardon my ignorance, but what does that saying mean in English?" The drawl had been replaced by the voice of an educated man.

"By the saints," the priest said. "I thought everyone knew the meaning of *Vaya con Dios.*"

"You ain't met too many ignorant ruffians from Missouri," Callahan said, again using that strange accent.

His smile widened, and so did the priest's.

"It means, 'Go with God.'"

Raindrops rolled off the brim of Callahan's hat. Extending his hand for another shake, he said softly, *"Siempre, mi amigo. Siempre."*

Clucking his tongue and flicking the reins, he rode past the church, turned right, and began whistling as the gentle rain continued to fall.

"Señor Capitán," the priest asked a moment later. "What is that Padre Callahan whistles?"

Already heading toward his horse and prisoners, Captain Rufus Lincoln did not stop walking, but just laughed before calling back:

"It isn't a song you'll hear in most churches. But he's not like most preachers."

THE END

Chapter 1

"Hey, Buck! Buck West! Is that you, you old hoss thief?" The loud, boisterous voice made Smoke Jensen come to a halt on the boardwalk. It had been a good while since he'd heard the name Buck West. When he stopped using it, he had figured he'd probably never hear it again.

But now here it was, coming from the mouth of the tall, rawboned man striding along the boardwalk toward him. The man's ugly face was wreathed in a grin. He wore a duster over canvas trousers, suspenders, and a flannel shirt. The brim of his battered old hat was turned up in front.

A holstered Colt swung on the man's right hip. Another revolver was stuck in his waistband on the left side. He had a lean, wolfish look about him that came from riding a lot of dark, lonely trails. Hoot-owl trails, some called them. Folks had started using the word "owlhoot" to describe the men who rode such trails.

Smoke had to search his memory for the name of the man who had just hailed him using that old alias. Sutcliffe, he recalled after a moment. Sort of a distinguished name for a gunman and outlaw. His nickname, Rowdy, fit him better. Smoke didn't think he had ever heard the man's real first name.

"Hello, Rowdy," he said, willing to be friendly as long as he could. "What brings you here?"

"Why, the same thing as you, I expect, Buck," replied Sutcliffe as he came to a stop and hooked his thumbs in his gun belt. "I heard that a fella name of Franklin was hirin' guns, so I come to sign on with him. This here is the town of Fontana, ain't it?"

That took Smoke by surprise. He frowned slightly and said, "You're a little behind the times. Tilden Franklin has been dead for almost a year. This is Big Rock. There's not much left of Fontana. It's fixing to dry up and blow away . . . like the memory of all the trouble that happened there."

Rowdy Sutcliffe cocked his head to the side and gave Smoke a quizzical stare.

"Franklin's dead?" he said. "Are you sure about that?"

"Pretty sure," Smoke said. He didn't add that he had been the one to hammer three slugs into the chest of the treacherous would-be emperor of this valley.

Sutcliffe peered at him for a moment longer, then shook his head.

"Well, dadgum it. Seems like I'm always late to the party. Don't know why I didn't hear about that. O' course, I was down in old Meh-hee-co for a while, takin' my ease with the señoritas, so I weren't really payin' that much attention to what was goin' on up here in Colorado." Sutcliffe sighed. "I reckon I'm plumb outta luck." Then he brightened and went on, "Unless you got wind o' some other work for the likes o' you and me. Shoot, Buck West wouldn't be here unless hell was about to pop!"

"Sorry, Rowdy. I don't use the name Buck West anymore, and there's no gun work to be had around here. Big Rock has grown some since the railroad arrived, but it's still small enough to be pretty peaceful."

"Wait." A frown creased Sutcliffe's forehead. "Your name *ain't* Buck West?"

"That's right. That's just what I called myself for a while."

Back in the days when he had been riding the hoot-owl trails himself, searching for the men he had set out to kill. Men responsible for the deaths of several people he had loved . . .

"Then . . . what *is* your name?"

"It's Jensen. Kirby Jensen. Most folks call me Smoke."

Sutcliffe's eyes widened. "Smoke Jensen," he repeated. "Dang. I've heard that name, all right. Fella's supposed to be the fastest draw on the whole frontier. The fightin'est son of a gun anybody ever saw." He let out a low whistle. "And now, come to find out, Smoke Jensen is none other than my old pard Buck West. What do you know about that?"

Smoke shook his head and said, "We were never pards, Rowdy. We were just in the same places as the same times, every now and then."

Sutcliffe squinted now, instead of staring, as he said, "Well, that's an unfriendly sort o' thing to say. If I weren't such a forgivin' fella, I might take offense at it. Could be you're puttin' on airs, since you're really the high-an'-mighty Smoke Jensen."

"Never claimed to be high-and-mighty," Smoke replied with a shake of his head. "Just another hombre trying to make his way in life."

"Looks like you've done all right for yourself," Sutcliffe said, sneering a little.

Smoke wasn't sure what the gunman meant by that. He certainly wasn't wearing fancy duds or anything like that, just common range clothes and a dark brown, curled-brim hat that had seen better days perched on his ash-blond hair. His boots still had a little mud clinging to them. The gun belt strapped around his waist and the walnut-butted Colt that rode in the attached holster were well cared for but strictly functional.

He looked like what he was these days, a hardworking, moderately successful rancher with a small but growing spread. He and his friend Pearlie Fontaine did most of the work around the place, with Smoke's wife, Sally, pitching in when she needed to. She was learning to ride a horse and use a lariat as well as most men.

Lately, there had been enough work to do that Smoke had hired a couple of extra hands, which had prompted Pearlie to start referring to himself as the foreman. The Sugarloaf—the name Smoke had given to the ranch—was still far from being the equal of some of the massive outfits in other parts of the state. Maybe it would grow to that point someday. Smoke hoped so.

One thing he knew for sure was that he never wanted to return to the bloody, dangerous, lone wolf days of his existence as "Buck West" . . . and Rowdy Sutcliffe was a living, breathing reminder of those days, standing right in front of him.

"It was good seeing you again, Rowdy," he said as he started to turn away. That was stretching the truth considerable-like, but he wanted to end this conversation as smoothly and efficiently as he could.

"Hold on a minute," Sutcliffe said as he raised his left hand slightly.

Smoke stopped, every muscle taut.

"Least you can do is let me buy you a drink," Sutcliffe went on. "For old times' sake."

Smoke hesitated, then nodded. What harm could that do? Maybe once he'd had a drink with Sutcliffe, the gunman would decide there was no reason for him to remain in Big Rock and would move along.

"Sure," he said. "Come on down the street with me to Longmont's. It's the best saloon in town."

"Longmont's," repeated Sutcliffe as he fell in step alongside Smoke. "That wouldn't have anything to do with Louis Longmont, would it?"

"Louis owns the place," Smoke said. "Are you acquainted with him?"

"Nope, just heard tell of him. He's supposed to be mighty slick with a gun and a deck of cards, both." Sutcliffe glanced around Big Rock's main street. "What's he doin' in a little wide place in the trail like this?"

Smoke thought the town had grown enough that it was more than a wide place in the trail, but he didn't waste the time or energy to argue that point. Instead he said, "Louis has put that part of his life behind him, just like I have."

Sutcliffe clucked his tongue and shook his head. "Smoke Jensen and Louis Longmont, both settlin' down. Never thought I'd see the day."

"Living like we used to can only have one end, Rowdy, and it's not a good one."

"I hope you ain't sayin' I ought to hang up my guns!" Sutcliffe let out a bray of laughter. "That ain't gonna happen. I'll take my chances and keep on livin' like I want to."

"That's your choice," Smoke said solemnly.

"Damn right it is."

A slight air of tension remained between them as they entered Louis Longmont's establishment. Louis had told Smoke that eventually he intended to make the place as much a restaurant as it was a saloon, since he appreciated superb cooking as much as he did fine wine, a beautiful woman, a good card game, and a perfectly balanced gun. For now, however, it catered primarily to men's thirst for beer and whiskey.

Louis stood at the far end of the bar, a glass of bourbon on the hardwood in front of him and smoke curling from the thin black cigar in his mouth. He took the cheroot from his lips and used them to give Smoke a smile of welcome.

"Good afternoon, Smoke," the gambler said. "What brings you to town today?"

"Sally and I came in to pick up some supplies," Smoke replied. "She's over at the mercantile and doesn't really need my help right now, so I thought I'd stop by and say hello."

"I'm glad you did." Coolly, Louis appraised Rowdy Sutcliffe. "Who's your friend?"

Smoke didn't correct Louis's incorrect assumption that Sutcliffe was his friend. He said, "This is Rowdy Sutcliffe."

"You probably heard of me," Sutcliffe said with a confidence that bordered on arrogance.

Louis was about to inform Sutcliffe that he had no idea who he was, Smoke could tell. Before that could happen, Smoke went on, "Rowdy and I met up a few times, a while back."

"Back in the days when you was usin' the name Buck West," Sutcliffe added.

Louis cocked an eyebrow. He knew most of the story of Smoke's background, although Smoke's laconic nature meant that prying it out of him hadn't been easy.

"Well, any friend of Smoke's is a friend of mine, as the old saying goes," Louis said. "How about a drink, Mr. Sutcliffe? First one's on the house."

Sutcliffe grinned and said, "I sure won't turn that down. I favor rye, if you've got it."

"Indeed we do." Louis crooked a finger at the bartender and told the man to pour Sutcliffe a shot of rye, then said, "What about you, Smoke?"

"I'd just as soon have coffee, if you've got it."

"We always keep a pot on the stove in the back room. I'm glad most of my customers don't have your moderate habits, Smoke. I'd go broke!"

"I like to keep a clear head."

Sutcliffe picked up the glass of rye the bartender set in front of him. He threw back the drink, wiped the back of his other hand across his mouth, and said, "Whiskey don't muddle me none. I draw just as fast and shoot just as straight, drunk or sober."

"I hope for your sake you're right, Mr. Sutcliffe," said Louis. "Being mistaken about a thing like that could have serious consequences for a man."

"You mean like he might get hisself shot?" Sutcliffe gestured for the bartender to pour him another drink. The apron glanced at Louis, who gave him a tiny nod. As the bartender splashed more rye in the glass, Sutcliffe snorted disdainfully and went on, "That ain't gonna happen. I know how good I am." He picked up the glass and swallowed the second shot of fiery liquor. "I know how good the fellas I have to face down are, too. Ain't none of 'em that can match me. Not even . . ." He thumped the empty glass on the bar and sneered. "Not even the high-and-mighty Smoke Jensen."

Chapter 2

Smoke kept his face carefully expressionless in response to Sutcliffe's challenging tone as he said, "I told you about that high-and-mighty business, Rowdy. I didn't set out to get any kind of a reputation—"

"But that didn't stop you from gettin' one anyway, did it?" Sutcliffe snapped. "Ever'where I go, people talk about Smoke Jensen and how he's the fastest gun there ever was. Bull!" Sutcliffe raised his left hand and pointed a dirty-nailed index finger at Smoke. "Don't forget, mister, I knew you when you was nobody! Just a snot-nosed kid packin' an iron like you know what to do with it. Hell, you ain't much more'n a kid now."

"I reckon I'm all grown up," Smoke said, his voice flat and hard. "I've got a wife and everything, and she's probably waiting for me, so I'll mosey on. I'd say that it's been good to see you again, but—"

"You ain't moseyin' nowhere," snarled Sutcliffe. "Not until I'm finished with you. Barkeep, put some more whiskey in that glass!"

Louis Longmont held up a hand to the bartender, motioning for him to disregard Sutcliffe's order. He said, "Mr. Sutcliffe, I believe you've had enough."

"Why? Because I ain't paid for that second drink?"

"I don't care about that. It's on the house. But I think you should move on now—"

"I know all about you, too, you damn tinhorn," Sutcliffe interrupted without taking his eyes off Smoke. "You're supposed to be fast, too. But you ain't near as fast as me, and once I'm finished with Jensen, I'll prove it."

Smoke said, "You and I are already finished. You can still walk out of here, get on your horse, and ride away from Big Rock, Sutcliffe. No harm done."

"There's plenty o' harm! I been away so long, folks probably done forgot all about me." Sutcliffe's shoulders hunched a little. His right hand hovered near the Colt on his hip, ready to hook and draw. "But they'll remember, right enough, once word gets around that I'm the fella who killed Smoke Jensen. Then anybody who needs gun work done will be fallin' all over theirselves to hire me. Yes, sir, once I outdraw Smoke Jensen clean as a whistle—"

Smoke knew what the words pouring out of Sutcliffe's mouth were designed to do. They were supposed to anger him and prod him into drawing before he was ready, or else they would distract him, lull him into a split-second of unreadiness when Sutcliffe abruptly made his move.

The rant didn't accomplish either of those things. Smoke just stood there stonily, and when Sutcliffe broke off and clawed at his gun, Smoke was ready.

The walnut-butted Colt appeared in Smoke's hand as if by magic. Rowdy Sutcliffe actually was pretty fast on the draw, even with two shots of rye whiskey burning in his belly, but he had barely cleared leather when Smoke's gun roared. And to tell the truth, Smoke could have shot him a little sooner than that, but he'd waited just to make sure Sutcliffe wouldn't realize his mistake and try to stop this.

The bullet slammed into Sutcliffe's chest, twisted him half around, and made him stumble backward against the bar. He would have collapsed if it hadn't been there to hold him up. A shudder went through him. Blood welled from the corner of his mouth. Still, he stayed on his feet, held up by a combination of rage, stubbornness, and being too dumb to realize he had only seconds to live.

With his left hand, he pulled the second revolver from his waistband. With a gun in each fist, he tried to raise them. Smoke shot him again, this time drilling a neat third eye in the center of his forehead. Both of Sutcliffe's guns thundered as his fingers spasmed and jerked the triggers, but they were pointed down and hammered their slugs into the sawdust-littered floorboards right in front of his feet. A cloud of powder smoke rose from the weapons, obscuring Sutcliffe's swaying form as if he were standing behind a dirty window, doing some sort of macabre dance.

Then the guns slipped from nerveless fingers and thudded to the floor, followed a heartbeat later by Sutcliffe's lifeless husk. He sprawled face down and didn't even twitch.

Smoke shook his head and started reloading the two chambers he had just emptied.

"We both tried to talk him out of it," Louis Longmont said into the silence that gripped the room as the echoes of the shots faded away. Louis lifted the cheroot to his mouth and took a puff, then went on, "He simply wouldn't listen to reason." He looked like something had just occurred to him. "Were the two of you actually friends at one time, Smoke?"

"Not hardly," Smoke said as he slid the reloaded Colt back into leather. "He was just another two-bit gun-wolf. There are too many of them in the world."

"And they all believe it would be a wonderful thing to be the man who killed Smoke Jensen." Louis smiled humorlessly. "It must be a terrible thing to carry the hopes and dreams of so many around on your shoulders, my friend."

Around the room, the men who had dived for cover just before the shooting started were beginning to poke their heads back up. Louis waved the hand holding the cheroot to encourage them and raised his voice.

"It's all over, gentlemen. A round of drinks on the house!"

A short time later, as Smoke walked up to the Big Rock Mercantile, he saw an apron-wearing clerk loading sacks and crates of supplies into the back of the buckboard Sally had parked there earlier. Smoke's big, powerful black stallion, Drifter, was tied to a nearby hitch rail.

"Howdy, Smoke," the clerk greeted him. "Miz Jensen's inside, just finishin' up her business." The man placed the keg of nails he was carrying in the buckboard and then dusted off his hands. "Say, I thought I heard a couple of shots up the street a little while ago. You know anything about that?"

"You know me, Stan," Smoke replied with a smile. "I always try to steer clear of trouble."

"Uh-huh, sure. I just thought you might—"

"There was a little unpleasantness at Longmont's," Smoke admitted. He didn't see any point in denying what had happened. The story would be all over town in less than an hour, whether he wanted that or not. More than likely, it had spread quite a bit already.

The clerk let out a whistle. "How many of 'em did you have to shoot, Smoke?"

"Just one man. One stubborn, foolish man."

"Well, he should'a known better than to go up against Smoke Jensen."

Smoke didn't reply to that. When he and Sally had first come to this valley, not long after they were married, he had been determined to leave his gunfighting ways behind him. To that end, he had used a different name, one that people wouldn't associate with either Smoke Jensen or his previous alias Buck West.

Inevitably, though, the truth had come out, and by the time the ruckus with Tilden Franklin and his hired killers was over, everybody in these parts knew who he really was.

And as it turned out, that was a relief. Smoke never had liked secrets, and he was proud of his family name. Keeping quiet about it seemed almost like a slap in the faces of his father Emmett and his brother Luke, both of whom had died in the service of what they believed was right and honorable.

So, for better or worse, he would be Smoke Jensen from now on.

He stepped up on the store's porch and was about to go in when Sally appeared in the open doorway. She smiled when she saw him, and he was struck once again by just how beautiful this dark-haired young woman really was. She was pretty enough to take a man's breath away.

But there was a lot more to Sally Reynolds Jensen than just good looks. She was smart as could be, both in book learning and common sense, and possessed of fierce courage that wouldn't allow her to hesitate in the face of danger. In fact, Smoke wished sometimes that she was a little less courageous and more inclined to be careful.

If she'd been different, though, he might not have fallen so completely in love with her.

"Ready to go?" he asked her.

"I think so. I got everything that was on my list. Did you enjoy your visit with Louis?"

"It was all right, I reckon." He had lived through the shootout with Sutcliffe, so he couldn't complain too much about how the visit had gone.

The clerk was still standing on the porch. He said excitedly, ignoring the warning glance Smoke gave him, "Miz Jensen, did you hear the shootin' while you were inside?"

Sally looked at Smoke and raised her eyebrows. "Shooting?"

"I'll tell you about it once we're on the trail," he said, after scowling for a second at the clerk. The man cleared his throat, looked a little embarrassed, and retreated into the mercantile. Smoke cupped his hand under Sally's elbow and went on, "Let me give you a hand climbing up there."

She could have gotten onto the buckboard's seat just fine by herself, but she let Smoke assist her. Then she picked up the reins attached to the two horses in the team and pulled the brake lever out of its notch. Smoke untied Drifter and swung up into the saddle.

Sally waited until they were out of town and on the trail to the Sugarloaf before she said, "All right, what happened?"

"I ran into a fella I used to know a few years ago, back in the days when I was calling myself Buck West."

"An old friend?"

"No, but we weren't enemies, either . . . until he found out my real name and decided that we were."

Quickly, and without dwelling on the details, he filled her in on the deadly encounter. Sally listened in silence, but she wore a frown of concern.

He concluded by saying, "Monte Carson came down to Louis's place, took my statement, and sent for the undertaker. That's the end of it as far as I'm concerned."

Monte Carson was the sheriff of Big Rock, a former gunman himself who had been on the wrong side in the war a year earlier, until he realized that and threw in with Smoke. After that, with the founding of Big Rock, he had accepted the offer to become the new town's lawman.

"Does this man Sutcliffe have any friends or relatives who are going to come looking for you to avenge what happened to him?" asked Sally.

"Not that I know of, but honestly, I never really knew the hombre that well."

Sally sighed as she handled the team and kept the buckboard rolling along the trail while Smoke rode beside the vehicle.

"I know that by now I should be getting used to the fact there are men roaming around who'd like to kill you," she said. "Your past is what makes you the man you are, and I knew that when I married you."

"What I used to be doesn't mean that's what I'll always be," Smoke pointed out.

"No, but it's hard to get away from all the things that have happened to us, all the things we've done. Our history

"That's like saying folks can't change."

"No, not at all," Sally argued. "But changing the way you go forward doesn't change everything you've done in the past." She paused, then went on, "Smoke, don't think I'm saying I regret marrying you. I don't, not one bit! I love you and I know you don't go around looking for trouble."

"But it seems to find me anyway, doesn't it?"

She smiled and said, "I suppose that's the way it is with some people. And honestly, I wouldn't change one thing about you, even if I could! Just let me hope that someday, peace will come to this land."

"It will. I'm sure of it." Smoke gazed off into the distance. "It may be a while before it does, though."

"Well, until then, I'm glad I have Smoke Jensen by my side."

"And I'm glad to have Sally Jensen by *my* side."

They smiled at each other and traveled on, but as he rode, Smoke couldn't help but think about the things they had said.

He truly believed that peace *would* come to the frontier someday . . . but there was still a lot of blood to be spilled before that could happen.